BRAZEN DESIRE

Brand looked down on Deirdre. "Tonight you seem to want to bathe, my lady."

Deirdre looked back into his eyes. "Tonight I want many things," she whispered.

Without another word, Deirdre slowly undid her tunic and let it slip to the damp floor.

Brand stared at her, intensely aware of the allure of her softly curved body now covered only by her near-transparent undergarment. Deirdre moved closer to him and carefully removed his leather vest, then his skirt. He was naked beneath, his hair curling on his broad chest, his hips lean, his legs straight.

Brand's arms flew around her and he cupped her perfectly round, lovely buttocks in his hands, drawing her hips close to him. Deirdre closed her eyes, allowing her body to enjoy fully every sensation. He was hard against her, and she wriggled in his grasp, not wanting to be free, but wanting—yes, wanting the reality of that, which till now, she had only dreamed.

"Do you fear me?" Brand asked, whispering in her ear.

"It is unknown to me—I fear and yet—"

"You desire."

"I desire," she gasped, as the pressure of his hand and the movement of his fingers worked pure magic.

Books by Joyce Carlow

TIMESWEPT

A TIMELESS TREASURE

TIMESWEPT PASSION

SO SPEAKS THE HEART

DEFIANT CAPTIVE

Published by Zebra Books

Defiant Captive

Joyce Carlow

Zebra Books
Kensington Publishing Corp.
http://www.zebrabooks.com

One

May, A.D. *890*

Brand moved his horse stealthily through the darkness. He was alone, deep into enemy territory, and well aware of the danger. Four days ago he had been sent by Lord Thorgills to reconnoiter this hitherto unexplored part of Hibernia, as it was once known to the ancients. Others now called it Ireland.

Several years ago Norwegian Vikings, led by Lord Thorgills, had raided and subsequently pacified Dublin. There, on the knoll above the river that flowed to the sea, they had built a fort. It was from Dublin he had ridden to this place called Meath. As he understood it, this area was ruled by King Odhran. Odhran was one of two kings of Meath, both of whom were subservient to the overkingship of the great king at Tara. Not that any of them offered much of a challenge to his own people. These Hibernians lacked the steel-tipped spears and arrows of his Viking comrades, as well as the axes and strong swords. Still, there were matters to be considered. From what he had seen, a raid on Tara would be ill-advised. It was well fortified and well guarded. Moreover, such a raid would have forced the two minor kingdoms to react with all their force. No, it was far better to take them one at a time, and, from what he gathered, there was already an uneasy truce and no love lost between them. He had been told that only the marriage of Odhran's daughter to the king of East Meath would bring permanent peace. But he had also heard that the princess was far younger than the king who desired her, quite beautiful, and reluctant to wed.

Brand surveyed the land. It was his job to decide whom to attack and where exactly the most vulnerability existed.

He smiled at the irony. Neither these people nor his own seemed to be able to stand unified. They fought among themselves as much as they fought with others. Indeed, were it not for the infighting, he would not now be gathering information for Lord Thorgills, a man whose very sight he detested though he was bound to be loyal to him . . . bound by an oath, bound by love for his father, who lived only because Lord Thorgills allowed him to live, and bound by his promise to the beautiful Erica.

Brand moved a little faster as his horse emerged from the glen and he began the trek across open farmland. The darkness cloaked him, daytime travel was most dangerous. But he would have to travel during the day tomorrow. Lord Thorgills was waiting for his return and would expect his report immediately.

Brand, son of King Jarls, looked up at the sky and found his direction in the stars. Dublin was still three days away even by the quickest route.

In order to keep awake, Brand pondered this land and its people. To him, they seemed inexplicably backward though they possessed treasure galore. Their churches and monasteries were filled with jeweled crosses, books bound in gold, silver and gold candelabra, as well as other bejeweled artifacts. Their priests wore rings of gold beset with jewels and even the frames around paintings were often made from silver. In the homes of wealthy landowners and in the castles of the kings there were still more jewels. He had seen brooches, golden combs, and necklaces of great value. Each raid yielded chests of treasure and in the fall, before storms rose, the treasure was loaded onto ships and taken home. And yet for all their treasure and elaborately decorated books, these people had little else. They were surrounded by water, but had no vessels capable of sustained sea travel. Their weapons splintered in the face of Viking broadswords, their hand-carved shields were beautiful but inferior, and their mallets fell apart. Yes, these people of Hibernia were less able to defend themselves than the people of Britannia, across the Hibernian Sea. "Britannia." He spoke the word aloud. Britannia was where he belonged. There, his own people, the Danes, had established Danelaw, where they ruled supreme. There, he thought, he would be free. But, of course, he could not leave. Lord Thorgills owned him.

Deirdre always thought of winter as the season of peace. The cold winds, which swept across the fields and down the rolling hills, combined with rain, wet snow, and ice to keep warring armies at home. Winter was the season for spinning wool and the weaving thereof. It was the season for playing the harp, for telling tales, and for singing old and familiar songs. But winter had fled now, its cruel winds blown out, its stinging rains of ice replaced with warm breezes. In spite of the fact that spring and summer brought renewed fighting among the kingdoms, Deirdre yearned for spring. She yearned to go outside and walk in the countryside and to pursue the many things which were of interest to her. War was, after all, intermittent rather than constant. Still, regardless of the season, her lessons continued.

"Meath, in our language, *Contae Na Midhe,* is the middle kingdom and divided into two parts: Meath and East Meath. East Meath is ruled by King Malvin while Meath is ruled by King Odhran, my father. Both Meaths are underkingdoms and together with Ulster and Connaught, are ruled by the great overking of Tara, King Niall."

"Excellent!" her tutor, the redoubtable Father David, muttered. He was a portly man with dark eyes and narrow lips. Deirdre counted the minutes she had to spend with him not because she shunned learning, but because he never taught her anything she wanted to know. Father David was a repetitious man, constantly making her repeat the lessons of her childhood, never venturing into unexplored subjects. Did the stars affect people's lives? What were the lands across the ocean like? Were there truly monsters in the sea? There were so many questions and so few answers.

Deirdre, the nineteen-year-old daughter of King Odhran, sighed deeply. The memorization of the *twathas,* or kingdoms of Ireland, also known as Hibernia, was part of her tutoring.

Not that it was as simple as a few place names. She had to know the names of all the kings of all the *twathas* as well as the names of all their descendants. And that was only part of her learning day. She was tutored in weaving and the mastery of the harp. She also had to memorize tales and practice the proper way to tell them in order to entertain her father's guests.

Deirdre was also made to learn long passages from the Bible, and it was this activity that formed the basis for her most important secret. Deirdre had learned to read from the laboriously copied manuscripts, and could indeed write as well. But this knowledge she kept secret from everyone but her brother. Women were not expected to know such things, and, in fact, she suspected that Father David would disapprove.

Not that Mistress Brigida, who taught her harp, or Sister Mary, who taught her weaving, were any great improvement over Father David. They were all quite boring.

The fact was, Deirdre had an enormous thirst for knowledge, but not for memorization, weaving, or the playing of the harp even though she was quite proficient at all three. The one formal lesson she did enjoy was Gifford's. Gifford was an old man with twinkling blue eyes and rough red skin. But he was a master of tales, and he not only made her commit them to memory, he coached her in accents and ways in which she could make their telling more dramatic.

Deirdre pressed her lips together and looked around the

room. It was a small room with no view of the castle courtyard below. Light came from two high windows and from candles that sat in the middle of an oblong table. It was a room without tapestries, warmth, or decoration. "All distractions!" Father David once declared.

Deirdre stole a look at the hourglass. The sands had run out. "Are we finished?" she asked.

Father David scowled. "Yes," he replied, a tone of resignation in his voice. "Send in your brother."

Deirdre scrambled to her feet. The days were getting longer, there was still time to go to Edana's. There, she thought with enthusiasm, she could learn something truly important.

Deirdre walked briskly across the green knoll. Beneath her hooded cloak she wore a dark ankle-length linen underdress and over it a modest tunic trimmed with gold threads. Her long, waist-length red hair was pulled loosely behind her head and bound with a thin strip of leather. As she was not wearing her hood, loose strands of her luxurious, thick hair blew in the gentle breeze.

It was May, and, as far as she could see, the land was lush with new-grown grasses and wildflowers. Behind her, at a distance she herself ordered, was the head of her father's household guard, Hagar. He was an unpleasant man who detested her wanderings into the countryside, but who—at her father's bidding—had to follow, in order to protect her.

Deirdre descended the gentle hill and then, entering the glen, walked along the rutted path toward the cottage where an old woman named Edana lived.

Deirdre was not certain how old Edana was, but many said she was in her eighties. She was certainly the oldest person Deirdre had ever known, and most probably the oldest in all of Meath.

Edana was small of stature, but clearly strong of will. She had survived many years in circumstances that would have been challenging for a man but for a woman presented almost insurmountable difficulties.

Deirdre often wondered how Edana had looked when she was young. Now the old woman's oval face was like leather, cracked and rough. Her hair was gray, thin, and scraggly. But regardless of her appearance, Edana was a crone, a woman who was accorded great respect and considered to be a fount of wisdom.

Edana's tiny cottage in the glen was a wondrous place, a never-ending source of fascination to Deirdre, who visited at least twice a week, weather permitting, and sometimes more often. But these visits were much to Hagar's displeasure, and he expressed his mood in the form of low grumbling and loud grunts as they walked.

As soon as Deirdre opened the door of the cottage her olfactory senses were assaulted by the sweet aroma of the dried herbs that hung from every rafter. Crude wooden shelves were filled with containers of carefully labeled medicines, and strange mixtures often bubbled on the fire.

Deirdre had met Edana a year ago while gathering wild roses with which to scent the floors of the castle. She had shared tea with her in her strangely furnished cottage. The old woman's story was as odd as the cottage. She told Deirdre that she had once been married to a seaman who had taken her on a long and ill-fated voyage in her youth. Sailing in the Mediterranean, they had been thrown off course and ended up in a land conquered by Infidels, believers in Islam. Edana explained that her husband was killed, and she was taken into the home of a wealthy merchant, there to serve his wives. She lived there seven years and learned medicine from the Infidels before the head wife, feeling she had earned her freedom, persuaded her husband to send her home on a Spanish sailing ship. Eventually Edana was returned to Hibernia and, after a time, she even found her way home to Meath.

After their initial meeting, Deirdre visited Edana often, and she quickly came to believe that there was much to be said for the woman's knowledge. She studied Edana's medicine and then tried various cures on both the ill in the village and the wounded who returned after battle. She found Edana's medicines superior to simple prayers and the use of leeches.

Deirdre turned about. "You may wait out here," she told Hagar authoritatively. She never allowed him in the cottage but always made him wait outside.

Hagar grumbled under his breath, and Deirdre immediately turned away from him. She knew he truly hated it when she gave him orders. Once she had heard him tell a fellow guard that it was unseemly that he should have to be ordered by a woman and that Odhran, though a fine king in many ways, had not properly reared his daughter to respect the natural superiority of men.

"Edana?" Deirdre called out softly as she carefully opened the door of the cottage and peered inside.

"Here," the weak and ancient voice called out.

Deirdre paused for a moment while her eyes adjusted to the shadowy interior of the cottage. On the opposite side of the small room she saw Edana stretched out on a pallet of straw covered with a piece of woven cloth. The old woman had a sheepskin blanket which, in spite of the warmth of the day, she had drawn around her. She looked tiny and shriveled beneath it.

"You're ill. What is it?" Deirdre asked with concern.

"I'm dying," Edana replied.

"Oh, no!" Deirdre hurried to her side and knelt. She looked at the old woman. The last few times she had visited she had noticed Edana was weaker. She was filled with guilt for not having acted sooner, for not having helped her. "Please, let me take you back to the castle, let me care for you."

Edana seized her hand. "No, but you are kind to offer, my sweet girl. Dear Deirdre, as knowledgeable as you have become in medicine, there is no cure for time. You must understand that this is right. My time has come, I want to die here. I've just been waiting for you. I wanted to say good-bye."

"Please—let me help you."

"Child, there is no help for one as old as I. I know the time has come, and I only want to close my eyes. I am tired, very tired."

"Please—" Deirdre pleaded.

"Princess Deirdre, you have given me purpose by soaking up all the knowledge I have given you. Take my medicines and make use of them."

"I shall stay with you," Deirdre whispered. "Please, let me stay."

Edana's bony hand squeezed hers. "Stay then," she whispered. "Stay and watch me leave this world."

Deirdre made herself comfortable by Edana's side. She held the withered hand and waited. It was as if the old woman had willed herself to wait for Deirdre to come and bear witness. Now she seemed to will herself to die. Edana closed her eyes, and it was only a few minutes before Deirdre felt her hand go limp and then begin to turn cold.

Deirdre did not let go. She rocked back and forth as she sat on her knees, humming an ancient tune and closing her eyes tightly. It was as if she could feel Edana's spirit rising, leaving her withered old body, hovering in the ramshackle cottage, and then dissipating into the netherworld.

"Edana?" Deirdre whispered in her ear. But there was no movement. And though she well knew Edana was dead and her spirit departed, Deirdre felt for the woman's heartbeat. But it was no more.

Deirdre's eyes filled with tears, and for a long while she sat, simply holding Edana's hand.

"Princess! It is growing dark!" Hagar's voice intruded on her mourning. Deirdre shook her head as if to return to the world. "I am coming," she called back. Carefully, she pulled the cover over Edana's face.

Deirdre stood up and shook out her skirts. She emerged from the cottage into the twilight. "You will send the priest to see to Edana's burial," she instructed. "And have these medicines brought to me."

Hagar nodded, and, as he did so, Deirdre noticed the expression on his face. He was pleased Edana had died because it meant he would not have to come here anymore. Deirdre glared at him and thought, *I shall have to find somewhere else to walk, someplace he will like even less.* Immediately she began to think of places she could go that would annoy him. *My friend is dead,* she thought, *and I shall make you pay for the momentary pleasure I see on your face, Hagar.*

Deirdre tossed restlessly in her bed and drew the heavy sheepskin closer around her. She was only half-awake, but fully aware of the sudden cool wind that always preceded the dawn. Although it was early spring, the dampness was all-pervasive this time of year, and the outside warmth of the day had not yet penetrated the thick castle walls.

A few minutes passed, and begrudgingly Deirdre opened her green eyes. Dim light shone around the edges of the heavy cloth which covered the long narrow window that looked out on the courtyard below. Beneath her layer of skins she stretched again and thought about getting up. But it was so much warmer in bed!

Deirdre tossed again on her stomach and buried her face in her mattress, sniffing it. Ah, it was so sweet! Only recently it had been restuffed with fresh straw, to which she had added dried rose petals so that she could awaken each morning to their sweet aroma. Naturally, the floors of the castle were strewn with dried flowers and sweet-smelling straw, too; but she insisted on the addition of wild roses and sachets of lavender. Still more dried flowers hung from the high rafters. They gave off a lovely smell and helped cover the odors of cooking or the often vile smells which arose from chamber pots left too long beneath the beds. She sighed deeply and thought that the only problem with floors covered with grasses and flowers was, that in the winter, mice and shrews invaded the castle to feed off the dried flowers, build nests from the sweet straw, and enjoy the warmth from the great stone fireplace.

Still, Deirdre knew she had cause to be grateful. She was after all, nobly born; she lived in a castle, had servants and even a bed. But the serfs who tilled the land lived in straw huts, slept on benches or on the hard ground, and often had no choice of food. Indeed, if the harvest was bad, they had little food at all.

Not that I am a wealthy princess, she thought as she visualized the great castle at Tara. Immediately her head filled with questions about life in the great castle. Again she sighed. It was enough of a gift to be a member of the aristocracy, enough to be the daughter of Odhran, a wealthy subking whose lands stretched as far as the eye could see, and whose cattle numbered in the hundreds. Her family ranked just below the king of Tara and his kindred, and just above the great landowners, their kindred, serfs, and slaves.

After a few moments, her thoughts turned to Edana. She thought again how much she would miss the old woman. Edana had been her link with those outside the castle walls. Indeed, Edana's stories of her life in the Idrisid Kingdom in a place called Fez were all she knew of the world beyond Hibernia. But it was not all she wanted to know. "I will know more of that world," she vowed. "One day I shall see foreign kingdoms."

Deirdre again turned on her back to stare up at the ceiling. As comfortable as her surroundings were, she did not feel at ease. There was always war. Rumors passed from mouth to mouth, whispered predictions of darkness, of terrible fighting, of unknown but feared changes. The heathen invaders from the north were coming, and they were ferocious and without mercy. None was more afraid than her brother, Alan. He was younger than she and, sadly, a frail young man with dark, brooding eyes and pale, sculptured features. Alan was an artist and musician. He abhorred hunting, riding, and fighting.

When Alan was nine, his father had turned him over to one of his commanders to begin his military training. Day after day he returned crying with minor injuries. When he was twelve, he was given his own sword and, while in training, cut himself badly. The men made fun of him as soon as he was out of earshot. But their father knew. Gradually, because he was such an embarrassment, the military training ceased. Yes, Alan was ill suited to be a prince, but he was especially ill suited to be the son of Odhran. Odhran, their father, had no time for his son and no tolerance for his son's artistic temperament. It fell to her to make peace between them, remind her father in a hundred ways that Alan was, after all was said and done, his son and heir.

One subject chased another away and was lost in this fugue of thoughts; her eyes had once again closed. She had almost returned to blessed sleep when she heard the bells and thundering hoofbeats . . . her father, King Odhran, was returning!

Deirdre literally sprang from her bed. Shivering with cold as well as anticipation, she quickly pulled on her undergarments, then her linen tunic. Last came her decorative cloak which she quickly pinned with a large intricate bejeweled brooch. The brooch was a badge of identification. It said to all who saw it, "I am the daughter of Odhran, king of Meath, underking of His Lordship, King Niall of Tara." It was one of three Tara brooches, each made of gold and each with a large golden amber stone.

Deirdre pulled on her leather shoes and hurried across the stone floor to the window. To see out of it she had to stand on a stool, and this she quickly did. She pulled away the skins that covered the opening and stared down into the castle courtyard.

The gates had been opened, and her father rode across the drawbridge that covered the moat and into clear view. He was in full battle dress and behind him followed his soldiers, well armed and proud. Last came a contingent bearing a prisoner.

Then Deirdre saw the cage. It was a great iron cage on wheels, and inside she could just make out the form of a prisoner. "What kind of monster is kept in such a cage?" she said aloud.

Deirdre wasted no more time. She hurried from her room and ran down the long corridor to the winding stone staircase. There was a prisoner! A caged prisoner! Such a thing was most unusual, and most certainly she must see this creature, this man who merited being brought back to her father's castle in a special cage.

She flew down the stairs and through the great hall to the open doors of the castle. She hurried outside just as her father's entourage and the men bearing the cage came to a halt at the foot of the stone steps leading to the tall, wooden castle doors.

Deirdre stared at the cage, her eyes wide, her lips parted ever so slightly in surprise. What manner of man was this? He wore no tunic and no cloak! Yet he did not shiver nor even appear to notice the cold dampness of the May morning. Instead he wore a vest of leather and a short skirtlike garment that fell only a few inches below his vest. He was a huge man, a veritable giant compared to her father and his soldiers. In fact, he was so tall he had to crouch in his cage. His arms were bare and bulged with strength, his legs were long, muscular, and covered with golden hair, while the blond hair on his head fell to his broad shoulders. His eyes were a deep intense blue, and, as they fastened on her, Deirdre felt him as surely as if he had reached out and touched her.

He was an animal, this heathen creature. And yet he was quite incredible, so splendid a male specimen that she could not take her eyes off him.

Her father dismounted, and, before she realized it, he was at her side. "Does our Viking prisoner interest you?" he asked a bit harshly.

Deirdre turned to face her father. "Is this giant truly a Viking?" Vikings . . . even the word was feared. They were the cause of the rumors, the reason for all the dark predictions. These Vikings were the instruments of terror and of change. Oh, it was well-known that they had invaded Leinster and occupied Dublin. Leinster was one of the Five Fifths—the overkingdoms of Ireland. If the other three had been invaded, she was unaware of it since she only had knowledge of those places under the control of Tara.

"Yes, he's a heathen Norseman," her father said, spitting on the ground.

Deirdre paid her father no mind. She lifted her tunic and descended the steps, walking as close as she dared to the cage. His arms were long, and for a moment she feared he might reach through the bars and grab her.

Here at close range she could see the prisoner more clearly. His shoulder was bleeding—or more accurately had been bleeding. He also had a series of deep cuts and many bruises and scratches. His whole arm was caked with dried blood, as were strands of his long unkempt hair.

She moved closer and tilted her head slightly. He did not look so ferocious—but surly he was. The reputation of the Vikings was one of ferocity and cruelty.

"Princess, stand back," Hagar commanded.

Hagar's command made her bolder. She hated his constant attempts to protect and shield her from everything that was of interest.

Was this caged person truly a savage? His eyes drew her closer as he stared at her, caressing her with a penetrating gaze.

Then a soldier came up and prodded the prisoner with his spear. The giant let out a great roar and shook his cage. The soldier jumped back, but Deirdre remained frozen to the spot where she stood. Could he only make the noises of an animal?

"We'll display him tonight at the banquet!" her father proclaimed. "Then we'll decide his fate."

Deirdre watched uncomfortably as the armed soldiers opened the cage and, poking away, drove the wounded prisoner out and up the steep stone steps of the castle on his knees.

"Take him to the tower," her father commanded.

Deirdre forced her eyes away from the prisoner to look into the hard eyes of her father.

"Well, what do you think of the heathen?" her father demanded.

A plan was taking form in her mind. *I really must see him alone,* she decided. *How else can I really learn about him?* "I think he is wounded and that his wounds need tending," she replied forthrightly.

"He's a barbarian!"

"And if we do not offer our help, what are we?" She lifted her head and confronted her father.

Odhran knew his son would never speak up as Deirdre had just done, and he was all the more distressed that his daughter, a renowned beauty like her long-dead mother, should also have inherited his fearlessness as well as her mother's beauty. If he dressed her in armor, he had no doubt she would have fought with greater proficiency than Alan. "We may kill the beast tonight," her father blustered.

"No matter. We should tend his wounds," Deirdre insisted. "We are God's children, we are a civilized people."

Odhran pressed his lips together. "Take a guard and go then! See to the heathen's wounds. Then prepare yourself for the banquet. King Malvin is attending and may well ask for your hand in marriage tonight!"

Deirdre forced herself not to react. Instead, she turned quickly and followed the soldiers who prodded the wounded prisoner toward the tower.

Brand stumbled up the stairs, aware of the throbbing pain in his shoulder and just as aware of the rare beauty who followed the guards at a safe distance. At least they were not putting him in some dank, dark dungeon. Any prison room in a tower had to be better—drier, cleaner, and healthier by comparison to a dungeon. And, it seemed, if he had understood correctly, that the delicate woman who followed was going to nurse him. However pleasant the latter thought, it was an arduous climb to the tower, and he knew that although the flow of blood was now stemmed, he had initially lost a lot.

He glanced around, and for his curiosity received a hard punch in the ribs. The beautiful woman had disappeared.

The stairs grew steeper, and, finally, they reached a narrow hall with a cell on each side. Each had a huge, heavy door with a small iron-barred window. The guard unlocked the great lock that held the chain, pulled the chain free, and opened the door. Brand was prodded into a small narrow room with straw on the floor. He was prodded to the wall, and he did not resist as they began to chain him.

The door was closed, and the room plunged into shadows. The only window was high above him. It was small and oblong, just big enough to allow light and air into the room. He sank to the floor. The woman was gone. He must have misunderstood.

Outside the door Deirdre stopped to catch her breath. She had run to the room where she kept her medicines, and now, holding her basket, she prepared to tend the prisoner. Hagar dogged her steps, and he, too, panted from the steep climb.

"Open the door," Deirdre commanded.

Brand looked up when the door swung open again.

Then he saw his beauty as she edged passed the burly guards.

"It will not be necessary to chain him," Deirdre said with authority. "He is a mere mortal, not one of the Viking gods."

"It is customary to chain—" Hagar began.

"He is wounded. I hardly think a wounded man who has lost so much blood could break through that chain on the door." Hagar was an unbearably officious sort, always trying to impress her father. Yet Deirdre realized her resolve to show no fear of the Viking was almost entirely due to her desire to appear in full control in front of Hagar.

Brand looked up at her and resisted a smile. The guard was angry, the lady was in command. He had not thought Celtic women so spirited. In fact, till now he had regarded them as a bit simpering compared to Scandinavian women. But this one was not only more beautiful than any woman he had ever seen, she was also strong of will. Yes, she was indeed a temptress with her waist-length red hair, white skin, and sea-green eyes. Such a woman would bring a fortune in the slave markets on the Mediterranean coast, where Celtic woman were, in any case, much in demand. Indeed, his compatriots raided these shores primarily to rob the wealth of its churches and to kidnap slaves for an ever-growing market.

Deirdre waited while he was unchained before she entered the cell and knelt beside the prisoner, forcing herself not to tremble or show any kind of fear.

"Be careful," Hagar again warned.

"He won't hurt me," she answered confidently. "Take your men and wait outside."

"Your father will be furious! What if something happens to you? He's a heathen animal!"

"My father won't blame you. He knows my mind and my will. Now go away, I am not afraid."

Reluctantly, and muttering under his breath, Hagar pushed his men back and out into the hall. He partially closed the door, but continued to watch through the narrow slit in the door.

"Such a fool," Deirdre said under her breath. "You wouldn't hurt me, would you?"

"No, my lady," Brand answered in a heavy accent. "You have nothing to fear."

"Oh, you speak my language."

"Only a little. I am learning it." He did not mention that his mastery of the language was the reason he had been sent forth to gather information. "I assure you I will not hurt you."

"I thought not," she said, wondering even as she spoke if he could hear the relief in her voice. He was large but clearly no animal. She leaned closer to examine his wound. Then, without speaking to him, she called outside, "Have one of the soldiers fetch hot water and some soapberry."

She listened as Hagar gave the order, and she heard a soldier scampering down the stairs. "It's not too deep, but it must be washed."

"I did not think the Celts washed," Brand said, a half smile crossing his face.

Deirdre did not smile back. "Not enough do," she answered crisply. *Yes,* she thought silently, *I would be happier if more of the men I know did wash.* As for the washing of wounds, she had learned the practice from Edana. Done promptly, it did indeed seem to prevent festering.

The soldier returned, and the guard brought Deirdre the iron pot filled with steaming water. Slowly, carefully, while the Viking watched her every move, she washed his shoulder, removing both the dried blood and the dirt.

Deirdre took a mixture of vile-smelling liquid made from fermented berries from her basket. She opened the crock and began to put it on his wound.

Suddenly, the Viking grabbed her wrist. "Why are you doing that?" he demanded. "It stings!"

Deirdre's mouth opened in surprise. His grip was powerful, yet controlled. She looked into his intense blue eyes and was all too well aware of her vulnerability. This man was filled with energy, and it seemed to flow into her as he held her fast.

"I must wash your wound with this," she whispered, "to prevent it from festering."

He held her for another moment, then dropped her wrist and nodded.

She finished cleaning the wound with the reeking liquid and, after that, carefully wrapped it in clean cloths. "If the wound begins to rot," she cautioned, "I shall have to bring maggots to clean it."

Brand grimaced. "Maggots and not leeches?" he questioned.

"You've already lost much blood, making leeches fat will not make you stronger nor rid your body of rotten flesh. Maggots, on the other hand, eat only the rotting flesh."

What she said made sense, though he had not thought of it before. "Where have you learned these things?" he asked, aware of how curious she made him. This woman's ways were unlike the ways of other Celtic women he had encountered.

"From a woman who studied with Infidels," Deirdre answered.

Brand nodded. He had heard the Infidels held secrets of healing. He let himself relax a little as he watched her with interest. As horrible as the smell of the liquid she had put on his wound, he could still smell the sweetness of the woman. She gave off the aroma of rose petals and the thought aroused him as he wondered if the nipples on her high, full breasts were as pink as the wild roses that grew along the side of every road in this part of the world. His eyes must have lingered too long on her breasts because she suddenly sat up straight, as if she knew what he was thinking, and moved away slightly.

"Do not look at me that way," she said sternly.

"You're in the full bloom of womanhood, my lady. You are a delectable flower. I should like to steal you away."

The feel of his grip on her wrist returned as if he still touched her. He was incredibly powerful and yet controlled. She was sure he could be gentle, too. But he was most forward.

"Stop it! Stop it at once! And mind your tongue, or you'll be lucky if you live to see another day."

He lifted his brows and drew back. "Are you so bad a healer?"

"As I told you, I have learned from a friend, and I enjoy the art of healing. I have nothing else to entertain me. As for your possible death, that is up to my father, not my medicine."

"Your father would be wiser to keep me to bargain with.

When my people come here they will take you, and he might be able to trade you for me."

As he spoke, she washed his other cuts and cleaned them. She looked up at him seriously. He was a bit hard to understand, but she could make out what he was saying, and it made good sense. After all, there were Vikings in Dublin, and raids were happening closer and closer to Meath. It was only a question of time. But then, he had been captured, and he had killed no one. Perhaps those who came would be defeated by her father's army. Perhaps these Vikings were not so unassailable. Certainly Tara would not fall easily. "Perhaps they will come, perhaps not," she replied. "After all, you were defeated and captured."

Brand laughed. "I was alone, my lady."

She frowned. "Oh," she answered softly, without asking why he was alone. Then, regaining herself, "I do not make the decision that concerns your fate."

"Ah, my lady, I know that is so, but I saw how you spoke up. Your father will listen if you argue well."

She did not respond, but rather stood up. "I have given you medicine and shown mercy, I must leave now."

"Ah, yes, of course. Leave before I begin to tell you about my land or threaten you with my gods. Leave before you want to stay."

"I do not believe in your gods," she replied, whirling about and leaving the cell.

"You may chain the door," she told Hagar. "And no beatings. I shall return to see to my patient's good health."

Hagar muttered again and turned away. Odhran seldom showed his enemies mercy. He behaved as a man should. But Odhran's son Alan was weak, and his daughter Deirdre was a shrew. He comforted himself with the thought that she would soon be gone; King Malvin would take her away and teach her a lesson in humility, a lesson she badly needed.

* * *

Deirdre sat in her bath with the steam billowing about her. The smell of roses permeated the room as it drifted from the vapors of her scented bath. She had played the harp for over an hour and Mistress Brigida had praised her talents. "Given by an angel!" she sang out. She had taken her two hours at the loom and again earned the praise of her teacher, Sister Mary. And for over an hour she had recited the genealogies of royal families for Father David. But no matter. She had performed these and other tasks without completely erasing the memory of her conversation with the Viking from her thoughts.

What had he meant, when he had said, 'Leave now before you want to stay'? It seemed a kind of challenge. Was he going to tell her tales of his adventures? Yes, she wanted to hear such tales. It was said that these Vikings traveled far, that they knew every country, even that they had magic powers bestowed on them by those outside the realm of earth . . . evil powers to be sure, but still magical, still potent.

"Nonsense," she said aloud, and she recalled her most recent discussion with Father David about these Vikings.

"Dark, dark powers," he had intoned.

"What powers?" she had asked.

"They can work with fire. It is how they make things of metal. Working with fire is the work of the devil."

"But we use metal objects," she had argued.

Father David had rolled his eyes toward heaven. "Using them is not the same as making them. Those among us who work with fire do the devil's work."

He was so absurd! She had to force herself not to laugh, and yet she knew that if she laughed at Father David, her own father would be more than just displeased.

No, she did not believe this Viking prisoner had dark powers, though she did admit she felt attracted to him. She felt the desire to speak with him again, to listen to his stories, and to find out more of the world.

Her thoughts began to drift, and the strength of his arms

came back to her. Never had she seen such large, bulging muscles and broad shoulders. And yet his skin had been smooth and white, his golden hair soft like the down of a baby duck. His eyes were a striking blue, both hypnotic and commanding.

And yet there were the stories. Women were tormented and raped, then sold to others. Houses were burned, everything was stolen. These Vikings were legend. They came down the river on their boats and stormed the towns, taking them by surprise and enslaving their inhabitants.

Nonetheless, this Viking was not like those in the stories she heard. This Viking seemed to be a gentle giant. At least he was gentle with her.

A slight chill passed through Deirdre, and immediately she shook her head and sat up straight. *I must hurry,* she thought as she began to scrub vigorously.

But no matter how hard she tried, the image of the Viking remained in her mind.

Two

Deirdre had put on a fresh white linen underdress over which she wore a deep green tunic trimmed with gold threads and embroidered with tiny golden roses. The color of the tunic made her eyes seem a deeper hue of green, and the gold embroidery matched her belt, necklace, and circular earrings. Her long hair was pulled back and tied with a golden chain. Over her hair she wore a translucent mantle which fell like a hood. Had she been going outside, or had it been winter, her mantle, which consisted of a cloak with a hood, would have been made of heavier fabric, but for tonight this diaphanous mantle better served the occasion and surely enhanced her appearance.

Considering Malvin would be her father's guest, she ought not be trying to make herself more attractive. "Better I should dress in sackcloth and cover my face with ash," she said aloud to no one.

King Malvin, who ruled the adjacent kingdom of East Meath, had made his intentions clear in a hundred different ways. It was only a question of time before he spoke to her father and asked for her hand in marriage.

Deirdre shivered in revulsion at the thought. But most certainly her father would agree. If Alan were a different person, her father's agreement might not so easily be had. But the fact was that her father would want a strong alliance with Malvin because Alan showed no interest in being his father's heir. Therefore, her father would marry her to Malvin and the two kingdoms would be united and inherited by their children. It was ideal for the future of the two kingdoms, but for Deirdre it meant a terrible sacrifice.

Deirdre stood up and shook out her tunic. She could only try to deal with the problem after her father made his own mind known. There was little point in worrying about it now.

She studied her image in the polished-metal mirror and frowned at herself as she did so. It was for the Viking prisoner that she dressed so well! She bit her lip and looked away. Why did she care if he found her desirable? He was a beast, a Viking. He was her father's prisoner, and, worse yet, he was a harbinger of more to come, of danger to her future, to her very world. And yet it was true. She wanted to see admiration for her in his blue eyes. She wanted him to see her as well as let her near to tend his wounds. She flushed at the very thoughts that circled the edges of her mind.

"The guests are arriving," Mistress Bryna called from the corridor.

"I'm coming," Deirdre answered. She left her own room and whispered her thanks to Bryna, her personal servant. The girl worked hard, and Deirdre hoped that if worse came to worst, she would be able to take Bryna with her to King Malvin's castle.

"Where is Alan?" she asked.

Bryna leaned close, aware of how sound carried down the long corridors of the castle. "With your father," she whispered.

Deirdre frowned. Meetings with Alan always put her father in a bad mood. A meeting between them did not bode well for the evening's festivities.

"I'll go and meet the guests," she said, heading toward the great hall and wondering at what point the Viking would be brought from the tower to the hall.

* * *

King Odhran rubbed his unkempt red beard and looked at his son through squinted, narrow, brown eyes. How could this clean-shaven, frail young man be his son? Alan was tall enough, but he was slender and without muscle. His face was as pale as snow, his eyes clear and heavily lashed, like those of a lovely woman. But none of this was as telling as his hands. Alan's fingers were long and slender, his hands smooth as silk. There were no calluses from the use of weapons, no blisters from the use of tools. And yet for all of Alan's sensitivity and lack of interest in being a warrior or even king of Meath, he did adore women and women adored him. He was a handsome lad; he was just no warrior and far too kind to be king. A king had to make tough decisions—life-and-death decisions. Alan would never make such choices. He would always seek the middle ground.

"I know you don't care, but we live in dangerous times," Odhran bellowed. "Did you see that Viking bastard? He was alone, but there will be others! They're going to kill and enslave us if we don't fight."

"I have no will to fight," Alan replied truthfully.

"You have no will for anything except to dabble with your paints. Everything I have fought a lifetime to preserve will be lost. Does that mean anything to you?" He narrowed his eyes and once again felt defeat in his soul. How was it he could vanquish his enemies on the field of battle and yet could say nothing to move, or even frighten, this young man?

"I know myself, Father. I would be less than useless in battle."

Odhran grimaced. He could not accuse his son of lying. "I shall have to grant Malvin's request to marry Deirdre," he said slowly.

"She dislikes him," Alan replied. "It would be wrong."

"Yes, the two of you are quite a pair. You stand up for her and she for you. Well, she is a woman, and her likes and dislikes hardly matter. She will have to marry Malvin."

"I think you do not like him either," Alan said. He felt

proud of himself. He hardly ever spoke with his father and almost never contradicted him. But he would have to argue with his father's decision to have Deirdre marry Malvin; he owed her that and much more. Deirdre had been his mother. Although she was only two years older than he, she had nursed him when he was ill, held him when he was frightened, and encouraged him to copy and illustrate books. "Please admit it, Father. Please admit you don't like Malvin."

"I do not trust him. But I suppose I shall have to trust him if he becomes my son-in-law."

"He's too old! It is wrong to force Deirdre into such a marriage."

"I don't need you to tell me right from wrong!" Odhran blustered. But he knew he did not sound genuine, and no doubt Alan saw through him. Malvin was powerful, but he did not deserve Deirdre, who was both beauteous and intelligent. Deep in his heart he feared Malvin would mistreat her, since he would no doubt be unable to deal with her intelligence or tame her will. What if he beat her into submission? It was a thought Odhran did not like, indeed could not tolerate. But still he had led Malvin to believe that Deirdre would be his.

"I shall think on these things," he allowed, letting some of his defenses down.

"Father, I have a request."

"And am I to entertain your request when you do not even consider mine?"

"This request, if granted, would rid you of me. Father, I want to enter the monastery at Bail Atha Truim. There I can pursue my artistic endeavor. Perhaps my illustrated translation of the Gospels would make you proud of me."

Odhran stared at his son. He had never thought Alan would gain the courage to ask this! There was most certainly something to be said for his son's request. Having a son in a monastery would surely find favor with the Almighty. And it would evidence his family's religious commitment to the entire population of Meath. Moreover, if Alan were a monk, Odhran's friends could no longer make unseemly remarks about Alan's masculinity, or—more precisely—the seeming lack of Alan's desire to ride, hunt, and defend the kingdom. A monastic life seemed a good solution, and the monastery at Bail Atha Truim, known to most simply as Trim, was an excellent choice. But he was not known for quick decisions. "Does this mean you never wish to take a wife?" he asked.

"I wanted to take a wife eventually, but if I remain here, I'll be a further embarrassment. This, I have decided, is best for all."

Odhran looked away. "I shall give your request some thought," he replied.

Alan suddenly felt filled with hope. Seldom did he and his father converse without an argument. Perhaps his request would be granted, perhaps his father was not as much of an ogre as he had thought. It had been Deirdre who had suggested this compromise and pushed him into this conversation. "And if you decide to marry, well, you will not be the first to leave the walls of the monastery," she had told him.

"Can I even broach this subject without a terrible argument?" Alan had asked.

"Of course you can," she had assured him. And she was right! He could hardly believe it.

The banquet table was long and sturdy, made of dark wood, with intricately carved supports at either end and in the middle. All of the high-backed chairs sat behind the table so that those who dined could look out on the great hall, where entertainments were provided for the diners' pleasure. There were twenty-four seats at the table, and the table and chairs all sat on a raised dais. Below them jesters, minstrels, or the occasional players performed during banquets such as the one being given tonight.

It was also in the great hall where her father's serfs and

vassals lined up before the throne to have their disputes settled or to present a petition for consideration. This ritual happened every Sunday after church. It was said throughout the kingdom of Meath that Odhran was a just king, far more just than King Malvin, who ruled East Meath with an iron hand and often settled disputes by killing one of the disputing parties.

Perhaps, Deirdre thought, *if I become his wife, I can change all that.* But in her heart, she knew it was not so. Malvin would go on abusing his power and no doubt, in time, he would abuse her as well. But if it meant Alan could have his wish and go to Trim—it would be worth it, she told herself. And Malvin would give her a child and perhaps she could forget Malvin and lose herself in love for the child, rearing him to be a good and honest king when he inherited his father's throne. Women did have opportunity to change things, and Deirdre vowed that if she were forced into marriage with Malvin, she would find a way to change the way the kingdom was governed, even if she had to wait for him to die.

"How pensive you are," King Malvin said, looking at her with his small, feral eyes. He had been seated next to her.

"I was thinking," she murmured, turning her head slightly away.

Malvin continued to look at her out of the corner of his eye. She was a stunning woman, but she needed discipline. She was far too outspoken, and she pursued her own interests. *But I can teach her respect,* he thought. In a matter of weeks he knew he could make her quite subservient. There were many ways to break a spirit such as Deirdre's, and he knew all of them.

Tonight, as always, Odhran's chair was the highest, with a tall back over four feet high. It also bore a hand-carved design. Tonight, Deirdre thought, the great hall looked impressive.

Not that the great hall of their castle was as grand as the great hall of Tara, but its design was the same even if the scale was smaller. Usually, the long table at which they now sat was kept behind her father's throne. But tonight the throne was placed behind the table and concealed by heavy drapes. Tonight, the table fairly groaned under the weight of huge platters of food, and wonderful aromas rose from the various dishes to mingle with each other and make the mouth water in anticipation. Everywhere servants scurried about, adding touches to the table and bringing more and more food.

Venison cooked to perfection sat on a silver platter. Around it were platters of roast hare, pig, chicken, and pigeon. There were greens and loaves of hot bread. Different cheeses were also on the table, as were bowls of wild berries. Large goblets held heady red wine brought from across the sea and mead produced locally. Deirdre had noticed when she was fairly young that it took only a few goblets of this brew to make men unseemly cheerful, uninhibited, and less warlike than usual. But if they drank too much, they became difficult and often started to fight with one another.

Generally, Deirdre did not find feasts to be unpleasant. She enjoyed the entertainments and felt relaxed because her father was less strict on such occasions.

But tonight was an exception. Sitting next to Malvin depressed her. Try as she might, she could not come to like him. Malvin was no more than a head taller than she, though he was a bear of a man, stocky and strong. He had shoulder-length hair that was now gray. His beard was full and badly trimmed. Indeed, all that could be seen of his face were his narrow, dark eyes, the eyes of a rodent, Deirdre thought uncharitably. Worse yet, his hair was greasy and matted. No doubt it crawled with lice. In fact, she was quite sure his whole body crawled with lice. Malvin might not have bathed less frequently than her own father, but he certainly looked and smelled as if soapberry and hot water were completely unfamiliar. She sighed inwardly. Not that Malvin's personal condition was much different from that of other men—none of them bathed enough, none of them washed or combed their hair. She suddenly pushed all thought of the odor which arose from Malvin from her mind. She envisaged the Viking. Even though his hair had been matted with blood from his wound, it was not tangled. Moreover, it seemed clean. Nor did his body reek. She had heard these Vikings were clean as well as strong. Rumor had it that they bathed in steaming water and then plunged into cold water. It was said that they also sat in small rooms heated by fires all around till they were very hot indeed. Such heat was said to rid the body of the little pests which were such a difficulty, and which she could not tolerate.

Deirdre suddenly jumped. Malvin's hand had just squeezed her thigh. She turned and shot him a nasty look, her green eyes flashing with anger.

Malvin laughed. "Beauty, you shall soon be mine. You may withdraw now, but soon I'll have you."

He whispered in her ear, and she shuddered at the very thought of him. Yet she knew her time was coming. Her father wanted to unite the kingdoms . . . and what other way was there? Her fate was sealed—and she regarded it as a cruel fate.

"Bring in the Viking!" her father suddenly shouted. All of those at the table simultaneously shouted, too. Deirdre's face flushed with anger. She hated it when prisoners were displayed like animals.

The Viking, now in chains, was dragged out of a side room and pulled into the great hall. He was positioned in the center of the hall, just below her father's chair.

Odhran laughed heartily. "A fine specimen! A great heathen warrior! How brave are you now?"

The Viking looked up, but not at Odhran. He sought Deirdre's eyes, and she looked back at him boldly, unable to take her eyes off his broad, naked chest, which glistened with perspiration in the torchlight of the great hall. One of the soldiers brought the lash down on the Viking's bare back and he jerked slightly, but did not cry out.

"What shall be done with this prisoner?" Odhran called out.

"Hang him!" Malvin shouted. "Or slice him in two, the heathen bastard!"

"Burn him!" another landowner shouted. "They burn our churches and steal holy objects!"

"Send his head to Dublin on a spear!" another shouted.

Deirdre had enough. She stood up, and as she did so the hall fell silent as all eyes turned toward her.

Odhran looked at his daughter. She was dressed in her finest tunic and wore a green cloak. Her magnificent hair fell to her tiny waist, and he could not help but think how exquisite she looked. How he hated marrying her to Malvin! It was his duty, but not his desire.

"I ask you to grant me permission to speak," she said clearly.

However much he disliked her tendency to speak out, he decided he would not forbid it. She often made sense, though he did not like to admit it. "Speak," he said with a kingly wave of his hand.

"We know that many other heathens like this man have built a fort and now remain in Dublin, whereas, in the past, they simply came and went. It would seem our shores will have to endure year-round raids now. This enemy grows in strength in spite of all our efforts. Killing this man—who might be important among their number—might be unwise. Suppose we are attacked, and some of our people held for ransom? Could we not trade this prisoner? No one trades a dead hostage for the living. I ask you to think on this, my father. I ask that you grant this man life, but hold him to bargain with should the need arise."

Alan suddenly stood up. "I agree with Deirdre. It is folly to kill this man."

"Is this a kingdom of simpering women!" Malvin roared.

"This is my kingdom!" Odhran returned, his doubled fist hitting the table. "We are Christians!"

Others muttered their agreement.

"Take the Viking back to his cell!" Odhran ordered.

Deirdre's eyes followed the prisoner as he was prodded from the room to be returned to the tower. Without saying so, her father had granted her request, and in a way he never had before, he had stood up for Alan as well.

Odhran turned and looked up and down the table. "I have an announcement to make." His expression was still unsmiling.

Deirdre shivered. *Oh, dear God,* she silently prayed. *Please don't let him announce my marriage to Malvin. Perhaps it is my punishment for speaking out. Please, a little longer, just a little longer to be free.*

"It is about my son, Alan."

Deirdre knew the color had drained from her face. Now she felt suddenly confused, as well as relieved. Alan? What had her father decided about Alan? Had Alan finally gained the courage to speak with Odhran?

"My son will enter the monastery at Trim. There he will devote his life to Holy Orders and the beautification of the word of the Almighty! He has been given a gift, and his gift must be given to God."

A ripple of "amens" filled the hall. Deirdre let out her breath slowly. It would not be tonight . . . not tonight . . . oh, how she wished she could she talk her father out of wedding her to Malvin.

"Have you no other announcement?" Malvin shouted. He pounded on the table, and all the goblets shook.

Deirdre stiffened. What was the matter with him?

Odhran turned toward them, and it was only then that Deirdre saw the deep anger in her father's eyes. Malvin's previous outburst had not been dismissed as that of a man who had drunk too much fermented liquid. Odhran had been made furious by Malvin's intervention . . . and now that she thought of it, she realized it was because she had spoken and her brother had supported her.

"This is no kingdom of women," Odhran shouted. "And

no woman from this kingdom will be leaving this night or any other night with you."

Malvin stood up with such force that his chair fell backward and hit the floor with a resounding crash that seemed to fill the now tensely silent hall. "Broken promises can have serious repercussions," he replied menacingly.

Instinctively, Deirdre moved away from Malvin. Had she actually been promised? She was filled with a combination of anger and relief. Anger that she had actually been promised without so much as a conversation on the subject with her father, relieved that Malvin had so angered her father that he had now reconsidered. And yet she was not unaware of the dangers. Her fist clenched automatically, and she forced herself to look entirely neutral and not frightened. Malvin, revolting as he was, was a powerful king. Now, at the very least, their adjoining kingdoms would be unfriendly, and at the worst, there could be war between them.

"You have forced me this night to reconsider my previous commitment," Odhran said evenly. "You have laughed at my son and his talent. You have also insulted me."

"I was promised Deirdre!" Malvin thundered.

"I would rather see her in a convent first!" her father shouted.

Deirdre almost smiled—this moment was as sweet as it was dangerous. Her father well knew she would not go to a convent.

"Go!" Odhran ordered. "Leave my kingdom!"

Malvin stomped away, his guard following in his wake.

Deirdre looked down, thinking that although she was glad her father had changed his mind, she was uneasy that Malvin had been humiliated. There were other ways . . . this was not at all sensible. But then, her father had been angered by Malvin's question, which more than implied Odhran's kingdom was a kingdom of women. It was an insult to Odhran's leadership, his bravery, his honor.

Odhran strode to her side. "Have I made you happy, my daughter?"

Deirdre nodded. "I hope you will not be sorry."

Odhran surprised her again. He agreed, saying sadly, "I have made a dangerous decision."

"And the Viking?"

"He has not been harmed. I considered your words and found them wise."

Others had slowly left the banquet or stood around talking. Deirdre realized this was a rare moment between them; it was as if she and her father were alone even though others were still milling about.

"Thank you, my father," Deirdre said, touching his sleeve.

Unexpectedly, Odhran bent and kissed her tenderly on the cheek. "Deirdre, Deirdre, if only you had been my son and not my daughter. You're brave and intelligent. And you have your mother's rare beauty."

Deirdre had never seen her father like this, nor heard this tone in his voice. "You compliment me too much," she whispered.

"And when I die I shall leave you too little," he said. Suddenly she saw moisture in her father's eyes. He rubbed them. "I have a cinder in my eyes," he protested. He looked at her. "I loved your mother, Deirdre. She was given to me by her father, but I loved and honored her, and she loved me back. It was a miracle."

"I love you, too, my father."

Odhran drew her close and held her. "Whatever happens Deirdre, keep your wits about you, and be safe."

"I shall," she promised.

The still-pale sun of late May filtered through the castle's high windows, a gentle breeze caressed the meadows and pastures beyond the castle walls, and flowers still in their calyxes strained to blossom. Deirdre felt her spirits rise with the coming of the new season and with the changes in her life that had occurred so quickly. The threat of having to wed Malvin was gone and with its leaving she found a new light-heartedness. Her husband-to-be was a mystery hidden in her future; the persistent nightmare of her wedding night with Malvin came to her no more.

"Deirdre!" Deirdre rose from her desk, where she had been memorizing passages from the Bible for her tutor, Father David, and opened the door to admit her brother, Alan.

Alan's face was aglow as he took her arm and gently squeezed it. "A messenger has come from Trim. I've received permission to take up residence there."

"I don't know whether to laugh or cry," she said earnestly. "We've never been separated; I shall miss you very much."

He put his arms around her. "Not as much as I'll miss you, my sister."

"And is this truly what you want?"

"I want to be able to practice my art. But I do not wish to take vows."

"Can you be happy there?"

"For a time—I will be able to work with others, to share the ways of painting I have learned."

Deirdre brushed some of the hair off her brother's forehead. They had been inseparable. When their mother had died, she had held Alan for hours while he sobbed. She had helped him learn to walk and talk and even to read. When Odhran got angry because Alan did not wish to ride and practice with the weapons of war, she defended him. Now she suddenly realized they would no longer be together. "You will come back to visit, won't you?"

"Dear Deirdre, I would perish if I were never to see you again. Of course I will come home to visit."

Deirdre fought back tears. "When will you go?"

"In two weeks' time," he answered.

"I shall save my tears for the hour of our parting," Deirdre said, forcing a smile.

She turned and looked at the hourglass. "It's time I went to the tower," she said, picking up her basket of medicines.

"You're so brave," her brother said.

Deirdre only smiled as she hurried away. There was no time to confide in her brother, no time to tell him about the Viking. And what would she have told him anyway? That she felt a strange attraction for this northerner? She certainly could not confide her daydreams about him, or the elaborate fantasies she enjoyed. But perhaps her fantasies and attraction would go away as she truly got to know him. That was it, of course. She really wanted to get to know him. She wanted to know why he fought and what his home was like. She wanted to know what he cared about and if he was honorable or not. She wanted to know how he was different from other men she knew. She wanted to know what made him laugh and what made him sad. She wanted to know what, if anything, frightened him. She had a thousand questions, but she knew she could learn from him. He had sailed the seas and been to foreign lands. He could tell her much.

She climbed the stairs to the tower slowly, pausing now and again to catch her breath. At last she reached the hall outside the tower cells. "I'm here to clean and change the dressing on the prisoner's wound," she announced authoritatively. "Open the door to his cell."

The guard fumbled about with his keys and finally undid the padlock and removed the chain. He swung open the door carefully, but Deirdre brushed by him. "Leave us," she commanded.

"But he is stronger now," the guard protested.

"He will not hurt me," she replied, sailing into the cell with newfound confidence. After all, she had saved him as he had hinted she should. Most certainly he would be grateful. In any case, she was here to help him.

Brand, who had been asleep, opened one eye and then the

other. She appeared as a vision poised beside the door. She was not dressed in the finery she had worn at the banquet, but rather she wore a simple dark green tunic and cloak. And her magnificent hair was not covered or pulled back. It hung loose, glistening in the ray of sunlight from the window high above. Her hair was something wondrous, a million strands of red-gold framing a perfect oval face.

"I've come to change the dressing on your wound," Deirdre said quickly, least he misunderstand the reason for her visit.

He sat up, his eyes still glued on her. "The reason does not matter. Your visit is my dream come true."

Deirdre felt the heat in her cheeks as her face flushed. His deep blue eyes were bold, and, for a single second, she allowed herself to feel complimented by his obvious expression of admiration for her. But playing such games with a heathen could be dangerous, she reminded herself. What, after all, might he have in mind? And more important, could she really trust him? "Does it throb?" she asked, coming nearer.

Brand's smile twisted slightly. "It throbs for you," he answered.

Deirdre jumped back from him slightly. It was more than liking! He desired her!

She turned her head sharply and tried to look stern. "I shall leave if you are crude with me!"

His expression changed instantly, and he laughed. "I'm sorry, my lady. I meant only that my wound throbs for your attention. What else might I have meant?"

Deirdre knew her face was now truly flushed. It seemed that men, no matter who they were, or what the circumstances, were always ready to mate. Malvin, old and wretched as he was, had certainly wanted to mate. Vaguely she wondered if she would like it, too—not with Malvin, of course, but with this Viking. But as quickly as she silently asked the question of herself, she rebuked herself. *What am I thinking?* she questioned. And she was certain that by now her face was crimson.

"You blush, my lady. What thoughts have come into your head?"

"Keep a civil tongue in your mouth," she warned. "My father has a temper."

"You spoke well for me at the banquet," he said. His expression had changed now, and he looked earnest.

"I spoke common sense," Deirdre replied.

"And because you find me handsome," he suggested. "Do you dream about me, my lady? Have you dreamt of us together?"

"Stop it! I demand you hold your tongue!"

He smiled. It was wicked to tease her. She seemed quite innocent. "I shall stop," he promised halfheartedly. "Still, may I offer my congratulations on escaping marriage vows with King Malvin. It is a reprieve at least equal to the one you gave me."

Deirdre half smiled in response to his words. Yes, she had also been reprieved. "How did you know this?" she asked, remembering he had been taken away before Malvin had left in a rage.

"I heard the soldiers talking. They're afraid of King Malvin, afraid he will now attack your father's kingdom."

Deirdre frowned. Might he attack? Yes, Malvin might well war with her father over such a thing. It had briefly crossed her mind at the banquet but for the past few days she had put it out of her thoughts and allowed herself only to celebrate her freedom from Malvin. A chill passed through her. Malvin was not used to being thwarted, and war did indeed seem possible. "I hope he has more sense," she replied, hesitating to let this Viking know her true fears.

Brand said no more for the moment, but he watched intently as she undid his bandage, cleaned his wound, and finally put on a new bandage. His shoulder had not festered and rotted. This woman's medicine was good. And once again, as she leaned close, he smelled the scent of roses. But it was not just the aroma of her skin that fascinated him. She had a soft touch, a gentle way. Her skin was like velvet, and she moved her hands expressively when she spoke.

"There," Deirdre said with satisfaction. "You're healing well. And I've brought you some honey to give you strength. I shall try to see to it that you are given meat several times a week."

"You are most generous," Brand said.

Deirdre nodded. "It is in our interests to keep you in good health. I am sure your compatriots would not bother to ransom an ill or emaciated hostage."

"Quite so," Brand answered, "and if you really want to keep me healthy, you could arrange for me to bathe."

"I can manage that," Deirdre replied. Yes, she would gladly arrange it. "I only wish the men of my father's kingdom wanted to bathe, too."

"Clearly they don't," Brand answered.

Deirdre did smile then. "I shall have the water and tub brought later today."

"I would be most grateful, my lady."

Deirdre nodded and quickly replaced her medicines in her basket. "I shall come tomorrow," she promised.

He smiled and put his large hand on her slender arm. "I should like to talk with you, my lady. I need to learn your language better. There are many things I wish to learn about this land."

"Why, so you will know from whom to steal?" She arched her brows, but did not shake free of his grasp.

"No, so that I will gain knowledge."

Deirdre looked into his stone blue eyes. They were indeed hypnotic, drawing her in, caressing her, delving into her innermost thoughts. Could he be telling the truth? Did he yearn for knowledge as she did? "I suppose we can speak of some things," she agreed hesitatingly.

He nodded and smiled. "I shall look forward to it."

"But in return you must tell me things—you have been to places of which I know nothing."

"I shall tell you anything you wish."

"I shall come back tomorrow," Deirdre agreed.

It was like a flash of lightning on a summer's eve, but there was no rain in the cloudless skies, only fear and the certain knowledge that the peace had been shattered. Deirdre clutched her brooch as she stood on the great stone steps of the castle. Her father was assembling his troops while those women and children who lived nearby sought shelter behind the castle walls. There was no time for farewells, no time for prayers, no time for contemplation. Malvin had attacked. Odhran would meet him on the plain with his army, or Malvin would besiege the castle. Clearly, her father had chosen to fight on the plain rather than see his castle destroyed and countless lives lost. Did her father anticipate defeat? Deirdre felt yet another shiver of apprehension run through her.

"It is because of me," Alan said from behind her.

Deirdre turned at the sound of her brother's voice and took his arm. "No, it is because of me," she said sadly.

"I want to fight with our father, but he has forbidden it."

Deirdre did not ask why. Alan was no soldier; on the battlefield he would have been more hindrance than help. "All my fault," she repeated.

"Why is this all your fault?" he asked.

"Because I spoke for the Viking, and our father agreed with me, but more because I did not want to marry Malvin."

Alan nodded. "We can only pray our father is victorious."

Deirdre thought for a long moment. If Odhran lost, Malvin would storm the castle. He would most certainly kill the Viking.

"Go to the chapel," she said gently to Alan. "I'll join you in a short time."

"No, I can't fight, so I will stand guard by the gate. It's the least I can do." Alan smiled weakly at her and kissed her cheek.

Deirdre watched him walk away. She waited for only a second, turned, and hurried inside. She ordered a servant to bring a horse and wagon to the back of the castle and to put a sword under the straw. The old man looked at her as if she were mad, but he disappeared to do as he was told.

Deirdre bolted up the steps, heading for the cells in the tower. Today there would be no guards to dismiss—they would all be with her father.

She reached the top of the steps and leaned for a moment against the wall to catch her breath. Outside she could hear the trumpets sounding the final call to arms.

She found the key hanging on a hook, unlocked the door, and fumbled with the chain. She flung open the door.

Brand turned toward her and raised his brow. "An unexpected visitor," he said with a broad smile. "Good day, my lady. May I ask the cause of all the commotion below?"

"War," she breathed. "Malvin attacks us, shattering the peace of the three kingdoms who pay homage to the great king at Tara. This may well be a sad day for my father's kingdom."

Brand looked over her head, past the open door, out into the hallway. "My guard is not here, my lady. Do you not fear for yourself? Do you not fear I will escape?"

Deirdre shook her head. "You have no time for frivolity. If Malvin wins, he will take this castle and kill you. As for escaping, it is my intention to free you."

Brand drew in his breath. How he would like to take this woman! How he would like to hold her, undress her, caress her, and lose himself in her red-gold tresses. Her skin was like milk, and he suspected her whole voluptuous body had the same silky feel as her hands. How he yearned to kiss her full breasts and bend her slender body to his will. But unhappily, there wasn't a moment to lose. She spoke sense. Time was of the essence, and he would not, in any case, force her unwillingly because she was his savior. "Are you really freeing me?" he asked.

Deirdre looked into his eyes. "Yes," she whispered. "Follow me. I'll show you a way out."

He followed her down the long, winding staircase and through the empty halls of the castle. She led him through the kitchen and down another flight of stairs. She paused long enough to enter a storeroom and return with some clothes—clothes that might be worn by an itinerant trader. "Put these on," she ordered.

He began to change quickly while she primly turned her back and watched for anyone coming. "I'm ready," he said.

She turned and, in spite of the situation almost laughed. The clothes fit, but only just. The pants, sewn for a poor man, were tied with a string around the waist, and while there was ample string, the legs were stretched over his muscular calves and thighs. Moreover, they were too short by inches. As if that were not absurd enough, the top could barely be closed, and he was obliged to leave several ties on the vest undone because it did not reach across his ample chest.

"Follow me," she bade, and again he followed her, this time down a narrow corridor and out into the courtyard. She led him past huddled peasant women and children to a narrow gate on the far side of the courtyard. "Take that wagon and horse," she commanded. "Travel south. The battle is on the western plain. You will find a sword in the wagon beneath the skins."

Brand looked down on her. Quickly, he slipped his arm around her tiny waist and drew her close, pressing his lips to hers for an instant. He breathed heavily in her ear, "Come with me, my lady."

"I cannot, I am the daughter of King Odhran."

"If your father is not victorious, King Malvin will claim you."

"I have to stay. I am my father's daughter."

He nodded as if he understood her responsibility. Yet he kissed her again and whispered, "Till we meet again, my lady."

Deirdre stood frozen to the spot as he climbed into the wagon and quickly rode through the gate out into the countryside. Her lips still burned from his kiss. As he disappeared from sight it was as if the feel of his forceful arms were still about her, still holding her close. His iron-hard body had pressed against her, and she had felt him torturously close—and she had pressed against him, too. What were these terrible, treacherous thoughts? What were these surging desires? This man was a Viking, a thief, a heathen!

And yet she thought about him in other ways—forbidden ways. She too readily imagined the feel of his naked chest against her, too realistically dreamt of running her hands across his body, too easily thought of being in his arms and of having him devour her with sweet kisses. No, no! This was not right! She turned quickly and hurried back into the castle. But her face was still hot and flushed with the memory of his lips and her own wild thoughts of him.

Three

The sun, which had been so weak at noon, sank into the western sea with a blaze of orange and gold. It was at this hour of the day's greatest beauty, that the horrible news came. King Odhran had been defeated. It was news that stunned Alan, caused Deirdre to weep with sadness and brought fear to the eyes of the serfs and vassals who had so loyally served her father.

The soldiers who had fought to defend her father's kingdom trickled back from battle one by one. Many were wounded and carried tattered banners. These were the soldiers from her father's personal guard.

Six of them carried Odhran back through the castle gates on a litter. Other soldiers, loyal to Malvin, followed. It all happened so quickly that Deirdre could not take it all in. Her father, Odhran, was mortally wounded, his army—now vanquished—had for the most part quickly sworn loyalty to the new king, Malvin, in order to avoid a harsh fate.

Deirdre ran to the litter and followed by its side. A long, vicious spear protruded from her father's stomach; his wound gushed blood, and his breath came in short gasps.

Even as Deirdre looked down into her father's face as he lay on the blood-soaked litter, Malvin rode triumphantly through the castle gates and into the courtyard, his battle banners blowing in the wind. He halted his horse by the litter and looked down at Deirdre.

"Nurse your father during his dying hours!" Malvin ordered.

Deirdre did not look up into the eyes of the man who had ordered her father struck down, or perhaps, who had struck him down himself.

Malvin laughed. "All Meath is now mine! See your brother, heir to your father's throne!"

Deirdre looked beyond Malvin and saw Alan. He was in chains, his head bowed. They had arrested him just outside the gates.

"You are without mercy," Deirdre said coldly. She turned to the guards. "Take my father to the steps in front of the chapel altar," she ordered.

The small chapel was just inside the castle walls. As directed, the soldiers set her father down on a wide step at the foot of the altar.

Deirdre knelt beside him, tears streaming down her face. King Odhran was strict but just; Malvin was, by contrast, mean, a man with a reputation for ordering undeserved punishments. King Odhran had ruled and was respected. Malvin was feared.

Deirdre shook her head and wiped the tears from her cheeks. He could be a harsh man, but he was her father, and she loved him dearly. Deirdre examined the spear and her father's wound.

Odhran's lips moved slowly, painfully. "This is where I married your mother."

"I know," she answered softly.

"And this is where you and your brother were christened." Her father's eyes had begun to glaze over. "Deirdre, what of Alan?"

Even now her father would not accept a lie from her. "In chains," she whispered. With all his strength she felt her father squeeze her hand. "Help him," her father pleaded. "Do not allow my line to die."

"I won't," Deirdre promised. She knew all to too well

what had to be done. It meant an end to her life of freedom. It would be the beginning of her terrible servitude to Malvin.

"You're strong," Odhran murmured. "You should have been my son."

He had said that before, and she knew he said it in admiration. But she was glad Alan was not there to hear it.

Deirdre pressed her lips to her father's forehead. "Your wound is too great for my medical knowledge," she whispered.

"I am a dead man who still breathes," her father managed to gasp. "Deirdre, give me a potion, I do not wish to suffer so."

Deirdre bit her lip. Such a thing was not right. The Holy Father forbid it, so the priest would not allow it. Still, if she did it before he came . . . it would be worse if her father cried out in agony. She had seen such wounds, it might take days for him to die. Yes, her father's painful cries were more than Malvin deserved to hear, more than she could bear. She fumbled in her basket and found the vial. She quickly held the vial of liquid to her father's lips. A fast and painless death, it would be their secret for eternity.

No sooner had her father drunk the potion than the priest hurried in. He came to perform the Last Rites and he hurriedly did so, even as Odhran closed his eyes and drifted into the longest of all sleeps.

"Go in peace, my father," Deirdre whispered. She waited silently, imagining his spirit leaving his body just as she had imagined Edana's spirit leaving her body. "Find my mother," Deirdre said softly. She closed her eyes and thought of them together, floating away on the summer breeze, united once again. She thought, too, of the talk she had with her father—a short talk. Too short. Yet that night, the night of the banquet, he had given her a precious gift. He had told her about her mother and how much they had loved one another. She smiled to herself and touched her fingers to her lips, then put her fingers on his forehead. How wonderful that in this imperfect world such a love could be found. "You were fortunate among men, my father," she said softly. "And you as well, my mother. True love is hard to find."

It seemed impossible—but maybe fate would intervene. Maybe she would not have to marry Malvin. Maybe she would also find a perfect love.

Lost in thought, Deirdre jumped when she felt a hand on her shoulder. There was no mercy. Her father breathed his last breath and it seemed that—even as it hung in the air—the messenger stood behind her, summoning her to the great hall, to kneel at Malvin's feet, to beg for mercy for her condemned brother.

I am living a long and horrible nightmare, Deirdre thought. *But this is a dream from which I will not awaken.*

Deirdre walked between the two guards as they escorted her into the great hall. There, on her father's throne, high on the dais, Malvin sat, his expression tense, his body rigid. To one side, her brother Alan stood in chains, his head bowed, his hands trembling. His face had been forced into the dirt and was muddy. Tears ran down his cheeks, making rivers in the dirt that covered him.

"Submit, daughter of King Odhran!" Malvin's head steward called out. He stood by the throne, tall and erect like a statue, his face impassive, Malvin's battle colors grasped in one hand.

Deirdre stood as if in a trance. Malvin looked like an ugly little frog, triumphant in his victory. Silently she heaped curses on him.

Deirdre came and knelt before Malvin as she was expected to do. She glanced at her brother. His face was a mask of misery.

"Before I decide on your brother's fate, I want entertainment," Malvin declared. "I've sent for the Viking prisoner. The beheading of a savage should improve my mood."

Deirdre did not look up; she forced herself not to react. Malvin would be furious when he discovered the Viking was not there.

It was a terrible wait and seemed like an eternity. The soldier returned at last. "The Viking is not in his cell! Sire, he appears to have escaped."

"And what do you know of this, Princess!" Malvin's voice thundered through the hall. He had jumped to his feet, and he towered over her crouched body.

Deirdre looked up, her eyes wide with innocence. "I know nothing, my lord. There was so much confusion . . . the guards must have gone to fight."

Malvin grumbled and gulped from his goblet of wine. "Then perhaps I shall behead your brother!"

"No!" Deirdre cried out. She stood up and immediately knelt again, throwing herself across Malvin's feet. "Spare him, I beg you. Send him to the monastery. He is an artist, his work belongs to God."

Malvin glanced at Alan and then at the lovely form that lay across his feet. "And in return, Princess? What will be my reward? Such an act would be pure generosity on my part. So tell me, what will you do for me?"

Deirdre looked up at him. "I shall consent to be your wife."

Malvin smiled broadly. He could not have forced her to wed as Naill, the king of Tara, would have objected. He could, however, have kept her prisoner. But this was a good bargain, her hand in marriage in return for her brother's life.

In spite of being a woman, Deirdre was aware of the unwritten, unspoken rules. Malvin wanted no trouble with the overkingdom of Tara, at least not until he felt himself strong enough to challenge its power. For many years now, Tara had ruled over the three kingdoms that were adjacent to its kingdom. In her heart she knew that Malvin would not have dared attack her father had Naill, the king of Tara, not agreed. No doubt he sanctioned the action because Alan was thought to be too weak to be king, and Odhran had no other male heirs. It seemed everyone's will but her own that she wed Malvin.

Malvin did not take his eyes off Deirdre, but with a wave

of his hand he gestured toward Alan. "Escort this boy to the monastery at Trim," he shouted to the captain of his guard.

Deirdre stared at the rough stone floor. She had fulfilled her father's last wish, she had saved her brother's life.

"I shall make the proper preparations and we shall marry before the month ends. Until our wedding, dear lady, you will keep to your rooms."

Deirdre did not answer. Malvin knew her well. He would keep her guarded till their nuptials; otherwise, she might try to conspire against him. *And conspire I would,* Deirdre thought . . . *if only I could think of someone with whom to conspire.* One thing of which she was certain, it would do no good to petition the king of Tara, nor could she kill herself or run away. To do so would anger Malvin, and he would have Alan killed.

I am trapped, Deirdre thought. *And there is no escape for me.*

The next morning, Deirdre was awakened by a loud pounding on her door. She threw her cloak around her and opened the door.

"Do not bolt your door, my lady!" Malvin's large foot kicked the door open and he stepped into her room, looking around, appraising everything.

Deirdre, who was wary of him and even more on edge because they were alone, stood still and stared at the floor. Malvin would take her posture to mean compliance, when in reality it was pure defiance.

"I could have you now," he thundered.

Deirdre did not reply. Perhaps her situation was hopeless. Did it really matter if he forced himself on her now, or on their wedding night? But yet her every instinct told her to buy time, to put off the inevitable for as long as possible.

"I look forward to the moment," Malvin said threateningly. "You will beg me, my lady. I will bend you to my will."

Still Deirdre said nothing. To show fear was to encourage him. He was a bully, and he took pleasure from the fear of others.

"Silence becomes you," Malvin muttered as he spit on the floor. "I didn't come to force you. That can wait till we're married and I have the blessings of King Naill. Your brother is leaving now. Go bid him farewell forever."

Forever—Deirdre again felt like crying, but she forced herself not to shed tears and give Malvin satisfaction.

"Where is he?" she asked.

"Below, in the courtyard, ready to begin his journey to Trim."

Deirdre hurried past Malvin and down the castle steps. When she reached the courtyard she saw her brother, and tears came to her eyes.

Alan was dressed in rough brown sackcloth and was to ride a mule.

Deirdre ran to him and embraced him.

"It is the final humiliation," Alan said, looking down. "I shall be paraded throughout Meath for all to see."

"Pride comes from within," Deirdre said softly. "Hold your head high, Alan."

"How can I? I have condemned you to a life of misery."

Deirdre kissed his pale cheek. "I don't know when and I don't know how, but I feel we will be reunited. Dear brother, be brave."

"I shall try to be as brave as you."

Deirdre forced a smile. He was still young, still a boy really. "We will meet again," she said firmly.

Alan kissed her and slowly turned and mounted the donkey. "It is a long way to Trim," he said with resolution.

Six days had passed since Brand had driven the cart away, leaving Princess Deirdre to her fate. Hardly a moment passed that he did not think of her, and now his preoccupation with her fate led him to the monastery at Trim. It was a huge compound, a walled city with a great church in its center. In addition to the church the compound held dormitories, cloisters, artists' workrooms, a bakery, a wine cellar, and an infirmary. Disguised in the clothes of a common serf, Brand made his way about and took silent inventory of the treasures the monastery offered.

But it was not treasure he sought. Brand peered into the rooms where artists toiled and finally he saw Alan, the soft-featured brother of the beautiful Deirdre.

Alan was alone, toiling over a large piece of parchment.

"Do not cry out," Brand said evenly as he put his hand on Alan's shoulder.

Alan turned and his face seemed to grow even paler.

"You—" he gasped.

"I mean you no harm," Brand said quickly. "Tell me what happened. It is time I go back to Dublin, but I must know what has happened to Deirdre."

"Deirdre set you free, didn't she?" Alan said, obviously regaining himself and grasping the situation.

Brand nodded. "Was your father victorious?"

Alan shook his head. "No, he died from wounds received in battle."

Brand felt his own blood run cold as a vision of Malvin filled his head. "Deirdre?" he asked. "What of your sister?"

"She gave her life for me. She must marry Malvin. But she only agreed in order to prevent my being killed."

Brand grimaced. He felt nothing but anger that a woman such as Deirdre would have to become the wife of a man such as Malvin. But he was angry with himself as well. It was unseemly that he should care so much! Why had he not been able to put this woman out of his mind? And not only was he weeks late returning to Dublin, now he was asking questions of her brother which would delay him further.

"You seem concerned," Alan said.

"Because she saved me. It is only a matter of honor."

Alan did not respond, though he thought the Viking might be in love with Deirdre. It seemed that all the men who met her wanted her.

It pained Brand to ask the next question, but he forced himself to say the words. "Are Deirdre and Malvin married yet?"

"No," Alan replied. "They will go to Tara to be married by the overking, Naill, at the end of the month."

Brand's heart leapt. She was not yet married! There was time!

"May I offer you the hospitality of this place? Some dinner perhaps? We make fine wine here," Alan said.

Brand shook his head. "I must return to Dublin. It is now even more important than before."

Yes, Brand thought. A plan was beginning to take shape in his mind. But he would have to hurry. Time was now most important; the days before Deirdre gave herself to Malvin were numbered.

Alan touched his arm. "Have a safe journey," he said softly.

"Thank you." Brand turned and left quickly, wondering about these Christians who offered their enemies food, shelter, and good wishes. It was beyond him, as beyond him as his own conflicting feelings about Princess Deirdre.

"Brand! Son of Jarls!" the captive servant proclaimed. Brand's name echoed down the long earthen corridor that led to the main room of the underground, sod-covered fort where Lord Thorgills sat at his solitary table eating a pork roast and quaffing red wine.

Thorgills was a massive man with a hairy face, pale blue eyes, and a narrow, mean mouth. He looked up and licked his chops, retrieving bits of food from his thick beard with his tongue.

"You've been gone a long while," he said, eyeing Brand and settling his gaze on Brand's wounded shoulder.

"I was wounded defending myself and taken captive."

"It would seem you were cared for well."

"I was looked after, and my wound dressed."

"Well, it would seem you escaped, and I trust that means you returned with information."

Brand nodded. "Perhaps of more import is what led to my escape."

"And what might that be?"

"The kingdom of East Meath, ruled by one King Malvin, attacked and defeated the kingdom of Meath, ruled by King Odhran. As a result of the battle and in spite of his victory, Malvin's forces are very much weakened."

Thorgills rubbed his chin thoughtfully. "If they spent their energies defending against us, we would not be so successful. But they war with one another instead. What invaders could ask for more? But the vital question is yet unanswered. Is there anything worth invading for—are these kingdoms rich?"

"The monastery at Trim is filled with treasure. It alone is well worth an expedition into Meath. And from what I have seen, both Odhran and Malvin have possessions well worth the trouble."

Brand answered forthrightly and did not bother to comment on the fact that the northern chieftains also fought among themselves. He himself served Lord Thorgills only because of such a war, a war that saw his father defeated and allowed to live only because Brand had been bound over for service.

"Tell me what you saw?" Lord Thorgills prodded.

Brand smiled and thought to describe a few of the things he had seen. But in truth his thoughts were not on treasure, they were on Deirdre and his own desire not just to see her again, but somehow to take her from Malvin. Perhaps, in spite of their arrangement, after all his years of service, he could persuade Thorgills to give him Deirdre rather than sell her with the other Celtic women to the slave markets of the Mediterranean. He would leave her here, of course. He would, in return for her kindness, set her free.

"Your eyes betray you, Brand. You think of more than war. I know you, too well."

Brand looked up at Thorgills and shook his head. "I am only tired. I've traveled far."

Thorgills shrugged. "Go rest, and when you return you will help me plan our attack. I'm bored, and there is always time for more conquest before we leave these shores."

Brand said no more. He left Thorgills and headed toward his quarters. They had wintered in this fort overlooking the river and now they had the summer to invade and conquer. In the fall most of them would head home. Home—it had been three years since he had dared think of home.

The river by which the monastery at Trim was built originated in a bog in Kildare. It then traveled some seventy miles to the Hibernian Sea, which it entered just below Drogheda. The river was more than a source of water, however. Like most rivers this one was a main transportation route. Travel by water, was, after all, far swifter than overland travel.

As a result of being on a main travel route, once a week, on Saturday morning, the pasture next to the monastery was turned into a large market. Farmers and artisans came from miles around to buy and sell. Women brought weaving and spindles of wool. Some brought fancy honey cakes and others various kinds of cured meats. Skins were sold, fresh vegetables and roots traded, and metalworkers displayed tools as well as fancy brooches and buckles. Horses were shod, games played, and dances held. When the sun set, as if by magic, the market stalls disappeared, the bells of the monastery rang in the sabbath, and the inhabitants all returned home to pray and keep the Holy Day.

The monastery itself was a repository for art from all over the Christian world. Its shelves held rows of carefully copied scripture, artfully executed and illuminated with silver and gold inks on the finest of heavy parchment. Each of these was written in a script which was itself ornate and a work of art.

The library held books mounted on silver, gold, and bronze and encrusted with precious jewels. The walls were covered with priceless tapestries and the vault held a cache of gold and silver coins. The monastery boasted a large group of artists who worked to copy and illustrate still more scriptures. It was to this work that Alan quickly dedicated himself. His pages of parchment soon burst forth with color and he designed wonderful delicate curlicues with which to surround his capital letters.

"Your work is exquisite, your talent a great gift," Father Paddrick said with admiration as he studied Alan's work. "It is difficult to believe you've been here only a few weeks."

Alan smiled at the monk's praise and thought how seldom anyone save his sister had praised him for anything.

"Do you find life here to your liking?" Father Paddrick asked.

"It's far different from the castle, but yes, I find it to my liking," Alan replied thoughtfully. But there was the unasked question—the question of Deirdre. He missed her with each passing day, and he was filled with sorrow for her. Malvin was a terrible and cruel man.

"How is it so different?" the monk asked.

Alan shrugged. "In the castle I had a large room and could roam anywhere. Here I sleep on the floor of a tiny cell." He thought of his small cell. For company there was only a plain wooden cross. It was a quiet existence, one which suited him. Each monk had his own work. Some cared for the crops, others cleaned, while still others worked as he did on the manuscripts for which the monastery was famous.

"But you have no real regrets?" the Monk persisted.

Alan shook his head.

"I'm glad you have no regrets," Father Paddrick said as he turned and left.

Alan watched him as he padded off. Regrets? No, he did not regret being here in the least. But again his thoughts returned to his sister. She had sacrificed everything for him, and he worried constantly about her. He could only pray that Malvin would not treat her badly and that, even though he knew she would never care for Malvin, perhaps she would have children to love. Deirdre deserved some happiness, and he felt misery that he had played so large a role in denying her that happiness.

He wondered, too, about the Viking. The man had dared to come here to make inquiries about her. Or perhaps, Alan thought, he had come to see the riches for himself. He felt confused and vaguely wondered if he should tell Father Paddrick. But on reflection, he thought better of it. Whatever the reason for the Viking's visit, the future had to be left to God.

Deirdre brushed her hair and stared into the mirror Malvin had given her. She drew her robe around her as evening brought a chill to the castle. She finished pulling the brush through her hair and quickly braided it, loosely. When she was done, she hurried to her bed and nestled beneath her skins, seeking warmth. But no sooner was she there then she was overcome with a feeling of dread. No matter how often she tried to put it out of her mind, she could not forget her coming marriage to Malvin. Unfortunately, her thoughts closed in upon her at the close of each day and during the night. "Fifteen days left," she whispered to herself. Fifteen days and she would be sharing her bed with Malvin. The thought was unbearable. It caused her to cringe. But there was no alternative. If she ran away, Malvin would surely kill her brother. Moreover, where would she run? No kingdom would give her sanctuary.

Once again, as they did at the end of every day, tears filled her eyes. There was simply no way out. She couldn't even kill herself. Malvin would execute her brother in anger. No, she had to marry him. She had to face giving her body to him, to bearing his children and to living in this castle, subject to his every whim.

Deirdre closed her eyes and sought blessed escape in sleep. She tossed first on one side and then the other. Finally she felt herself slipping away as she crossed the boundary between half wakefulness and sleep. At first she had no dreams and was lost only in the silent darkness. She found herself in the meadow behind her father's castle. It was summer, and the wildflowers danced in a soft breeze; the summer sun warmed her and she walked alone, gathering herbs.

Unexpectedly, from just below knoll she saw the Viking. His golden silken hair glistened in the sunlight, his muscular legs gripping a black steed. His arms were bare, and his broad shoulders seemed even broader. He drew his steed up and slipped from the saddle. His arms surrounded her, and she felt tiny yet secure in his grasp. His body was hot against hers, and she felt the outline of him as his large hands caressed her roughly. It was as if their clothing fell away and they were together, he pressing to her, she moving against him. His lips were everywhere, kissing her breasts, her neck, her lips, and even her mound of red hair. "Tighter," she whispered in her deep sleep. "Never let me go." She felt a gentle release, a feeling so wonderfully pleasant that it awakened her.

Deirdre's eyes opened suddenly and she was aware that her whole body glowed in warmth as she felt the gentle pulsating; a pleasurable flush surged through her. Instinctively her hands flew to her cheeks. They were flushed in the darkness of the room, as flushed as if her dream had been a reality. She touched her lips and thought of the Viking's kiss—it lingered, the memory as pleasant as the all-too-fleeting reality. Where was the Viking now? Surely he was safe— her dream had been pleasant, not foreboding.

Deirdre turned again on her side. She urged herself to sleep. The cold reality of morning would come all too soon.

Deirdre turned over and faced the dark wall next to her bed, and in the darkness she saw Malvin's face. Forcing the image of Malvin from her mind, she instead thought of the Viking whom she had helped escape. Why did she always think of him? Why could she still feel the imprint of his lips on hers? Why could she still remember the outline of his body pressing against hers? Still, when she thought of the Viking, she forgot Malvin.

Deirdre finally closed her eyes, and, even as sleep crept over her, she saw his face, felt his fine blond hair caress her cheek, and squirmed contentedly in his strong grasp. Sleep . . . yes, return to dreams, she thought, as she allowed herself to be carried away to a far more pleasant place than this room in Malvin's castle.

Deirdre's eyes opened, and she sat up suddenly, all her senses alert. There was shouting in the courtyard as well as in the castle. She heard the alarm, the familiar gong that signaled attack. That was followed by the certain clatter of armed soldiers running down the castle corridors and steps. They were shouting in panic, as if the Devil himself were pursuing them.

For a second, panic seized Deirdre, too—she had been bathed in the security of a warm and tender dream, a dream where she was held, caressed, and loved by a handsome stranger—no, not a stranger, the Viking! Her cheeks again flushed at the thought of her dream. It had seemed so real, he had seemed so close . . . but the Vikings were the enemies of her people, he was the enemy, and it was wrong of her to think of him or even to dream of him as she had.

"We're being attacked!" There was an incessant pounding on her door. It was followed by more shouting.

The words carried her back to that morning only a few weeks earlier when Malvin had attacked her father's kingdom. The memory of her father mounted on his great black steed and clad for battle filled her mind. Her eyes suddenly filled with tears as she thought of him being brought back, his once strong body mortally wounded, the life seeping out of him. And Alan—her brother—who had been sent away. She missed him terribly and wondered if he was happy at Trim. In all of these weeks she had heard nothing from him, but it was entirely possible that he had written to her and Malvin had confiscated his letters.

Deirdre shook her head to dispel her all-too-recent memories. The pounding on her door had ceased, but she still heard shouting. The cries were still punctuated with the clang of the great iron gong that called the men to arms.

Was it possible that survivors of her father's army had rallied and were now attacking? Or maybe the great king at Tara had decided to squelch Malvin's ambitions. After a moment's reflection neither of these possibilities seemed likely.

And it was hardly light! This was very different from Malvin's attack on her father, very different from the way the Celts fought among themselves. The morning of the attack on her father's kingdom, the alarm had been sounded and the armies had met on the open plain . . . no, something strange was happening here. No sooner had she thought how very strange it was, when the very floor seemed to shake and she heard screams of real pain from the courtyard below.

Deirdre jumped out of bed and ran to the slit that served as a window. It was so high she had to stand on a stool to see out and down into the courtyard. She bit her lip as she stared at the melee below. There was fire! Great fireballs were being hurled by catapults over the castle walls. Men lay dying, and Malvin, only half-dressed, was running about trying to organize some sort of counterattack. His greasy gray hair blew in the wind, his scrawny legs danced about in growing agitation. There were shouts of "Viking hordes!" and "Surrender before you're killed!" Still Malvin danced about, his mouth moving as he issued orders no one followed.

"Viking hordes," Deirdre whispered to herself. She had heard the stories of their raids, of how they fought, of what happened when they won. There was no meeting on the plain when the Vikings came.

"Dear heaven," she whispered. "Am I responsible for this?" She had let one of them go, freed one of their warriors to fight this day. Of course he might not be one of them. There were many different groups, and each had its own leader. Not that she cared about Malvin's fate or the fate of his commanders. They had, after all, killed her father. No, Malvin was of no concern to her. But the landowners and the villagers did matter. It was said the Vikings made serfs of all men and sold the women into slavery. That they burned, stole, and looted seemed the lesser of their sins.

It immediately crossed her mind that she might not have to marry Malvin, but she forced that thought away, however pleasant it was. Such a thought was selfish given the fact that the circumstances which would free her from Malvin would deliver others into slavery—and of course, she herself might be enslaved. But somehow she felt no fear for herself. Escaping Malvin was enough—she could not imagine a worse fate.

Deirdre ran back to her bed. Her clothes lay over the foot of it, and she hurriedly dressed, binding her cloak about her and pinning it with her Tara brooch. She grasped her basket of medicines and ran from the room even as she silently asked the question which haunted her—was the Viking she had helped among the attackers?

I must be evil even to think of such a thing, to want such a thing, she said to herself. No, she told herself. It was unlikely. In any case, what if he were among them? What made her think that he was really any different than the others . . . except for the fact that she had helped him and thought, somehow, he might help her. But it was an idle thought . . . the fantasy of a silly girl.

She hurried down the stairs. The screams she heard when she reached the grand entrance hall were no fantasy. "They're storming the gates!" she heard a panic-stricken soldier shout.

Deirdre stood stone-still, unable even to run as the others

did. She felt sorry for the soldiers and for those who would suffer. But she had no sympathy for Malvin. "You killed my father," she said under her breath. "I curse you." Deirdre smiled with satisfaction. Malvin himself was defeated!

Deirdre ran toward the entrance to the great hall. She stopped short; four soldiers were bearing Malvin's body. "He's dead!" one of them yelled at her. "Run for your life! Hide! These savages ravish our women and enslave them!"

Deirdre did not move. The man who spoke was the captain of the guard. His arm was gashed and his eyes narrowed as he looked at her, unafraid now of insulting his dead master's future wife. "And a woman like you . . ." he muttered. "They'll rip the clothes from your body! They'll rape you and enslave you!"

Deirdre stepped away from him. He might have been the very one who killed her father. Only now, at this moment, did she realize the depth of her anger. She felt no compassion for these men who had been close to Malvin, none at all.

"Enslave me?" she said, allowing her brow to rise slightly. "I am not free now. Your lord, King Malvin, already enslaved me!"

Something in her wanted to laugh at the terrible irony. How many times could she be enslaved? Besides, perhaps the stories about the Viking hordes were not all true.

She stood rooted to the spot as she heard the screams. The castle doors were forced open, she heard the thundering troops as they entered the castle, shouting victorious cries in their strange northern tongue. They swarmed through the entrance to the great hall, their swords drawn. Deirdre stood in the corner, her back to the wall.

The captain of the castle guard turned, his sword drawn also. It was a miniature compared to those of the Vikings, who wielded great steel broadswords and were taller and stronger, seemingly a race of giants. The castle guard was immediately outnumbered and surrounded. In a moment most were dead, lying on the floor, a dying curse on their lips.

Deirdre had closed her eyes when the first man was felled. Her nostrils filled with the smell of blood; her ears rang with the cries of the dying. But she herself did not scream. She stood with the hard wall to her back, her eyes closed tightly, her lips pressed together. If she were killed, so be it. At least she would die free, untouched by her father's murderer.

It was not until she felt a large hand on her arm pulling her that she opened her eyes to look up into cold steel blue eyes, strangely pale eyes surrounded by snow-white facial hair.

"What have we here?" Thorgills asked, his sword still drawn. He looked down at her. She was a rare beauty, clearly nobly born. He half smiled.

Deirdre read the look in his blue eyes. His expression was twisted, the same expression she had seen on Malvin's face. It was the expression of lust.

"Seize her, Brand!" Thorgills ordered.

And from the rear of the group her Viking strode forward, his face expressionless as if he did not even recognize her. He grabbed her roughly, pulling her hands behind her, holding her in a tight grasp. Deirdre was so surprised she couldn't utter a sound.

Thorgills walked up to her and ripped off the brooch that held her cloak. The cloak fell to the floor, but she made no move. She was stunned by this Brand's lack of recognition. *What a fool I was,* she chastised herself, *for dreaming of this man!* Now that he was no longer vulnerable, he had reverted to kind and was just like all the others.

Thorgills held her brooch up and turned it this way and that, allowing the morning light to catch its amber surface. "Very nice," he said, watching as the golden jewel in its center sparkled. He turned his attention back to her, and roughly, as if she were a prized animal, forced open her mouth.

"Good teeth!" he said, turning to spit on the floor.

He ran his large hand over her hair and touched her throat.

Deirdre could not have moved even if she had not been held. She was utterly frozen to the spot. But she knew at this moment he was assessing her as a piece of merchandise. It was all true! They would ravish and sell her.

Thorgills opened her tunic and parted it.

The men who stood about laughed and she felt herself turn red with embarrassment as bold eyes stared at her. Thorgills's large hand ran over the thin material of her underdress, circled her breasts, moved down her hips.

"Yes, a rare beauty," he whispered as he drew closer. "A suitable birthday gift for Olaf, don't you think, Brand?"

Brand did not answer, but only nodded. It took all of his restraint to allow Thorgills to touch Deirdre, but a wise man chooses his moment to act.

Thorgills turned to another of his men. "Take her upstairs and lock her in her bedchamber. And see you keep your hands off her, she's for Olaf!"

Deirdre wanted to shout at Brand, but her pride would not allow her to beg him for help. How could she have been such a fool!

The guard moved quickly. He threw her over his shoulder as if she were a sack of flour. She was so miserable she could not even scream as the guard carried her up the staircase. She could not even contemplate her fate. Who was this Olaf? What would he do with her? What would become of her when he was finished with her?

She was dumped onto the bed in her room, and her hands were tied as if she were some dangerous criminal. She forced herself to be silent and strong until the guard left her, bolting the door behind him. Then and only then did she allow the tears to flow down her cheeks.

"Dear heaven, what will become of me?" she whispered.

Four

Deirdre stood near a side entrance to the great hall with a burly guard on each side of her. Did they think she would try to run away? As if she could overpower two such strong men; as if there were anywhere to run.

She looked around at the great hall. Never during Malvin's reign had it looked as it looked now. Deirdre was amazed at the transformation. Noise, smoke from the fireplace, and the aroma of food filled the still air. Everywhere groups of men seemed to be arguing as they shouted at one another. This was no formal gathering, it was a beehive of activity.

The long table which usually sat on a dais, just as it had in her father's castle, had been moved into the center of the hall. It was covered with a great variety of food. A large roasted stag had been brought in, as had a huge leg of mutton. Greens and puddings, fish and fowl filled other bowls and platters. But no one sat at the table; rather all the men present simply went to the table and took food and wine as desired. When they had filled their plates, they sat or stood where they pleased.

But it was not just the manner of eating which had changed. The great hall itself seemed barren and cold. The heavy rich tapestries which had hung on the four walls had been ripped down, rolled up, and carried away. Chests containing jewelry and household objects had been filled to overflowing, and clearly these, too, would be borne away.

But most disconcerting were the women. The village girls and daughters of wealthy landowners were treated in the same way. Their finery, if they had any, had been taken away, and they were all dressed in plain brown garments which were held together with heavy cords. They waited on their new masters, bringing them wine and mead. They willingly lifted their faces to be kissed, and few, if any, seemed to resist the advances of the Viking men.

It is always so, Deirdre thought. The victors, any victors, claimed the women of the vanquished as among the spoils of war. And most woman quickly learned compliance; it was a form of survival.

"This feast is to our God of War, Odin," one of her guards said.

It was a heathen feast, and Deirdre watched silently with a combination of horror and fascination. She had been brought from her bedchamber and now stood waiting. But for what? Would she soon be among those women stripped of their clothing and made to wear the rough robes of slaves?

"Inside!" Lord Thorgills shouted, as he looked toward her and motioned to the guard. The guard pushed her forward so hard that Deirdre almost lost her balance. Her hands were still tied behind her, but her feet had not been tied.

Deirdre's eyes moved quickly about the room as she attempted to take in everything. Brand sat near the man they called Lord Thorgills, who was obviously their leader. Next to this Thorgills was his younger image—a huge man with dark blond hair and narrow pale blue eyes. His nose was flattish, his lips too full. And even though he was a big man and no doubt strong, he was also fat. Worse yet, there was something about his expression that made him seem not too bright. Unlike Brand, he lacked quick intelligent eyes and lean muscular strength. He was not attractive in any way, and even at a distance his mannerisms seemed brutish. Deirdre took a deep breath to prepare herself. In her heart she knew this giant was Olaf, son of Thorgills, the man to whom she would be given. It seemed impossible, but he appeared to be even worse than Malvin.

Lord Thorgills pushed Olaf forward. "I saved her for you! A birthday gift! A princess!"

She had been propelled forward and now stood only a few inches away from Olaf, who leered at her, even as he seemed to twitch with anticipation.

Olaf had been eating, and he thrust a giant greasy hand toward her and ran it over her hair.

Deirdre closed her eyes and pressed her lips together so she would not scream. He felt her breasts, squeezing one so that she winced in pain. She kept her head down, trying in some way to separate her mind from her body, though her face burned red and she was sure she was trembling.

Unexpectedly, he dipped his hand into her dress and she felt him touch her bare breast and pinch her nipple. She closed her eyes and shook violently—he wanted her to scream, and she vowed she would not give him the pleasure.

Brand leaned over to Thorgills and, sipping his own wine with a certain lack of concern, shook his head. "This is not wise," he whispered. He made a gesture that took in the whole room.

Thorgills turned around. "What's not wise?"

"These are our most valuable warriors; Olaf is among the most valuable. It's not wise to allow them to spend a night in dissipation when we have to fight tomorrow. This revelry should be postponed until we have taken Trim. After all, we ride at dawn."

Deirdre strained to hear what was being said in spite of Olaf's huge probing hands. Trim! Alan was at Trim. He could be killed! Quite suddenly it was as if Olaf did not exist. Her thoughts focused on her brother, on finding some way to save him.

"Everyone now knows we are in the vicinity and there will be opposition," Brand continued, a serious tone in his voice. "We need our best warriors alert and not drunk with wine and weakened by the pleasures of the body. Olaf should wait and take this woman only after our battle is won. The others, too, should be restrained."

Lord Thorgills turned and looked at Brand. It was true that Brand served him in order to keep his father safe. But Lord Thorgills judged Brand to be twice the warrior his own son was and possibly ten times more intelligent. He was a fine strategist, and he understood the ways of both men and the gods. He was an honorable man, untempted by the large number of available women, and he remained loyal to Erica. Brand drank, but was never drunk. Yes, Lord Thorgills thought, there was much to admire in Brand. Still, the very aspects of his personality that were admirable, would no doubt destroy him one day just as his father had been destroyed. *The honorable man trusts too much,* Thorgills concluded. Still, his comments about tomorrow were well-taken. The time for celebration was when all the battles had been won.

"Today's victory was only half the victory; we shall celebrate tomorrow night when we return here," Brand said, pressing his point.

Thorgills grunted and looked at Olaf. Clearly he was pleased with his little princess. But a gift worth having was a gift worth waiting for. Brand was right, they had to fight tomorrow. "Olaf!"

Thorgills's tone was sharp, and his voice filled the hall. Olaf reluctantly turned away from Deirdre, and virtually everyone fell silent.

"Have your woman locked up, and the rest of you put away your pleasures—we'll leave them here under guard, and they'll be here when we return. We need to be strong for tomorrow's battle. Look at this beauty! Olaf, she'll wear you out! Wait and take your time with her."

Olaf's mouth opened slightly, and his expression twisted in anger as his pale blue eyes narrowed. "I want her now," Olaf grumbled.

Anticipating his son's howl of displeasure, Thorgills raised his hand. "No argument! We fight tomorrow and need not be weakened by wine and women!"

Brand lifted his goblet. "To Thorgills, our leader!" he thundered. Everyone joined the toast, and Olaf turned back to Deirdre. "Take her away!" he ordered. "Lock her up! Let no one near her! I want this virgin beauty on my return!"

Temporary relief flooded over Deirdre. But it would be a short reprieve—they would return, and, when they did, this pig Olaf would claim her. As she was prodded once again toward the staircase, she glanced back at Brand, who ate contentedly and did not even look at her. Pigs! They were all pigs! Not, she reminded herself, that Malvin had been any better.

But this Brand was worse! He was not concerned in the slightest with her fate even though she had tended his wounds and freed him, allowing him to escape certain death. She stared at the stone steps as the guards led her onward. They were taking her back to the bedchamber, where they would again leave her with her hands tied. That meant she could not even take her own life! Deirdre fought to hold back hot tears. Olaf was a cruel, miserable beast! He would use her and discard her to a life of disgrace and misery or perhaps sell her into slavery to be used by others. It was too horrible to contemplate.

The guard kicked open the door to her bedchamber prison. She was carried to the bed and dropped onto it without concern. The guard pulled a skin cover over her, and laughed. "So you won't be cold," he said.

Deirdre felt the hot tears begin to run down her cheeks. It didn't matter now. It was too dark for her captors to see her. They were laughing, and she could easily imagine what they were laughing about even though she could not understand much of their language. Doubtless they were laughing at her humiliation. Doubtless they were talking about what would soon happen to her. She turned on the bed, wondering, not for the first time, why when men were defeated in battle, it was the women who paid.

Brand eased himself through the din and finally reached the door. Soon everyone would be finished and would retire for the evening as Thorgills had commanded.

He walked outside into the courtyard and wiped his brow. The hall was unseemly hot and the noise annoying. Outside it was quiet, and above the stars shone brightly in a cloudless sky. "I have only bought her time," he said to himself. All he had accomplished was to forestall the woman's cruel fate. But I, too, have time, he reminded himself. Time to think of some plan, time to in some way to help her escape to safety. But how could he help her when he could not even help himself? Little did she realize it, but he was as much a prisoner of Lord Thorgills as she.

He cursed under his breath. This was not how he had planned it. He had planned to attack Malvin and claim the princess as his prize. Instead, Lord Thorgills had given her to Olaf! His lovely little Deirdre had gone from the pan into the fire.

Brand lay down on one of the stone steps and fastened his eyes on the stars. It was a bright night, the moon full. Inside the men had locked up the women and dragged themselves into secluded corners where they now slept. Most would fall into sleep easily because they had drunk too much wine already.

Brand's eyes searched the walls of the castle, seeking the window of the bedchamber where Princess Deirdre was locked and under guard. He thought about her for a long moment. She was brave and beautiful. How he had fought for self-control when Olaf had touched her! One day, maybe tomorrow, the opportunity would arise, and he would kill Olaf. It would be easy if he thought of that moment, of Olaf's hand on her flesh, of the look of terror and humiliation in her compelling green eyes. *You will pay, Olaf,* he vowed. *If not tomorrow, then indeed soon.*

No, he could not let Olaf have her—he would not let it happen—although he could not immediately think of just how to prevent it.

Again, he sought the stars as if in their patterns he might find the answer to his dilemma. But of course he could not endanger his father—how could he save the woman and at the same time avoid Thorgills's wrath?

Five years—it seemed like a lifetime, Brand brooded. He closed his eyes and thought of home and of the circumstances that had brought him to this moment.

His home was in a land shaped by the gods and carved by the sea. As its full streams rushed down narrow canyons to the choppy gray ocean, the voice of Thor could be heard thundering across the waters. It was a miraculous land of islands, white chalk cliffs, and dense forests. Freyr, the god of the World, had created peaceful beauty as well as breathtaking seascapes. Waves on hard rock, it was a land of contrasts, a land of green pines and barren ground, of wind and calm, of war and peace.

Vivid images of Heorot, his home, filled Brand's mind. The castle was seemingly carved from the hillside, and its outer walls were decorated with stags' horns.

Inside, its rooms were hung with skins, and flames rose from giant fireplaces to bring the comfort of heat to the long, dark, cold winter nights. It was a fortress, yet it was home—a place where childish laughter had once echoed through the halls. He remembered sliding on snowbanks and ice fishing with his father. He remembered his first hunt and how his mother's gentleness had tempered his father's strict discipline.

Brand felt moisture behind his closed lids. His mother had died when he was twelve. Her death had sent his father, Jarls, into a deep depression. When his father emerged from the jaws of his sorrow, he was a kinder man; too kind, Brand admitted. Kindness had been his father's downfall. It was his father's kindness that had led him to trust Lord Thorgills. They had ventured forth together and when they returned, Thorgills had tried to claim everything—all the land and all the treasure which they had taken together. Lord Thorgills was full of deceit. He was a man without honor, a man for whom the word justice had no meaning.

A great battle ensued between Jarls and Thorgills. Thorgills emerged victorious. But as crude and bellicose as Thorgills was, he was not stupid. He needed Jarls's troops, and he needed someone to lead them. And so a bargain had been struck. It was a bargain which deprived Brand of his own independence, of his own freedom of action. Brand had been forced to pledge his fighting skills and loyalty to Lord Thorgills in exchange for his father's life and freedom.

Brand opened his eyes. The stars were still bright overhead. He pressed his lips together. Tomorrow they would go to Trim in search of the riches he knew were there. Odin, the God of War, would guide them, and those who fought bravely and fell in battle would go to Valhalla—the Hall of the Slain Warriors. Tomorrow he would have to think of how to repay the woman who had saved him. It was a matter of honor. Somehow, he had to get her out of Olaf's clutches.

He thought of her, and his thoughts surprised him. Yes, he had hated having Olaf touch her and might have hated it in any case, whether or not she had saved him. The truth was, he couldn't stop thinking about her. No, it was wrong. He had no right to want her himself, and yet he recognized his desire for her.

He forced himself to think only of the debt he owed her. His heart was already pledged to Erica, whose strength, beauty, and fighting skills were renowned. Erica of the blond hair and blue eyes awaited him, her long white silky limbs beckoning him from afar. Soon they would return, and soon he would go to her. Yes, he was a Viking, a Dane, and Erica was destined for him as he was destined for her.

No, he told himself, this delicate Celtic maiden was no more than a favor to be repaid. And yet he could not keep from thinking about her sea-green eyes and yards of red-gold hair. He had kissed her, and the sweet taste of her lips lingered. She had spirit, too, spirit and strength. On the whole, Celtic woman did not stand up to men, and, unlike Viking women, they were certainly not warriors. Yet this one had a fire about her. Brand smiled. He was attracted by fire.

Brand closed his eyes and pulled his sheepskin over him. It was warm enough to sleep outside, and it seemed even warmer if he allowed his imagination to run free.

Yes, his Irish princess was very much with him. He imagined her in sheer robes held only by a gold rope around her tiny waist. He imagined himself loosening her bound hair, freeing it to fall over her slim shoulders. Her breasts pushed against the thin fabric of her robes as if they wanted to be free, and he could see her white billowy breasts, hard and firm beneath the garments.

Perspiration broke out on his brow as he reached out for her, drawing her close. He inhaled, and in his dream, as in real life, the scent of wild roses surrounded her.

With anxious fumbling fingers he undid the golden knot that held her robes and, pushing the fabric aside, stood looking at her naked body. His hands moved over her slowly, so slowly she moved against them, wanting more, desiring him as he desired her. Heat emanated from their bodies as he took her breast into his mouth and gently teased her nipple. She squirmed in his arms—pushed against him, held his throbbing organ—

Brand felt himself fulfilled and once again stared at the sky. He had not given himself such pleasure since boyhood, but he could not help it, his desire was too great. A peace settled over him and he closed his eyes, letting sleep consume him.

* * *

"Brand! Are you asleep?"

Brand opened his eyes and looked up into the craggy face of Cnut. He swung himself up so he was no longer lying down. He shook his head. How long had he been asleep? Surely no more than an hour. Or was he still asleep?

"Can that be you?" he asked, squinting. The night was bright, but was this really Cnut? He had not seen Cnut in over a year, and he was surprised to see him now.

"Yes, it is really me! I landed in Dublin four days ago and rode like the wind to join you here. One of those inside said you were out here."

Cnut and he went back a long way. When his own father, Jarls, had been the overking, Cnut's father had been one of his underkings just as Lord Thorgills was an underking of Halvdan. Cnut's father had been loyal to his father, they had been friends since they were boys. Now Cnut also fought with Lord Thorgills, though there was no lost love between them. For both he and Cnut, their alliance with Lord Thorgills was a waiting game. When the time was right they would join forces and try to overthrow him. Once Thorgills was gone, Cnut, as was his right, would once again be called Lord Cnut.

Brand seized his friend's arm. "In the name of Thor, sit down my friend. You bear precious news—you've been home."

"I have, but my news is not precious, Brand."

Brand studied Cnut's expression. It was serious, and his eyes were clouded with concern. "You have bad news—"

"Yes."

"Tell me now. Don't hesitate."

"Your father has died, Brand."

Brand's mouth opened slightly. He closed it and pressed his lips together. Again memories rushed back, images of the past, moments of intense pleasure spent with his father, memories of happiness to ease the terrible pain that now filled him. "How——?" he managed.

"Peacefully, Brand. He died in his sleep. He had been ill."

Ill? No doubt. Since the day Thorgills had borne him away, since the day the bargain had been struck; his father had not been the same. He had heard the stories. His father, once strong and robust, had weakened. He had no inner strength with which to fight illness. Brand felt his own hatred for Lord Thorgills fill him. Thorgills had killed his father as surely as if he had run him through with a sword. He had killed his father's spirit, and when the spirit died the body fought to follow.

"You have said nothing, but I can feel your anger," Cnut said after a few moments.

"I must control it till the time is right," Brand muttered. "But when the time comes——" his hand caressed his sword— "Lord Thorgills will be repaid tenfold."

For a few moments they were silent, and Brand thought of the mythical three sisters whose faces were covered with dark scarves. According to legend they sat by the roots of Yggdrasil, the tree of the world. They were Norns—the spirits of light and darkness who spun out the thread of life and death like a spider spins its web. There were brilliantly well-spun webs—symmetrical and intricate—and in the early morning, the dew shimmered on their magnificence. These webs were like good lives. But there were other webs, haphazard and hanging, filled with uneaten insects and broken here and there. These webs were like badly lived lives; they were messy and reflected greed because more had been caught than could be eaten.

He turned to Cnut. "Who knows of this?" he asked. "Who knows of my father's death?"

"No one. I disembarked, asked for you, and rode straight here."

Brand nodded. "You must tell no one. As soon as Thorgills

knows, he will realize his hold over me is no more. He won't trust me and might even have me killed."

Cnut nodded. "It is our secret."

"Tell me now of my father's burial."

"He was returned to your home and buried with honor. His body, together with your mother's remains, was put into the finest ship in his fleet. The ship was filled with their belongings and it was buried beneath the knoll behind your home."

It was the custom. His mother and father would sail into eternity with those material possessions they loved most. Brand stared off into the distance. "It is good," he said abstractedly.

But already Brand was thinking of revenge. His mind was beginning to formulate a plan. As saddened as he was, his father's death would make things easier. He no longer had to worry about Thorgills's anger. "Best we sleep," Brand suggested as he squeezed his friend's shoulder. "Tomorrow we fight."

Cnut smiled. "There's a small room by the castle gate. It's ideal for a good sleep away from the rest of the snoring warriors.

Brand stood up and stretched. It was good to see Cnut again. Like so many others, Cnut had remained loyal. But unlike with the others, his friendship with Cnut was special.

The bells in the cathedral pealed forth a warning and immediately the compound of the monastery at Trim was filled with people running this way and that.

Alan stepped outside his monk's cell and watched. He was both horrified and fascinated as the walls were quickly breached and fierce Viking warriors rode into the courtyard, shrieking and screaming oaths, their battle banners flying in the wind, their swords glimmering in the summer sun.

He saw Brand, and he froze. Brand leaned from his horse

and looked directly into Alan's eyes. His voice was low and his eyes steady. "No matter what happens, do not acknowledge me. Remember, I am trying to save your sister."

Alan's mouth opened and closed in surprise. Brand shouted, as if he had not spoken to him previously, "Where are your treasures!"

Alan pointed aimlessly toward the sanctuary, feeling confused and puzzled.

Gradually, the Vikings drove the monks into the center of the courtyard. Some of them guarded their hapless prisoners while others rooted through the cathedral and private belongings.

Great chests were brought and filled. *They are like insects,* Alan thought. *They swarm over everything as if they were ants with voracious appetites.*

"A wondrous thing!" Olaf cried out. In his hand he held a silver goblet encrusted with jewels. He turned it toward the light and roared again with an idiot's delight. Without a moment's hesitation, he seized a bottle of wine and filled the goblet, drinking from it greedily.

Thorgills watched his son, then turned away and began to examine a book which was written in gold and silver leaf, its pages delicate works of art. "What is this?" he said, turning to Brand, who had handed it to him in the first place.

"A priceless treasure," Brand said. "An illustrated copy of one of the Christian Gospels."

"Who is responsible for this!" Thorgills shouted.

Lord Thorgills looked at the rows of dejected men who stood before him. They had put up no fight, and to his eyes they were as women, dressed in long robes and muttering prayers.

"I am," Alan answered. "It is a holy book."

"Ah," Brand said quickly. He leaned and whispered to Lord Thorgills, "This is the son of King Odhran of Meath, I saw him when I was held captive. And this book is most valuable. He could be sent to our homeland, there to copy and illustrate a book about our gods. Think of it, Thorgills. You would do Odin great honor, and you would have a slave who was once a young prince."

Thorgills turned and laughed at Alan. "We have our own gods!" he roared. Still, he turned the pages carefully. They were written on heavy parchment. "But our gods have no books such as these," he allowed. Yes, Brand had a fine idea. "That is what I desire! I desire the stories of Odin, Thor, and Frigg written out in such a hand and on pages decorated with gold and silver such as this!"

Alan felt puzzled. He had expected instant death from the Viking heathens. And even if he had been spared, the last thing he expected was to have one of the heathens—apparently their leader at that—be impressed with his art.

Thorgills did not wait for a reply, but rather stepped up to Alan, whom he physically dwarfed. "Can such a thing be done?"

Alan looked into Thorgills's eyes and knew instantly that a negative answer would be a death sentence. And why after all couldn't the tales of these strange gods be set down in an illuminated book? It would be sinful for him to worship this heathen's gods, but surely transcribing stories on decorated pages was no crime. "It can be done," he answered slowly. "Indeed, I can do it."

"Will you go willingly to my homeland to work?"

What could he expect if he refused? To be sold into slavery? At the very least the monastery would be destroyed, and he would be deprived of his work. His father's kingdom was lost, Deirdre was either dead or in the hands of these people although it did not seem possible that this Viking was trying to help her. Perhaps she, too, would be taken to their homeland. Heaven knew she was beautiful enough. Perhaps he could find her, perhaps if this Viking liked his work he could even arrange to have her freed. After all, she had sacrificed mightily to save his life.

"I will go willingly," Alan replied. And, sweetening the

bargain to gain favor he quickly added, "I will even teach artists in your own land how this work is done."

"Let this man gather up his belongings and his supplies. We will send him home, and there he will teach artists. He will work setting down our stories! Odin should be as exalted as this . . . this"—Thorgills studied the illuminated page— "Matthew," he managed in a heavy accent.

Brand was pleased, and though he did not look at Alan, he smiled to himself. Deirdre's brother would at least be safe for the time being. It surprised him that Lord Thorgills had liked the book, but on reflection he realized it should not have. Lord Thorgills was as complex as Olaf was brutal and simple.

Olaf looked at the rest of the men and tapped his father on the shoulder. "And what of these men?"

"They are nothing to us. Set them free in the countryside," Thorgills said with a dismissive wave of his hand. "Gather up this treasure, and we'll return to the castle."

Olaf grinned stupidly. "I shall have my birthday gift when we return, and, afterward, I shall drink from this fine goblet."

Brand forced himself to maintain a neutral expression. So, Olaf liked the goblet. Well he would take the goblet, the treasure, and the woman. Olaf would be denied his treasures. All of them.

"And what treasure do you claim, Brand?"

Brand glanced at Lord Thorgills. The wretched man had come to trust him over the years. Of course he had worked on that. He wanted Lord Thorgills to trust him, so that when he took his revenge it would be all the sweeter. Still, Lord Thorgills was no idiot. Thorgills adored Olaf, but he knew Olaf was neither quick of wit nor a great warrior. Time and again, when Thorgills had to choose one to stand by his side in battle, he had not chosen his own son. *He chose me,* Brand thought with some pride.

"Have you lost your tongue? What treasure do you claim?" Thorgills asked again.

"I claim none, Lord Thorgills. I only ask permission to ride ahead and prepare the feast. When you return we can celebrate. Our fighting will be over, our treasure taken."

Thorgills smiled. "Have the treasure loaded. Take twelve men and go. We will come later when we've finished gathering whatever treasure those who live about here have in their homes."

There were many homes belonging to obviously wealthy landowners in the vicinity. It would take some time for Thorgills and Olaf to finish looting them. This was his opportunity. Brand wasted no time. He gave the orders and selected the men carefully. Cnut would stay with Thorgills. Brand wanted none of those loyal to him to be involved in his plan because those who let him slip away with Olaf's treasures would surely be punished. This was a solitary mission. He would claim those loyal to him later, but for now he had only one thought. He would take Olaf's precious goblet and the sacks of loot in order to sell them, and he would take the woman. If they could escape, he could head for Jorvik, the largest city in Danelaw. At Jorvik his fellow Danes had a huge encampment. He would be safe there. Thorgills was Norwegian, and there was no love lost between Thorgills and the Danish ruler of Danelaw. Yes, in Jorvik he could find allies and help. He would be able to go home and raise an army. He would defeat Thorgills and take back all that was rightfully his. Brand's spirits soared.

Within the hour he was off with twelve men and the treasure. When Olaf and Thorgills returned to East Meath, they were in for a great surprise, Brand thought with pleasure. But it would certainly not be the surprise which they expected.

"See to this, see to that." Brand liked commanding, and no sooner had they reached Malvin's castle then he dispersed the men and sent them scampering on a thousand missions to prepare for the feast and victory celebration. Without a moment's hesitation he wrapped the goblet, took the sacks with the most valuable treasure, and prepared two fast horses. He packed the vital necessities and, recalling his travels through the area, planned the best route of escape. Then, as quickly as possible, he hurried to the bedchamber where Deirdre was held.

"I was told to guard the woman!" the bored guard protested.

"And I was told to prepare her. Would I be here if Lord Thorgills had not sent me?" Brand shouted at the guard, advancing on him threateningly.

Intimidated, the guard shook his head and handed over the keys. He had seen this man in battle at Lord Thorgills's side. He was not a man with whom to take issue.

"Go to the banquet hall and help ready the feast! I have little time to waste on you," Brand ordered.

He waited till he heard the guard scamper off. Once alone, he quickly unlocked the door and entered the partially darkened room.

Deirdre looked up at him in surprise. "Have you come to taunt me?" she asked. "Or perhaps you are disloyal and will force yourself upon me before your lord and master has the opportunity."

Brand suppressed a smile. Far from weeping and far from having a broken spirit, the Irish princess was as spicy as ever. "That is an appealing thought," he said, sitting down at her side.

"Vile heathen! I should have let Malvin kill you!"

"Now, now. If I were dead, I would not be untying your hands, my lady." He expertly undid the ropes and rubbed her wrists.

Deirdre shook her hands free of him. "I don't know what your game is. I only know you are one of them. And I'm sure you are just like them. You let that beast touch me!"

Again Brand suppressed a smile. "It was difficult, especially as I had wished his hand was mine."

"You're vile!"

He pulled her upward.

"Don't touch me!"

He looked at her flashing sea-green eyes, at the way she turned her head defiantly. She was truly a magnificent creature. "Be good, or I shall have you now. I have nothing to lose, Olaf and Thorgills will want me killed in any case."

Deirdre looked at him. What was he up to? Should she trust him?

"Now come along or stay here and wait for Olaf. The choice is yours."

What was he talking about? She had seen him with Thorgills. "Why would he have you killed? You seemed willing enough to do his bidding."

"I have no time now for explanations. Either come now or remain. As I said, the choice is yours."

What choice? There was no choice. The revolting image of Olaf filled her thoughts. No, it would be better to take her chances with this one. Maybe she could escape from him, especially as he appeared to be on the run. "I'll come," she agreed.

"I should hope so. Follow me, my lady, and make no noise."

Deirdre followed as they descended the steps and walked down a long corridor and out one of the many doors that led to the back of the castle. "This is oddly like the morning you helped me escape," he said with a laugh. "Put these clothes on," Brand commanded. He handed her a plain tunic and simple cloak. She modestly moved to the shadows near the wall to change her clothing. When she returned she was surprised to see that he had also changed. He had discarded the clothing that identified him as a Viking warrior and wore instead the kind of clothes any local peasant might wear. He said nothing as he lifted her to the black stallion, climbing up behind her and pulling her closer to him as his arms encircled her. The second horse carried two large sacks.

Deirdre sat rigidly in place, aware of the heat from his body, aware of his arms around her, and all too aware of his breath on her neck. He signaled the horse and they were off. Deirdre's hood blew off, and she felt the wind in her hair.

"Prison or no prison, my lady, you still smell of roses."

He spoke into her ear, and she felt a chill pass through her even though she was definitely not cold. What was it about his breath in her ear? It was most pleasant. In fact it was almost indecently pleasant. She stiffened, willing herself not to respond in any way to this new and interesting sensation or to his words. "Where are you taking me?" she asked.

"To Danelaw, dear lady."

"Danelaw—" She repeated the strange name slowly.

"I will be protected there," he said without further explanation.

"Where is this place?" Deirdre asked.

Brand squeezed her. "Across the sea, my lady."

Deirdre was stunned into absolute silence. Across the sea? What sea? How would they get there? Not that she was unaware of the lands across the sea. Across the turbulent Hibernian Sea lay the land of the Angles and Saxons—Britannia. To the south lay the land ruled by Charles the Fat, the great grandson of Charlemagne, and even farther south beyond the kingdom of Charles the Fat lay the land that had been conquered by the Moors, whose miraculous medicines her friend Edana had studied. She had been told the Moors had skins as black as coal. Long had she wanted to see the world! Surely it was filled with wondrous things.

But Danelaw? It seemed a long journey, and such a journey seemed laden with danger.

"I do not understand," she finally said.

"I have betrayed Thorgills, and I am trying to find my countrymen. Can you understand that?"

Deirdre nodded. "I am not a simpleton."

Brand laughed. "That is the last of my thoughts. Indeed, you are far too smart for your own good."

"Just what do you mean by that?"

"Only that sometimes your tongue is too stinging."

"Some people deserve a tongue-lashing."

Brand laughed. "Nonetheless, Lord Thorgills is dangerous."

"Will he pursue us?" she asked.

"Yes, my lady, and if we're caught, he'll kill me. If such a thing happens, tell him I took you by force. It will go easier on you."

Deirdre fell into silence. Was he trying to help her? No, she could not trust him. He was one of them. There was no telling what he might do. Perhaps he just wanted her himself and, like the clanging bags of what was obviously treasure, she was just one of his stolen prizes.

After a time, he seemed to draw her even closer. Deirdre said nothing. The warmth of him was comforting, his arms made her feel secure, and, unhappily, she admitted she found him exciting. Well, he might also enslave her, but she was sure he would be a far better master than either Malvin or Olaf. Indeed, there was no comparison. The other two revolted her—this one, well—this one was very different.

Five

They rode south toward Dublin as the blazing sun set in the West. They could not see the ocean, but both knew it was not far away because the smell of salt was in the air. To Deirdre the land over which they journeyed seemed a land deserted. The peasants clearly knew there were Viking warriors in the area and took precautions. They remained inside their hovels and did not even venture out to tend the land.

As for the landowners, it seemed obvious that most of them had fled, taking refuge in castles or burying their valuables and hiding out among the peasants.

Deirdre and Brand rode for hours across green pastures and through meadows. They passed grazing animals and two deserted nunneries.

Deirdre's legs ached from riding and from time to time her eyes closed and she leaned against Brand, whose strong arms still held her fast. She was, in fact dozing lightly when she felt the horse being drawn to a halt. She opened her eyes to find it had grown completely dark while she slept.

"Here, my lady. We need to stop and rest for a short time. The horses need water, and we must relieve ourselves and take some nourishment."

"Could we not have stopped where there is shelter? We passed two deserted nunneries."

"No. That is just the sort of place we might be expected to stop. We are far safer out in the open."

Brand slid down from the horse and lifted Deirdre to the ground. She was as light as a feather in his arms.

To her own surprise Deirdre staggered, and he caught her. "Oh," she gasped. "My legs have turned to water." She tried to sound cheerful, but the truth was, she was in considerable pain.

Brand saw the look of distress on her face. "Your legs are sore, aren't they?"

"I can hardly stand," she admitted.

"Here, hold on to the horse for a moment."

Deirdre did as he asked and waited while he spread the saddle blanket out on the grass. "Sit down on the grass, my lady."

Gratefully she did as he suggested, sinking to the soft ground, relieved to be able to stretch out.

Brand walked the horses to the stream and waited while they drank thirstily. When the animals had their fill, he tied them where they could graze on the young oats that stood only a foot high in the nearby pasture.

He returned, and without a word, moved closer, kneeling beside her. He parted her dress and began to rub her legs. She was so stunned, she could not speak for a moment.

After a moment, she tried to pull back. "What are you doing?"

"Getting your blood to circulate, my lady. You've been too long in the saddle."

"Oh!" She twitched. It suddenly felt as if someone were sticking pins into both legs. "What a horrible feeling," she said. But in a moment she smiled. "Not your rubbing—the sensation it has caused."

"Just the feeling returning," he assured her.

Her instincts told her she should protest this intimacy, but she could not. Her legs truly ached, and the feel of his strong hands was soothing as he kneaded and massaged her taut muscles.

"I am only letting you do this because I really am very stiff," she said, trying to recover a modicum of dignity.

Brand laughed again. "I am only doing it because you are stiff, my lady." But in a moment he looked up at her, and, without smiling, said, "But I will do with you as I wish."

Deirdre dug her fingers into the blanket. "Does that mean you intend—"

"I don't 'intend' anything right now, my lady."

He looked away from her eyes and continued his massage, and after a time he finally stopped. "Better?" he asked.

"Yes, thank you," she answered crisply.

He stood up and got her cloak. He wrapped it around her shoulders. "This night is as bright as last night," Brand said, looking up at the sky. "But it's a bit cooler." They were in a small clearing in a wooded glen, but the trees were not tall, and the sky was visible. In fact, there were stars everywhere. It seemed as if one could reach up and touch them.

"It is cooler," Deirdre agreed. "Will you build a fire?"

"No, my lady. We travel in darkness, and we rest in darkness. They will begin to look for us soon, and while we have a good start, we must travel through the night to reach the sea."

"The Hibernian Sea?" Deirdre ventured.

"Yes, that sea. We must cross it to get to Danelaw."

He unfolded one of the packs. "I have brought some bread, and we'll have a little wine to warm us."

Deirdre pulled her cloak even closer. He unwrapped some bread and tore off a piece for her. After a moment, he drank some wine from his wineskin and handed it to her. It seemed a bit unmannerly, but she knew it would warm her, so she took the pouch and gulped down a mouthful of wine.

"It's good," she acknowledged.

"When we get to Danelaw we can rest in peace."

"But the Hibernian Sea . . . if we cross it, won't we be in Britannia, the land of the Angles and Saxons?

"Ah, yes. You seem quite knowledgeable."

She did not react to his comment. Had he thought her stupid? "If it is the land of the Angles and Saxons, where is this Danelaw?"

"In the land that was once the land of the Angles, my lady. Many years ago my people came to the land of the Angles. At first they just raided, but after a time they settled down. King Alfred, who rules Wessex and is the strongest of the Saxon kings, signed a peace treaty with my people. He recognizes all the land that lies to the east and west of Wessex as ours—as Danelaw."

"I did not know," she admitted.

"It did not happen that long ago. News travels slowly."

"If at all," she replied. "Men often speak of these things, but they do not bother to tell women much of anything. If a woman is to know anything, she has to listen and learn on her own. My knowledge of the world is most limited. My father had some drawings that show the location of various lands—maps?"

"Yes, maps."

"Danelaw was not on the maps I saw. Tell me, where in this Danelaw will we go?"

Brand's eyes twinkled. "I would say you listen well to have learned so much, my lady. We will go to Jorvik."

"This is a village?"

"It is a big settlement. I must go to King Guthrum and ask for help. He was once a friend of my father. I'll give him some of the treasure, and I think he will give me a vessel that will take me home."

Deirdre looked at him steadily. She could not see his face in the darkness, and she did not want to ask too many questions when she could not see his eyes and read his expression. Did he intend selling her, too? Would he just leave her in this Jorvik? Or did he intend taking her with him? She decided to save her questions for another time. After all, Lord Thorgills might well overtake them, and that would render all of her conjecture irrelevant.

"What is our immediate destination?"

Brand grinned. "Dublin."

"Dublin! Are you mad? There's a fortress there, a Viking fortress. I heard Lord Thorgills speak of it! It is his stronghold."

Brand laughed. "Exactly, my lady, exactly. Lord Thorgills will expect us to travel northwest, sail across the sea, and land in Scotland. If we followed that course we would have to travel many miles south to reach Jorvik. No, this is the better way. First, because Lord Thorgills will not suspect we circled round him and are headed back to his own stronghold, and second, because many vessels are anchored there, and we can find one in which to cross the sea."

"This is a dangerous game," Deirdre said at length.

"It is the game of life"—Brand laughed, then more solemnly—"and death."

"War," Deirdre murmured. "I always said that winter was the season of peace and summer the season of war. In the summers—for as long as I can remember, my father and his armies set out to war with rebellious landlords or nearby kingdoms. I understand the need to protect one's lands, but I don't understand why there must be constant war."

Something inside Brand agreed with her, but another part of him disagreed. He knew full well that most of his comrades set forth to make war in order to increase their wealth. Certainly that is why Lord Thorgills fought. But he had only served Lord Thorgills because he was forced to. No, he did not fight to increase his wealth. Indeed, when next he fought it would be to settle a blood feud. It would be to gain full power over the lands once ruled by his father, King Jarls.

"You are a Viking," Deirdre said. "Surely you of all men can answer my question. Why must there be constant war?"

"Because few men are happy with what they have," Brand replied simply. "Greed, my dear princess. It makes animals of us all."

Deirdre lay down and stared up at the stars. "I do not

understand the bellicose character of men. I do not understand why they can't till the land and tend their flocks and relish their children."

"Ah, my lady, that is it. Not all men have lands and flocks and children. As long as there is dissatisfaction there will be war. I expect to die fighting."

"And what do you fight for?"

"For what is mine and was my father's. I will fight to avenge my father."

"I understand that desire; I am not so virtuous as to have lived without wishing vengeance. I wished Malvin dead, and a wish is as good as a deed. Now King Malvin, my father's killer, is dead and vanquished, and certainly I do not mourn for him. Still, hatreds must end somewhere. Who wins if everyone dies?"

Brand laughed. "You are too honest. But all right, sometimes I, too, yearn for peace."

Deirdre ate some more bread and took some more wine from the wineskin. This was the first time in her entire life she had ever had such a conversation with a man. It was a revelation to her. She had wanted vengeance, but also dreamed of peace. He seemed in many ways to be the same. "This land, this Ireland, is a sad place. We'll war for two thousand years."

He could tell her thoughts were far away, that she was contemplating her country's difficulties.

"Are we to sleep here?" Deirdre asked after a few minutes.

"We have no time for sleep. We are just to rest."

She yearned for sleep, but Brand did not seem at all tired. No doubt he had great stamina. She studied his craggy profile in the darkness. *If only I trusted him,* she thought. And naturally she silently asked the more important question, *What are his plans for me?* Her eyes closed, and sleep, as sudden as a summer storm, overtook her.

His fingers were in her hair, moving through it like a giant comb, caressing her neck, rubbing her back gently.

"You have beautiful hair, my lady. I would see it cascading over your bare shoulders and covering your lovely breasts. I would feel your hips undulating beneath me; I would have you clinging and sighing in my arms—"

Deirdre opened her eyes suddenly and sat up, her face hot and flushed, her breath a little short. Her mouth opened to say something, but Brand's hands were not in her hair, nor was he touching her in any way.

A dream? Had she dreamt of him again? Or had he run his fingers through her hair while she was asleep? Had he spoken to her? *Dear heaven, I can't tell dreams from reality! And why do I keep dreaming about him? This has to stop, especially now that we are together.*

"You fell asleep. I thought I would let you sleep for a few moments."

He looked somehow bemused. Had she said anything in her sleep? Did he guess that she dreamt of him? A chill ran through her, perhaps she had called out to him.

"I'm fine," she said stiffly. "Did I . . . did I sleep long?"

Brand smiled. "Not long, my lady, but blissfully."

Deirdre's face burned red in the darkness. *I must get control of myself,* she thought.

"When can we sleep?" she asked.

"Not until we're at sea, my lady. I have no desire for you to see Lord Thorgills display my head on his spear."

"And you are doing all of this to rescue me?" she asked sarcastically.

His laughter filled the glen, and though she had been sarcastic, she was a little hurt that he laughed so hard. "I wasn't serious," she said sharply. "I'm quite sure you are doing all this with only yourself in mind."

Suddenly he reached out toward her and grasped her by the side of her throat, pulling her face close to his, so close she could feel his breath on her neck. His lips touched hers and pressed against them hard. His other hand wrapped about her, and he held her tight as he kissed her. The hand on her throat moved ever so slightly, and his fingers danced round her ear, playing on her flesh. A chill passed through her, and for a moment she responded to his lips. But she pulled away, and though he could have held her, he did not. Even in the darkness she could feel his eyes boring into hers.

"That was to remind you that you are a woman, and I am your temporary master. Do not play with me, my lady. I have not yet decided what to do with you."

"I knew you weren't saving me from Olaf out of mere kindness!"

"You think you know many things, my lady. But you are not the master of the universe, and you do not know everything that is in my heart and mind. Be good, and you will be treated well; behave badly, and I shall punish you."

Deirdre looked back at him in stony silence. Why had she shown even the slightest weakness with this man! She felt angry with herself and frustrated because she had no choice but to stay with him for the present. *And yet—Heaven help me,* she thought. *I am drawn to him.*

The horse trotted off into the darkness, and Brand once again encircled her with his arms. How sweet her lips had tasted, how very much he desired her. He could not rid himself of thoughts of possessing Deirdre, nor could he escape thoughts of Erica. Yet, he sadly admitted, his thoughts of Erica were unlike his dreams of Deirdre. He was betrothed to Erica, and to him her very name meant duty. But he knew he did not love her.

He thought back to only moments ago, when he had kissed Deirdre. He had never kissed Erica in such a way. But his thoughts settled on his sleeping princess. She had moved seductively in her sleep and she had whispered his name. She never said his name that way when she was awake! He smiled to himself as he had at the time. His little princess dreamt of him, dreamt of him and perhaps desired him as he desired her.

* * *

Alan sat beneath the cover, midship, wrapped in warm robes. His belongings and supplies surrounded him, and much to his surprise, he was treated more like a guest than a captive.

He had expected to be put with the other slaves and ordered to row for long hours, but this was not the case. Apparently, the order had been sent forward that his hands must be protected.

After a time, a man came and sat next to him. "You're the artist," the man said.

Alan nodded. The man was in his thirties, and though he wore the clothes of a Viking warrior, he wore no metal helmet as the others did.

"Yes," Alan answered, even as he drew his robes around him. Even though it was summer, it seemed that cold winds blew down the Hibernian Sea from Norway. "Do you know how long this voyage takes?"

"Five days with good winds. But they are long days, the sun hardly sets at all the farther north we travel."

"I've heard of days when the sun never sets," Alan said thoughtfully. "Where are you from?"

"I'm a Swed. I'm from farther south than Norway. You're going to the castle of Lord Thorgills at the entrance to the Oslo Fjord."

Alan contemplated the information, but the geography was meaningless to him.

The young man shoved a wineskin into his hands. "Hot mead," he offered, and with a grin he introduced himself. "I'm Bjorn."

"I'm Alan, son of King Odhran."

Bjorn laughed. "I could tell you were of noble blood. Your hands are smooth."

Alan looked at his hands. He turned them over. Yes, they did give him away.

"I am to copy tales of your gods and illustrate them," he said.

"You will be busy, our gods are many," Bjorn said good-naturedly.

"You say you are a Swed, yet you are aboard one of Lord Thorgills's vessels—I do not understand."

"Ah . . . well, let me try to explain. My people fought with the Norwegians and the Danes for many years. Then a strong king emerged in Oslo. He created underkings, chieftains to rule various parts of the land. There were more wars, but Lord Thorgills led King Halvdan's men and eventually conquered King Jarls, his last remaining enemy. There are many who still support Jarls, many who would fight to restore him."

Alan hung on every word. The Viking who had come to him and who wanted to rescue Deirdre was the son of Jarls. "Perhaps one day the kingdom of Jarls will be restored," Alan ventured.

Bjorn laughed. "I think not. Halvdan is a strong and ferocious king."

Outside of Dublin, Deirdre waited while Brand changed back into his Viking clothes. He wore leather strapping on his bare legs, a leather jacket over his skirt, and a helmet. He carried a shield, a sword, and a spear. Unlike warriors who might have been sent forth from Meath, Brand's arms were as bare as his legs above the leather strapping. She could hardly keep from noticing, as she had noticed before, that he was covered with thick blond hair. His hands were large enough to span her waist and when they both stood she did not even come to his shoulder. But she did not stand close to him. She was growing well aware of the effect he had on her, and she certainly did not want him to detect these strange feelings that she seemed unable to control. And, alas, it was not just that he was strong and handsome. There was more to him than that. He had brooding eyes, he was intelligent, and he seemed to yearn for knowledge as she did. If only she could completely trust him. But she admitted, perhaps she did not trust herself.

"This is Dublin," Brand proclaimed as they paused momentarily atop the hill. "We found much treasure here."

The monastery was a tight cluster of buildings made of stone. It was like a small, walled village and was indeed, a small self-sustained town. The center of the monastery was the abbey church, with its tall, massive tower. To one side of the courtyard was a cloister where the monks walked and prayed. There were also a dormitory, a dining hall, a bakery, and a wine cellar. A second dormitory for novices was on the other side of the courtyard.

Around the perimeter were other buildings, linked by a high, defensive wall. They included an infirmary, guesthouses, shops, latrines and storage buildings. "When we came here we found that inside this place a hundred monks were living together with some one hundred craftsmen and artists. There were laborers, too. In all, we discovered there was room for over two hundred wayfarers and visitors, and we were told that such visitors would be guaranteed shelter and food by the church."

"Is this like the monastery at Trim?"

Brand shrugged. "It's much larger than the one at Trim. But this monastery has been taken over by Vikings—we also built a fort on one side of the river."

Deirdre was silent. The sight of the monastery made her think of her brother.

"What are you thinking, my lady?"

"That I have lost my brother. God knows what they will do with him. He is a gentle soul. He is no warrior."

"I have seen your brother, my lady. I remembered him from the night at your father's castle. He is safe, though on his way to Norway, I fear. Lord Thorgills was quite taken with his work. He ordered him taken to Norway, there to copy and illustrate the tales of our gods."

Deirdre's mouth opened in surprise. "Thank heaven," she murmured.

Brand did not say that it was he who had suggested it.

"Alan is very talented," Deirdre said. "Will he be well treated?"

"I imagine so. It is far better than being sold into slavery."

"I had him sent to Trim," Deirdre said. "It was my father's wish that he should survive. I promised Malvin I would marry him if Alan were allowed to enter the monastery."

"Is it a monastic life he seeks?"

"No, he only wanted the opportunity to work on his art."

A sudden wave of real sympathy flooded over Brand. A life for a life. Deirdre's bargain with Malvin was similar to the bargain he had made with Thorgills in order to save his father. "I'm sorry," he said. "You miss one another, but as you are both alive, there is hope you may one day be together."

Deirdre ran her hand abstractedly through her hair. He sounded genuine, and his voice was far softer than usual. "Alan will go to the castle of Lord Thorgills, and you will take me to the ends of the earth."

Brand tried to smile. "Perhaps to the end of the sea, but not to the ends of the earth."

Tears suddenly filled her eyes and began to roll down her cheeks. "My brother has gone to an unknown land," Deirdre wept.

Brand reached across the distance between them and touched her hand. "Thorgills cost me my father. I know your sadness, my lady. Do not assume I am a stone."

Deirdre could not respond. Words escaped her. She did not know his story, and he did not really know hers. "I assume nothing," she replied.

Brand walked toward the horses. "We must find a vessel.

Cover your hair and pull your cloak up to cover your face. Your beauty will cause suspicion."

Deirdre turned away slightly. Did he think her beautiful? Silently, she did as he asked.

"I shall have to find old friends," Brand said, looking at her. "It would be advisable if you held your tongue no matter what I say. Your pride could end this escape for both of us."

Deirdre frowned. That was it, of course. He thought her a beautiful idiot. Well, he would find out differently. Once she had toyed with escape, but now she thought she must stay with him till she was reunited with Alan. For the time being she decided to say and do nothing. The memory of Olaf's brutish ways lingered in her thoughts.

"What feast is this!" Lord Thorgills's voice carried and echoed off the walls of Malvin's castle. But no one answered. Thorgills, deeply furious, tromped about, shouting curses into the emptiness. Clearly some preparation had been made, but the food was not cooked, and all the entertainments seemed to have vanished, along with Brand and the twelve men he had brought with him.

The women had been unlocked and all had fled, and where was the treasure? There were some sacks, but the most precious of the prizes, including the priceless goblet and the beautiful Tara brooch, were gone.

"She's gone!" Olaf wailed in anger, and shouted epithets and threats. He reached his father and stopped short. "He's taken her!"

"And most of our treasure," Lord Thorgills muttered.

"Where are the twelve men he brought with him? They were all loyal men," Olaf stuttered. "Could he have killed all of them?"

"Be still and let me think." Thorgills smoldered. The fact that they were not here did not mean they were with Brand. Once they discovered his disappearance and the disappear-

ance of the women and treasure they would run away simply
to avoid Olaf's wrath. Doubtless they would seek some
nearby hiding place till Olaf's ferocity subsided.

"He's stolen my woman and my goblet!" Olaf shrieked.
His huge body fairly vibrated with fury, and spittle ran from
the sides of this mouth and down into his unkempt beard.
His already small eyes narrowed, and he whirled about to
face his father, who had come up the steps to join him.
"Vengeance shall be mine!" Olaf vowed.

Thorgills felt his chest tighten as his own anger rose. He
had trusted Brand, treated him like a son. "He and Jarls are
as good as dead!" Thorgills muttered.

Cnut, standing nearby, and fully armed, said nothing. The
revelation that Jarls was already dead would only have further infuriated Thorgills. But he himself could hardly sup-
press his smile. Brand had planned well. Those loyal to Brand
were not implicated, but those who had accompanied him,
some of Thorgills's best men, were not just implicated—they
were condemned.

"Find me all the men who accompanied Brand!" Thorgills
ordered as if he had read Cnut's mind. "I'm certain they're
nearby."

"He never should have been trusted," Olaf said, turning
on his father. "He was a hostage warrior; you treated him
too well."

Thorgills looked at his son and felt the sting of Olaf's
jealousy and hatred. Olaf had always disliked Brand. Brand's
fighting skills were superior, as was his intelligence. And of
course Brand was handsome and Olaf was not. *But Olaf is
my son,* Thorgills reminded himself. He had forgotten the
most important of lessons—blood was all that mattered. And
what existed between him and Brand was no less than a
blood feud. Olaf was his true son, his only son.

Thorgills touched Olaf's arm and narrowed his eyes.
"Bring me Brand's head on a spear! And when we get home,
I will let you kill Jarls as well."

A snarling half smile covered Olaf's face. "I shall leave at once," he vowed. "And I shall return with Brand's head."

Brand circled the little vessel suspiciously while its owner, a small, poor-looking soul watched, his face expressionless. This Irish boat was no more than wickerwork covered by skin. "It hardly looks seaworthy," Brand observed.

Deirdre did not agree or disagree. "It's called a currach," she said in a matter-of-fact tone. "The fishermen have used them for hundreds of years."

"That does not make such a thing safe," Brand muttered. He knew full well that the Romans had never reached this island as they had reached and ruled Britannia. As a result, the Celts who lived here were woefully unaware of advances in both shipbuilding and weaponry. But amazingly these Irish artisans were the envy of all Europe for their illuminated manuscripts, their intricate wool weaving, and their fine leatherwork.

"Have you ever sailed on one of these, my lady?"

"I have not had the opportunity," Deirdre replied. She had wanted to say, 'thank heaven, no,' but she restrained herself. It really would not do for him to discover how truly terrified she was of setting forth across the water in a currach, or in anything, for that matter.

"Why not use one of your own ships?" the fisherman asked.

Brand ignored him and returned to his examination. Brand turned again to the fisherman. "Have you actually sailed this thing across the Hibernian Sea to the shores of Britannia?" Brand's voice was full of disdain for the fishing boat.

"I've sailed it all over the Hibernian Sea. It's seaworthy . . . unless, of course, there is a storm."

"As if one could count on good weather. It looks to me as if it were intended for childish play on some tranquil pond."

"I said it's seaworthy," the old man replied angrily.

Brand shook his head. Having escaped Thorgills, he had no intention of dying in a boat no better than a wicker basket. Brand turned away and nudged Deirdre. "We must look elsewhere. I must find us a real vessel."

Deirdre did not hide her relief.

They led their horses down the narrow path that ran parallel to the river's edge and away from the place where the fishing boats were tied.

"What next?" Deirdre asked.

"The larger vessels are farther downriver, closer to the sea," Brand said. "We either go there and take our chances on finding a small knorr, or we go into the fort and risk everything by trying to brazen it out—I could say I was sent by Thorgills to take a ship—"

"He would not have sent me with you," Deirdre said. "Let us look for a knorr—whatever that may be."

Brand smiled. "It's a small sturdy cargo boat, built for rough water, which, my lady, I know the Hibernian Sea to be. Mind you, if we take this choice, we will lose time if we don't find one. We will have to return to the fort."

"I have a feeling," Deirdre said. "Call it what you like—instinct—that danger lies in the fort."

Brand wet his lips. "I suppose Thorgills might well have sent someone by now. All right, we'll try to find a knorr."

Several fires burned furiously in the center of the Viking encampment. Olaf roasted a large piece of meat on a skewer, turning it slowly this way and that above red-hot coals. Fat dropped from the roast and caused an occasional sizzling flame.

"When I find Brand," he boasted, "I shall have him on the end of a spear roasting in a fire!"

Thorgills said nothing. His expression was set. His anger knew no words. How could he have trusted Brand? Yet Brand had stood by him in battle and not flinched. There had been a thousand opportunities—why now had the son of Jarls betrayed him and run away? Brand certainly knew what the punishment would be—the theft of the woman was bad enough, but the theft of the treasure would mean a death without mercy.

He tried to think. Was this woman so desirable that Brand would risk everything for her? It seemed unlikely. After all, Brand was betrothed to Erica, and Erica was beautiful and a skilled warrior. No, Brand's reason for departure, his theft, his betrayal was not at all clear to him. It was quite true that Brand had been more or less forced to fight with him, but over the years he had grown to trust Brand, and indeed thought of himself as nothing short of paternal. "Gratitude," Thorgills said, spitting on the ground. Well, no matter. Brand must be caught and punished. He could not allow Brand to set an example like this for the others. The first thing he knew all his men would be acting independently, taking what they wanted and ignoring his leadership.

Olaf narrowed his eyes and turned toward his father. "This is your fault. You should have killed Jarls and Brand when you had the opportunity! Now they will rise again to fight us!"

"You will get your chance to do with Brand what you like," Thorgills promised.

Olaf bit off a piece of meat and chewed it angrily. His father did not realize how many followers Brand had, even among their own men. He looked around; he didn't trust any of them. If Brand beckoned, they might well follow.

Lord Thorgills touched Olaf's arm. "I am returning to Dublin. You will follow Brand till you find him. But think, it is most logical for him to go to Danelaw. He cannot get to Danelaw without sailing the sea and stopping at Monapia—the Isle of Man. Look there."

Olaf half smiled. Brand would pay for everything.

* * *

"Lady, your instincts are very good indeed." Brand drew up his horse in front of a small knorr, anchored to the shore. It was a perfect vessel, neat and sturdily built. Its square sail was strong.

Even in the dark Deirdre could see that the vessel was far from the wicker basket they had previously considered. Still, the idea of crossing the sea frightened her.

Quite suddenly, the outline of a man sprang from the silent deck of the knorr, his sword in his hand. "Who goes there?" he called out.

"Oh, dear," Deirdre said, biting her lip.

Brand did not draw his sword. Rather he slipped from the saddle. "A friend," he called out.

"What's your name? You woke me up."

"I am Brand, son of King Jarls. Are you to guard all these vessels?"

"Brand? Is that really you?"

The sword was replaced in its sheath, and the square figure jumped over the side of the boat. "It is I—Fredrik. Remember? I am the son of Hanna, your mother's servant."

Brand embraced Fredrik with a great bear hug. "I did not know you had joined Lord Thorgills."

"Join is such a grand word, old friend. When your father was defeated, I was taken, with the others. We either pledged ourselves to Thorgills or died. But naturally, you know all about that."

"My father is dead," Brand said, grasping Fredrik's shoulder.

Fredrik looked down. "I'm sorry to hear that."

"I intend to raise an army," Brand said firmly. "I intend to challenge Lord Thorgills."

Deirdre stood stock-still. She supposed she should have guessed as much. He had rescued her, but his real concern was a rebellion.

"I'm going to Danelaw to seek support from King Guthrum, and, if he grants it, I shall sail for home."

Fredrik smiled broadly. "I hope you do not intend to sail this vessel alone, my lord Brand."

Brand grinned. "Does this mean you will sail with me?"

"I shall chance it."

"I must warn you, there is no doubt a price on my head. We have escaped from Lord Thorgills. I have taken his treasure from Trim and Olaf's birthday gift, this comely Irish princess."

Fredrik laughed and slapped Brand on the back. "A prize worth having."

Deirdre fought not to scowl at both of them. She kept quiet only because Brand had warned her he would have to treat her in a certain way. Still, it was galling. She was being spoken of as some object—as a part of the treasure.

"Come aboard," Fredrik said, stepping aside. Brand took the bags with the treasure and threw them over the side. He lifted Deirdre into his arms and put her into the knorr. That done, he, too, climbed over the side.

Fredrik undid the ropes that tied the vessel and jumped in. "We have supplies, and are quite ready to sail."

Brand turned to Deirdre. "Your instincts are good, my lady."

Deirdre looked around. Her nightmare would now begin. She shuddered slightly. After all, who knew what lay beneath the sea?

Fredrik grasped a large paddlelike piece of wood—a mastfish, attached to the stern on the starboard side of the boat.

He positioned himself as oarsman, and in a few moments they were gliding down the river toward the black sea. "It's good to sail by night so we can navigate by the stars," Brand told her.

"We must head for The Isle of Man," Fredrik called out. "It's the island where we must land. It is more than halfway."

"I've heard tell of that island," Deirdre said. "St. Patrick was there, and it is said many monks live in the monastery."

"The island belongs to the Danes now," Brand told her.

For a time he and Fredrik spoke. It was, Deirdre thought, a most interesting conversation. They spoke of the stars, of different constellations, and of how to tell direction from their position in the sky during different seasons. It was something of which Deirdre had never thought, and she found herself absorbed.

Deirdre pulled her cloak tighter, then availed herself of a fur. As they drew closer to the sea, it grew more windy.

"Come, sit by me," Brand called out to her.

Deirdre made her way to his side and for a time sat silently while he rowed.

"Soon the wind will catch the sail and I can retire," he laughed.

"I have never been on the sea," Deirdre whispered.

Brand put his arm around her shoulders and squeezed her. "That is unbelievable to me," he said. "I was born at sea; even my mother had her own vessel."

"I have much to learn," Deirdre said, looking into his eyes.

Brand looked back into hers. "I, too."

He was such an unusual man. From moment to moment she didn't know what to expect of him. Sometimes he treated her like an object and sometimes like a precious individual. Sometimes he was crisp, even a bit mean, while at other times he was gentle and loving. On the one hand he seemed to care for her and about her—he had, after all, thought enough to tell her about Alan. But at other times, it was as if she did not exist. Was she destined to be his slave or something more?

I have given myself over to fate, Deirdre thought. *I must go where it takes me.*

Six

Deirdre watched with great interest as the knorr left the estuary of the river and entered the sea. Once, long ago, the sea to which this river led was called Oceania Hibernicus, more recently it was simply called the Hibernian Sea though some called it the North Sea since the Norsemen had sailed south on it to become the scourge of all Europe. She knew of the sea's names only because her father had been in possession of some drawings or crude representations of the countryside and the seas surrounding it.

Her father had ridden many times to Dublin, but she herself had never been this far from her place of birth. The thought that she would travel still farther both excited and frightened her. She tried to keep thinking of Edana and the wonderful adventures she had experienced. Edana had spun a thousand tales of lands across the seas, of strange people, of odd languages, of lands without fog, of cities surrounded by sand, of men dressed in turbans and women whose faces were covered. Yes, no matter what happened she found herself filled with curiosity.

Never before in her entire life had it occurred to her that she might one day cross the sea and journey to Britannia. A thousand stories ran through her mind. Stories of monsters which lived beneath the seas and emerged to devour travelers on the water—stories of lost kingdoms. But once again she thought of Edana. Edana had traveled the sea, and no harm had come to her. Moreover, she had learned much. She spoke of her adventure as if she missed it, and was sorry she had been returned.

Deirdre looked back toward the shore. In retrospect Dublin was not what she had expected, though she was not sure just what she had imagined. It was quite an ordinary market town with a large monastery and a Viking fort. The populace moved about as if in hopes of not being noticed by their unwanted rulers. Still, it was a pleasant place. The river which wound through the town was pretty and grass grew on each side of it.

Deirdre wondered what the largest town in the whole world was—she tried to imagine what living in such a place would be like. Dublin would likely grow and become larger, she decided. Perhaps she had been a little disappointed in Dublin because she was ill at ease there.

The Vikings in Dublin who saw them did not question them because Brand was so obviously one of their number. But soon Thorgills would come and tell them otherwise, and the hunt for them would begin. She was glad they had found this knorr. Now they were on their way.

"We're fortunate," Brand said. "The stars are bright to-night. Some nights there is thick fog here, and one can hardly tell the difference between land and water."

Deirdre pulled her cloak even closer. Apart from the fact that they would have become lost, she almost wished there was fog. Fog was soft and peaceful; like clouds, it had an ethereal quality and somehow made her feel safe. Alan always said that fog was naught but clouds visiting from the heavens. But as Brand noted, the sky was bright and the moon full. That enabled her to feel the enormity of the sea, to know there was no land in view, to know that all around them there was nothing but black water which could swallow them up. In fact, now that they had reached the sea, the water was choppy, and she imagined it had little teeth trying to snap at her.

"Seldom is this sea so calm, especially when the moon is full," Brand explained.

"What has the moon to do with it?" Deirdre looked up at the glowing white ball. "It looks like a flat white plate. Surely it has no power here."

"I don't understand it," Brand confessed, "but one learns from observation. It is just a simple fact that when the moon is full, the tides are higher, and, more often than not, high tides bring turbulent waters."

"Observation is important in medicine, too."

"Perhaps listening and watching is real learning," he suggested.

"Perhaps. I've never thought about the moon and the stars much. How can such a small thing so far away have such power over the waters in the sea?"

"I do not know, except I am certain it is not small but rather large."

"Large? But it looks—"

"Yes, of course it looks small because it is far away. Just as when you first see land from the sea. It looks smaller and as you get closer it becomes larger."

"Yes, you are right. I understand, I just never thought about it. I suppose we cannot know how large the moon is, or even how far away it is."

"One of the secrets of the heavens."

"All my life I've asked questions about the land—I mean I never thought much about the sky or the sea until tonight."

"I've always lived near the sea," Brand told her. As he spoke, his voice grew softer and dreamier, far away. "As I told you, I was born at sea. When I was a child my father took me to sea. At sea there is nothing but water and stars, and you soon learn how important the stars are."

"I did not notice the patterns of the heavens until I heard you talking. Please tell me more about it."

He smiled, and she could see his teeth, white and gleaming

in the moonlight. "Look up there. See that group of stars which looks like a ladle?"

"Yes, I see it." A little chill went through her. It really did look like a ladle.

"Now, see the last star in what would be the handle of the ladle?"

"Yes, I see it."

He moved his finger across the sky. "That bright star, the one you can trace from the end of the ladle, if you follow that star, you go toward my home."

Deirdre felt excited by the conversation. There was so much she wanted to know, so many mysterious things she did not understand.

"What if it is daylight? How do you know in what direction to sail?"

Brand laughed. "By day you follow the sun. When the sun seems highest, it is due south. This high point will be closer to the horizon the farther north you sail. By measuring this distance, you can tell how far north you are."

"He's a wealth of knowledge," Fredrik called out good naturedly from the mastfish.

"I confess I am afraid to sail on the sea because I cannot see the bottom. Is the water in this sea deep?" she asked.

Again Brand smiled. "It is many embraces, my lady."

"Embraces? I do not understand."

"We use a lead weight to measure the depth of water. If we then outstretch our arms and measure from the tip of our right fingers to the tip of our left fingers across our body, we say that is one fathom, or an embrace. But I think to embrace you I would not need the full length of my arms, to embrace you is less than a fathom."

Deirdre blushed and was glad it was night. Even by the light of the moon, the hue of her complexion could not be seen. "Are you teasing me?" she asked, trying to sound a trifle annoyed.

"Not at all, my lady. You watch. You will see my countrymen measure the depth of the water, withdraw the line, and count the lengths as I have described. They will then say how many fathoms it is, and as I have said, a fathom in my language means embrace."

Deirdre did not immediately reply. After a time she said, "But we do not know how deep this water is."

"That is true, I have no lead weight. But I've been told this sea is deep indeed.

"Do you miss not having a lead weight to measure?"

Again Brand laughed. "No, my lady. I miss a dozen oarsmen.

"I feel the wind," Fredrik called out from his position on the mastfish. "You will not miss the oarsmen for long."

Even in the darkness, Deirdre could see Brand's sinewy arms as he plied the oars. His physique was mighty, and he exuded a raw virility that excited her on a level she had not known existed till he had first kissed her.

"Why do you ask of depth, my lady?"

Deirdre looked across at him. "Among my people there is a legend about an island in this sea—a large island with a remarkable civilization. It is said that one day the sea rose and submerged it, drowning all its inhabitants."

"I was not in your land long. But I was there long enough to know that tales abound. Still, the tale of which you speak is a common one. I have heard it in many lands, or at least one like it."

"Are there no tales in your land?"

"My lady, we can spin the night away on tales and the adventures of the gods who play with us."

"I do not believe in your gods," she said firmly.

"You shall, my lady. When you hear Thor roar down the fjords, you will believe."

Was he really going to take her to his land? She dared not react for fear he might change his mind. It was her only hope of finding her brother. The thought comforted her; perhaps she and Alan would not be separated forever.

"My lady, this rowing is a boring job. It would go easier if you would tell me a tale."

Deirdre leaned back and looked up at the stars again. "I have misled you," she said slowly. "I believe in only one god, but there was a time when my people believed in many gods and in many manifestations of those more powerful than we mortals. Many of our tales involve such immortals."

"Spin away—the night is long."

"I shall tell you of Conn, a fair young prince with fiery hair."

Brand pulled on the oars and listened. The cadence of her voice was marvelous, and he was certain, had he been able to watch, that her hands moved expressively when she spoke.

"Conn was the son of Connaught of a Hundred Fights, a bellicose king who warred constantly. One day Connaught and his son were standing on the mountaintop, listening to the wind and speaking of yet another battle. Then Conn turned away. He saw a beautiful maiden walking toward him. She wore a filmy dress and garlands of flowers in her hair. Though the ground was cold, she was barefoot. Her golden hair fell to her waist and she spoke softly, dreamily so as to enchant Conn. 'I come from the land of the ever-living,' she told him. 'In this land there is no sin, no death, only everlasting youth. We are a people who are all pleasure, for we have no strife.'

"Conn was enchanted, but his father, the king, was beside himself. He could not see this maiden, but could only hear her voice.

" 'I bid you come with me,' the maiden said to Conn.

" 'Wait,' the king commanded. 'Bring my Druid.'

"Now the king's Druid was a powerful man of many spells. The king told him of the maiden who could be heard by all but only seen by Conn, who wanted to follow her.

" 'Let me go!' Conn begged. 'I love her and must be with her.'

"But the Druid cast a spell, and the maiden disappeared even to Conn's eyes. But as she vanished, she tossed Conn an apple, which he caught and hid from his father the king and his powerful Druid.

"For one month, Conn ate only from the magic apple. Each bite was replaced so that the apple was never gone, and Conn was never hungry. But each day that he ate, his desire for the maiden grew greater.

"One day the king, his Druid, and Conn were walking by the river, when suddenly the maiden again appeared to Conn.

" 'Come with me,' she called out to Conn.

" 'I love my home,' he replied.

" 'The sun is not as strong as thy longing,' the maiden cried.

" 'Make her go away, the king begged his Druid.

"But before the Druid could cast his spell, Conn ran to the river's edge and climbed into a crystal boat and sailed into the setting sun. The king, the Druid, and the people never saw him again except for a very few lovers who said they saw a crystal boat at sunset as it sailed on the shimmering waters of the river."

"A wonderful romantic tale, my lady. You have made light my work."

"And it has taken my mind off being on the dark sea."

Brand laughed. "I count myself fortunate you are not moaning with illness."

"Should I be?"

"Many women get seasick. I remember another voyage when we took ten or twelve captives to market. They were sorry sights when we arrived, and I'm sure their value was diminished."

"As I am a captive myself, I cannot mourn for your loss."

"I do not intend selling you," he said evenly.

Deirdre did not know how to respond. Was she to be grateful? "Nor can you return me to my home."

"My lady, your home is no more. Nothing ever remains the same. Think of your tale. Perhaps we are going to the land of pleasure."

"There is war in your land. We are pursued by those who would fight you."

"When it is over, it will be over," he answered. But she was right. He would fight again, and probably all too soon.

"I am concerned only for my brother. I long to find him. But now Thorgills has taken him, and I shall see him no more."

Brand shrugged. "One never knows, my lady. One never knows."

Brand rowed on. After a time he lapsed into silence, and Deirdre found herself closing her eyes and drifting off into sleep, even as they plowed across the sea. Vaguely, she was aware of their moving more swiftly and the fact that the motion of Brand's rowing had ceased. The wind had caught the sail and now propelled them.

The sensation of cold water on her face woke Deirdre, and in a sudden panic she grasped the side of the boat. "I'm drowning!" she gasped. Then, realizing that they were still afloat, she let out her breath.

Brand laughed at her. "I would let you know if we were in danger."

The sail had indeed caught the wind, and they were moving swiftly across the choppy water.

"Much better than rowing!" He grinned at her. "I suspect we're near land. I hope it is the island."

The sun was coming up, and across the far horizon a single orange line of light heralded its coming. She reveled in the thought that soon the sun would be beating down on them, drying their damp clothes and warming them.

"There!" he said, pointing off into the distance.

Deirdre squinted. "Is that land?"

"It is!"

Brand once again took up the oars in order to make sure the boat went where he wanted to go. Fredrik, still at his post, manned the mastfish.

Deirdre watched silently as the land grew closer.

Finally, Brand jumped into the surf and pulled the boat onto the sand. He scooped her up into his arms, carried her ashore, and set her down. Next he brought their supplies, and, finally, he and Fredrik pulled the boat ashore and secured it.

"Why don't you remain here?" Fredrik suggested. "I'll go in search of the village."

"You must be as tired as I," Brand protested.

Fredrik shook his head. "Tending the mastfish is not as arduous as rowing. Wait here, I shall return."

Deirdre sank to the sand.

Brand quickly built a fire, and when it was roaring he stood up and began to take off his clothes.

Deirdre's mouth opened in surprise. "What are you doing?"

"I intend to dry my clothes, my lady. I suggest you do the same. The sun and the fire will keep us warm."

He was quick, so quick she could not turn away. He dropped his sleeveless leather tunic and his broad, bare chest was revealed. Without the slightest hesitation, he removed his skirt. His hips were lean, his thighs strong and like his arms, muscular. She glanced at his organ and then quickly turned away, her face red with embarrassment.

Brand roared with laughter. "And, my lady, it is at ease!"

Deirdre covered her face with her hands. "I do not wish to see you."

Again he laughed. "Of course you do! Just as I should like to see you."

"I shall remain wet," she said indignantly. But she did stand up and, discarding her cloak, turned her back to the fire. "My clothes will dry on me," she added as she stood looking away from his nakedness.

Brand stared at her. It mattered not. Her wet clothes clung to her voluptuous body. He could clearly see the firm roundness of her buttocks, the tiny waist, and full, upturned breasts. Her long and beautiful hair fell to her waist, and vaguely he wondered the color of the hair which hid her zone of pleasure. Doubtless, it was also red, and doubtless each wonderfully curved young breast was crowned with a soft pink circle. "A pity," he sighed. "I was looking forward to seeing you."

"I will certainly not willingly reveal myself," she said, attempting to muster some dignity as she stood staring at the trees beyond the beach. It was difficult knowing that behind her he was standing naked. She shivered, but not from cold. A vision of him pushing her to the ground, of removing her clothes, of taking her filled her thoughts for an instant. And just as quickly she rebuked herself. What was she thinking! This man was a heathen thief! This desire she felt was something terrible!

"I'm afraid you shall see me naked more than once on this voyage."

"Why should I?" she asked, still staring off into the distance, trying to forget what she had already seen. Why in heavens name couldn't she purge the mental picture of his handsome body from her thoughts?

"In order to protect you I shall have to tell everyone you are my slave. I suggest you do not contradict me. I am afraid you shall have to act the slave."

Slave? Was she now to pretend she was this heathen's slave? Well, she supposed she was, in a way.

"Your silence disturbs me. I need your promise, my lady."

Deirdre nodded slowly. "I shall not betray you," she finally agreed.

"Who is there? Who builds a fire to warm themselves?" a voice shouted out from the woods beyond the beach.

Deirdre quickly wrapped her cloak around her. Behind her she heard Brand quickly dressing. "Brand, son of Jarls, a Dane!" he called out in answer. Then he added, "My slave and I are on our way to Danelaw."

Deirdre was surprised to see ten or so armed men emerge from the woods. "Welcome," one of them offered. "Come along, follow us."

"There is another with us, he went to find the village."

"We'll send someone after him."

Brand said nothing more, but shouldered their pack. "Come along," he said, taking her arm and guiding her across the rock-strewn beach toward bent trees that grew beyond. They entered a glen and followed a narrow path.

After a time, they came to a fortress. It consisted of a small castle, several other buildings, and a sod-covered wall. It was not unlike the fortress in Dublin. The castle itself was not as large as the castle in which she had grown up, but it seemed large enough. On this island, Deirdre noted, the Vikings seemed settled indeed.

"Take food from the table in the great hall," their host, Leif, invited. "Then feel free to avail yourselves of our sweat rooms and baths, and take a good night's sleep in any one of the empty bedchambers."

"I shall not forget your hospitality," Brand promised.

Leif smiled. "It is our pleasure to have the son of Jarls stay with us. Your father was well-known and well liked."

"Thank you," Brand said, bowing slightly.

Deirdre said nothing as Brand propelled her toward the great hall. Her hunger was too great, and her weariness too acute. She felt that as soon as she closed her eyes she could sleep for a million years, and she knew she would close her eyes as soon as her pangs of hunger were sated.

Deirdre, at Brand's bidding, did not speak while they were in the great hall. She ate heartily of bread and cheese, after which she drank some wine and ate some berries sweetened with honey. Brand quaffed down several goblets of wine, ate venison and chicken, and also had bread, cheese, and fruit.

"Can we sleep now?" Deirdre asked. She felt she would soon not be able to keep her eyes open.

"We must bathe first," Brand replied. "It would be considered impolite if we didn't wash before sleeping in a clean bed."

Deirdre said nothing because the thought of bathing was

really quite appealing. She was grimy from their long trip and felt sticky from the seawater.

Brand led her down the corridors and out behind the castle to a small wooden building. It was almost as if he had been here before, as if he knew where everything was located.

"Where are we going?" she asked.

"To the bath. We always build them right outside," Brand answered.

"But surely this castle was built by others."

"Of course, but it's been added to."

Brand pushed open the heavy door of the wooden structure. Steamy vapors poured out of it. It was like a hot fog.

"I can barely see," Deirdre said.

To one side was a stone pool filled with steaming water. By its side were great iron pots boiling over roaring fires.

"Hot water is put into the pool," Brand explained. "More water is kept boiling to provide steam. Beyond here is a pool of cold water. First we bathe in hot water, after that we sit on the bench and allow the steam to cleanse us, and finally we dive into the cold water."

Deirdre could not even ask the question, "Together?" Nor, indeed, did she have time.

"Get out of your clothes," Brand ordered.

Her mouth opened. "I shall do no such thing," she protested.

He leaned close. "You are my slave, remember? Do as I say, or I shall rip them from your body, my lady."

Deirdre stood paralyzed for a long moment. But the look in his eye made her realize that this was no idle threat. And she reminded herself that her life might depend on her performance. She turned away from him shyly and began to undo her tunic.

Hardly had she finished than she heard a splash behind her. It was Brand in the hot pool. He made a sound of satisfaction.

Deirdre, feeling only partially hidden by the rising vapors, finished disrobing and slipped into the blessed hot water.

Brand soaked up to his neck, trying to ignore the other presence on the far side of the pool. She was submerged in the water up to her neck, too, but he could see the gentle curve of her shoulders, and beneath the water, her lovely rounded buttocks. She washed her long hair, and rubbed the sweet-scented soapberry into her skin.

Deirdre dared not turn around. Behind her a few feet away in the water was Brand, his magnificent body glistening.

"When you're finished, wrap yourself in one of those cloths and go and sit by the steam."

Deirdre did not answer, but continued to wash herself and enjoy the warmth of the water and the glorious feeling of cleanliness.

After a time she said, "Close your eyes."

Brand could hardly control himself he wanted to laugh so much. Did she really expect him to be so devoid of interest? "Yes, my lady," he replied. It hardly mattered; she would not turn around.

Deirdre climbed out of the water. She hurried to the bench and wrapped herself in one of the cloths.

Brand did not close his eyes. He watched as her perfectly formed snow-white body emerged from the water. Her luxurious rounded bottom was more lovely than he had imagined when revealed without the distortion of the water. Her legs were lovely and shaped to perfection. He was sorry that he had not seen the front view . . . but perhaps later in the cold pool where the ice-cold water would make her breasts hard and turn her lovely nipples to rosy stones . . . perhaps there he would get his wish. But did he wish only to see her unclothed? No, he wished for much more. He wished to feel her writhe beneath him, to hear her cry out for him. He wished to possess her, and he was well aware that day by day, hour by hour, his passion for Deirdre had blurred his memory of Erica and all but blotted out his sense of duty.

He withdrew from the water, and shook himself off.

Deirdre could not draw her eyes away. The warmth of the

water had made him rise. Never had she seen a male organ ready to mate. He was a huge man, and she shivered violently, quickly turning her head before he could see her. *I'm weak!* She chastised herself yet again for the longing she felt, for this savage craving which seemed to consume her. What would it be like to have him take her?

Edana had told her stories—"How wonderful is a good lover—his hands, his lips, his movements inside you can make you hot with wantonness, can make you scream for him. Your whole body will throb with fulfillment, your breasts will ache for his lips. Ah, my child, fear not—you're young and beautiful, great pleasure awaits you. Eventually you will know the perfect lover."

Deirdre had wept and told Edana that she feared she would know only Malvin, but Edana has shaken her head. "Edana sees the future. You will not marry Malvin. You will know many things, among them true love."

Was Brand her true love? No, he was a Viking and she was his prisoner, she reminded herself yet again.

Brand stood up. "Come along," he beckoned.

With the cloth wound about her, Deirdre followed him to another room, a large room with a glistening, cold, clear, stone-lined pool.

Suddenly, without warning, Brand seized her cloth, unwinding it from around her body, and simultaneously pushed her into the icy water.

Deirdre shrieked. She was too shocked even to realize she was unclothed.

Brand looked down at her, his face filled with amusement. She was beautiful! Her full breasts were as he had imagined, though, he thought, even more lovely. Her nipples were now tight and hard, made rosier and harder yet by the shock of the cold water.

Deirdre's arms flew to cover herself, and she quickly scrambled from the pool and drew her cloth around her. "Vile pig!" she shouted.

But Brand was in the ice-cold pool. He looked down. Regrettably, his organ had shrunk to normal size. Yet he knew, even in this ice water, if he thought much about Deirdre he could change that. Ah, temptation. He wondered if it would make him stronger to resist.

After a moment he, too, emerged from the water. He wrapped himself in the cloth and picked up their bundle of clothes.

"Come, my lady, we both need a good night's rest."

"I will not sleep in the same bed with you," she announced, trying to sound dignified.

"So sleep at the foot of it on a skin. I'm sleeping in a bed, my lady."

Deirdre tried to muster her last bit of dignity. "My name is Deirdre. You may call me by my name."

Brand knew she already knew his name. He took her small hand in his. "Come then, Deirdre."

Deirdre awakened feeling as if she had slept for a thousand hours. She stretched and uncurled herself. True to his word, Brand had made her a bed of skins at the foot of the bed he claimed for himself. Nonetheless, she had slept well and long.

It was a glorious morning. The sun shone through the windows, and she had bathed and felt wonderfully clean. She stretched again and after a second, struggled to her feet. The bed was empty. Brand was gone!

A sudden panic seized her. Had he left her on this strange island? Should she stay here in this room or should she seek him?

Deirdre quickly dressed and, when she was finished, slowly opened the door and peered into the deserted stone corridor. "I am the slave of Brand." She practiced the words as Brand had taught her. Oh, it was such a peculiar language!

Deirdre walked slowly down the winding staircase and

into the great hall. It was deserted. Hearing voices, she followed their sound down the path toward the beach.

Deirdre stopped short. There, offshore, bobbing in the
water, was a most magnificent sight! Deirdre gasped; it was
a great Viking ship, beautiful as well as fearsome. It appeared
to be at least as long as the great hall in the castle, at least
seventy-five feet. As long as it was, it was also shallow with
a great red-and-white square sail. On its curved bow, a huge
carved serpent served as figurehead. But on this occasion,
it was turned, facing the back of the vessel and thus the sea.

She turned her eyes away from the amazing sight to see
Brand talking to several other men.

Brand glanced at her, but did not speak when she walked
up to him. When he finished speaking to the men, he turned
to her, "We will continue our onward voyage in a proper
ship. We'll sail in four days' time for Danelaw."

"Is this your slave girl?" one of the Vikings asked.

Brand nodded. "Yes, and a rare find."

"You have only one slave girl!" the other roared. "I have
two slave girls! Both do my every bidding, and my wife likes
them, too."

Brand said nothing; he only shrugged. But, nonetheless,
the mention of the man's wife made him think of Erica. He
did not, however, wish to have both a mistress and a wife.

It was true that sometimes a wife and husband would share
a slave girl, but he did not think that such an arrangement
was for him. Truth be known, he wanted only one woman.
When he had defeated Lord Thorgills, he wanted that woman
to bear him children and sail with him to the new land.

Brand looked again at Deirdre, who now pretended to be
his slave. How convenient it would be to turn pretense into
reality! But then he thought again of her spirit and knew it
would not be easy. He could call her a slave, but she would
never be one. No, to have this woman he would have to free
her and marry her.

Deirdre was enough like the women in his land to survive

there. In his land free women inherited, they fought, they had power.

"Is that the vessel on which we will travel?" Deirdre asked, interrupting his thoughts.

"Yes, she's a trading vessel that sails between this island and Danelaw."

"It's a large vessel," Deirdre allowed, then hesitatingly, "the awesome serpent on its bow looks like those described in tales of sea monsters. Why is its head twisted away, toward the sea?"

"Because it is meant to frighten the spirits of the sea. When in port it must be made to face the sea so as not to frighten the spirits of the land. That's the making of another tale."

She was not certain if Brand believed in stories of land and sea spirits or if they were like the legends and tales her people told about fairies and little people. But perhaps he did believe. He, after all, was not a Christian. He believed in strange gods. And, she admitted to herself, she did believe in sea monsters. Many people had seen such creatures and no doubt there were waterborne dragons like the image depicted on the bow of the vessel.

"Are you sure we should not leave sooner?" Deirdre asked. "Olaf may well be in pursuit."

Brand looked thoughtfully down at her. "The journey between here and Danelaw is across a rougher part of the sea. This vessel is safer, even if we must take the chance and wait."

"I'm sure you're right," Deirdre said, looking again at the magnificent ship. Still, in her heart she was afraid. She was certain that Olaf would not give up easily.

Deirdre repacked the bundle which contained their change of clothes. She wrapped it carefully in the oilskin Brand had given her and tied it tightly with leather straps. Brand had already taken their food and two animal skins under which to sleep to the vessel. He had explained that they would need these things after they were put ashore because from where they would land, it was a journey of several days to Jorvick.

The sun was about to rise in the eastern sky; they would leave on the high tide a little after dawn.

Brand was already on the beach helping to prepare the vessel. It was part of the bargain; Brand would help row if the wind did not take the sails.

Deirdre acknowledged a strange feeling of excitement, of anticipation. She wondered what the land of the Angles was like, she wondered what this Danelaw was like. Here, on the island called the Isle of Man, there seemed to be a semblance of order, a peacefulness to the way of life. In spite of everything, she found seeing new things intriguing. And reluctantly she admitted that Brand made her feel safe. She felt certain he would not hurt her; she knew she was beginning to feel secure in his presence.

Deirdre looked around quickly to make certain she had forgotten nothing. Seeing that everything was packed, she hurried to meet Brand by the edge of the sea to board the vessel that would take them to Danelaw.

Midway down the winding path, she heard the sound of the huge metal hammer hit the great metal plate that hung at the bottom of the path. It was the alarm. Deirdre moved off the path instinctively, seeking shelter amid the rocks. In seconds fully armed Viking warriors swarmed onto the beach, ready to defend their settlement.

Deirdre moved closer, and when she heard Brand's voice she ran toward it. What was happening? A feeling of apprehension surged through her.

As soon as she saw the beach she stopped short, frozen in terror. A second ship was anchored and on the beach she saw Olaf in full battle dress, surrounded by others who had come to fight alongside him.

Brand was being held. He was surrounded by warriors, not Olaf's warriors, but those who had welcomed them to this island. Without hesitation, Deirdre ran to Brand's side. Surprisingly, the warriors let her pass. Brand's eyes burned into hers—they seemed to say, 'you should have saved yourself.'

"The woman is mine!" Olaf spit. "And he stole a treasure, too! No doubt he carries it in his pack!"

Deirdre said nothing, but she felt afraid. What if something happened to Brand?

"I demand his life!" Olaf shouted. "And I demand my property back."

He glared at Deirdre, his narrow eyes filled with hatred—a terrible hatred, for it was hatred mixed with raw lust.

"You are Olaf, son of Thorgills," one of the elder warriors said. He assessed Olaf somewhat unsympathetically.

"Yes! I demand my property."

"We are no friends of Lord Thorgills," the warrior said slowly. "On the other hand, this man has told us he is the son of Jarls, a much-respected king. Do you deny that he is the son of Jarls?"

"No!" Olaf stormed. "But the property is mine!"

The older warrior nodded. "We have laws—laws which even Olaf the son of Thorgills must obey. We will go to the Thywald—to our place of decision, and there twelve warriors will decide who will be given what. We will listen to each of your arguments."

Deirdre, who had understood little, looked imploringly at Brand, whose mastery of her language was much greater than hers of his. "What does this mean?" she whispered.

Brand held her arm. "That I must state my case before a jury of twelve. They will decide how to resolve this matter."

"But what if—"

"Deirdre, this is the law of my people. I must obey it."

Deirdre looked downward. She did not wish to admit how afraid she was, nor did she express her fear that the twelve men could not be trusted to render a just verdict.

Moving as a single group, they all took to the wider path that led across open ground, away from the shore. Olaf marched at the head of his own men while the older warrior, who appeared to rule the island, led the rest. She and Brand moved along in the center of a guard.

After some time they came to a wall, and twelve of the elder warriors from the island seated themselves on the grass, the stone wall at their backs.

"Olaf, son of Thorgills! Come forward and tell your tale."

Olaf looked about suspiciously, then stepped forward. "This one, Brand, son of Jarls, stole my treasure and took my slave, this woman." He motioned toward Deirdre, then pointed at Brand accusingly.

"And what do you ask of the Thywald?"

"I ask that Brand be killed, that my treasure be given back, and that the woman be severely beaten and returned to me!"

Deirdre could not even look at him. He sneered when he spoke, he was a horrible creature.

"And you Brand, son of Jarls. What do you say?"

"I say that I was forced to fight for Thorgills who took me in return for my father's life. I say that Thorgills stole from my father and that this treasure and this woman are rightfully mine. I have served Thorgills well, but now my father is dead and I will serve him no more."

Olaf's eyes flickered with surprise when Brand said his father was dead. But he said nothing.

"We shall deliberate," the elder warrior said, holding up his shield.

The twelve men retired behind the wall to discuss the claims made by Olaf and Brand.

Brand held fast to Deirdre's arm. She could feel the strength of his body, and she tried to convince herself that all would be well.

After a short time, the twelve men returned, and one stood up and addressed the others loudly, "We have decided that this is not our battle. We command Olaf and Brand to fight alone, and to the death! To the victor go the spoils!"

Deirdre felt the blood drain from her face. Brand was strong and swift, but was he a match for Olaf? Strangely, at that moment she realized she was more afraid for Brand than for herself. She looked up at him, and pleaded, "You must not leave me," she whispered. "You must win."

Brand looked down on her beautiful face. He gently touched her ravishing red hair and then her white throat. Oh, he did want her so. If he won, there would be no denying his own desire for her any longer. And looking into her concerned eyes, he knew full well she would not struggle or deny him.

"Worry not, Deirdre, you are a prize for whom I shall return," he whispered as he furtively caressed her ear and kissed her neck.

Deirdre felt her face flush. *Yes, I want you,* she thought. She kissed his cheek, pressing her lips against his skin.

Brand smiled at her and turned away. "I am ready," Brand said, looking at Olaf, whose hand was already on his fearsome hatchet.

"Let nothing happen to him," she whispered, looking heavenward. Did she pray to her God or his gods? Deirdre admitted to herself that she wanted him and that she would willingly follow him. *Free or as your willing slave,* she thought as she watched him walk toward Olaf. *Dear heaven, how can I bear this? Do the good ever win?*

Malvin had won over her father, a good man. Thorgills had won over Jarls, a just king. Would Olaf now kill Brand? It wasn't fair! First Alan and then her father! If the fates deprived her of Brand, too—what would she do?

Seven

As if in a trance, Deirdre was moved along with the others, hardly aware that she was guarded—a prize to be won, a vital part of this terrible contest.

They walked to a great open space beyond the wall. It was a large, flat, grassy circle rimmed with huge boulders. All around the circle, the ground rose gradually so that people sitting on the gentle slope could see into the middle of this natural arena. Deirdre was made to sit down, and most of the others sat down as well. In the distance she heard the gong being rung to summon all to the deadly duel.

They sat on the dewy grass for what to Deirdre seemed an eternity. The time passed slowly as a large, noisy crowd of men, women, and children gradually assembled. They, too, sat down along the outer rim of the circle, well behind the boulders but high enough up the incline so all could see. Clearly this was more than a contest that would settle an argument; it was also a form of entertainment, and the islanders seemed to be making the most of it. It would have been the same in Meath, Deirdre reflected. Duels, like sporting events, always drew large crowds.

After a long while Brand and Olaf appeared. Deirdre watched with consternation as the space between them was measured off, and they were placed some two yards apart, unarmed, in the center of the circle and facing the island's leader and the twelve men of the Thywald.

They were each clothed only in a leather loincloth. At this moment they carried no shields; nor did they wear helmets. Brand's blond hair blew slightly in the breeze, but Olaf's greasy mane clung together, framing his froglike face.

How could they fight? Deirdre asked herself. They were attached to one another at the wrist by a length of leather. Their weapons, a sword, a frightening two headed ax, and a shield, were arranged in two pyramids a few feet from each of them.

Brand and Olaf were signaled and each turned so that they stood back-to-back, leaning against each other. Suddenly the leader blew a ram's horn and all became silent. He climbed onto the highest boulder and declared, "This is a fight to the death. You must fight unarmed until you can reach your weapons. At the next sound of the horn the contest begins!"

This was nothing like a duel in her land would have been, Deirdre realized. In Meath, the participants would not have been tied, and both would have been on horseback. She wanted to turn away so as not to know what was happening. She could not.

The combatants bowed to the island's leader. He lifted the ram's horn to his lips and again the peculiar sound filled the now still arena.

Brand and Olaf were not of equal weight. Brand was taller, leaner, and more muscular, and Olaf was bearlike, and somewhat fat. They each pulled at the leather rope in the opposite direction, straining desperately toward their pile of weapons. Brand, unable to pull Olaf forward, wound the leather around his arm so he could get closer without allowing Olaf to move. Olaf responded by virtually planting himself where he stood. Brand did the unexpected. Instead of continuing to resist, Brand quickly ran toward Olaf, causing him to fall backwards. Brand pounced on him, hitting him in the head with his fists. Olaf used his huge knee to push Brand in the groin and off him. They both scrambled to their feet, Olaf holding the rope taut with his left hand so he could punch Brand with his other doubled fist. Brand was swift and artfully dodged the blow, landing a counterpunch to Olaf's soft midsection. Olaf fell toward his pyramid of deadly weapons and pulled Brand with him, knocking them down with a clatter.

Behind her, around her, the crowd roared, but only Olaf's men roared for him. The rest were Danes, not Norwegians like Olaf, so they cheered for Brand. Deirdre was so frightened she could not find her voice.

Hands reached out to grab the sword. There was slack in the leather, and Olaf rose to his feet sword in hand. Brand, seeing Olaf coming at him, adroitly sidestepped to avoid a blow to his head and pulled the leather around Olaf's feet, tripping him.

Deirdre let her breath out. Her body was as tight as the leather strap; her heart was beating wildly.

Olaf's next blow cut the leather, which Brand had raised in front of him. Olaf picked up his shield and pursued Brand, who raced for his own sword and shield. Brand heard the whistle of the blade as it came toward the back of his head. He spun about, moving his shield to deflect Olaf's blow. He then countered with a strike at Olaf's head. Back and forth they pounded on each other. Each blow was punctuated by cries and hoots from the crowd.

Whenever Olaf swung, Deirdre closed her eyes, opening them quickly to see if Brand was all right.

Perspiration poured from both combatants as each grunted with the other's attack. The crash of swords hitting shields filled the air. Every muscle of both men was taut, and their near-naked bodies glistened in the sun. Brand struck hard, but this time Olaf turned sideways and the blow missed him.

Deirdre gasped. Surely Olaf's next blow would strike Brand on the back of his head. But no! Brand used his own momentum to roll, and, keeping his sword arm out, he turned aside Olaf's blow.

The crowd made a collective, "Ah!"

Brand tried to slice Olaf's legs, but Olaf jumped out of

the way with shocking agility and came down on Brand with a withering blow. Brand felt his grip on his shield loosening, and he slipped on the grass under the next blow. Olaf's sword cut into Brand's right shoulder.

"No!" Deirdre screamed.

Sharp pain then numbness shot through Brand's body as he grabbed his shoulder. His concentration was broken, yet he saw Olaf's thrust coming straight at him as he rolled to the side. As Olaf came down toward him on the ground Brand swung his dented shield into the side of Olaf's head, knocking him away so he had time to get up, although he left his shield behind.

Olaf groaned, but recovered. He thrust his sword at Brand, who suddenly struck Olaf's wrist. Finally he hit Olaf hard in the head with his fist.

Olaf looked stunned. He fell back, but was able to reach his ax as Brand moved in for the death blow.

Deirdre's hand covered her mouth. Her eyes were large and she felt ill. Behind her she heard a man whisper, "A good match!" Yet no matter how she felt, she could not turn away. Her attention was absolute. She was riveted on the duel, willing Brand to win and to live.

Brand missed with his next blow, and Olaf knocked Brand's sword out of his hand. Brand, barely avoiding Olaf's swinging ax, retreated and grabbed his own ax to block Olaf's next strike at his head.

Then Deirdre leaned forward, a silent scream of terror grasping her.

Brand's ax handle snapped, leaving him on his knees with just a sharp-pointed stick to defend himself. The crowd yelled wildly. Brand's shoulder was bleeding badly, and his movements indicated his dizziness. It was the same shoulder that had been wounded before. Perhaps, Deirdre prayed, it was not too deep.

Brand looked into Olaf's pale blue eyes. The son of Thorgills raised his ax over his head, ready to deliver the final blow. An image of his own father flashed across Brand's mind, and then it was Deirdre he saw. Olaf would not have her!

Olaf's blow was about to come, and Brand summoned every ounce of strength left in his battered body. He thrust the pointed end of his ax handle straight into Olaf's chest and moved quickly to the side as Olaf's ax came down. Olaf's eyes bulged, and he gasped with surprise as he fell to the ground impaled on the ax handle. There was a sudden silence and then cheers. Brand struggled to his feet.

No power could hold her. Deirdre bolted away from the two men between whom she had been sitting and ran to Brand. His arm encircled her tiny waist and he held her against him. "Quickly," she whispered, "I must see to your wound."

Brand nodded, and together they walked away from the circle. A large Viking smiled at Brand. "I'm the captain of the vessel you were to sail on."

Brand nodded.

"We've missed the tide. We'll wait and sail tomorrow instead."

"And we with you," Brand told him even as he wiped salty perspiration from his brow.

Deirdre tugged on him gently. "Come, I must dress your wound. You have lost too much blood already."

He smiled at her through the grime and dirt on his face. "I have enough."

Deirdre stood on the edge of the steaming pool and this time, she faced Brand who stood opposite even as the clouds of white vapor rose between them, filling the room like a soft spring fog. His wound was no deeper than the first, and it was now securely bandaged.

Brand looked down on her. "Tonight you seem to want to bathe, my lady."

Deirdre looked back into his eyes. "Tonight I want many things," she whispered.

Without another word, Deirdre slowly undid her tunic and let it slip to the damp floor.

Brand stared at her, intensely aware of the allure of her softly curved body now covered only by her near-transparent undergarment. Her young breasts were high and firm, her waist tiny, her hips gently rounded. He had seen them before, but tonight there were no stolen glances. Tonight she presented herself for his approval. 'Tonight I want many things,' she had said. She extended an invitation to him, a willingness to seek paradise together. She was irresistible. Her words beckoned him, and they were equal to the legendary song of the sea sirens. He could not resist her magnetism.

As he stood transfixed by her eyes, her lips, her expression, she slowly let her filmy undergarment drop to the floor. It slithered about her as she seemed to shed it like an outer skin.

His eyes widened, his mouth felt dry. Her skin was as white as new-fallen snow, and the hair which covered her pleasure zone was like the hair on her head, a delicious red-gold indication of the fire within.

Deirdre moved closer to him and carefully removed his leather vest, then his skirt. He was naked beneath, his hair curling on his broad chest, his hips lean, his legs straight.

Brand reached out for her, stroking one of her lovely breasts with his large hand. He toyed with it for a minute till her nipple was hard, and then he bent and kissed it, drawing it slowly into his mouth and suckling till she moaned and rubbed against him.

His arms flew around her and he cupped her perfectly round, lovely buttocks in his hands, drawing her hips close to him.

Deirdre closed her eyes, allowing her body to enjoy fully every sensation. He was hard against her, his organ a growing sword of flesh pressing against her in such away that she wriggled in his grasp, not wanting to be free, but wanting—yes, wanting the reality of that, which till now, she had only dreamed.

In a playful mood, Brand pulled them both downward into the warm water.

It was wonderful this feeling! The warm water all around her, Brand's mouth on her breast, his hands moving all over her body, slowly, as if he were a blind man memorizing its curves and crevices, its softness, and its heat.

In a moment his mouth released her breast and moved to her lips for a long kiss. But his hands were not idle. He massaged both breasts now, rubbing her nipples till she groaned with deep-felt pleasure. Yes, this was the delight of which Edana had spoken. Ah, but the reality was far finer than had been the description.

His hand enclosed hers and directed her to his organ. It was huge, and she touched it with a sense of wonder, gently holding it, moving now and again.

"Do you fear, me?" he asked, whispering in her ear and causing a chill to run through her—a chill such as the one she had the very first morning he had kissed her.

"It is unknown to me—I fear and yet—"

"You desire," he finished her sentence, even as he ran his hand between her legs, rubbing in a way which caused a pleasure she had not dreamed existed. It was much more intense than in any of her dreams.

"I desire," she gasped, as he parted her hair and touched her in an area so sensitive she almost screamed. The pressure of his hand and the movement of his fingers worked pure magic. All she knew was a kind of hunger. She rubbed against him like a cat, shamelessly wanting more and realizing he was taunting her.

"You are more than I had hoped," he whispered, once again nursing on her breast while toying with the other.

"Please . . ." she breathed. Please what? She did not want his lips to leave her breast, but she wanted something—she wanted him to touch her in that place once again. She tried desperately to move against him in order to feel again that divine sensation.

He again kissed her neck and held her buttocks. "This is your first time, isn't it, my lady."

"Yes," she whispered.

"I must prepare you, my love."

She again felt him. He was large; she wondered if it would hurt. "Prepare me?" she questioned.

"I must make you more desirous. I must make you flow with the nectar of love to ease my passage."

Again his hand slid down her body, pausing for a long while on that place, gently rubbing it till again she felt herself holding her breath—waiting—waiting.

"Not yet," he whispered. His hand moved on till now his arm rested on that spot, but his fingers were elsewhere. She felt him rubbing her gently, and then a finger slipped inside her. It moved slowly this way and that inside her secret passage. She groaned and tried to rub against his arm. It was pure wantonness this desire!

She rolled about, moaning and wriggling as his fingers explored her secrets. He withdrew his finger and once again, her body now hot and almost feverish, he grasped her buttocks and lifted her from the water, setting her on the side of the pool. "Lean back, my lady."

Deirdre, already anxious for his touch, leaned back on her hands. He gently spread her legs and kissed her in that place even as his hands reached up to toy with her breasts.

It was more than she could stand. His fingers playing with her hard nipples, his soft tongue in a wild dance on that place. She actually screamed and felt her whole body shake when the pulsating descent began. She was completely out of control, and she collapsed, writhing on the floor, not wanting this sensation to end. He was out of the pool now and holding her while she shook in his arms.

When she opened her eyes she looked into his face. "You're ready now," he said carefully, a smile creeping across his mouth.

He rolled over to a nearby fur skin and, lying on his back,

lifted her onto him as if she were a feather, lowering her slowly downward. She closed her eyes as she felt him teasing at her entrance and she moaned aloud as he slowly, ever so slowly, eased her downward, holding her hips tightly, pushing himself upward and ever deeper into her.

It was agonizingly wonderful. He filled her completely and yet he touched that place and pressed against it as he moved slowly. His hands kneaded her breasts, which caressed his lips, allowing him to flick across her tight nipples with his tongue.

He began moving beneath her more rapidly, and, as he did so, he rubbed her till once again she felt the pressure building, that wild unbridled desire mounting inside of her. She began to tremble uncontrollably, and she felt him tremble, too. She felt for an instant as if she were atop a wild stallion. He moved up and down with abandon, perspiration covering his forehead. His arms suddenly wrapped around her as he made one last thrust.

Deirdre felt her sudden release at almost the same instant. It was deeper and longer than before, and, in spite of the slight pain she had felt when he had first filled her, she felt only pleasure now as she collapsed atop him, panting wildly.

After a time during which they remained joined, he rolled on his side and pulled her close. They were lying on the fur, and the steam swirled about their moist bodies. "My lady, you are sheer pleasure."

Deirdre cuddled closer, fitting her body into the curve of his. Never had she dreamed of anything so sensual, so pleasurable. Edana's tales were no exaggeration! And though she felt tired, she knew she would want to do this again and again. This man knew how to touch her, he had awakened her, and distractedly she kissed his chest as he lifted her and carried her to their bed.

* * *

The first light of day had only just appeared when Deirdre felt Brand's warm hands awaken her. He kissed her back, her shoulders, and finally her neck. "We must leave," he said, whispering into her ear. "Our ship sails on the high tide."

Deirdre rolled over and into his waiting, eager arms.

"It's much better to have you in my bed than at the foot of it."

Deirdre kissed his chest, nuzzling him. "It is better to be here," she whispered.

He eased down in the bed and began to tease her again. His movements were so knowing, so intended to taunt and rouse her. But the memory of last night lingered, and it took little before she was moaning in his arms, begging for his touch, wanting him again to enter and fill her.

"This morning I must be swift," he whispered, as he touched her intimately and lingered long enough for her to feel her hips undulating, reaching for him. He kissed her breasts and massaged her slowly till he heard her breath come in short gasps and felt her hands on his back. Then he entered her, moving slowly against her till she groaned with pleasure. Sensing her ready, indeed anxious, he allowed himself fulfillment and felt her plunge with him into ecstatic release.

After they had both rested for a moment, Brand climbed from the bed and quickly dressed.

"You must wear this," he told her, handing her a long, white, pleated dress.

Deirdre examined it curiously. It was sewn at the shoulders and down the sides, but on each side there were spaces that were not sewn. "This is a strange garment," Deirdre said.

"It is what you must wear. It signifies your status as my slave. And you must wear this around your waist."

Deirdre looked at the long, thin, silver chain. On the end it had a round coinlike piece of metal with runic writing.

"This identifies you as mine," he told her, as he pointed to the odd marks and read them for her.

Deirdre put on the garment without comment. It was necessary for her to continue to be his slave in order for him to protect her. In any case he had fought Olaf and won. He had cared enough for her to risk his life. *And perhaps,* she thought, *I am his slave in a way.* Then she smiled to herself. *At least that is so when we are making love.* But inside, Deirdre knew she retained her own self. A garment and a pendant did not a slave make.

Deirdre stood by the rail of the Viking vessel. Above her the great, green, carved sea serpent on the bow of the ship stared out to sea. It seemed to Deirdre that what lay ahead was a vast distance, an endless expanse of choppy greenish blue water. Never had she been able to look so far into the distance, for here on the Hibernian Sea there were no rolling hills to obstruct her view of the faraway horizon.

There was no cutting through the water on a swift breeze because the wind was reluctant this morning, and thus the vessel was rowed. Deirdre looked at those whose strength drew them through the water. Among them was Fredrik. He had pledged himself to Brand and would stay with this vessel till it returned to Denmark in a month's time. After he arrived, he would make his way to a friend of Brand's, there to wait with others who would make up Brand's fighting force.

Brand, who was to have rowed, but could not because of his wound, was treated as an honored guest aboard the vessel.

Deirdre drew her shawl around her. It was all she had left of her previous clothing. Her tunic had been discarded and now she wore only the long white dress he had given her and her leather shoes. Around her waist the silver chain dangled, an ever-present reminder of her status.

Again she asked herself if she really was his slave or was this merely a charade? She was not sure. But she was sure she enjoyed their lovemaking, and if she was to be a slave, though it was certainly not her desire, she felt fortunate that it was to this man. No, she was not really a slave. She was certain he loved her as much as she was certain she loved him. Naturally, in front of the others, he had to treat her as a slave, and she was forced to act the part, sitting demurely at his feet when he spoke with others, bringing him his food, and caring for his wound, which she would have done in any case.

"You're thoughtful—are you thinking of the past or the future?" Brand asked, his arm encircling her waist even as he breathed lustily into her ear.

A chill passed through her as it always did when she felt his hot breath on her neck. Again she marveled at how sensitive her body was to his touch, to his lips. "I'm taken with the sea," she replied. "Never have I been able to see so far."

"Seeing is not knowing. Tell me, are those distant clouds or distant mountains?"

"I cannot tell."

He smiled. "I think they are clouds, but even I cannot be certain. Do you think only about the sea?"

"No, I think about my people, too."

"What about your people?"

"My people do not set forth in boats—except for a few religious hermits who seek the solitude of some deserted isle. Tell me why your people sail the seas—is it only to rob, pillage, and take slaves as I have seen you do?"

Brand shook his head. "Our land is beautiful and wild. It is the land of the gods, but too much of it is barren. And there is constant fighting. King Halvdan the Black is ruthless—Lord Thorgills is one of his favorite chieftains. Halvdan makes slaves of his own people as well as others. Many of us seek a new land, a land away from the fighting and tyranny of Halvdan. We seek a refuge. It is why so many of us now live in Danelaw and why even Lord Thorgills prefers his settlement at Dublin."

Deirdre continued to look out to sea. "My land is also ripped by rivalries and war."

Brand knew full well that what she said was true. Blood feuds fed the flames of fighting all over the known world.

The constant fighting among small kingdoms made it easy for his people to make conquests.

"Those Norwegians who want peace have found a new land," he told her. "I would like to go there. They say that hot pools bubble from beneath the ground."

Deirdre half smiled. "Such a place cannot be. It is just one of your stories."

"No, my lady. It exists. Fire bubbles forth from the ground just as the fire in your body comes forth in desire when I touch you."

He stood in back of her now, and his hand slipped beneath her white robe. Was this why it was so designed? Was it fashioned to make the body of the slave girl always accessible to her master?

She quivered and pressed against him, hoping no one would come up to them, that no one would see them. His hand found that magic place, and she shook violently—wanting to pull away, but unable to do so.

"Adventure, my lady. Our raids are adventures that bring us furs from Russia, gold, silk, and spices from the East, wine from the Mediterranean and jewels of great value. I shall see you in furs; they're soft against the skin."

He breathed into her ear and his hand was persistent. She felt as if she might faint.

"Steady, my lady. Lean against me."

Deirdre could do nothing else. To cry out would draw attention to both his explorations and her all-to-obvious response. His fingers danced on her, she grew feverish with desire and knew that in spite of the brisk wind, her cheeks glowed with heat.

His other hand sought yet another entrance in her gown and he grasped her breast, toying with the nipple even as his fingers caused her to wiggle and gasp in his clutch.

"Were I another, my lady, I would now spin you about and force you to your knees to fulfill me while everyone watched."

The image filled her mind and he grasped her hard, just

as the wonderful pulsating release engulfed her. She shook against him, thinking that she wanted to fulfill him, too, and he kissed her neck again. "I like pleasuring my slave," he whispered. "Ah, sweet and lovely slave who always has the aroma of roses."

Still breathing hard, but trying to disguise it, she leaned against him even as he continued to hold her close, a smile of satisfaction on his face. He was surely as hungry for her as she was for him.

Brand continued to hold her till her breathing returned to normal. Then he let her go, but did not leave her side.

"I have something for you," he said, reaching into his vest.

"My brooch!" Deirdre exclaimed. He held her precious Tara brooch, its amber jewel sparkling in the sun.

"I took it from Thorgills, but it was with the other treasures in a sack, and it has taken me some time to find it."

He looked into her eyes. "Wear the emblem that says you are mine, but wear this, too—it says who you are, my lady." He pulled her shawl closer around her shoulder and pinned the brooch in place. "There, my princess."

Deirdre turned and, standing on her tiptoes, kissed his cheek. "Thank you," she said, touching the brooch. "It will always remind me of my father and brother."

"And the life you lost," he concluded.

Deirdre looked into his sky-blue eyes. "I have not lost a life, only a way of life. I will gain another. It is my father and brother whom I have truly lost."

"Perhaps only your father," Brand said. He did not want to hold out too much hope. But if he won—if Thorgills were defeated, he could reunite brother and sister. Still, he did not say anything. Dashed hopes could be painful indeed.

Brand held her close and inhaled her hair. It was the texture of silk and the color of fire. This woman was intelligent, spirited, and sought fulfillment. She was everything he could want in a woman, everything and more. He was in love with her. No, it was more than love. He was obsessed with this

Celtic beauty. She responded to him with a fiery hunger that made his own enjoyment tenfold what it had ever been with any other woman.

"What shall we do when we are set ashore?" Deirdre asked dreamily.

Brand squeezed her again. "Eat, make love, and begin our journey to Jorvik."

"And when we arrive in Jorvik?"

"I must obtain pledges from the king of Danelaw."

"Pledges?"

"I need him as an ally. I must have his support."

"To fight Lord Thorgills?"

"I must challenge Halvdan, too."

"I feel great happiness and great fear . . . is it unnatural?"

"I think not, my lady. I feel it, too."

Brand held her close, and yet again his previous obligations crept into his mind. He was pledged to Erica and she to him. He could tell Erica and intended to, but there were other concerns. If he failed to defeat Halvdan, Thorgills, and those chieftains who supported them, he would be killed and so would Deirdre. Was it fair to take her into such a situation? Perhaps, he thought, it would be better to leave her in Britannia until he was secure in victory. But the only place he could leave her, if it were allowed, would be with King Guthrum in Jorvik. He could send for her when it was safe and they would be reunited. But could he part with her? These were questions he vowed to think on.

"This is not how I imagined Britannia," Deirdre admitted, as they walked along. It was barren here, and the land was flat and rocky. Overhead, gulls circled, swooping now and again to examine them with bright, intelligent eyes.

"This is land's end, my lady."

"The rest is not like this?"

"No. It is forested and hilly. But this is a long stretch of land that reaches into the sea. I will see to hiring a horse and wagon here, and we shall proceed onward toward one of the many rivers."

"How?" she asked, a look of puzzlement on her face.

"Long ago, my lady, this land was conquered by the Romans. They built roads, and those roads are still here."

"I do not believe such people came to my land. We have no roads such as these."

"You are correct, my lady. And it is for that same reason that the weapons your people fight with are inferior to ours. The Romans sent an army, but the army also brought knowledge."

"How do you know so many things?"

He laughed. "I am the son of Jarls, a once-powerful king. I was tutored by a wise man, who taught me much."

"In my land only monks are learned. Of course we were tutored, but I was taught differently than my brother."

Brand smiled. "We have no monks, all men know about our gods. By our fire tonight I will tell you tales of Odin."

"You owe me a tale," she said playfully. "Will we travel all the way to this Jorvik by horse?" she asked curiously.

"No, my lady. It is too far, and such a journey would take far too long. We will travel by river—it is much swifter."

Rivers—yes, he was right. River travel was far more desirable than travel on foot or by cart. But rivers could be dangerous. It was the rivers that had allowed the Viking armies to penetrate deep into Ireland.

Brand led her into the village. It was an odd place, not underground, but with houses the roofs of which were covered with sod. The chimneys appeared to be reaching up from inside the earth, and doors and windows were visible on only one side of these strange hillside dwellings. The houses above the ground were made of stone with thatched roofs, but the others appeared to have been covered with earth and grass.

"Why do people here live like moles?" Deirdre asked as he propelled her along.

"This is a cold and barren place, my lady. Those who live beneath the sod are protected from the cold winds that blow mercilessly down the Hibernian Sea from Norway in winter."

Brand led her to an enclosure with horses, and there he negotiated with an old man whose language was the same as his. He still spoke more of her language than she spoke of his, but daily she was becoming more proficient in the Nordic tongue.

It was only then that it occurred to Deirdre that this area as well as what lay beyond was populated by Vikings and no doubt ruled by them as well. Yes, they were in Danelaw now. Deirdre recalled the treaty with the Saxon king that recognized this area as belonging to the Vikings.

A driver, a wagon, and a horse were soon arranged for them, together with food and a pile of sheepskins for warmth.

"Your language is so difficult," Deirdre said, as he lifted her into the wagon.

"You're doing very well, my lady." He smiled and winked as he climbed up beside her. "But we both speak one language that is the same, don't we?"

His look was penetrating, and she knew he meant the language of their lovemaking. Yes, it was the same. He seemed never to have enough of her, nor she of him. When he touched her the fire of her yearning sprang forth immediately and ceased only when she lay exhausted in his strong arms.

Brand climbed in beside her, and presently the driver appeared. He nudged the horses forward and Deirdre fell back against the straw that filled the back of the wagon. Brand crawled to her side. "Rest," he whispered. "This is only the beginning of our long journey."

The fire flickered, and Deirdre sat wrapped in her sheepskin. Around them a low fog clung to the ground, giving everything an eerie appearance, an illusion of other worldliness.

"Odin is the highest of our gods," Brand told her. His

deep voice took on a faraway quality, and it was as if someone else were speaking.

"Odin is the all-pervading spirit of the universe, the personification of air—the god of wisdom and victory, the leader of and protector of warriors. Odin is sometimes called 'Allfather' because all the gods descended from him. We are taught that he sits on the highest chair and can see all the other gods, the world, the giants, elves, dwarfs, and men."

"And only Odin uses this honored seat?" Deirdre asked.

"No, his wife Frigg may also use it. But usually it is he who occupies it. On his shoulders there are two eagles who fly forth each day to bring him news, and at his feet, two wolves stand, poised to protect or to obey if ordered to seek something for Odin."

"Allfather," Deirdre whispered. Brand's stories were strange, indeed. But was this Odin so different from the god in which she believed? He, too, was the ruler of heaven and earth, sat on a throne, and was the source of everything good. Perhaps she could make Brand understand the god her people worshiped and perhaps, if she did, he would love her as man loved a wife rather than keeping her a slave. And she was intrigued by what he had told her earlier about a strange new land.

"Twice now you have mentioned a strange new land. Tell me more about this place across the sea—the place where hot water bubbles from beneath the ground."

"It is a strange paradise," Brand said slowly. "Settlers began to go there only twenty years ago. All the houses there are built of turf and sod on a stone base. It's a good life I've heard, a peaceful life."

"Is there farmland?"

"Yes, but it is limited. Most of it is ideal for raising cattle and sheep. And there are plenty of fish to catch and animals to hunt."

Deirdre closed her eyes. "Does this mysterious land have a name?"

Brand laughed. "Iceland."

"That sounds cold indeed."

"It's a land of ice and fire, Deirdre. It is the land of Thor, where heat bubbles forth from the ground and pools are filled with steaming water called hot springs."

"It sounds as if it's a magic place," Deirdre said dreamily.

"It's a peaceful land."

Deirdre sighed. Yes, deep inside, this Viking warrior also yearned for peace. No matter how great his desire for revenge, he wanted more. He wanted what she wanted.

Lord Thorgills's castle fortress was filled with the mounted heads of dead animals, with skins that hung from the walls and covered the floors, and with treasure from the four corners of the earth. Its long stone corridors were illuminated by great torches which cast long, strange shadows, and its furnishings were heavy, wooden, and massive.

Alan, among others, had been herded up winding staircases and down long halls, and he stood in the great hall awaiting the appearance of whoever was in charge while Lord Thorgills was in Dublin.

Alan shivered slightly in the dampness even though it was summer. Or perhaps, he reasoned, he shivered in fear. What kind of person would Lord Thorgills leave in charge? His journey here had been long and difficult, but he had not been mistreated except by his own body. His stomach rebelled against the sea and complained at the roll and heave of the vessel in which he traveled.

The vessel on which he had traveled had sailed from Dublin south to Brest on the coast of France, where it had picked up three Viking passengers and four slaves. After that stop, it had continued North through the Hibernian Sea to Norway.

Although the vessel was not huge, Alan had not seen the slaves taken aboard at Brest during the entire voyage. Now he found himself standing among them. There were three men and one young woman. She was pretty, petite, and obviously very frightened. Alan glanced at her several times and once, while they had been climbing the stairs, he had tried to smile at her, to set her at ease. But how was that possible? Who knew what their mutual fate might be? She had looked away, and, still keeping to herself, stood slightly apart from the men, with her head bowed.

In a moment a door opened and a woman entered the room. She was dressed plainly in a dark underdress and a black tunic, embroidered only along the bottom with silver threads in a symmetrical design. Her brownish hair hung in two simple braids.

Somewhat nervously, or at least Alan thought her nervous, she sat down on the throne seat, a seat far too large for her rather small derriere.

"I am Ingrid, daughter of Lord Thorgills," she said in a voice that strained to be heard.

Alan stared at her. Could this girl actually be Olaf's sister? It was difficult enough to think of her as related to Lord Thorgills. She seemed to be the antithesis of them both.

"While my father is away, I rule here. Obey and you will be well treated, disobey and you will be punished."

She looked out at them and frowned. No one said anything.

"I am told one of you is an artist, here to copy manuscripts."

"It is I," Alan said, as the others turned toward him.

"You will be taken to the sod house beyond the castle, there to work in peace. The guard will escort you and show you all you need to know. Make a list of what you require, and it will be filled."

Alan nodded.

"You men will be taken to the fields and you"—she looked at the young girl curiously—"you will come with me," she finished.

Alan had wanted to say something, but he was quickly taken by the arm and escorted toward the door.

"Be good to him," he heard Ingrid call out. "He is to be treated as our guest; he is to copy our sacred tales."

The guard dropped his arm, and Alan smiled back at Ingrid. He had wanted to thank her, but he was afraid he should not speak.

As they left the great hall, he glanced once again at the dark-haired girl. Her head was still bowed, but Ingrid was speaking softly to her. Alan felt relieved to discover that she would be in the hands of this woman who, on the surface at least, seemed kind and most unlike her father and brother.

Eight

The castle of Lord Radnor the Wolf appeared to be carved into the side of the jagged cliff. From the top of its walls one could survey an expanse of cold silvery gray sea and view at least four other islands as they floated in and out of the mist like disappearing and reappearing lands of legendary fame.

It was this part of Denmark, the Jutland Peninsula and the northern outer islands, that came closest to touching the shores of Norway and Sweden. Neither Norway nor Sweden was as fertile as Denmark, where the land was flat and often bare heath. Yet for Erica, daughter of Lord Radnor the Wolf, Norway was the true land of the gods. Its forest-covered mountains dropped to the sea and were guarded by vicious rocks which, according to lore, had been scattered by giants to protect the land. The narrow, misty fjords and river valleys were filled with the songs of the sirens and the thundering commands of Thor.

Erica was tall and slender. Her skin was white, her eyes a penetrating blue, her hair thick, long, and blond. She was a beautiful woman, but not a soft woman. Her features were strong, her nose a trifle too sharp, her lips too often pressed together. Seldom did Erica smile or laugh. And yet when she wanted she could use her wiles to good advantage and Erica "wanted" often.

Some years ago Lord Thorgills had subjugated her father as he had King Jarls. Still, she was betrothed to Brand, Jarls's son and Thorgills, as part of the peace arrangement, had recognized that betrothal. But Brand had been gone fighting with Thorgills for over three years now, and Radnor, her father, had been gone almost as long a time raiding lands to the east.

Erica had grown restless as well as lonely, and so it was, with some anticipation, that she watched from the castle ramparts as a proud Viking vessel laid anchor in the sea below her father's palace.

Erica turned quickly and returned to her quarters, where Ludmilla, a slave girl from the banks of the Volga, waited nervously for her mistress's command.

"Prepare me," Erica commanded imperiously. "It would appear I have important guests."

Ludmilla did not hesitate. She was well aware of her mistress's erratic temper. "Shall I have hot water brought for a bath?" she inquired.

"Yes, of course. And I shall require a special braid for my hair, and what shall I wear—yes, the finely pleated white gown and embroidered royal blue overdress. I shall want my gold brooches."

"Yes, mistress. I shall fetch them immediately and have the water brought."

"And give the order that my guest, whoever it may be, be given refreshment while I prepare to meet him."

Naturally, it was a man who awaited her. Women never came to see her, and in her father's absence it was she who was in charge of everything. Erica admitted she liked being in charge. But the knowledge that she would be displaced as soon as her father returned ate at her soul. Yes, he would once again take over, strip her of all responsibility, and treat her like a child. *But I am not a child,* she told herself. *I can rule as well as any man, better than most.* She pressed her lips together. Who was her father to take advantage of her talents when he needed them and ignore them when he was home? After all, as was happening at this moment, important men came to see her. They came to seek her counsel and to ask for her help.

"My large gold brooches!" Erica called out. "Fetch them!"

Ludmilla moved quickly. Fortunately the water was always kept at the ready on the fire, as Mistress Erica seldom gave warning of her desires. Ludmilla scurried away and gave the order for the water to be brought and for the visitor to be given refreshment. Hurriedly she returned to lay out Erica's elegant clothes and rich jewelry.

The wooden tub was located in a room just off Erica's bedroom. It was a small room with its own fire, a long wooden bench, and a rich fur rug.

It was Boris, the huge Russian slave from Kiev, who led the parade of slaves hauling the water. Erica smiled meanly when she saw him. He was the source of one of her favorite entertainments.

She moved to one side of the tub while Boris poured water into it. When one bucket was empty, he went to the door to get another left by a departing slave. The others were not allowed in her private quarters, only Boris had earned that honor. Intent on his duty, Boris carefully alternated between hot and cold water in order to ensure the perfect temperature for her bath.

Erica watched him for a moment. One could not but admire his muscles. They rippled beneath his tawny skin. And his beard was intriguing. Unlike the beards of her countrymen, his was black and tightly curled. He was, in fact, a hairy, monstrous man. Like a great bear compared to most Viking men, whose body hair was usually blond and, while thick, was fine rather than coarse and curly.

Erica stared at Boris, then without hesitation, she began to disrobe slowly while Ludmilla kept her eyes down and busied herself with laying out the clothes in the bedchamber.

As Boris poured the water his hands began to tremble.

Erica smiled and allowed her underdress to fall to the floor.

All that remained were her woven shoes. By the side of the tub, its perfumed steam rising toward the ceiling, she stood naked, her lovely full breasts leaning toward poor Boris, whose eyes fell first on her erect nipples and then on her mound of golden fleece. His face flushed, and he strained to avert his eyes.

Yes, he was a tame bear, she thought with considerable pleasure. Ignoring him, Erica lifted first one leg and then the other. She slipped into the water. "Stay in my bedroom," she called out to Ludmilla, "and prepare my clothes."

"Yes, mistress," Ludmilla answered with a quivering voice.

Erica looked up at Boris. "Wash me," she said, staring into his eyes. "Slowly, Boris. As I have taught you."

Erica leaned back and closed her lids as his large, trembling, pawlike hands applied the scented soap to her body, lingering on her breasts, carefully washing her erect nipples with the rough sea sponge. How hard it made them! It was almost as if she could feel the blood filling them. How sensitive they were to the roughness of the sponge! Vaguely she wondered how Boris's mouth would feel. Would his rough beard do as well as the sponge? In a few moments she opened her legs slightly and felt Boris's fingers probe her eagerly. He thrust his large middle finger inside her, and with his thumb he rubbed her eager spot of sensitivity. Small pleasures, she thought as her passion mounted. She threw her head back against the rim of the tub, her lips parted as her breath came in short gasps, and a moan of pleasure escaped from deep inside her throat as Boris held her magic place tightly and she felt the ever-pleasurable release surge through her.

It took a long minute for Erica to get her breath, but at length, without opening her eyes, she ordered Boris away with an imperious wave of her hand. Naturally, as soon as she had gone to greet her guest, Boris would exercise his own pent-up desires on Ludmilla who adored him. *Well,* she thought callously, *I must have some pleasure while men are away fighting.*

Within the hour, Erica, adorned in her refinery and smelling of musk, sailed into the reception room.

"Henrik! You are an unexpected guest!" Henrik was a man close to Erica's own age, a handsome first cousin to King Halvdan and an equal to Lord Thorgills.

"It has been too long since I visited the land governed by Radnor," he replied, looking her over appreciatively.

"I cannot remember when I last saw you," she replied, smiling.

"I have just returned from Dublin," he told her.

Erica hesitated. Was she to ask of Brand? But of course everyone knew they were betrothed. It would be expected. "What news is there of Brand?"

"Much news," Henrik replied. "Disturbing news."

Erica looked at him intently. "Tell me," she pressed.

"Brand has betrayed Lord Thorgills. He learned his father was dead, and he ran away with an Irish girl, a Princess Deirdre who had been given to Olaf. Olaf followed, and, on the Isle of Man, Brand killed Olaf in battle. It is said that Brand will now raise an army to avenge his father and defeat Lord Thorgills."

Erica felt like a stone statue. What was she supposed to say? Her relationship with Brand was well-known. And he had clearly betrayed her! How could he! She felt a seething anger fill her. Not that she loved him, though she was the first to admit he was a fine lover. No, it was not losing him that made her angry; it was not possessing him that filled her with fury. Who was this Irish princess? If he had taken a beautiful slave for them to share, she could have accepted it. But had that been the case he would not have fought for her. Slaves were not worth fighting for.

"Such an action would most certainly threaten Halvdan,"

Erica responded, carefully weighing her words. She wondered if her own rising anxiety showed—her very relationship with Brand could be life-threatening.

"It is why I am here. Halvdan does not want the daughter of Radnor sharing Brand's fate. I've been sent to ensure your loyalty."

"I am betrothed to Brand," she reminded him.

Henrik smiled. "One cannot be expected to marry a dead man."

Erica did not immediately answer. Sometimes silence was the best response. But most certainly she had no intention of allowing her head to become one of the skulls that decorated Halvdan the Black's castle walls. In Erica's mind it was all a matter of power and politics.

"We need your help to trap Brand and avoid loss of life."

Erica looked steadily into the eyes of Henrik. He was a large man and ever since he returned from Russia several years ago, he had taken to dressing as the Slavs dressed. He wore full trousers bound tightly to his legs below the knees, a belted tunic, a cape, and a fur hat. His steel sword dangled at his side, and his now graying beard covered his face. Nothing in his eyes betrayed his inner thoughts. If he had fears, they, too, were a mystery. But at the moment, she reminded herself, Henrik was not her problem. *I am locked in a dilemma,* she thought. Brand might well raise an army large enough to take Thorgills and threaten Halvdan. If this were the case, she should remain loyal to Brand. At least until she could plan her own revenge. On the other hand, if Brand lost and she remained loyal to him, she, too, would be killed by Lord Thorgills and King Halvdan.

"What exactly is wanted of me?" she hedged.

"We want you to see Brand when he comes, find out his plans, and tell us."

Erica nodded. Yes, this was a way out. She could decide what to do after she had the opportunity to find out which side was the strongest. She could pretend to be helping both, and then betray the one that was weakest. "Of course I shall help," she replied. "I am Halvdan's loyal subject." She knew that to be disloyal to Halvdan was a terrible death sentence. Halvdan was a cruel, perverted man, who was known to commit unspeakable acts.

"Halvdan will be pleased," Henrik intoned.

"Now that is decided, perhaps we can go on to other matters," she suggested.

Henrik smiled expectantly. "What other matters might we go on to?"

"Dear Henrik, you have been to Russia and found riches. I want to know about all of it, every detail. And of course I want to know about this, this Dublin." She did not say she wanted to know about the woman Brand had run off with— the woman that had been given to Olaf. *I shall have to kill her,* Erica thought. At the same time, she decided, it was important to show Henrik she did not care about the woman or about Brand.

"That might take all night, my northern beauty."

Erica touched his knee with her hand, and moved it in a slow, suggestive circle. "I have nights to spare."

It was an exceedingly bright night. The forest through which they traveled was sparse, and moonlight from the unclouded half-moon filtered through lacy summer leaves to the forest floor where Deirdre and Brand slept wrapped in their sheepskin while the wagon driver slept in his wagon, covered only with straw.

The sounds were part of her dream. Horses galloping across a plain—her father's army riding into battle. Deirdre opened her eyes suddenly, realizing the sounds were real and not dreamt, and, in sheer panic, she wrapped herself in her sheepskin and struggled to her feet. Brand, who seemingly slept like a cat, had already sprung into action. His sword was drawn, his feet set wide apart, his body at the ready to fend off an attack. Deirdre glanced at the wagon. The driver prudently remained hidden beneath the straw.

Deirdre felt a chill sweep over her. There were five riders in all, their swords drawn. But from whence had these riders come? They did not look at all like her countrymen, and they did not dress at all like those Vikings she had encountered—either those from Brand's Denmark or those from Norway, the land from which Thorgills came. They did not brandish broadswords but rather each carried a spear, a bow, arrows, and a shield. One, apparently the leader, did have a sword. But it was long and slender and it glinted as the moonlight caught the jeweled decorations that embellished it.

For what seemed like an eternal moment, no one moved or spoke. The riders had halted, their apparent leader had drawn his sword, and Brand stood poised to defend himself against all five warriors.

"Who art thou? And where do you travel?" the leader of the riders asked.

"I am Brand, son of Jarls, once king of Falster—I travel to Jorvik in Danelaw. Who are you that brandish weapons on sleeping pilgrims?"

"I am Wilfred, an emissary of King Alfred, ruler of Wessex, sent to Danelaw to discuss our treaty."

Brand let his sword drop to his side. "If there is a treaty, then we are at peace with one another."

"Perhaps, but the terms of our treaty state that no Dane will take a lady of high birth and make of her a slave."

Even as he spoke, Wilfred was dismounting. His riders were poised to attack Brand if he were interfered with. He strode to Deirdre's side. "Let me see your hands," he demanded.

Puzzled, Deirdre held out her hands. Wilfred turned them slowly in his. "Soft and smooth," he said, turning toward Brand. "Clearly she is nobly born, and yet she wears the garb of a slave girl—I have seen others like her though few are as beautiful."

"She is nobly born, but not of this land. She is from across the Hibernian Sea."

Wilfred turned his back on Brand and again faced her. "Who are you?" he asked bluntly.

"Deirdre, daughter of Odhran, king of Meath."

"I know not this place Meath, but clearly you are of noble birth and our treaty is clear. I must take this woman," Wilfred said, turning toward Brand again. "If you fight, you break the treaty, and even your own will not defend your actions."

Brand did not speak. This Wilfred was right. If he fought and won against these odds, it would be a miracle, but he would not truly win since none would defend his breaking of the treaty. He needed his countrymen in Jorvik and, most of all, he needed the support of King Guthrum. And, of course, there was the obvious—he probably could not win against so many.

Deirdre looked from one to the other. What did all this mean? Was Brand going to allow these strange men who did not even speak her language take her with them into the night?

"You will come with us, my lady." Wilfred's tone seemed to leave no room for argument.

"Where will you take her?" Brand asked.

"To Wessex, where she will receive the hospitality of King Alfred."

Brand could not look at Deirdre. He had been awakened from a deep sleep with Deirdre at his side. He loved her, loved her so much he wanted desperately to protect her. Perhaps this was the solution to his problem, the dilemma with which he had struggled. If he let her be taken to Wessex, he could return to Denmark and raise an army, defeat Halvdan and Thorgills, and tell Erica the truth—that he could not marry her because he loved another. After confessing to Erica, he could return to Wessex and find Deirdre. She would be safe there, and together they could then go to Iceland. But he knew she would not leave him willingly. She was too brave and far too stubborn. And now, provided by the gods came this solution—a way to make certain his love was safe.

"It would seem I have no choice but to yield to you," Brand said, sheathing his sword and backing away.

"No—" Deirdre protested. "What are you saying?"

"Come, my lady, we will take you back to Wessex, where you will be free and protected."

"Brand—" She did not want to go. What kind of world was this that you could be rescued against your will? And how could Brand let her be taken away by strangers in the night? As Wilfred lifted her to his horse she felt bewildered and betrayed. Just hours ago they had made love. Was he tired of her? How could this have happened? How could Brand let it happen?

"I do not want to go with you," she protested.

"Lady, you are nobly born. Our code demands you be returned to your kingdom."

"My kingdom is no more." She felt desperate. But yet she could not bring herself to fall to her knees and beg Brand to protest her taking, even to say he wanted her.

"Then you shall remain in Wessex."

"No—"

Brand took a step toward her. "It is for the best, my lady. I must war on my father's enemies. In Wessex you will have protection." It wasn't what he felt, it was far from what he wanted to say. Letting her go was not what he wanted to do, but perhaps it was for the best. He did not wish to enslave her, and he had a duty. For a time his need for her had caused him to forget his true purpose. Yes, she should go to Wessex, and he should raise and army and defeat Thorgills. And there was Erica—yes, this was best for Deirdre, for him, and for Erica. But silently, he vowed that when Thorgills was defeated, he would return for her.

Deirdre looked at him and fought to keep the tears from welling in her eyes. How could he do this? But pride enabled her to stand straight and tall. She turned to the stranger, Wilfred. "Take me to Wessex," she murmured, not daring to turn around and look into the face of Brand, the man with whom she had made passionate love—the man who she believed cared for her. But clearly not. She had been but his chattel, and he had acquired her as such, only to repay her for saving him. Now, able to rid himself of her with a clear conscience, he did so without hesitation.

Wilfred turned his horse into the darkness, and the tears began to flow down Deirdre's face. *Now I shall never find my brother,* she thought desperately. *I have lost everything: Alan, my father, and now—now I have lost Brand.* She cursed herself for loving him and she cursed him for not loving her.

The sun was overhead when, after many days of arduous travel, they reached Winchester, the place where, Deirdre was told, King Alfred, ruler of all the Saxons resided.

Wilfred drew his caravan to a halt at the top of a hill.

"Below, Princess Deirdre, in the valley of the River Itchen, lies Winchester, our destination."

Wilfred was a learned man and Deirdre assumed him to be in his late thirties or early forties. His skin was fair, and his hair, though sparse, was a light brown. He was not a tall man, as Brand was, but was rather like her own people, shorter of stature though broad of shoulders.

As it had turned out, Wilfred and the soldiers who had surrounded them while they slept were not alone. After she was taken, they journeyed for less than an hour before joining a larger group which included ten more soldiers, two priests, two nuns, and Sir Wilfred's wife, Lady Adaline. It was into Lady Adaline's care she was given. Now the three of them stood looking at the valley below while Sir Wilfred pointed with pride down on Winchester.

His pride was justified, Deirdre thought. The town was dominated by three structures. One was obviously a huge cathedral, and one was clearly a magnificent castle. The third was a large stone building surrounded by acres of rolling lawns.

"Behold the castle of King Alfred," Sir Wilfred said, pointing to the many-turreted castle.

"It is the finest castle I have ever seen," Deirdre admitted. "It is larger and greater than even the castle at Tara."

"And that is the cathedral," he said, moving his hand.

"It is a glory," Deirdre replied.

"And there lies the place where churchmen and others study. Our king values education above all else."

Deirdre nodded. Beyond the great buildings there were houses and what appeared to be a huge market. Beyond that, as far as the eye could see, there were farms and farmhouses. Her eyes strayed back to the place of learning. Only men of God studied there; still, she had to admire a king who stressed education and gave learning a high priority. Months ago she would have wanted to be here, and she would have wanted to absorb all she could from the scholars of Alfred's kingdom. But now she felt only emptiness. She had found the idyllic kingdom of which she had so often dreamt only to have lost the most exciting man she had ever known. *It was not meant to be,* she told herself for the hundredth time. *But I am here, and I owe it to myself to take advantage of this place, perhaps even to have an audience with this great king who alone has protected his people from the Viking raiders.*

Lady Adaline took her hand. "Come, my child. We are close to home, and I must prepare you."

"I have no fine clothes," Deirdre said, stating the obvious.

"You shall wear something of mine, child. I feel certain the king will want to hear your tale."

Deirdre felt stunned. Was she to meet this king now? She had expected no such honor. "I—I'm unprepared to be presented."

Lady Adaline smiled. "Nonsense. You seem an intelligent girl; the king will be impressed."

Deirdre blushed slightly and, in spite of her personal lone-liness, the adventure which lay ahead still intrigued her.

The day had begun with a clear blue sky and the discordant songs of a hundred birds by the water's edge. The grass of the fields was green, the trees lacy with leaves. But now clouds were moving across the sky and soon, Brand realized, the sun would be obscured. Such was the weather on this island of the Britons. No matter where one was, the sea was never far away, and the gods of the sea could be pernicious at worst and unpredictable at best.

"Concentrate on the task ahead," Brand said aloud as he paddled down the River Ouse toward Jorvik, which the En-glish called York. "I am betrothed to Erica," he added, as if to remind himself yet again of his obligations. "I shall go to Hel if I do not fulfill those obligations or somehow end them honorably." His mind filled with all the tales he had been told as a child by his nurse.

"The earth on which we live is flat," she told him. "And it is surrounded by ocean beneath which lies Hel, a dark and freezing place—colder than the coldest winter, darker than the blackest winter night. If you do not heed your obligations, you are destined to spend eternity in Hel. But you know that the ash tree, Yggdrasil, touches the heavens with its branches and that it has three roots. One root grows beneath the earth, one reaches to Hel, and one to the mountains where the giants dwell—that is a place beyond the world's end."

"And if I am true? If I live honorably and fulfill my prom-ises?" As a boy he had asked that question often. His old nurse would smile and rock him in her arms. "Then you shall walk across the rainbow and find Asgard, the home of the gods, and you will be rewarded."

Even as he vowed to see to his obligations for the hun-dredth time, the memory of Deirdre flooded over him, en-gulfed him, and his vows faded. Her long hair caressing his bare chest, the recollection of her sweet aroma—the scent of roses, the touch of her soft lips, and the memory of her passion-racked body as she clung to him haunted his every thought.

Brand looked ahead. The river, which had previously meandered through the flat countryside, was now straight and wide. On either side farms stretched out, and the houses of the farmsteads built by his countrymen could easily be seen. By traditional design he knew these to have been built by his countrymen. Such farmsteads usually consisted of three buildings grouped around an enclosure. A path linked the long house to the kitchen, and across the yard was a smithy. They were sturdy houses, far sturdier than those built by the people of Britannia. These houses in which his countrymen lived had walls which were at least three and one half arm length's thick. The thickness served as insulation and kept out the cold.

Beyond the farms lay the town. It was a thriving market town, and small Viking trading craft bobbed in the water at the foot of the street which led from the center of town down to the water. He had already passed St. Peter's Minister, a school where Christian priests were trained. At first his countrymen had eschewed Christianity, but later many had converted, and the two religions existed side by side.

Until he had met Deirdre he had thought little about such things—but now he found he thought more about his own beliefs. He shook his head—no matter what he thought, no matter how hard he tried, thoughts of her always returned to him. Was there no subject on which he could think that did not lead back to her fair image, the memory of their adventure together?

"An obligation," he said again. "I have an obligation." Slowly, Brand drew his oars out of the water. There was going to be no peace unless he went back for her. "Damn," he muttered. "She has bewitched me." But he knew she had not. He loved her and wanted her. It was as simple as that,

and regardless of the complications, even the dangers, he
had to find her again. His will now set, Brand continued
toward Jorvik, vowing to get supplies and then travel to the
kingdom of Alfred, leader of the Saxons, the most powerful
king in all Britannia. "I should not have let you go," he said
to no one. "Somehow I will convince Erica to free me."

Lady Adaline had a narrow face and sharp features sof-
tened by her lively brown eyes. Beneath the loose folds of
her wimple, which was not unlike those worn by nuns except
for the embroidered headband, she had long brown hair,
which she wore tied in a knot at the back of her head. Her
figure was slight, and it seemed more so because her underdress was dark and full and her tunic straight and unadorned
except for the identical silver brooches which clasped it together over her shoulders. Her garments—elegant but at the
same time somewhat plain—gave her a matronly look, an
appearance heightened by her maternal demeanor.

The clothes she gave Deirdre to wear were not so maternal.
The underdress was a rare light blue, and it fit her snugly,
drawing in at the waist and falling gently over her hips. The
overgarment was sheer and hung from the shoulders, held
by gold brooches. Her hair was brushed smooth and tied
with a ribbon. Like all the women, she wore a wimple the
same color as her underdress. It fell in gentle folds and set
off her face, making her eyes seem larger and even more
luminous than usual.

"You look lovely," Lady Adaline cooed. "You're a bright
young addition to our court."

Deirdre smiled shyly. The great hall of this palace was
somewhat cavernous but extremely elegant, with heavy, rich
tapestries hanging from every wall. Most depicted scenes of
battle, though some were pastoral in nature. Large pieces of
heavy, dark, carved furniture lined the walls. Most of the
furniture consisted of tall high-backed chairs, taller indeed

than her father's throne had been. On a dais, the throne of King Alfred dominated the room. It was covered with red tapestry and trimmed with heavy gold cords. It was massive, ornately carved, and dwarfed every other piece of furniture in the room.

In front of the throne a long carpet extended from the massive wooden doors of the hall to the throne itself. On either side of the carpet some twenty trumpeters, smartly dressed in military uniforms, stood at attention.

Deirdre, Lady Adaline, and Sir Wilfred stood together with some fifty other nobles in the back of the great hall.

"You are so at ease," Deirdre whispered to her sponsor. "I have never met such a great king. I shall faint."

Lady Adaline smiled and took her hand. "I think not, my dear. True, our king is a great man, but he is also an easy man to know. He is warm and friendly, and he is the wisest ruler this great Saxon kingdom has ever known."

Hardly had Lady Adaline spoken when the trumpeters lifted their instruments and saluted the king. Everyone in the great hall fell silent. The men bowed deeply, and the women curtsied as the procession passed them.

"King Alfred of Wessex! King of the Saxons!" the page announced. Down the line others repeated the greeting, and once again the blare of the trumpets filled the hall.

The king strode down the carpet followed by his wife, the still-beautiful Ealhswith, who was descended from Mercian kings. Mercia, Deirdre had learned from Lady Adaline, was one of the kingdoms of Anglo-Saxon Britain. Unlike Wessex, it had been conquered by the Danes and was now part of Danelaw.

The king himself was taller than many of his subjects. He stood erect in a strict military posture, yet Deirdre thought his face seemed kind. Deirdre had been told that King Alfred had been born in the year 849 and was thus forty years old. His facial lines revealed a man who smiled readily, and his eyes flickered with interest for all around him.

He took his throne easily, sitting in a relaxed manner. "What business is there?" he asked in a loud voice.

The page stepped forward and read from a long scroll. Two noblemen had a land dispute which they wished to bring before the king. Another wished to postpone his tariff, and yet another had come to discuss his son's desire to serve in the royal household. At the end of the list Deirdre heard the page announce, "Lady Adaline and Sir Wilfred wish to present Princess Deirdre, daughter of the late King Odhran of Meath in the country of Hibernia across the sea. Princess Deirdre was rescued from Viking slavery and seeks the protection of this court since she was removed from her homeland, which has been overrun."

King Alfred's eyes strayed to where Sir Wilfred, Lady Adaline, and Deirdre stood. He smiled and gave a slight wave of his hand. "I shall receive this fair maiden in a short while, forgive me, my lady, if I deal with these other matters first."

Deirdre did not answer, but only curtsied to indicate her reply. She tried to listen as the king attempted to settle justly the disputes that were brought before him and to consider the young man who wished to be of service. But she could not concentrate. It seemed dishonest to allow them to continue to think she had been forcibly brought to this land by Brand, when in fact she had wanted to escape her own land. But still he had made her a slave, and though he had not forced her to do anything, she did feel betrayed. *I gave my love so freely,* she thought. Again, she reminded herself how foolish she had been. *A lesson learned,* she told herself. He had not loved her as she loved him. Yet no matter how harshly she tried to think of him, she could not sustain her feelings of betrayal or of anger. She could not cease wanting him. His face crept into her every thought. The memory of his smile still warmed her, and she could easily imagine the touch of his large hands on her body. She could remember all too clearly how he pleasured her again and again till she wept in his arms and curled herself into his form to sleep, his arms wrapped about her. Why did it have to end? Why had he given her up so easily?

Suddenly she heard the king summon Sir Wilfred, who took her arm and escorted her toward the throne.

"I wish to present Princess Deirdre, daughter of the late King Odhran of Meath in the land of Hibernia," Sir Wilfred repeated what he had said before.

King Alfred smiled. "I know of your land. I know of the great monastery at Trim."

"My brother Alan was an artist there. But it was sacked by Viking raiders from Norway and my brother was taken prisoner."

"I'm sorry, Princess. Was that when your father was killed?"

"No, Your Majesty. My father was killed by King Malvin, a neighbor."

Alfred shook his head knowingly. "It is why the Vikings defeat us so readily. We fight too much among ourselves and ignore education. The Vikings are sent as a punishment for our willful ignorance."

"My brother was learned."

"And you do not seem ignorant," the king said, smiling.

Deirdre smiled shyly. "I try to study," she said softly, without trying to sound as surprised as she was that a king would even take notice of the extent of a woman's knowledge.

"Approach the throne, Princess Deirdre."

Deirdre did as he requested and when she reached it, she fell to her knees as she had been taught to do in the presence of a great king.

"Rise, please, and sit down on the step a moment."

Deirdre felt puzzled, but she did as he requested.

"Tell me what you have tried to learn," he asked.

Deirdre told him all about Edana and her study of medicine. She told him she had learned to read in Latin by herself and that she had taught herself to write as well.

King Alfred smiled. "I am impressed with your endeavors,

Princess Deirdre. I shall hear more of your medicine. You shall remain here in my court and serve as a lady-in-waiting to the queen. And I shall see your writing—I am in need of a scribe."

Deirdre was too stunned to speak. Could a woman be a scribe? She had never heard of such a thing. But she did not say no. This was a great opportunity to learn about the Saxons. In spite of her misery and loneliness since Brand had turned her over to these people, she would put herself to work. *Time,* she thought, *will send the memory of him from my heart.*

Brand pulled his oars out of the water and allowed the current to carry him along while he rested for a few moments and enjoyed the fine spring air. This Britain was an odd place, different in so many ways from his homeland. Even in winter it did not get cold enough to freeze the waters of the many rivers solidly enough to support a man's weight. He remembered how as a boy he would fasten the long specially carved bone to his shoes and skate the river by pushing himself along with a spiked stick. And seldom was there sufficient snow here to ski. It was a swift way to travel for those accomplished in the art, as most people in his homeland were. Even as he pictured himself on the river skating and on the snow skiing, he saw himself teaching Deirdre the art. She would smile and find it an adventure. Her cheeks would be rosy and her laughter would echo in the stillness of the mountain valley behind his home.

He did not exactly know what he would say to her, or to this King Alfred. He could not marry her until he settled matters with Erica, nor could he enforce her enslavement. No, she would have to come with him of her own free will. It was she who would have to convince this Alfred, king of the Saxons, that she wanted to be with Brand, as much as he wanted to be with her.

He pictured her in the bath, her flesh glistening, her breasts full and hard when he toyed with them. He could all but feel her legs wrap about him, hear her moans in his ears, feel himself fill with desire—but it was not just their lovemaking, passionate though it was. There was so much more! She had a wonderful thirst for knowledge, and she was brave and intelligent.

"I must find her," he voiced. "I was a fool to let her go."

Alan was deeply engrossed in his work when he heard the pounding on the door of his dwelling. He had been here several weeks now and had not seen a soul save an irritable guard who brought food.

But his stomach told him it was not yet time for food. He put down his brush, and called out, "Just a minute."

Alan went to the door and opened it. There, to his surprise, stood the irritable guard and the young girl he had seen the day of his arrival. She was dressed in a slave's brown garment, and her long curly hair was loose. Her dark eyes were huge, and she looked even more frightened then she had on the day of her arrival.

"Lady Ingrid says you need a slave," the disgruntled guard said.

With those words he shoved the young girl inside roughly and followed her.

"I don't think I need a slave," Alan protested.

The guard laughed and rubbed his beard. "You're a fool. Every man needs a woman. Here, look at her!"

With that, he yanked the garment off the girl, and she stood naked and shivering. Her hands flew to her well-shaped breasts, and she drew her legs together trying to hide herself. Her face was crimson with shame, and she looked down as she trembled.

Alan felt his mouth turn dry. She was terrified.

"You can use her as you like," the guard imparted. "And she can cook and clean for you, too."

"But I—"

"Lady Ingrid has no need of another house slave. If you don't want her, she'll be sold in the barracks."

"No!" The girl cringed and fell to her knees. She wrapped her arms around his legs and whimpered, "Please take me, please."

The guard leered at her bare buttocks. "A prize if you ask me. Lady Ingrid is most generous."

"Yes, most generous," Alan repeated. What was he to do? If he did not take her, she would face a horrible fate, and apparently she had already suffered. "Tell Lady Ingrid I am grateful."

"Send her to the kitchen for food," the guard mumbled. "I'll not be coming anymore. She will take care of you."

The guard turned on his heels and left. Alan hurriedly closed the door behind him. The poor girl was lying on the floor sobbing.

Alan picked up her robe and took it to her. "Put your clothes on," he said in a gentle voice. He reached out and touched her rounded back. "Please, stop. I won't hurt you."

She did not look up at him, so he stood up and turned away from her. He went to the small samovar he had been given and poured some hot tea into a cup. When he turned back to her, she was again clothed, though her face was still flushed and her eyes swollen.

He held out the tea. "Drink this, it will make you feel better."

She approached him warily, as if she were a wild animal. She took the tea and he saw that her hand was still shaking. "My name is Alan," he said, carefully pronouncing his name for her.

Her eyes were huge. "Charlotte," she murmured. "I'm Charlotte."

Alan turned and poured some tea for himself. She was

very beautiful, even more beautiful than when he had first seen her. And her body was exquisite, well formed and well rounded. Her breasts were high, with full, dark nipples. Her face was oval, and she had full lips and large, dark, heavily lashed eyes. Her skin was like cream. But she was like a frightened animal, and he was certain she had been abused.

"I won't hurt you," he repeated. He meant what he said, but at the same time he realized she was to live with him. *I am only human,* he thought, wondering how long he could resist the temptation of her.

"We'll make another bed for you," he said, pointing to a corner far from where he himself slept, "and put it over there."

Her eyes seemed to be studying him now. "You really won't hurt me?" she asked in a hesitant voice.

"No. Just rest a while and later, when you feel like it, we'll talk."

"May I lie down for a while?"

"Yes. I'll go back to work."

With that he walked back to his worktable. Perhaps, when she knew him, she would be more talkative. And, he thought, he did truly get lonely here. Having her here was good. He could only wish it had been her choice.

Nine

As clear as it was this day, it was obvious that it had rained during the night. The narrow streets that wound through Jorvik were muddy and bore the footprints of both the humans and animals that had passed before. Brand inhaled deeply of the early-morning air. It was a blend of smells as the smoke from cooking fires and roasting meat mingled with the aroma of newly baked bread and the singular scent of the ground after a summer rain.

It had been more than twenty years since his countrymen had conquered and begun to settle Jorvik. Since then Jorvik had become a thriving settlement, the largest town in Danelaw, and the second largest town outside of London in Britannia. Even so, Brand well knew that Danelaw, and Jorvik specifically, were constantly threatened by Norwegian Vikings led by Lord Thorgills and his ilk, who worked to fulfill the ambitious dreams of Halvdan the Black. Halvdan temporarily united the warring chieftains of Norway, Denmark, and Sweden. Many of those chieftains would now rise against Halvdan if given the opportunity—Halvdan had seized authority and ruled by fear, which was not the same as being given the authority to rule. Most chieftains would have preferred a unified rule, with regular meetings of *The Thing*.

The Thing was a kind of parliament. Once a year the underkings would meet and settle their differences. They would make decisions, and their decisions gave legitimacy to the overking.

In turn, each underking would meet with his landowners and nobles in a local *Thing*. Loyalty given was far different than loyalty forced. Jarls, his own father, had ruled his subjects with their permission. The local *Thing* had met with regularity twice a year. Disputes were settled, laws passed, and each year the authority of Jarls was reaffirmed by his own subjects. This was also the way King Guthrum of Danelaw ruled and Brand believed it was the way the overking should rule. But Halvdan had sent the members of *The Thing* home. He ruled through fear.

"No more a mere settlement," Brand said to himself as he trudged along up the hill from the river. The beautiful, sleepy little town had turned into an industrious center of production. Fine combs of bone and sharp bone pins were made here, as was pottery and many household items carved from wood. A little farther down the Ouse, just beyond the main dock, boats to ply the river were built, while in the area called Coppergate, which he now passed through, iron, pewter, bronze, silver, and gold were all worked. Indeed, the smell of metal in fire filled the air; it was like inhaling iron.

A great deal of cloth was also made here; beautifully woven clothes and cloaks. But these were made mostly in individual homes and sold on market day together with homegrown produce and freshly killed game. In all, the citizens of Jorvik worked hard and prospered. As did their neighbors, with whom they had begun to intermarry.

Brand decided he would need new and, most certainly, finer clothes. He would also need a boat and a letter from the king of Danelaw to this Anglo-Saxon king, Alfred. Alfred's was a palace he could not storm. Rather, he had to be admitted freely and offered the hospitality of the court. In order to obtain all that he needed, it would be necessary for him to convince King Guthrum, ruler of Danelaw, to help him. But then, he needed Guthrum's help for other reasons as well. He sought him as an ally against Halvdan and Thorgills, and felt certain he would succeed if for two reasons. Guthrum disliked the two, and they had broken the treaties they had signed.

Steeling himself for what might lie ahead, Brand headed for the palace from which Guthrum ruled Danelaw. As the son of a king himself, he knew an audience would be easy to obtain. Oddly, the Viking rulers in this land were less formal than were the remaining royalty in Britannia.

The palace of King Guthrum was on top of a hill that overlooked the town as well as the River Ouse. It was not as grand or as protected as would be a fortress in his homeland, but it seemed the need was not as great here. The land was relatively flat and tilled for agricultural purposes, so an invader could be seen approaching. Not so at home, where dense forest, great rocks, and long, narrow, misty fjords could easily hide an invading army.

The palace was a stone building behind a stone wall with a single tower to offer a good view of the countryside beyond Jorvik. Inside, its rooms were large and well furnished. Most of the furniture was hand-carved from light wood and made in Jorvik. Every room he passed through was furnished with tables, the usual high-backed chairs, chests, stools, and stone lamps. Jorvik was clearly a place of affluence as well as industry.

King Guthrum was a huge man whose physical prowess and uncouth demeanor belied his intellectual strengths and basic decency. Brand was ushered into the great hall to find King Guthrum sitting at the head of a long wooden table rather than on his throne. Spread out before the king a huge roast of venison lay surrounded by greens and mashed turnips. Guthrum's large hands dripped grease, and his beard was embedded with bits of meat which had fallen from the bones of the roast as he gnawed on them.

Guthrum let the bone on which he was chewing drop to his iron plate with a clang. Then, assessing Brand silently, he quaffed down several large gulps of red wine from his goblet.

"I am Brand, son of King Jarls," Brand said, bowing slightly.

"Brand," Guthrum repeated his name slowly as if savoring it almost as much as he had savored his juicy bone. "I have not seen you since you were a boy, and your father brought you to *The Thing.*"

The Thing, yes. Brand remembered now that he had indeed met Guthrum before. *The Thing* at which he had met Guthrum was before the advent of Halvdan the Black, the overking and subjugator.

But Brand remembered the past. His father had taken him to that last meeting of *The Thing*—he must have been nine or perhaps ten years of age.

"I am honored that you remember meeting me at an event that happened so long ago," Brand said.

"I pride myself on my digestion and my memory," Guthrum said, with a deep belch and a smile. He pulled on his beard and raised a bushy brow. "I recall the feud—something about the division of plunder."

"Yes, with Lord Thorgills, underlord of King Halvdan."

"And Lord Thorgills was victorious. You were bound over into service to him."

"Yes, but I have freed myself. My father is dead. I will raise an army and take back all that is rightfully mine."

Guthrum grinned, revealing a missing tooth. "News has already reached me that you killed Olaf, Lord Thorgills's son, in a challenge."

"I am surprised you know that."

"A ship came to the coast and messengers were sent. You see, Thorgills and his allies are a great bother to us. They attack constantly. As a result, I have found spies useful. Yes, Halvdan and Thorgills greatly desire to conquer us."

"There is nothing Halvdan and Thorgills do not desire."

"You will have no trouble raising an army," Guthrum predicted. "Halvdan and Thorgills are hated."

"I intend to sail for Denmark as soon as possible, but first I must go to King Alfred. There is a woman—I took her as a slave, but now wish her for my wife."

Guthrum grinned again. "A man should have something to fight for," he muttered, leering slightly. "Is she Saxon?"

"No, Irish."

"With red hair, no doubt."

Brand's face flushed slightly. "Yes, and she is Christian."

"I myself have been baptized," Guthrum admitted. He rolled his eyes heavenward. "So have many of our people. There is something to this Christian god—something compelling."

Brand did not know if he was surprised or not.

Guthrum laughed. "Not that baptism can wash away our pagan myths—they are deep, they burn in our souls. I still hear Thor when he roars in a storm, and in battle I know Odin is there."

"Will this baptism make you stronger?" Brand asked.

"Surely the hammer of our God of War, Odin, is stronger when combined with the sword of St. Peter," Guthrum replied.

"I cannot argue that two gods are better than one."

"You are not yet ready for conversion." Guthrum laughed. "A man must strike a delicate balance between the tales of his youth and the beliefs he holds true."

Brand did not contradict him. "I come to ask for help," he finally said.

"What can I do to help the son of Jarls?"

"I need clothes that denote my rank, I need a proper rivercraft, and I need a letter of introduction to King Alfred."

"My letter will not get back your woman. Under our treaty the nobly born are to receive protection."

"If I can see her and speak with her, I believe she will come with me willingly."

"Yes, of course. These women—the Irish and the Saxons alike, prefer us because we bathe more often." Guthrum laughed loudly. "So you want a letter of introduction?"

"Yes."

"Sit down young Brand. Have some wine and venison. We'll see to your clothes and your letter, but first you will rest for a time here. I know your father schooled you well. Do you play chess?"

"I do," Brand replied.

"Bring my chessmen!" Guthrum shouted.

Almost immediately a young blond girl appeared, bearing a large box.

Brand helped himself to some venison and greens. He took the wine and poured it into a goblet. He drank the ruby red liquid, grateful for the warmth it brought.

While Brand ate, Guthrum unpacked his chessmen. They were wonderful pieces. Each was carved from bone, intricate pieces in detailed dress.

"Those are works of art," Brand commented.

"Made by one of our master craftsmen."

Master craftsman. The word made Brand remember Deirdre's brother Alan. Vaguely he wondered if Alan had yet reached Norway and what had become of the talented young man. Deirdre had spoken of her brother every day when they were together, and he had vowed to help her find him. He smiled to himself. That vow was yet another reason why he believed she would come with him.

Never in her entire life had Deirdre dreamt that such a room could exist. It was two floors above the great hall and had large windows, which faced the inner courtyard of the palace. These windows were unlike others. They were not built to point weapons through, or to observe an enemy below or beyond the castle walls. Rather, they were built to allow in the sunlight, and they had overhangs to ensure that when it rained, water did not come in.

On the long wooden table in the center of the room there were four huge candelabra. A stone fireplace took up one wall while heavy hand-carved chests lined the remaining walls. Inside each chest a treasure trove of meticulously copied manuscripts was carefully stored. A few were illuminated manuscripts like those her brother made.

Alfred sat at one end of the table, his current manuscript before him. "I am pleased with your handwriting," he said, looking at Deirdre who sat, at his bidding, a short distance away.

"I do not understand all that I write," she said honestly. "This English is a terrible language. It is very difficult indeed."

"Ah, but you have learned quickly, and your letters show an artistic tendency."

"Oh, Your Majesty, how I wish you could see the letters made by my brother, Alan. He is an artist and illuminates his manuscripts in inks of gold and silver leaf."

"This is the brother who has been enslaved?"

"Yes. I have only one brother."

"I presume he copies Holy Scripture."

"Yes, Your Highness."

"Such work is needed. Still, there are other worthy manuscripts, and Latin is not the language of all, indeed it is spoken by few. Why should we continue to write in this ancient tongue which hardly anyone speaks and few read? I have decreed that all freemen in my kingdom must learn to read English. Toward that end, I have employed translators, and I myself often translate, to make available English versions of those books which I believe most necessary."

Deirdre sat on the edge of her chair listening intently. What were these books which held such knowledge? As if he read her mind, he walked slowly to the chests.

"First, *The Ecclesiastical History of the English People,*

by the Venerable Bede. He was a great man who has recorded our history. Next, the *Seven Books of Histories of the Pagans* as recorded by Orosius. These two books tell us of the divine purpose of history, my child. We must come to understand what has come before. And, of course, there are more religious works such as the *Pastoral Care of St. Gregory I* and his *Dialogues*. I myself am working on the *Soliloquies of St. Augustine of Hippo* and Boethius's *Consolation of Philosophy*. I have set others to work on a chronicle of our times, which we will call *The Anglo-Saxon Chronicle*."

"I am in a room that contains much of the knowledge of the world," Deirdre said reverently. She felt awestruck.

"There are other rooms with greater knowledge," Alfred said pensively.

Deirdre was not certain to what rooms he referred. "Where?" she asked.

"There are great libraries in the East, my child. They hold the mysteries of the pagan world, they tell the story of the world before—"

As he spoke, Alfred's voice grew more strained, as if he were distracted. He moved around as if trying to get more comfortable.

"Are you all right, Your Highness?" Deirdre leaned toward him with concern.

Suddenly King Alfred grasped his sides as his face became contorted with pain.

"My king, are you ill?" Deirdre asked with alarm.

"I have a disease, my child. It is most mysterious, and yet it plagues me greatly. It is very painful, it is as if I am being squeezed by an internal snake. I have pains here and here and sometimes I vomit."

His face was unseemly pale, and he leaned back and clutched himself.

"Is the pain constant?" Deirdre asked.

"No, it is acute now and will remain so for several hours,

then it leaves me and I feel as if it never was. Perhaps it is a punishment."

Deirdre shook her head. "I do not believe that the body's ills are a punishment, Your Highness. I believe pain and illness have causes, but that we simply do not yet understand those causes."

"Some say suffering is the pathway to God."

Deirdre shook her head. "Though it may be blasphemy, I cannot accept that. I think the alleviation of suffering is a much surer path."

"I think more people should have your beliefs," the king said as he tried to put his head down on the table, but quickly sat up because it seemed the position hurt him more.

"Let me help you," Deirdre offered.

"I must lie down," Alfred gasped. "It is not so acute when I am flat on my back."

"My king, I beg you to let me observe your attack. Edana, of whom I have spoken before, taught me much medicine she gleaned in the East."

Alfred forced a smile. "God knows my own doctors are useless enough. I shall give instructions for you to observe."

Deirdre nodded, and Alfred shouted for his servants. In moments he was being carried to his bed, and Deirdre followed. In her room she had already begun to gather medicines and had been happy to discover that local plants were not unlike those of her homeland.

The king was laid out in a large bed, and great woven covers were pulled up around him.

He shivered for a short time and when she felt his brow she knew he had a slight fever. But the fever grew no worse, though he cried out in pain and held his sides.

"Forgive me," Deirdre said softly. "Can you describe this pain?"

"It is in my back and shoulder blades, and here just below my chest, as well as in my sides. It is as I said, it is like being squeezed tightly from the inside."

"And does this pain come daily?"

He shook his head in misery.

"Do you have thirst?"

Again he shook his head.

Deirdre sat down beside him in a large chair.

"My doctors once gave me wine, but it made it worse."

Deirdre nodded. "But it gives you comfort to hold your stomach, there." She pointed to the area just below his chest and he nodded.

"I have been bled as well, but it did not help."

"It seldom does," Deirdre said. It was her personal, though unuttered theory that bleeding, in fact, almost always made matters worse.

"Does your knowledge extend to this disease?"

Deirdre smiled kindly. "The essence of what I have been taught is to observe fully first, Your Highness. I think I shall want to keep a record of what you eat."

"Am I poisoned?" he asked with concern.

Deirdre shook her head. "I think not, my lord. But it is said that one man's nourishment is another man's poison. I must consider everything."

Alfred managed a smile. "You are a wise young woman of many talents, Princess Deirdre of Meath. If you succeed in treating my illness, I will reward you."

Deirdre smiled at him. "To help you is reward enough. The world needs knowledge, I admire you more than I can say."

The day was far from beautiful. The sky, from horizon to horizon, was filled with dark gray clouds, and while it had not yet started to rain, a heavy mist filled the air and lingered over the River Ouse as if the water were being drawn to the heavens rather than falling from it.

This was, Brand knew, the more natural climate of this place, indeed of the whole British Isle. It was the rain that made the grass so green, the flowers so abundant, the soil so dark and rich. The rain was a gift from the gods, it enabled the farmers to produce sufficient foodstuffs.

Brand glanced at the clouds. They did not look overly ominous. The rain, when it actually came, would in all likelihood be a gentle rain, a reasonably warm rain.

And if the weather were less decent than the day he arrived, his departure was taken in a far grander fashion. King Guthrum, judging him an asset in his battle against Lord Thorgills and King Halvdan the Black, had been more than generous. King Guthrum insisted he be outfitted in royal garments, the likes of which he had not worn since being forced into military service by Lord Thorgills. He wore fine leather shoes, tight leggings, and a belted tunic embroidered with gold threads. Over this he wore a cloak that was held in place by his own massive neck ring, which was made of almost four pounds of gold. His sword hung under his cloak, so it was always at the ready. Over his thick blond hair he wore the traditional steel helmet.

The vessel provided by Guthrum was a Viking dugout with a good steering device and a cover over part of the vessel so he could keep his supplies dry and seek refuge from the elements. So generous was King Guthrum that Brand bore a gift for King Alfred as well as a letter of greetings and a recommendation explaining that although Princess Deirdre had been a slave, he desired to marry her.

"You will return here to Jorvik before setting sail for our homeland," King Guthrum said as they stood on the river's edge.

"I will," Brand promised.

"I am counting on you, Brand. Lord Thorgills must be defeated, and Halvdan the Black must fall as well. He has ruled badly."

Brand bowed before Guthrum. "To a new era," he said firmly.

* * *

Outside it continued to rain, as it had for several days now. It was a fine spring rain, a sort of warm drizzle that, although it filled the air with dampness, did not seem to penetrate the way the cold, drenching rains of winter did.

Deirdre looked out for a time on the green fields behind the palace, then she went to her table in the corner, which contained a variety of small crocks, each of which had herbs soaking in a substance stronger than the strongest mead or wine. The substance was obtained by boiling fermented barley mash and covering the steaming mixture with a piece of sheepskin which had itself been boiled to make it clean. The steam from the mash soaked into the skin and finally the skin was wrung out and the result was what Edana called pure alcohol. After that, the desired root was put into the alcohol and the result, as Edana had taught her, was a tincture which could be taken in water.

Deirdre peered into the crock which sat nearest the end of the table and smelled of it, deeply inhaling the aroma of its contents. It was root of wormwood, and now after six weeks, the tincture was almost ready.

Deirdre then turned away and left her room to join the king in his library.

"You are like sunshine on this rather gloomy day," King Alfred said, holding out his hand to greet her.

Deirdre smiled and curtsied. This was her favorite room in all the palace, but as much as she liked reading and learning, she still found her mind wandering. Her memories of Brand and their time together did not seem to fade as she had thought they would. On the contrary, as time passed she felt more desirous of him, and more betrayed because he had given her up so easily. And yet logic prevailed. What was he to have done? To fight for her against such odds would have been folly. Still, he did not give her the opportunity to speak and express her desire to stay with him. If only she had spoken up! Probably Sir Wilfred would have listened to her, and in all likelihood she and Brand would have continued on their journey to Jorvik. Yet dozens of questions remained. Would he have kept her as a slave only? Was she only a temporary amusement for him, or did he really care for her? And if he cared, why had he—? She forced her thoughts away from her own questions. They led her mind in circles and always ended with one word: why?

"You seem troubled this morning," King Alfred noted.

Deirdre forced a smile. "No, Your Highness. It is just the weather."

"I had another attack last night," Alfred said, slowly. "It lasted several hours."

"I'm deeply sorry to hear that. I have made many notes, and I have prepared a medicine."

"Have you come to some conclusions about my illness?"

"Yes, Your Highness, but I fear the treatment I suggest will not be pleasant."

King Alfred smiled. "Can it be worse than more attacks or being bled? My court physicians are men without imagination."

"They will resent me."

"Their resentment is of no concern to me. They need not know about you or your medicine. Now tell me what you conclude?"

"I believe your pain is not a disease, Your Highness, but what might better be called a continuing condition. I believe it has to do with what you eat."

The king frowned. "It is true that following the pains I must always go to my closestool."

Deirdre nodded. "I should like you to eat no meat but the leanest meat and I should like you to eat more greens and grains."

"Grains? How so?"

"Gruel, Your Highness. Gruel and greens and only meat and foul without fat or skin."

"Oh, my favorite part."

Deirdre smiled. "It will be worth giving it up if your pains leave you."

"You are quite correct. Is there anything else."

"Yes, no eggs. It is my observation that they cause you great difficulty. And you shall also take a few drops of medicine. I shall bring it to you later today. It is taken in water and will make you belch loudly."

"And this is desirable?"

Deirdre smiled. "Yes, such a substance kept inside the body can indeed cause pains."

"You are right, I do always feel better after I have belched. But why would not this happen naturally?"

"I do not know," Deirdre answered honestly. "The mystery of medicine involves why one thing works and another does not. We can only know from observing you if the regime will help you. If it seems to, we will wait for a time, and then give you fatty meat. If the pain returns, you will know that what I recommend is the correct path to follow."

"I find this plan quite satisfactory, Princess Deirdre."

"It is my pleasure to try to help," Deirdre said modestly.

"You are intelligent and compassionate as well as beautiful. There is a young man of the court, the son of an earl, who would like to visit with you. Might I suggest he would make an excellent suitor."

A suitor? Deirdre had not thought of acquiring a suitor. But of course it would be the natural way of things. The king's desires for her were well-meaning, yet how could she give her heart to another? "I am not certain I am ready to be courted," she replied, looking down and away.

The king smiled and nodded. "I suspect your heart is not yet free."

Was this an invitation to confide in the king? No, she could not. As kind as he was, she was not yet ready to discuss her mixed emotions, her constant dreams, her thoughts of Brand who seemingly had enslaved her heart as well as her body. "I have many things to think on," she said, and, from his expression, she knew that King Alfred understood her hesitance.

"Take your time, Princess Deirdre. The young man may seek you out, but you need not respond to his overtures."

Deirdre smiled, "Thank you, Your Highness."

"Princess Deirdre, I beg you to walk with me in the garden." Gilbert, son of the exiled earl of Catterick in Northumbria, was as handsome a young man as the court of Alfred had to offer. He was tall and slender, though well built. He had soft brown hair and brown eyes, the pupils of which were ringed with gold.

Deirdre smiled shyly at him and wondered if she should accept his invitation. He was well mannered and pleasant; indeed all her instincts told her he was kind. She had been honest with the king, but he had seen fit to introduce them in any case, and now she wondered if it would be fair to encourage him. "I am not of this kingdom," she said softly.

"Nor am I, my lady. Like you, I am a refugee from afar. My kingdom is now a part of Danelaw."

"It isn't only that I am from across the Hibernian Sea. I have—well, a past."

"A past love?"

His words were incredibly blunt, and she wondered how she should respond. Perhaps it was best to be equally blunt, equally honest, so that there would be no misunderstandings between them. "Yes, there is someone whom I loved."

His smile was kind. "I, too, have lost someone," he admitted. "She was stolen away, as you were stolen away."

Deirdre felt a chill. If his loved one were stolen, he would not likely understand her if she admitted she had been willingly taken and had, in fact, loved Brand who had taken her. No, not had loved—still loved. It was hard for her to admit it even to herself, but in spite of everything she still longed for him and wondered how he could have hurt her so by giving her up so easily.

"Was she taken by the Vikings?"

"Yes, my lady. They are a hard and cruel people."

Deirdre knew he was right, but were they truly harder and more cruel than Malvin had been? All her instincts told her that no people had a monopoly on hardness and cruelty. Furthermore, she had been told more of these Vikings than he. She knew how they lived and loved. And on the Isle of Man she had seen them with their children and she knew about how they governed themselves. In many ways they were advanced over her own people, in many ways they were not. "Many are hard and cruel," she said vaguely. "But most are not. Still, few are as enlightened as this king."

Gilbert nodded. "With that I must agree, my lady. Now will you walk with me?"

She knew she had made herself far from clear, but perhaps at least he understood her reluctance. "Very well," she agreed. And immediately she began asking herself why not. Brand was gone. Perhaps she should be at least trying to forget him. But it was not easy. Even as she vowed to try to forget him, his touch came back to her, his smile, the sound of his voice, the feel of him against her. No, he would not be easy to forget.

Yet she let Gilbert take her arm and escort her into the garden. It was a lovely garden and, as summer was at hand, it was in full bloom, its blossoms filling the night air with the scent of oleander and roses, with lilac and carnations.

"You are most beautiful, Princess Deirdre."

Deirdre could tell by the tone of his voice that he was shy.

"You're good-hearted," she replied, as they came to the well and paused.

"I should like to court you, Princess Deirdre, but the king says since you have no guardian, it is you who must give permission."

"I cannot be dishonest with you, Gilbert. I am in love with

another, and I cannot forget him. I do not yet know my own heart."

"I understand that, my lady."

With those words, he dropped to his knees and taking her hand, kissed it tenderly. And still she imagined Brand! Not that he would kiss her hand, no. He would pull her to him roughly and slip his large hands inside her clothes, running them over her, commanding her with his every movement to respond to his desires. There would be no pleading and no asking. In heaven's name, what was wrong with her? She preferred Brand's rough passion, she yielded to his desires and shared them, she did not want to be asked, she wanted to be taken by her Viking bear, whose arms threatened to crush her and whose kisses were intimate and not polite.

"At least tell me we may walk in the garden once again, or that you will entertain me with a tale of Hibernia."

Deirdre smiled at him. "I can promise you that," she replied.

Alan relaxed in the hot bath just outside the sod house. He contemplated the unexpected turns his life had taken. He admitted to himself that this place was far more comfortable than the monastery and that he was more creatively fulfilled copying and illustrating these heathen tales than he had been merely illuminating Scripture. And now there was the girl, Charlotte. She had been with him over a week, but sensing her discomfort, he had not approached her in any way. She slept in a far corner. She cleaned daily and cooked, after which she went to her loom. In the evening, she took her meal to her corner and ate there. She was like a frightened little kitten. He shrugged with frustration and admitted his own loneliness. If only he could get her to talk to him. But one could not rush these things. Alan closed his eyes and thought of his most recent discovery. In a chest in his house he had found some maps, and so, he thought with satisfaction, *I at least have an idea where I am.*

Lord Thorgills's stronghold was at Grunstat, overlooking the Skagerrak, an arm of the North Sea that separated Denmark and Sweden from Norway. His abode was at the end of the long Norwegian peninsula which guarded the entrance to the fjord that led to Oslo and King Halvdan's castle fortress. To the south lay Denmark and a castle-fortress labeled King Jarls's. To the east lay Sweden, where a fortress which dominated the northern coast was labeled Lord Henrik's. He had further learned that most of Sweden's coastal areas were ruled by, or at least paid homage to King Halvdan the Black. The rest of Sweden had no one leader but was instead governed by a variety of constantly warring chieftains. He found it all quite interesting but, of course, useless to him. Unless he had a vessel and a crew, where could he go? And even if he had them, where would he go? Reluctantly, he pulled himself from the bath and dressed.

Alan walked hurriedly back toward his domicile and workplace. It was surely a strange building, the oddest he had ever seen, though since being here he had grown to appreciate it as well as other features of Viking life. And he had to admit he was not treated badly. In fact, since he had been here he had been left pretty much to himself until Charlotte was brought. Food was brought to him several times a day. His bathhouse was nearby, adjacent to a small, and now frozen stream. No one mistreated him, and no one oversaw what he did, though each time he finished a page, it was taken away and sewn into a large book that was to be the finished product of his labor. Whenever he needed supplies, they were also brought.

Alan walked more rapidly. He was cold in spite of the furs in which he was wrapped. How these people could roll in the snow after a hot bath was beyond him, though he knew they did it, because he had seen them.

He opened the door to his spacious house and hurried

inside, glad for the heat that greeted him. His sod house was oblong. Its walls were stone and its roof made of wood. There was a huge fireplace in its center. But from the outside the house looked as if it were a hill. It was a turf house with layers and layers of sod over the stone foundation. The roof was covered with a thinner turf. When he had first come here, there were flowers blooming on his roof, but as it was completely covered with snow except for the part near the chimney, it looked like nothing more than a snow hill.

Inside it had more furniture than he had in Meath. A long table and several chairs were placed near the fireplace. A bed, which was built like a wooden box and filled with furs, was placed in one corner.

At the other end of the room was a very long table on which he kept his art supplies, and five stone lamps which burned whale oil or sometimes animal fat. They gave off a bright light, enabling him to see to work.

Alan was finished with work for today and had every intention of eating his evening meal, and then working for a short time on an oak storage chest he was building. He had been told that since it was August, the days would grow shorter and shorter and that by December, the sun would disappear for all but a few hours a day. He shrugged, wondering what he would do. Somehow when the sun set, his body seemed to want to sleep. And what about next June when the sun would shine all night? Would he be awake all the time?

Charlotte was setting the table. He watched her, hoping she did not notice he was doing so. Her lips were like rosebuds, and her skin was a creamy white. She was very pretty.

She was dressed as all slave girls were dressed, in a common rough woolen tunic tied at the waist with a leather cord. It was the same tunic she had been stripped of by the guard when he brought her to Alan. Perhaps that was why she would not talk to him. He was certain she had felt greatly humiliated to be treated in such a fashion.

She was, he decided, the most appealing woman he had ever met. She seemed sweet and terribly vulnerable. In fact, her beautiful dark eyes had a haunted look.

Alan summoned himself. After all, if they were to live under the same roof at least they should be able to talk. "Charlotte, please sit at the table with me. You've prepared much too much for me to eat."

Charlotte looked at the food and then at him.

"Please," he added. "I am very lonely."

She continued looking down, but then nodded and set another place.

He poured some wine into his goblet. "We'll have to share the goblet, since there is only one."

She shook her head. "I do not drink wine."

"It warms you on cold nights," he suggested.

Again she shook her head. "For me its taste brings unpleasant memories."

Alan set the glass down carefully and felt himself fill with pain. He remembered Thorgills's conquest, and he remembered the women. Wine was poured down their throats to make them more pliable.

"I'm sorry," he said softly. "Did they hurt you much?"

Charlotte lifted her eyes to his and looked into them. He was so kind and so gentle. Perhaps Ingrid was right, perhaps he could be trusted. She had not told him, but Ingrid had sent her to get her out of the castle before her father returned and before she was molested by the guards, whom Ingrid readily admitted she could not always control.

"I was given to one of them, one of the leaders of the invasion party that attacked Brest. He had me many times and beat me. When he tired of me, I was turned over to the Viking master of the ship on which we came. When we arrived, I was given to Ingrid. She is strangely kind to me. They are not all like the one who took me—some are good to their women. But the one to whom I was given was a monster."

Alan reached across the distance between them and took

her small white hand. "My sister was taken by them. I have no idea where she is."

"Sometimes they sell women in the slave markets of the Mediterranean, many times they are brought here to serve in homes."

"Deirdre was very beautiful and learned. She was a master of tale telling, medicine, and could even read."

"It is not always good to be beautiful," Charlotte said slowly.

"You're beautiful," Alan said, still holding her hand.

"You've been kind to leave me alone."

He squeezed her hand. Then he leaned over and kissed her cheek.

Charlotte jumped up and stood by the table, her hand gripping its side, tears filling her large dark eyes.

Alan, filled with guilt, hurriedly stood up by her side. He gently put his arms around her. "I did not mean to frighten you. I didn't mean to bring back terrible memories, dear little Charlotte. I promise I will not hurt you. Please, sit down and eat. Later we'll talk."

She seemed to relax slightly as she looked into his eyes. "I will try," she murmured. "I, too, am lonely."

Deirdre walked in the garden with Gilbert at her side. It was a cool evening, and she pulled her shawl around her. The insects were all singing their night songs, mating melodies that called them together before the onset of fall.

"Day by day I grow to admire you more," Gilbert said.

Deirdre did not know what to say. Her feelings for Brand had only grown stronger. She dreamt of him nightly and thought about him at her loom. Only her work in the library kept her from thinking about him.

"Thank you," she answered, realizing it was not the answer he wanted to hear. How terrible this was—she did not want to be courted this way. She wanted Brand, she wanted him to seize her and hold her. He knew her so well . . . no one else could make her feel the way he did. But how can I truly know that since I have never had another?

As if reading her thoughts, Gilbert pulled her into his arms and kissed her. His lips were filled with warm passion, yet she felt nothing. And when he kissed her neck as Brand had so often, there was no chill, no leaping response from within her.

"Please," she whispered. "My heart is not yet free."

He pulled away and pressed her hand, "I'm sorry, I understand, Princess. I will wait."

Lord Thorgills ran his hand through his rough, unkempt beard. Outside the summer sun glistened off the River Liffey, but he could think of nothing save revenge. Summer was a time to fight, a time to plunder, a time to seek the man whose sword had taken his son's life.

He paced in front of his throne and turned and spit on the floor. "Tell me again!" he thundered.

Ulf Bloodax pulled on his beard and chewed as if he were a cow with a cud. "Brand has left Danelaw! King Guthrum has given him aid and treated him like royalty."

"In Guthrum's time he was royalty!"

"In any case he is no longer there. Those we questioned said he was going to seek an audience with King Alfred."

"King Alfred! I curse his name!"

"That's all we know."

"It's good that he's left Danelaw. We're not yet ready to attack them. Guthrum is too strong. But this Anglo-Saxon king—perhaps."

"It is said his defenses are excellent. And he has a treaty with Guthrum."

"Guthrum would defend a Saxon king?"

"Guthrum has been baptized."

Lord Thorgills spit again. "He has been weakened! Odin will protect him no longer!"

"Then we should attack him."

Thorgills shook his head. "Perhaps," he grumbled. "It is Brand I shall see dead! Why has he gone to this Saxon king?"

"We do not know. But the Irish princess was not in Danelaw with him."

Thorgills frowned as if trying to work it all out. "Defenses or no, we shall test this Alfred's forces before we see to Guthrum. And if we find Brand, you will be rewarded—doubly so if it is you who brings me his head."

Ulf touched the ax that hung by his side. He would be happy to see Brand dead and happier yet to collect a reward. "Shall I rouse the men and have the ships readied?"

"Yes. We'll sail on the first tide next Monday. We'll see of what stuff this Saxon king is made."

Ten

Brand entered the great hall of King Alfred's castle and found that, except for the guard and the king who sat on his distant throne, he was quite alone. This was a new experience for him, and he walked toward the throne slowly, taking in the gigantic room. Long shadows were cast by the huge pillars of stone that stood on each side of the hall.

In a way, this great hall was like a Christian cathedral, he thought. It was a cavernous room lit by flickering candles and a few torches that were on the walls. And a strange aroma permeated the whole of the room. It was, he concluded, the scent of lilac. Yes, that was it. The floors had been sprinkled with lilacs to chase away the odors of winter. And from each wall hung a great tapestry. One depicted a warrior and a dragon in mortal combat, others were of simple crosses or pastoral scenes of some winding river or distant mountains.

The king on his throne was an imposing man though it was not his physical prowess that Brand noticed. Even sitting silently, this king seemed to project a quiet intelligence. His expression was intense, and it seemed obvious that he noticed everything—the way a man walked, his expression, how he moved his hands.

When Brand reached the foot of the throne, he bowed. "I am Prince Brand, son of King Jarls. I bring to you a letter from King Guthrum of Jorvik." With that, Brand withdrew the letter and handed it to the king.

Alfred read the letter slowly. Then he handed it back to Brand. "You are welcome in my court, since you come from Guthrum and you come in peace."

"I come to plead my case," Brand said without hesitation.

"Do you feel you have been wronged?"

"May I tell you my story, Your Highness?"

Alfred nodded and waved his hand. It was a rather rare and unusual circumstance for a Viking to come before him to plead a case. And although the letter he had just read stated a few of the facts, the details were missing.

"I was bound into the service of Lord Thorgills of Norway when my father's kingdom was conquered by him some years ago. I served him only to prevent the death of my father," Brand began.

"I've heard harsh words of this Lord Thorgills," King Alfred said, rubbing his chin. "Indeed, he is among those who have threatened this kingdom."

"Some months ago, in the early spring of the year, he attacked the kingdom of Malvin, the king of East Meath in Hibernia."

Alfred leaned forward. The mention of Meath had brought him to full attention. Was the woman mentioned in the letter Princess Deirdre? And was this her lover, or the man who had killed him?

"The king of Meath had been defeated by Malvin. But I am ahead of my story. I was taken prisoner by the other king, King Odhran. When Malvin attacked Odhran, Odhran's daughter, Princess Deirdre, who had been seeing to my wounds, let me escape. I in turn, helped her to escape when Lord Thorgills attacked Malvin."

"You helped her escape?" Alfred queried.

"Lord Thorgills was planning to give her to Olaf, his son."

"And so you set her free?"

"We escaped together. I made her my slave in order to protect her."

Alfred touched his chin and frowned. "And you were on

your way to Danelaw when my men found the two of you and liberated the nobly born lady."

"Yes, Your Highness."

"And you want to claim her back again, is that it?"

"I understand the treaty. I do not wish to enslave Princess Deirdre. I love her and believe she loves me."

Alfred smiled. "I believe you might be right, but why did you allow her to be taken so easily, why did you not insist on accompanying her?"

"There are several reasons. First and foremost, I intend to raise an army to defeat Lord Thorgills. I wanted Deirdre to be safe. Thorgills will seek me out. I am a dangerous man to befriend, a more dangerous man to love. Second, I did not know of you or how you ruled. I assumed I might be imprisoned."

"But you are here. Has the danger lessened?"

"I have tried to forget her. I cannot. I have come to talk with her, to find out her wishes."

King Alfred smiled. "I suggested to her that she might find someone here to marry, and though there is a young man who desires her, it is clear to me, at least, that her heart belongs to another. She is without a guardian, so whatever she decides I will abide by. Though, mind you, she is treating me for an unknown disease, and I shall not be pleased to see her leave my kingdom."

"Princess Deirdre is an unusual woman."

"Princess Deirdre can read and write. She is most intelligent and not just an unusual woman but an exceptional woman."

"I am well aware of all her assets," Brand said.

"I shall arrange a meeting for you two. But rest now, I am certain your journey has been arduous."

Brand nodded and bowed again to the king. How could he sleep under the same roof as Deirdre without seeing her? His heart pounded with anticipation. *Let her take me back,* he thought. *Let us begin again.* He imagined her swirl of red hair, the flash of green eyes, the softness of her body and eagerness with which they had always sought one another. He could all but feel her now that he knew they were so close. He wondered if she felt the same, if she sensed his presence. *We will be together soon,* he silently vowed.

Alfred raised his hand, and a servant appeared. "Take our visitor to the west wing. See that he receives refreshment and bring him tomorrow morning after breakfast to the garden."

Brand did not argue. He willingly followed the servant, wondering at each door they passed if Deirdre were behind it sleeping.

The rain of the day before had ceased, but the sun and blue sky had not yet returned. It was a silver day, with high gray clouds that moved lethargically across the sky and were illuminated only by a weak sun that occasionally burned through their thickness.

Deirdre stood by the well and waited patiently as King Alfred had asked her to do. Was this some prearranged tryst with Gilbert? Had he gone to plead his case with the king and was the king trying to convince her she should consider him?

Abstractedly Deirdre tied her kerchief in a knot. King Alfred had been wonderful to her, and Gilbert was kind and charming. But nothing erased Brand from her thoughts. For a short time she had thought a kiss was a kiss—that perhaps any man could arouse the passion in her that now lay dormant. But it was not so. Gilbert's kiss meant nothing. There was no chill, no anticipation, no desire. It was a terrible truth, only Brand could arouse her.

"My lady, you are as beautiful now as you were the night you were taken from me."

At the sound of Brand's familiar voice and the words cloaked in his peculiar accent, Deirdre spun around, her mouth slightly open in shock, her well-shaped eyebrows lifted. Her first instinct was to throw herself into his arms, but instead she stood stock-still, wondering who knew he was here, and if this were the reason King Alfred had sent her to the garden. A second wave of emotion flooded over her as her anger at being left in the first place returned to her. That he had given her up was one thing, but that he had not said he would come back for her, or even told her that he loved her was another. That was what angered her.

"It's been weeks since you sent me here without so much as a struggle or even a word of hope that you might come for me," she said at length.

"I came as fast as was possible," he answered, taking a step toward her.

"And you expect me to behave as if nothing has happened? I thought I would never see you again."

Brand decided to be a little less than honest. On the night she was taken he supposed he could have insisted on being taken as well. But who could guess how he would have been received? In any case he had not thought through his arrangements with Erica, and had not realized the depth of his own feeling toward Deirdre. Now he knew he would have to end it with Erica in spite of their childhood betrothal, and he knew he loved the woman who stood before him, her loose hair blowing in the breeze, her eyes staring at him openly. In spite of her words he could see her feelings for him in her eyes. He was certain she loved him as he loved her.

"I could not come here for you without the support of King Guthrum."

"You should have said you would try to come for me. You should have said—" She stopped short of saying:" *You should have told me you loved me.*

"Well, I have come for you now. King Alfred says it is your decision, Deirdre. If you want, you can come with me and be mine. If you do not wish to come, he will take care of you here."

Be his? Did he mean to return her to the status of his slave if she wished to be with him? "King Alfred has been very good to me. I like it here."

He ignored her declaration. He could hardly blame her for being reluctant. He had let her go too easily, and her confidence in him was not so easily restored. "King Alfred tells me your knowledge of medicine is extraordinary and that you have helped him."

"I have tried to repay his kindness. King Alfred is a learned man. He has done me great honor by allowing me to study in his library."

He saw the flicker in her eyes, he had seen it before. She loved learning, her curiosity was boundless. "There are books in my library as well."

"Stolen, I imagine."

He smiled. He even loved her temper. One woman in a million would dare to speak to him this way. Or to any man, for that matter. It was her spark that had drawn him to her, that drew him to her now as he took another step toward her. He was close enough now to smell the rose scent of her body. "Deirdre, I want you back."

Deirdre still did not move. She couldn't throw herself into his arms, nor could she run away. Oh, how she wanted to trust him! How she wanted to think he had returned because he truly loved her and had not merely lost an amusing possession. Perhaps she could goad him into saying the right words. "There is someone here," she said slowly. "He has asked to court me."

Barely had the words escaped her mouth when Brand took more steps. He now stood so close she could feel his breath on her neck. She felt weaker and more vulnerable with him so close. "His name is Gilbert," she managed.

"Then you must choose between us," Brand said, reaching out for her. His arms went around her, and he bent and kissed her neck and then her ears. Chills passed through her. His touch—the memory of him, she felt faint in his arms. No one else could make her feel this way. He held her to him and she could feel the outline of his body, the strength of him as he devoured her throat with kisses. When he kissed her lips she knew she responded, pressing against him, opening her mouth to his probing tongue.

"Deirdre—!"

At the sound of the male voice calling, Brand let go of her and stepped back.

Deirdre clutched the side of the well with one hand. She was trembling all over. It was Gilbert. Thankful he had called out to her as he came down the path, she quickly brushed her hair off her forehead and tried desperately to compose herself.

"Princess Deirdre—"

Gilbert stepped from the path into the clearing. He looked at her and then at Brand.

"Ah, and you must be Prince Brand."

"I am," Brand replied. He felt wonderfully confident now. Deirdre's kiss had told him everything. She loved him as he loved her. Still, he could not blame her for being angry at him.

"King Alfred has told me about you," Gilbert revealed. "You are, I believe, my competition for Princess Deirdre's hand."

Brand nodded. How he loved the English turn of phrase. He fought the temptation to say he was interested in all of her, not just her hand. These Saxons had such quaint expressions they made him laugh. "I guess I am," he answered.

Deirdre frowned. They were speaking of her as if she were not there. "It is possible I might choose neither of you," she said, turning toward the path. "It is almost time for the noonday meal. I shall see both of you later."

Deirdre lifted her skirt and walked briskly toward the palace entrance holding her head high. *Yes,* she thought, *I will choose. But in my own good time, Brand. After you have learned to appreciate me.*

* * *

The noonday meal was the largest meal of the day. It consisted of bread and cheese as well as meat and greens. At night less was eaten, though often considerable mead was consumed.

Deirdre watched as King Alfred chose his food. He ate what she had told him he must eat, and he had told her privately that his pains had ceased. To be sure, he looked healthier and spent more time at his translations. But today he looked concerned.

Brand sat far down the table, and Gilbert sat next to her. Deirdre paid neither of them any attention. Her eyes were on the king. He looked preoccupied, and thus she was not surprised that after a time he hit his goblet with his knife as a sign asking for silence. Then he stood up.

"I have received distressing news," he said, looking at those gathered round the table. "Our coastal sources tell us that Lord Thorgills has set forth from Dublin. He is headed our way, and we must increase our defenses."

"Lord Thorgills—" His name escaped Deirdre's lips before anyone said anything. The very thought of him in Alfred's kingdom made her fearful, and she knew her face had paled.

"We will turn him back," King Alfred said confidently.

"I shall take a contingent to the coast immediately to reinforce our troops," Gilbert said.

Brand stood up. "I shall go too; I shall fight for you. This man is my enemy, and in all likelihood he comes after me. It is I who killed his son, Olaf."

"I except your offer, Prince Brand. But fight for us with the knowledge that your Lord Thorgills may have attacked for other reasons. He has threatened this kingdom before."

"I shall fight in any case."

King Alfred smiled. "Under the terms of our treaty, Guthrum must also contribute troops. I should like you to lead those troops, Prince Brand. I think perhaps we might arrange a little surprise for Lord Thorgills."

Brand nodded even though he was puzzled. How exactly

did King Alfred know of Thorgills's departure from Dublin and who were the mysterious "coastal sources." Moreover, it had taken him two days to reach Wessex; how could Guthrum be notified and send troops in time?

"Let us finish our meal," Alfred said, looking at Gilbert and Brand. "When we are done, we'll adjourn and plan our strategy, gentlemen."

King Alfred turned to Brand and smiled enigmatically. "I shall take the time to answer your unspoken questions as well."

When all had finished their noonday meal, Deirdre planned to return to her work in the library. But she watched as King Alfred and Brand disappeared up a spiral staircase that led to the tower. She remembered with some curiosity that she had seen the king take this staircase to the tower many times before.

"Come, Brand," King Alfred said as he opened the door. "It's a steep climb, but you will understand."

When they reached the top of the narrow staircase King Alfred pushed open a door, and, to Brand's surprise, it led, not to a cell in the tower, but to the outside top of the turret.

Brand stepped out and inhaled. "The view is magnificent," he breathed. And it was so, he could see for miles and miles across the rolling countryside.

"My kingdom," Alfred offered. "Or some of it, in any case."

Brand continued to look into the distance, but he turned at the sound of cooing. There, against the wall, were a number of large cages filled with pigeons. "Ah, is this where fowl for meals is raised?"

Alfred laughed. "No, young Brand. And I would thank no one who ate these particular birds."

Brand went to the cage and studied the birds. They seemed quite tame, and certainly they were fat enough to eat.

"You have wondered how I know about the coming of Thorgills, and you also wonder how I will notify King Guthrum in time."

"You read my mind, Your Highness. Are my questions stupid?"

"Hardly. But you will understand that this is a secret I share with few—not even those within my kingdom. Gilbert knows, of course, and some of my other commanders. But generally it is a secret of which we do not speak."

"I am honored."

"I can only judge you by what you seem to be. I judge you to be a man of honor, and so I will trust you with my secret."

Without further explanation, King Alfred went to one of his cages. He took from his pocket a scrap of paper which he rolled carefully and put in a small metal tube which he held up. "Delicate workmanship this. It's made by one of the craftsmen in Jorvik."

Brand was completely absorbed as he watched King Alfred lift one of the fat pigeons from the cage and attach the metal tube to its leg. It fit on a small chain attached to the bird. Then, throwing the bird into the air he cried, "Go home!"

Brand watched as the bird flew away, circling once before it headed off in the direction of Jorvik.

"I do not fully understand," Brand admitted. "What miracle is this?"

Alfred laughed. "No miracle, an ancient secret. It was one known to the Egyptians three hundred years before the birth of Christ. It is simply long forgotten. It is based on nature. These birds, you see, will always fly home. That bird's home is a roost in Jorvik atop the palace where King Guthrum rules. The bird will travel much faster than any messenger could."

There was a bench next to the roost, and Brand sat down. "This is astounding."

"Knowledge is important. There are a series of roosts throughout my kingdom. Some even farther away," Alfred confided.

"I understand the full of importance of this," Brand said. "So much so that I will never again eat these birds."

"I do not know if they would survive so well in your harsh land."

"I'm certain they wouldn't. But the knowledge is still priceless. Tell me, I still do not understand how Guthrum's troops can arrive in time."

"I must send another message to their commander. He is not in Jorvik, but much closer. I will send the message now and they will join with us near the coastal village where Thorgills will land."

"I think Lord Thorgills will be surprised to have a welcome party greet him."

"Come, let us return below to plan our strategy exactly. But first let me send the second message."

Brand watched as Alfred repeated the process and sent a second bird into the air.

In the study below Gilbert was waiting. "I see you have met our little birds."

"I have," Brand said, taking the wine offered.

"Thorgills, like other Viking raiders, will attempt to come up the river and take us by surprise. Thus we must surprise him first," Alfred said. "We will meet Lord Thorgills and his horde of warriors outside the village where they will disembark.

Gilbert opened a wooden chest and withdrew a large map, which he unrolled and placed flat on the table, adding a weight at each corner to hold it.

"Here," Alfred said, pointing to the river. "He will land here and bring his vessels this way."

"I have a plan," Brand offered. "What if you and Gilbert take your troops and meet Lord Thorgills here and I come from this direction with Guthrum's troops."

"Lord Thorgills will essentially be caught in the middle," King Alfred observed. "Yes, I like that plan."

Brand sat down and looked at the map. He took a sip of wine and, warming to the task at hand, moved his finger across the map. "Let's get more detailed. Weapons, hiding places, signals—there is much to do."

It was early morning and the smell of cooking meat and fresh bread still permeated the lower part of the castle. But the scene in the great hall was far from domestic and for Deirdre, who stood in the archway which led outside, it was nothing less than frightening.

King Alfred was a man transformed. He was no longer the quiet, gentle scholar. He was a soldier in full battle dress, a king who had every intention of leading his own army into the battle against the invading Norwegians.

Sir Gilbert was there, too. He looked dashing and handsome, his bejeweled sword hanging at his side. But it was Brand she watched most closely; Brand who occupied her every thought. Was she to lose him just as he had returned to her? Why had she not accepted him yesterday—told him the truth, told him she loved him? She cursed herself a hundred times for waiting for him to commit himself to her—surely he cared and cared deeply, or he would not have returned for her.

She watched and listened as Brand moved about, talking to the king, examining the weapons that had been brought from the storage vaults beneath the castle.

He looked far different from the man she had first seen in a cage in her father's castle. He was dressed now as a prince, and he looked strong and handsome in his beautifully embroidered tunic and leather belt held with its gold buckle.

"These weapons are vastly superior to most used in this part of the world," Brand said as he examined the steel swords, knives, and shields.

"They are from Danelaw, a part of our peace agreement. Guthrum, too, fears an attack by Lord Thorgills. In a sense we are his first line of defense. He agreed to supply us with weapons, and I paid him for them. Most of these arrived only a few weeks ago. We are in great good luck that Lord Thorgills chose to wait to attack," Alfred said. "We've just finished training with these weapons."

"And Guthrum's men?"

"They will meet us, or more specifically, you. You will be with them as planned."

"Lord Thorgills will be expecting different weapons—the kind of weapons usually used by the Irish. He will not expect these."

"Nor a contingent of Viking warriors."

Brand smiled. "Nor me."

"Are we ready to ride?" Alfred looked about.

"We're ready," Brand agreed.

Gilbert said nothing. Instead, he strode across the room to Deirdre. "I shall think of you Princess Deirdre, and I will return eagerly to hear your decision."

Deirdre looked into his open, honest eyes. She could have told him now that there was no decision to hear. She could have told him that she loved Brand and would go with him. But she could not send him off into battle without hope. That she already decided was worse than the truth. She smiled nervously at him and nodded. He turned away and left her to Brand who also crossed the great hall to stand for a moment by her side.

Deirdre's expression revealed her thoughts. Brand smiled at her. "Don't worry, Princess Deirdre. If either Gilbert or I do not return, you will have no choice to make."

"Do not say such a thing. Do not be so cruel."

He brushed her cheek with his hand. "I didn't mean to be cruel."

"I fear for you," she said softly. "Lord Thorgills will show you no mercy. He will be looking for you."

Brand nodded. "I do not want his mercy: I want his defeat."

"But his defeat here will not solve your problems at home."

"Well I know it, my love. But his defeat here will frighten him, give him cause for concern, and hopefully send him scurrying home to King Halvdan the Black seeking protection for his lands."

Deirdre touched her brooch and then looked into his clear blue eyes. He had called her "my love." She prayed he meant it. God how she wanted him! It was shameful! "My thoughts go with you," she murmured. She reached up and undid her cloak. She pinned her Tara brooch on him. "For luck," she whispered. Gilbert was gone; he could not see and be hurt by her action.

"Only your thoughts, my lady? Come now, I think your desires must go with me as well."

He was right, but his arrogance irritated her. She was on the verge of disagreement when he suddenly bent and kissed her. "You will not forget me," he whispered in her ear. "You will remember our baths together, you will feel me within you."

His lips touched her neck, and she sagged slightly in his arms. If only there was time to be with him—but he moved quickly back for fear of insulting Alfred's hospitality by being too brazen with her. Yet their eyes locked and she felt the power of unspoken vows, the power of their mutual need for one another. "Be safe," she whispered. "Please be safe."

He touched the brooch, lifted it, and kissed it. Without further delay, he turned quickly and strode across the room. Outside the trumpeter was calling the men to arms. The time was right for them to ride, to defend the kingdom once again.

The floodplain was flat, the only visible hills low and rolling and some distance from the river. The cold, predawn wind blew across dark land carrying its special chill. Brand sat silently behind a huge boulder near Gilbert, four other commanders, and King Alfred himself. The difficulty was keeping the horses quiet and convincing the men that they must remain at the ready, silent and poised to spring from the ditches they had dug the day before.

"Surprise has always been their advantage," Brand said. "It was easy to overrun villages and terrorize the inhabitants because they were usually asleep and unsuspecting. Our boats are run ashore and everyone leaps out—men and horses."

"I have seen your boats; they are masterfully constructed," Alfred allowed. "They tilt gracefully to one side so horses and men can scramble ashore, yet they are perfectly stable when they are afloat."

"Lord Thorgills and his men will disembark and ride across this plain toward the village." Brand grinned. "But they don't know of the ditches, nor can they dream an army awaits them."

"If we surprise them as they intend to surprise us, we will easily win. Lord Thorgills does not like to fight battles he cannot control," Brand added.

"He will not control this one," Gilbert said confidently.

"It is important for us to remain hidden in order to have the complete element of surprise. Let them get close enough so that when we spring from our ditches, they will be startled," the king said.

"Pass the word to the men. No one rides or emerges from hiding till my trumpet sounds," Gilbert instructed.

"It will not be too long," Brand predicted. "Lord Thorgills likes the surprise of morning. He wants his fighting done by noon." Brand smiled. "I must return to my men."

He hurriedly mounted and rode across the plain. There, as well hidden as the men of Wessex, were Guthrum's warriors. As his horse slowed, Brand stopped and touched the Tara brooch. It was under his own cloak, so Gilbert had not seen it. It was clear to him that Deirdre had chosen him; poor Gilbert would have to be told later.

Brand suddenly turned when he heard the sound of hoofbeats on the wind. The spies were right. They had predicted the time and day correctly, and the defense forces had just had sufficient time to dig their ditches and select their hiding places among the plentiful rocks that marked this land.

From the far side of the plain, Brand heard the sound of the trumpet.

Lord Thorgills's men had landed and were riding across the green expanse toward the village. Men and horses slowed, then came to a confused halt as Alfred's forces emerged, a Saxon war cry on their collective lips.

Brand saw Lord Thorgills's black stallion rear in the confusion. Everywhere men were locked in hand-to-hand combat while those on horseback attempted to topple one another, thus seeking the advantage.

Then one of Thorgills's commanders whirled about and shouted, and Brand's men emerged, coming from behind and partially surrounding Thorgills's forces.

It was Brand's last view of the battle. He was now in the thick of it, fighting for his own life, trying to work his way closer to Lord Thorgills, his personal foe. To defeat and kill him here on Saxon land would be the greatest of all revenges—the taking of his territory in Norway would be nothing.

Brand was swift and efficient. He knew the fighting techniques of his foes so well he was able to surprise them at every turn. A few he recognized, but most were strangers, reinforcements who had come to Dublin to fight with Lord Thorgills.

Brand heard a muffled cry and turned suddenly to see Sir Gilbert in mortal combat with not one, but two warriors on horseback. One toppled him easily from his saddle using a long pole, the other was bearing down with his ax.

The man who wanted Deirdre as much as he was about to be killed by his own former allies in battle. But he had kissed Deirdre and felt her lips. She was his. Deirdre would come with him. But even if that had not been the case, he was honor-bound to help Gilbert. He and Sir Gilbert had traveled here together, shared food, and now fought under the same banner. Brand raised his sword and swore loudly as he bore down on the nameless warrior, who in turn stood ready to deliver the death blow to the young Gilbert.

Brand did not see the expression on Gilbert's face, he looked only at his opponent. He ran him through and watched him as he crumpled, falling partially on the slightly wounded Gilbert. The second warrior, seeing Brand, rode away a curse on his lips.

"My life is yours," Gilbert muttered.

Brand looked steadily at him. "Your life is your own. Get back on your horse, my Saxon friend. Hurry!"

He held the animal, and Gilbert awkwardly climbed into the saddle, grateful to be off the ground. Brand turned his own horse and moved away—there was no time to talk, the battle still raged.

"There! It is Brand the traitor! Lord Thorgills has put a price on his head!"

Brand whirled around to see two men bearing down on him. He fought off an attack by the two ax-wielding Vikings, whose vicious weapons were swung wildly at him. "Traitor!" they shouted as they attacked him.

"I am no traitor!" Brand retorted. He used his shield to protect himself and dislodged one rider with his spear. The other bore down on him, but Brand was too quick, too well trained. Again he used his spear, but rather than running his opponent through, he used it to push the man from his horse. Only when his opponent was on the ground, did he spear him. Brand was blind with rage. A traitor? Was that what Lord Thorgills had told his men?

"I am no traitor!" Brand repeated as he turned his steed and pursued Lord Thorgills himself. "I avenge my father!"

Two partially armored Vikings appeared from over a slight knoll. They wore the colors of Lord Thorgills's personal guards and they moved swiftly and purposefully toward him and him alone. Others were locked in battle, but Brand could see that Lord Thorgills was escaping—his gallop for open ground was covered by his guard. His swift boat in the river waited to take him aboard and to safety.

But there was no time to think, another warrior had found him. Brand again used his spear as a lance, jabbing a warrior hard and tumbling him from the saddle.

He turned quickly as he heard a muffled warning cry and opened his mouth when saw the second warrior poised, and ready with what might have been a death blow. It was only a split second, but Brand could not ready himself against the blow—and yet the blow did not come. Instead, the warrior doubled forward, emitting a terrible scream as his ax slipped from his hand.

Behind him, Brand saw another Viking, and beneath the helmet, he immediately recognized Cnut.

"I owe you my life," Brand breathed.

"I owe you mine many times over," Cnut said smiling.

"There is no turning back for you," Brand said. "Come, my friend. Now is the time to declare oneself."

Cnut nodded.

The Viking horde which less than thirty minutes ago had ridden across the plain unobstructed had been surprised and destroyed, its survivors sent away in disarray.

The trumpet once again sounded, and Alfred's men, save those who had given pursuit, began to assemble.

"Surprised and outnumbered," King Alfred said as he reached Brand and Cnut.

"They were surprised we were here and doubly surprised by our weaponry. I wanted to pursue Lord Thorgills," Brand admitted.

"Another day. And is this man your prisoner?" Alfred asked.

Brand shook his head. "This man is one of my oldest friends. He will fight with me to regain my father's land and property."

Alfred smiled and handed Cnut a red sash such as those worn by his other men. "Wear this to signify your allegiance."

Cnut laughed. "You didn't hear them! Seldom have I seen Lord Thorgills and his men so frightened. It will be a long while before they come this way."

"Never again will Saxon lands be in such danger," Alfred said confidently. "Lord Thorgills now knows we are his match, and he will seek to attack those who are weaker than we."

"He was never one for a fair fight," Brand said. "The Irish tribes with their wooden swords and badly made shields of wood made him brave. But faced with swords, spears, axes, and shields of metal, he will think more than once against attacking your kingdom."

King Alfred laughed. "I do not want him to think of it at all." Then he turned to Brand and winked. "And he does not even know about the birds. Come, we must ride for home."

Sir Gilbert who rode at King Alfred's side turned to Brand. "A princess waits for you, Brand. She loves you, and she is yours."

Brand shifted uncomfortably at Gilbert's words. Beneath his cloak he could feel her brooch, and he touched it, visualizing her face, her touch. "I'm sorry," he said, looking at Gilbert. "Deirdre and I were meant for each other, our bond is strong."

Gilbert smiled. "I know, my friend. I have known from the beginning. She gave me no encouragement—she was always yours alone."

Brand smiled. "I value friendship," he answered.

"You are a man of honor," Gilbert said.

Eleven

A low fog shrouded the valley, giving it a mysterious appearance, an appearance enhanced by the eerie sound of men singing in the distance. It was a rousing song they sang, yet coming as it did from the fog-enshrouded land it seemed strange.

Deirdre listened as she stood near the gate to the castle courtyard. She wanted desperately to be able to discern individual voices—was Brand among them? Gilbert? The beloved King Alfred? But no, they sang as one, and there was no choice but to wait until the disembodied voices appeared, materializing out of the fog.

Deirdre wanted to shout, to cry out, to run forward. But she did not, even though her heart leapt with both hope and joy as soon as she realized that the voices raised in song were Saxon voices singing in the English language, and singing of victory rather than humming a dirge of defeat.

It seemed an eternity that she stood there with other women and children who awaited their loved ones. Brand— would he be among the survivors of what surely had been a fierce battle? "Let him be all right," she murmured. It was selfish of her to think only of him—of course she cared greatly about both Gilbert and the king . . . indeed about the fate of all who had fought. But Brand was first in her thoughts. And desire overcame all else, wicked desire, the desire to be with him entangled in lovemaking, satisfying her long pent-up hunger for him.

Deirdre closed her eyes, praying that if she looked away the time would seem shorter, that the riders would appear sooner, that her questions would be answered more quickly. With the closing of her lids against the reality of the day, she could see Brand in her mind. She could see his face, his jaw set, his eyes looking into the distance. What would he do when he saw her? Would he sweep her into his arms as she wanted him to do, or would he wait for the king's permission to take her? And Gilbert—how could she tell him of her decision? He was a kind man, a good man. She did not want to hurt him. He had been good to her when no one else was there. He had offered her the protection of his love and his name.

"I see them!" The shout that filled the air came from a young boy, and Deirdre opened her eyes to see the band of riders emerge from the fog like cheerful ghosts.

"They ride at full gallop toward the castle!" the boy shouted.

It was truly a sight to behold. The banners of the Saxon army blew in the wind, the sound of the horses were like thunder in the morning air, the shouts of victory were a soothing song to the ears of wives and children who waited for the defending warriors. How rare it was! Deirdre thought. How rare for those who fought against the Vikings to return with tales of victory on their lips, with prisoners, and with booty seized from those prisoners. Never in her experience had she heard of such a thing. The defenders of Dublin had been defeated, Meath had fallen with hardly a murmur, and most of England had tumbled before these Northern invaders. Not even God seemed to be victorious. The holy monasteries were sacked, their treasure taken back to the heathen land. Yet she well knew they were not all so heathen. And one day, if all went well, she might hold a child in her arms whose blood was Viking, whose father was Brand and whose destiny lay across the sea.

"Deirdre!" she heard her name and saw Brand. He rode with King Alfred, and Gilbert was at his side.

She ran to him and then slowed as all three of them dismounted.

It was not Gilbert's face she wanted to search out first, nor indeed did she want to waste precious moments. But there was duty. "Gilbert—I must speak with you," she said softly.

He smiled at her and touched her arm. "My lady, you have no need for words. I would not be here were this man not so honorable. I believe it is he with whom you wish to speak."

She was sure she looked surprised, and her lips parted, though the words she wanted seemed to have disappeared into the same mist from which the army of the king had appeared.

"In battle men learn about one another," King Alfred said. "My lady, you have cured me of my illness, or at the least you have found a treatment that makes my condition bearable. I would grant you any favor you ask."

"I ask to be returned to this man," Deirdre said, turning to Brand.

"Your wish is granted, my lady. I know he will fight for you as he has fought for me."

"I am grateful, Your Highness."

"Take your leave, my young lovers," Alfred said with a wave of his hand.

Brand slipped his arm around her waist. "Come, my woman."

Deirdre said nothing, but allowed him to guide her away. All around them wives had found their husbands and children their fathers. There was laughter and shouting. There were tears, too. Not all had come home. Some wept for their losses.

Brand had lifted her off the ground now. He carried her as he would carry a feather. She lay in his arms, limp with her own desire, her heart pounding inside her as if it would jump from her breast.

He took her to the room he had been in during his stay in the castle, and set her down in front of the bed.

"I've waited long for this moment," he said in a deep voice.

Deirdre trembled. Memories flooded through her, fear gripped her. Would it be as wonderful as she remembered?

He lay down on the bed and propped up his head with his arm. He smiled at her, a wonderfully twisted kind of smile, a smile that held promises.

"Take off your garments, my lady. Do so slowly in order to pleasure me after this battle."

A chill ran through her. His eyes held her, his eyes commanded no less than his voice. And it was, after all, an order she desired to hear, indeed, an order she desired to obey.

Slowly, as he asked, she undid her tunic and let it slip to the stone floor. Beneath it she wore a pleated underdress, and she lifted it over her head to reveal her nakedness to him without shame.

Brand stared at her and it was as if his hands were already on her. His eyes caressed her, and her nipples hardened as if his lips had drawn them and bitten them gently between his teeth.

"Lean over," he said. "Lean over me."

She moved toward him and leaned forward. She had thought he would caress her breasts, but instead his fingers parted the red hair which hid her mound and sought a more intimate caress, a caress that caused her to gasp and shiver. Then his other hand touched her nipple ever so gently, and she shivered again, this time more violently.

She started to lie down next to him. "No, not yet," he said. "Stand still, let me drink you in."

She closed her eyes and felt him run his hands over her

as she leaned toward him. It was the most sensuous of moments. He was a divine lover, a commanding lover who knew how to bring her sensations to a fevered pitch.

Without her realizing it, he swung about and drew himself into a sitting position on the side of the bed. His hands seized her buttocks and drew her close to his face.

"Oh," she groaned as he parted her hair with his tongue and touched her in the most intimate of all caresses. But what was he doing? He did not withdraw but rather held her buttocks tightly in his hands while kissing and nibbling at her in a way that drew moans of pleasure from her tormented body.

She wiggled, and her hips thrust forward and back.

"Stand still, my lady." His voice commanded her.

As if she could stop herself! He squeezed her buttocks and she shuddered again with deep pleasure as he drew on her, touching her in ways she had not imagined possible. His tongue was a soft, warm, darting instrument of pure joy. He took such pleasure in taunting her, in denying her till she could stand it no longer.

Then suddenly it stopped. She was panting, and her body was aglow with desire, her cheeks pink, her skin warm. She still thrust her hips forward seeking him, wanting him. "Why did you stop?" she breathed. Again she tried to lie down, and again he stopped her.

"Stay still."

He lifted his face and drew the rock hard nipple of her breast into his mouth. He sucked on it long and hard while tormenting the other with his touch. Again her hips moved, "Please," she begged. "Please."

He left his hands on her breasts and again his tongue sought that special place. She felt him draw her in, hold her tight, touch and withdraw, touch again. Suddenly his hands slid away from her breasts and he held her bottom tightly as he held his tongue against her till she shook all over and felt the pulsating release surge though her whole body. Never had it been so strong! Never had she felt so incredible.

It was then that he drew her down to the bed and held her tightly. It went on and on as she lay next to him. Only when she stopped shaking did he devour her lips with kisses. "I am for you, my lady," he whispered. "Now you touch me."

Deirdre did not hesitate. She reached down and felt for him. He was like a sword: hard, erect, and ready. Then, she began to undress him as slowly as he had made her undress. When all his clothes had been discarded, she kissed his chest and again sought a more intimate caress.

She stroked him gently, then harder, and finally slithered down and touched him as he had touched her.

"My Deirdre, you learn quickly."

Encouraged by his words and consumed with desire for him anew, she took him full into her mouth and caressed his member as it seemed to grow even stronger and harder. He was a huge man—wide as well as long.

"You must stop now, my lady."

"You did not stop when I was so aroused."

He laughed and pulled away from her slightly. "You can enjoy your pleasure several times to my once. And your pleasure arouses me. Taking you arouses me. But pleasure is to be prolonged."

Yes, Deirdre thought as he fell upon her hungrily and again began to suckle her breast. That was the secret. Pleasure was to be prolonged and prolonging it was the sweetest of tortures.

She moved beneath him as seductively as she could, and he pushed her legs apart and entered her, moving slowly, touching her now with his member as he had touched her before with his darting tongue.

"I shall find new ways to torment you," he laughed.

She sighed, and breathed into his ear, "Oh, please do."

* * *

The tables in the great hall fairly groaned with food and both mead and wine flowed generously among the victors. Deirdre sat proudly by Brand's side, and Brand, in turn, was honored by being given a place beside King Alfred.

"We shall miss our newfound friends," the king declared. "But if, as a result of their leaving, an army is raised in Denmark to defeat Lord Thorgills, we shall be more than pleased."

And while others dined on venison, goat, lamb, fish, and foul, King Alfred drank his tea and dined only on chicken. "Deirdre, I cannot thank you openly as I can Brand—it would make the court physicians jealous. I can say honestly that your medicine is strong and your knowledge well beyond that which we know."

"It gives me happiness to help, Your Highness, but it is not my medicine, it is the medicine of the East."

"Yes, Infidels they may be, yet it appears they have the knowledge possessed by the ancients—a knowledge mostly lost to our own people."

"Why must this be so?" Deirdre asked.

Alfred himself chose to answer her question. "Because, dear lady, those who are all powerful in Christendom will not listen to the voice of the Infidels. Muhammad's sword, like the ax of the Vikings, is seen to have been sent by the Devil to test us in our faith."

"But it is not really the medicine of the Infidels, rather it is the medicine of the ancients and is only preserved by the Infidels."

"No, not till we learn it for ourselves and make it ourselves will it be accepted. This is why written records are so important. It seems that each of us is born knowing nothing and we must learn all the lessons our parents had to learn— not just how to walk and speak, but how to love and what the meaning of true kindness is—but it is not just an individual matter. As a whole, we must learn from the past."

Deirdre understood what the king meant.

"Still," Alfred said thoughtfully, "I will think on these matters. Perhaps someone could be brought to teach a few of our more enlightened physicians. One must be enlightened in order to accept learning."

Deirdre smiled. King Alfred was a wonderful scholar. "I knew you would not turn away from knowledge."

"And you, my lady, I wish you good fortune in the land of the Norsemen. May you and the man you have chosen have good fortune."

Deirdre's thoughts turned to the future. Her mind was full of questions. What was Jorvik like? What indeed was Denmark like? Would she be accepted? Yet for all her questions, she knew it would be an adventure. What twists and turns her life had taken in only a short time! But for fate she might have been married to Malvin, shut away in his castle never to see the world nor learn its wonders. And perhaps, she thought, that would have been even worse than ending up with Olaf.

"I have known Cnut since I was a boy," Brand said as the three of them sailed north toward Jorvik. "He would have joined me in Ireland, but I had to come for you alone."

Cnut was blond like Brand, but neither as tall nor apparently as strong, though he was hardly a weakling. Like Brand, he had been pressed into Lord Thorgills's service by threat. Cnut's sister, Astrid, was taken prisoner as was Brand's father. Cnut fought for Lord Thorgills to save her life. Eventually she was given in marriage to Bjorn, one of King Halvdan's underkings.

"Bjorn," Deirdre repeated. "What a strange name."

"It means bear," Cnut said.

"Is he a bear?" Deirdre asked as she leaned over and dipped a long reed into the water of the Ouse. It pleased her to watch the gentle trail the reed left as she allowed it to drag in the calm water.

"Yes, he is aptly named," Cnut said grinning. "And if we can get Bjorn on our side, there is more than a little hope of our winning against Lord Thorgills."

Deirdre turned to Brand. "And what does your name mean?"

"It means firebrand, a sword."

She looked at him and blushed as she thought of their love-making. Yes, he too was aptly named, for more than one reason.

As if guessing her thoughts he reddened, "Not that sword, my lady."

Deirdre, hoping that Cnut was not paying much attention, turned her full attention to the reed as it cut through the water.

But Cnut laughed.

Brand slapped Cnut on the back. "And his name means as steadfast as a rock. He is as well named as Bjorn."

"What does your name mean, my lady? It is a strange name with a strange sound to it."

Deirdre looked up, a faraway expression covering her face. "In my Gaelic tongue it means wanderer, but we are a complicated people, so naturally there is a legend that accompanies each name."

"You are wandering, my lady," Cnut replied. "But tell us the rest, as you know we Norsemen like a good tale."

"A good tale is not always a happy tale," she warned. "It is said that Deirdre was the ward of a great king. She fell in love and fled to England with her lover. When she and her lover returned to Ireland, her lover was killed, and she died of a broken heart on his grave."

"You, too, have come to England with your lover, lady," Brand said. "But rest assured we will not return, nor will you die on my grave. You shall live to bear my children, and we shall live a long while."

Deirdre smiled at him.

Brand turned and steadied the mastfish. "Jorvik lies ahead."

Deirdre stretched and looked into the distance. It was a sizable town and apparently one bustling with activity.

"It's market day," Brand observed. "A fine day to arrive."

Cnut inhaled. "I can already smell the cooking of my homeland. I've had enough of Saxon food."

"King Guthrum will welcome us," Brand said confidently. "And then, as soon as we can, we'll leave for Denmark."

A thousand and one new things were going on, Deirdre thought as they walked the streets of Jorvik. Woodworkers made buckets the likes of which she had never seen. They were made with staves and banded with iron. Their wide bases made them difficult to tip over. Women kneaded bread in elongated, hand-carved wooden troths while something called frying irons were placed over hot fires to cook bits of meat. The metalworkers of Coppergate made ladles, forks, and meat skewers as well as all manner of knives, weapons, and jewelry.

"I have never seen such things," Deirdre said as she watched, engrossed, as metal was worked over fire.

"My lady, your people probably believe that only devils can work metal over fire."

"You're right," she agreed. "It is like the medicine the Infidels preserve—we fear what we do not understand."

"You are as wise as you are beautiful," Brand said, pausing in the bustle of Coppergate, through which they had to pass in order to reach the castle.

Brand stopped in front of a jeweler's place of business. "It is time I bought you a ring," he said to Deirdre.

He examined those made. They were silver—though the cheaper ones were made of iron. On them were words scratched in runes. "I shall have our names put on the ring."

Deirdre watched enthralled as their names were put on the silver ring in runes. When it was finished, Brand slipped the

ring onto her finger and pressed her hand in his. "We will
be together always, my lady. The four winds will carry us to
the ends of the earth."

He took a coin from his leather purse and paid the artisan
for the silver ring. "From Lord Thorgills's treasure," he whispered.

Deirdre smiled up at him lovingly. Still, her mind wan-
dered. What did lie ahead? He would do more battle—what
if he did not survive? No, she could not think of that—especially on this day. Today, Deirdre thought, the future called
out to them. Soon they would sail to Denmark, and a whole
new world would open before them.

Norway's coast was far different from that of low-lying
Denmark. Its fir-covered mountains descended directly to the
sea, creating narrow fjords with rushing rivers. But between
the coast and the sea there were millions of islands, many of
which were rugged fortresses guarding the mainland. On her
way to Halvdan the Black's castle, Erica's vessel had threaded
its way around the islands like a needle on an intricate embroidery. She had entered Oslo Fjord just as a fine rain began
to fall, a rain that resulted in a lingering fog that danced above
the tall treetops. It was some sixty miles up the fjord to
Halvdan's fortress, a great castle built into the side of a rocky
cliff that jutted out into the middle of the fjord and offered a
commanding view of all the surrounding area. As her ship
docked, Erica looked upward to the castle walls. Halvdan the
Black was a fearsome man, whose castle reflected his nature
in every way. The top of the castle wall displayed more than
two thousand skulls, all victims of Halvdan's effort to con-
solidate territory. Rumor had it that among them were two of
his own brothers, who had balked at paying homage to him.

Yes, fear was Halvdan's loving ally.

* * *

Erica was ushered into a small but richly furnished room. Its huge fireplace offered continual warmth against the early-fall chill that permeated the air. Its fur rugs insulated the cold stone floor, and rich tapestries, clearly from somewhere in Italy, hung from the walls. A silver samovar from an expedition up the Volga brewed strong tea, and on a small table, jewels were arranged artistically in the form of a circle. A soft fur-covered bench with a wooden back stood against one wall. Erica looked at it and sat down to wait. Vaguely she wondered if Halvdan would come here, or if she would be summoned to the royal chambers.

It was only moments before her question was answered. The wooden door opened, and King Halvdan the Black stood before her.

She sprang to her feet and bowed deeply.

"You may rise," he intoned.

Erica stood up and forced a smile. Halvdan was not a man whose appearance brought an automatic smile to anyone's lips. His face was utterly sharp and bony. It was as if someone had taken a skull from the castle wall and stretched skin over it tightly. His pale, cruel, blue eyes were sunken in his head, and his nose was long and sharp like that of a bird of prey. His hair was shoulder-length, thin, straight, and truly fine, like thread. His chin was sharp, and even the crown on his head, with its blood red jewels and sharp crests, had an ominous quality to it.

Halvdan did not smile back, but he did take her hand and lift it to his pale narrow lips. His hands too were skeletal—he had long fingers and long, yellowed nails. There was no moisture as his cold lips touched her hand.

"Erica, daughter of Radnor. You have braved my castle."

"Yes, Your Highness." Erica dropped her eyes, not out of respect but more because he was so hideous she could not bear to look at him.

"Did my emissary, Henrik of Lade, come to you?"

"He did," Erica replied.

"And did you give him your answer?"

"I did, Your Highness."

"If Henrik bears your answer, what brings you here, daughter of Radnor?"

"I come to give my allegiance in person, Your Highness."

"Is this because you do not trust Lord Henrik?"

"It is because my father taught me to trust only myself. A relayed message is not as forceful as one delivered in person."

A trace of a smile crept round the edges of Halvdan's mouth. "Your father has taught you well, Erica. I would so regret adding your skull to my collection, though it is indeed a most attractive skull."

Erica said nothing, but continued to look down at the rug. It seemed she could almost count the hairs on her own skin as she fought to detach herself from all feeling. Few people frightened her, but Halvdan frightened her. He was, at best, a lunatic.

"Pledge your undying allegiance to me, Erica. Get down on your knees and pledge before me."

Erica dropped to her knees in front of him. "I pledge my loyalty to you, Your Highness."

"Your undying loyalty," Halvdan said sternly.

"My undying loyalty," Erica repeated.

"I accept your pledge, or will when you have proved yourself."

Erica said nothing. His skeletal hand descended and touched her chin, lifting her face. With his other hand he touched her face, slowly running his finger around her full lips in a slow agonizing circle. "Pleasure me," he commanded. "So I will know your pledge is genuine."

Erica shuddered. She hated touching him. He even gave off the odor of death. "Yes, Your Highness," she whispered, steeling herself for the unspeakable task ahead.

* * *

The vessel with which Brand had been provided was a Viking longship. It was larger, but not unlike the vessel in which they had crossed from the Isle of Man. This one was twenty-one meters in length, and on its prow there was a great green dragon. Its large square red-and-white-striped sail hung from a single mast. The midportion of the vessel was covered, and a warm sleeping compartment lay therein. The ship held more than a hundred men, all of whom pledged loyalty to Brand because, like Cnut, their fathers had fought for his father.

The day on which they sailed was clear and warm, and Deirdre looked into the distance enthusiastically, trying to imagine Brand's homeland from all the tales he had woven. And Alan! She was not just on an adventure, she was a step closer to finding her brother and being reunited with him. How she missed him! Deirdre thought of all the knowledge she now had to share with him—knowledge of King Alfred's court, knowledge of Danelaw. She wondered if Alan were well, if he still loved his art as he once had and if it would be the same when once again they met. *Please be well,* she thought. *Please let us find you so we can all share a new life.*

At first the ship was rowed, but within the hour the wind caught the sail and they were cutting through the water, the wind to their backs.

Brand's arm slipped around her waist, and he held her close. "There is no feeling like the feeling of the wind at your back," he said, inhaling deeply. "I love the sea—I have always loved the sea."

His arm was warm, and the feeling of him next to her immediately, as always, caused a surge of excitement to ripple through her. He had a way of subtly touching her that made her wonder what he would do next. *I do love you with all my heart,* she thought as she leaned against him. And silently Deirdre dreamed of their marriage, of living peacefully at his side, of bearing his children and of making love with him forever. Then her eyes caught a side glimpse of the open mouth of the dragon on the ship's bow, and she felt a sudden questioning—a rippling fear that all her dreams would not come to pass.

His hand slipped beneath the fold of her dress and she felt him touch her skin. His fingers moved over her flesh, and she pressed herself to him, her apprehension fleeing with her rising excitement. "We shall be happy," she whispered. "I will find Alan, and we will be happy."

"Very happy," he replied, kissing her neck.

The sky was a deep blue, and the northern sun shone brightly. But in the distance, to the far north, great dark clouds were gathering, and Deirdre felt a distinct chill in the air.

"Winter is coming," Brand said in a matter-of-fact tone. "You will see how it is here. It is a white world, a world reborn each time the snow falls from the heavens."

"It sounds very cold. I have heard about the winters here."

"I shall keep you warm," Brand promised.

"And when you are not about, who will keep me warm?"

"No one, but you shall have furs and warm boots. Our fires burn hot, and our baths steam. You will soon get used to it."

The vessel had left the sea and now sailed up a fjord. On either side tree-covered cliffs rose several hundred feet, and, in the distance, even through though the sun was shining, a light ghostlike mist floated on top of the water.

"There, up there," Brand said, pointing into the distance.

"Is that your home? Is that Heorot?"

"No, my lady. That is Dragon Head, Ivar's fortress."

"We do not go to Heorot?" She felt puzzled as she looked at the great stone edifice that loomed in the distance.

"I feel it would be unsafe. King Halvdan and Lord Thorgills would like nothing better than to trap me and these loyal men at Heorot before I have the opportunity to raise an army. So I have come to Ivar, a man whom Halvdan believes to be his loyal ally."

"Are you sure he is not?"

"I have been gone for some time. It is true that the political winds can easily shift. I have no choice but to test the waters."

"This, too, could be dangerous," Deirdre said. Again her eyes strayed to the clouds beyond the blue sky.

"Dangerous, but not as dangerous as walking into a trap at Heorot."

Deirdre nodded. So far, in her experience with Brand, she had found his instincts to be good. She could only hope he was right and that this Ivar would welcome them and aid Brand's cause.

Ivar was known to all as Ivar the Boneless and that, Deirdre soon learned, was because he was double-jointed, being able to bend his wrists and fingers in both directions. This he did with little encouragement, sometimes to entertain and sometimes to frighten.

Ivar was a tall man who walked slightly hunched over, as if he wanted, in reality, to roll up into a ball. Still, he did not have an unkind face, nor did he seem at all hostile when he greeted Brand.

"You have been gone a long while," Ivar said as he filled large goblets with a deep, red, spiced wine.

The room in which they met was of medium size. But the fireplace was not against one wall as it might have been in castles in Ireland and Britannia. Indeed, the place from which the heat emanated was a thing of wonder, vastly more efficient than any such thing Deirdre had seen before. It was a great stone edifice in the very middle of the room. On its bottom there was a hearth which was open on four sides and supported by thick columns. At its top, there were smaller openings on each of its four sides. The fire in the hearth burned steadily, but the heat came not only from the hearth, but from the holes at the top as well as from the stones on all four sides. In all, it made the room extremely comfortable in spite of the fact that outside the sun had set and a cold wind whistled up the fjord from the sea.

They sat on wooden chairs covered with thick fur mats that appeared to be stuffed with something . . . perhaps seaweed, Deirdre thought. The walls were draped with furs rather than tapestries, and these gave added warmth. Light was provided by not only the flickering fire but by strange metal lamps filled with burning oil. It was all much more comfortable than anything she had known previously.

"I bring greetings from King Guthrum of Danelaw," Brand said seriously.

Deirdre turned away from her observations to listen to the two men talk.

"And not from Lord Thorgills in Dublin?" Ivar asked, his brows rising slightly.

"I do not know if Lord Thorgills would greet you or not. In any case he would not send greetings by me."

Ivar smiled. He was, Deirdre decided, older than Brand by ten or more years.

"I've heard rumors," Ivar said carefully. "I've heard you left Lord Thorgills and that you killed Olaf in a contest."

"Your ears are good," Brand allowed.

"Vessels come and go. News such as that travels on the tongue of every warrior," Ivar said.

Ivar sipped slowly from his goblet, as did Brand. Deirdre was reminded of a cat and a mouse. Brand was stalking Ivar's true thoughts, and Ivar, in turn, was being not only reticent but cagey.

"I know from the past that you harbor no love for either Thorgills or Halvdan," Brand finally said. His eyes were fastened on Ivar's eyes, and Deirdre knew he was looking for any and all signs of agreement or disagreement.

"Halvdan the Black taxes us all too highly. But his wealth has made him stronger, and we are all commanded to love him and obey him. Lord Thorgills is the most fearsome, and thus the most valuable of his underlords."

"Lord Thorgills is away, and the force he left behind is vulnerable."

"There is Lord Henrik. He, too, is strong."

"He, too, is vulnerable. Many of his men fight with Lord Thorgills in Ireland. Many were lost when Lord Thorgills attacked King Alfred, the Saxon king."

Ivar smiled and ran his finger around the rim of his goblet. "I've heard of that battle, too. Tell me, is Halvdan vulnerable?" Ivar asked.

"If enough join to defeat him," Deirdre suddenly said.

Ivar turned toward her in surprise. "What is this, Brand? A woman from Ireland with a mind to speak?"

Brand smiled. "With a mind to speak, with courage, with stamina, and with a heart to love."

Ivar grinned. "And with the ravishing red hair of her people. Ah Brand, I see now that this was a woman worth killing Olaf for."

Deirdre blushed and turned away. Even though their comments were flattering, they embarrassed her.

"Ah, and modest, too." Ivar took another sip of wine. He turned to Brand with a most serious expression on his face. "So, you want a pledge from me? You want my men to fight with yours."

Brand nodded. "Cnut has gone to raise his men, and I am certain Lord Radnor will commit his men as well."

Ivar raised his brow and looked at Brand as if the two shared some secret. "You don't think that Radnor will be a problem?" he asked.

To Deirdre, Brand seemed uneasy. It was as if there were something of which he did not want to speak.

"I'm sure Radnor will not be a problem," Brand said with conviction.

"If that's the case, I believe we can secure a pledge of support from at least five others," Ivar said, rubbing his chin. "But first, tell me what you want. The others will want to know, Brand. Indeed, I want to know. Will you become overking?"

Brand shook his head. "It is not what I desire. Ideally, I would like Harald, Halvdan's young son to become king with you and Cnut as his advisors. I should like to see *The Thing* reinstated."

"And you?"

"I intend to sail to Iceland with Deirdre and seek a life far from the blood feuds which have haunted my family for generations."

"I give you my pledge. How shall we proceed?"

"By raising a strong army and planning. We take Thorgills first in the early spring," Brand said with a smile. "Then we attack Halvdan."

"I look forward to an end to taxes," Ivar grinned. "Spoils to the victor, not to the king."

Brand raised his goblet. "To our alliance. I pledge all."

Ivar leaned toward him, and their goblets touched. "In the name of Odin, I, too, pledge all."

Both men drank and leaned back, more relaxed than they had been. "I have need to impose on your hospitality, Ivar. If I return to Heorot, I shall be attacked immediately. My arrival must be as much of a secret as possible if surprise is to be our ally."

"You are welcome here," Ivar said, pouring more spiced wine.

"I shall send for Erica," Brand said slowly, not daring to look at Deirdre. To himself he thought, *I shall get it over quickly. I shall tell her about Deirdre and set her free from our betrothal. Certainly her hatred for Halvdan and Lord Thorgills will prevail. She may be angry, but her anger will not prevent her father from committing his fighting force to the cause.*

Wisely, perhaps because he sensed the delicacy of Brand's problem, Ivar only nodded.

Twelve

A layer of wet white snow that fell during the night covered the ground and flocked the pines. But now the sun shone brightly, the sky was blue, and the snow had begun to melt.

"When it is really winter," Brand had warned, the water in the fjord will freeze. There will be no battles till spring. Winter is for raising armies, spring is for fighting."

"And so," Deirdre said, talking to herself as she stood on the castle wall surveying the new white world around her, "I will not find you till spring, dear Alan, wherever you are."

Brand and Ivar were plotting strategy in a room where Brand had laid out crude models of Thorgills's castle and Halvdan's stronghold. Great, white, fluffy clouds moved across the sky, and Deirdre thought of the tales that Brand so often told her.

"Frigg, the wife of Odin, has a palace of her own. There she sits and spins thread to weave into clouds." Deirdre smiled; she liked that tale. She drew her fur cloak around her more tightly. The wind here atop the castle was strong—it swept down the fjord from the sea. But although the weather here was colder than in Ireland or in England, it also seemed less damp, and thus did not seem to penetrate so deeply.

Deirdre looked down once again and suddenly, from around the bend in the fjord, a vessel appeared. It was a Viking knorr, far smaller than the longboat in which they had come to Scandinavia, but similar to the knorr in which they had crossed the Hibernian Sea. Its square sail was filled with wind as it sailed toward the wharf in front of Ivar's fortress. Deirdre watched carefully as the vessel docked. A tall woman disembarked and Deirdre could see her dress rippling in the brisk wind. She felt mildly curious as she headed for the stone stairs that led back into the castle. Was this visitor for Brand or for Ivar?

Brand stood by the hearth, staring into its embers.

"Brand!" Erica stood in the doorway.

At the sound of his name Brand turned quickly, lifting his brows in complete surprise. Erica smiled devastatingly and began to walk toward him. "Darling, it's been a long time. Too long."

Deirdre stopped short when she heard a woman's voice. She was just on the other side of the far entrance to the room. The woman had called Brand darling. Deirdre was frozen to the spot and could not make her legs move forward.

Erica's appearance startled Brand completely. The messengers he had sent could not possibly have reached her. "How did you know I was here?" he asked.

"I didn't," she admitted. "I just stopped here on my way home. But is this a way to greet your lover?"

Brand looked at her in silence for a long moment. She seemed taller than he remembered, and even more self-confident. She wore a pleated white underdress and bright red embroidered tunic. Her rich hair was pulled back and wound into an elaborate thick braid. She had taken off her heavy mink cloak and held it in one hand. As she got closer, she draped it over a chair and, turning, walked up to him. She encircled him with her long white arms. As she leaned over his broad shoulder, Erica saw the girl at the other doorway, the entrance toward which Brand's back was turned. It could only be the woman of whom she had heard. The woman for whom Brand had killed Olaf. She was small and petite with red hair which flowed to her waist. She was there for an instant and then disappeared. But Erica sensed she had not gone far, not out of earshot. *So, little witch, I will give you something to hear,* she thought.

"Darling! You've come home to me! And what is this I hear? You brought me a beautiful princess for a slave."

Deirdre had only stepped to one side of the doorway; her mouth was still open in surprise as she saw Brand's arms encircle the blond woman. A slave? Had Brand brought her to serve this woman? To serve him? Did he not intend to make her his wife? A cold chill passed through her. Brand was kissing this woman, and she was pressed tight against him. Deirdre's eyes filled with sudden hot tears, and, before Brand or the woman could see her, she turned and ran down the castle corridor toward her room.

Brand felt Erica's full lips on his mouth. They moved seductively, and she probed his mouth with her tongue even as she pressed to him. At the same time he felt her hand on his leg. It was not unpleasant—her perfume was heady, her body strong and well built. But she was not his Deirdre, and he pulled away, breaking their embrace.

"Is this how you treat me after so long?" Erica stared into his eyes, her lips pouting ever so slightly. "I was so looking forward to your return. I am not the child you left five years ago, Brand. I am a woman, a woman with cool skin and hot blood."

She started to embrace him again, but he held out his hand. "Erica, there are things of which we must speak." He studied her for a moment. He did not remember her being so forward. Nor did he remember the sharpness of her features. Erica seemed to have changed drastically, but he felt at a loss to define those changes.

"After so long, I should think you would want actions before words," she said sharply.

"Erica, things have changed. I have changed."

She smiled. "And you think I have remained the same?"

"No, I am quite sure you have changed, too."

"For better or worse, Brand?"

Her brow was raised. No, he did not recall that she was so vain. He forced a smile. "Better, of course." It was a lie; he did not like this Erica as much as the one he remembered.

"If that's true, why do you pull away from me?"

"Because I have changed, Erica. I did not mean to betray you. I did not mean to have my feelings for you change. But I love another, and I cannot marry you."

Erica's expression remained the same. "The slave girl?"

Brand nodded. "She is a princess. I did not take her as a slave."

Erica stood up straight and looked him in the eye. "I suppose I should have guessed. Is that the reason you are here and not at Heorot or with me at my father's?"

"I'm here because Heorot is not safe for me just now. I am here to build an army with Ivar. Erica, I need your father's men to defeat Lord Thorgills and King Halvdan. We've known each other since we were children. I need your military pledge even though I wish to end our betrothal."

"Dear Brand, I want what you want, and I want you to be happy. I would not hold you to our betrothal against your will even if I could. I wish you only great happiness and the blessings of the gods."

Brand exhaled, aware only now that he had been holding his breath. He felt great waves of relief swept over him. She was a generous woman after all, a woman without jealousy. He should not have feared her reaction. "Thank you, Erica. Your heart is generous." But still he felt mystified. There was something about her, something ingenuous. He could only hope she meant what she said.

Erica reached across the distance between them and took his hand, "And of course, dear Brand, you have my military pledge as well. My father is away, but due to return soon.

In fact, he may be home when I arrive. He would fight with no other. Tell me your plans."

Brand took her hand. "Follow me, Erica. I shall show you the beginning of our plans."

Deirdre lay on her bed and cried into her pillow. What was to become of her now? Brand would marry this woman he called Erica, and she would be their slave. She supposed that meant he would avail himself of her when he wished, perhaps when Erica, his rightful wife, was with child, or having her monthly blood.

I will be his convenience, she thought bitterly. And what of Alan? Would Brand really free him? Or was his promise to her a ruse to get her to cooperate and follow him? It seemed evident that he only cared for her body and not for her. He had returned here to marry his own kind, and to enslave her.

Deirdre turned on her back and stared at the beamed wood ceiling. How cruel he was to lead her on! Well, she would give him no pleasure. If he wanted her, he would have to take her by force. At first she had not trusted him, then she had, then for a time she doubted. But he had come for her and even fought for King Alfred, and she had believed him. *What a fool I am,* she thought to herself. *I could have remained in the court of King Alfred.* More tears spilled from her eyes, and she murmured, "I could have become a nun!"

The strategy room as Brand called it was well heated and well lit. In its center was a large table, and on the table was a model of Thorgills's stronghold and the surrounding countryside.

"It's most impressive," Erica said as she examined it. "And so is the one over there of Halvdan's castle." The second model was on a table against the wall.

"Thorgills is my first concern," Brand said. "He will

doubtless return in the spring, and we will attack before he is able to recuperate from the long voyage."

"The fjord is well guarded," Erica said carefully.

"We will come from the rear. Down this fjord and then overland, so we approach Thorgills's castle from behind."

"Oh, Brand, how very clever of you. It is certainly not the usual approach."

"While his forces are distracted, Ivar's men will sail down the main fjord and attack from the front."

"Thorgills will most certainly be defeated," Erica said.

Ivar, who stood in the doorway, entered the room. "Are you with us, Erica?"

"Would Brand share his plans if I were not?"

Ivar grinned. "We're glad to welcome you."

Erica turned and poured herself some wine from the silver jug. "I would not miss it for the world. Too long have Halvdan and Lord Thorgills demanded tribute from us. When I tell him, my father will most certainly agree."

Ivar clanked his goblet to hers. "To victory," he said.

"To victory," Erica agreed. Then she turned to Brand. "And tell me, when shall I meet this woman of yours?"

Brand smiled. "At dinner I imagine."

"I look forward to it. Now if you will excuse me, I must go and bathe. I've had a long trip."

Both men watched as Erica left the room, then Ivar turned toward Brand and slapped him on the back. "You have a way with women, my friend. I did not think Erica would be so understanding. It is certainly not every woman who would give up so easily."

Brand shrugged. "We've been apart many years. We're no longer the same. I cannot imagine that Erica has remained loyal to me either."

Ivar said nothing. He had long heard rumors about Erica, but there was no need to share them with Brand now that they were all allies. In any case, he himself did not intend making an enemy of Erica. Deep inside he thought she was like the legendary Loki, who could change shape and appear in many forms. Loki was spiteful, though. He hoped Erica was not.

"Deirdre, it's time to bathe and dress for dinner. We have a guest!"

Deirdre sat up, and Brand saw her reddened eyes.

"What is it?"

"As if you had to ask!" Deirdre jumped from the bed, wiping her cheek as she did so. She had not wanted him to find her in tears. Damn him!

"What is it?" he repeated.

"I saw you with her! I heard you both. You're betrothed to one another! She said I was your slave! How could you lead me on so . . . ?"

Brand felt empty inside. "We were betrothed—we're not now."

"And you expect me to believe this? I saw you kissing, I saw her pressed to your body as you press me to your body. No, I will not believe you again. You want only one thing from me, and I shall give it freely no more!"

"Deirdre! Listen to me!"

Deirdre covered her ears with her hands. "No! I shall not be a fool again. If you command me, master, I will sit at your feet! I am, after all, only a slave!"

"Stop it!" He grabbed her arm and pulled her forcibly into his arms.

"Leave me!" Deirdre cried. She wiggled like a tigress trying to break free of him, but he did not let her go. Instead he forced his lips to hers, pressing hard and probing her mouth with his tongue. She was stiff at first, but desire took over, and, in spite of everything, she almost stopped struggling.

With his other hand he disrobed her quickly until she stood naked before him. His hands held her buttocks firmly, his lips ravished her taut breasts. Her nipples were hard, her gateway moist and ready. But she protested softly even as he pushed her on to the bed and fell on her, kissing and taunting her, holding her while she half fought, half writhed in his arms. "You are mine!" he said again and again. "You are the only woman I want. You did not understand what you heard!"

Deirdre felt the growing need and cursed herself. There was no controlling it! When he touched her it was like magic, and she could not resist no matter how she felt. He continued till she thought she would go mad as his fingers pressed and withdrew, pressed and withdrew. Then he entered her, filling her utterly, as if they were one entity. As he moved inside her, her passion spilled over her, carrying her down, down into throbbing relief.

"You will always be mine," he whispered urgently in her ear.

But he felt her body go stiff as she attempted to pull away from him. "Only when you take me," she replied.

He kissed her neck. "Then I shall take you often till you know the truth."

Erica looked about the room Ivar had given her. It had a fine chair, a desk, and a bed covered with furs. Its large fireplace was in the center of the room, as was the custom. On the wall above the bed was the head of a wolf, its mouth open in angry surprise.

She sat down on the chair and stared into space, trying to clear her mind. *This is a dilemma,* she thought. Coming to Ivar was a pure accident. She had come here to gain allies, to ensure who would be on whose side in the spring when the ice melted and armies once again moved against one another. She had come to make certain Ivar was committed to Lord Thorgills and King Halvdan. Instead, when she docked she had learned that Brand was there.

"How very smart of you," she muttered. She knew full well that Lord Thorgills's men waited at Heorot for Brand to return. But who would suspect he would come to Ivar,

once a fearsome supporter of both Lord Thorgills and Lord
Henrik. No, Ivar was a man Halvdan certainly did not suspect
would turn against him. "But turn against you he has," she
said, shaking her head. How many would join Brand? Cnut
was out raising men to fight, Ivar could certainly influence
several other chieftains—if not more. How far had this gone?
To know the strategy of battle was one thing, but the vital
information was how many would rise against Thorgills and
Halvdan, and that neither Ivar nor Brand had revealed. Perhaps because they did not yet know.

"And what are we to do?" she asked aloud. If she and her
father betrayed Ivar and Brand and they won, they would
lose everything. If they fought by their side, and they lost,
Halvdan would exact a terrible punishment. Worse yet, Erica
was certain her father would want to fight with Brand. He
might even be angry that she had allowed Henrik and
Halvdan to believe they would be allied to them.

"I must find a way," she said aloud. Again she thought of
the girl. Brand really seemed to love her, and that was the
most galling part of it. "Perhaps the girl holds the key," Erica
said thoughtfully. It was a half-formed thought. But the more
she concentrated, the more it seemed to her that this Princess
Deirdre might be the key to controlling Brand. How much
had she heard, Erica wondered. She had been there, and she
had certainly seen her kiss Brand and speak of him bringing
her a slave. Did she run away at that point feeling betrayed?
Or was she there to hear Brand declare his love? Well, Erica
would find out the answer to that sooner or later.

"Halvdan," she said at last. The image of Halvdan came
into her mind. His bony hands and skeletal features—his body
which seemed eternally cold as if ice ran through his veins.
It was as if he were actually dead. Erica shivered as she
thought of his hands on her. She loathed him, and yet he was
powerful—if Halvdan were dead, Henrik, his cousin, would
become regent for young Harald. Henrik was a more than
tolerable bed partner. A vision of her and Henrik ruling all of

Scandinavia side by side warmed her. Yes, somehow this Irish princess could be used to control Brand, and Halvdan's death would provide for her own future. Still, Henrik's forces combined with Halvdan's and those of Lord Thorgills had to prevail. Thus, first and foremost, Brand must be stopped, she reasoned.

Deirdre soaked in the steaming bath and vaguely wondered why her own people had not thought of such an ingenious way to bathe. There were several baths in Ivar's castle, each one in a small building a few feet from the nearest outside door. A covered walkway led from the castle to the bath. Ivar's baths were more sophisticated than those she had seen on the Isle of Man or in Danelaw. The floor was made of stone, and there was a drain to carry away excess water. The walls were made of wood, and benches lined one side. Two fires burned brightly, one heated water for a hot water pool and another heated great rocks. As in other baths, first one submerged in the hot pool and bathed. When finished, one sat on the bench and cold water was poured over the hot stones, creating a hot foglike vapor which Brand called steam. It was the amount of steam in Ivar's baths that made them far better than those she had been in before.

Brand had taught her that to help the cleansing of one's body it was customary to be beaten with a bundle of twigs. This brought the blood to the surface of the skin and made one warmer. When that was completed, Brand went outside and jumped into a pool of ice-cold water. He had told her that when there was snow on the ground, he rolled in it. But Deirdre did not like going in the cold water, and she could not imagine rolling in the snow naked.

But she loved the hot-water bath and the steam. It seemed to renew her, and as she sat in the tub, the steam rising about her, she vowed to stop crying. *I will get dressed and go down to dinner,* she vowed. *I will not cry. No matter what else hap-*

pens, I must make Brand keep to his promise to help me find Alan.

"Ah, you are here, enjoying the bath."

Deirdre, who had been lost in thought, looked up, startled, as the tall blond Erica slipped into the water. As quickly Deirdre climbed out, wrapping herself in the white drying cloth. She moved through the misty vapor and sat down on the bench tentatively.

"Have you no tongue, Princess Deirdre?"

"I have a tongue," Deirdre replied.

"Brand seems to like you. He tells me you are from Ireland."

"I am from Meath."

"You will be our slave when Brand and I marry."

Deirdre did not look at her, not that she could really see her through the steam. "I may be Brand's slave, but my soul is free."

Erica smiled to herself. The girl had run away; she had not stayed to hear Brand declare his love. How lovely. It meant she was angry with Brand and felt betrayed. *How can I use this?* Erica wondered. Time, she needed time to work out some kind of plan. She quickly finished her bath and climbed out, sitting at the other end of the bench. Deirdre looked up only once. Erica was switching herself with the twigs.

"It is so much more fun when Brand does this to me," she said, looking toward where Deirdre sat obscured by the rising steam.

The bath was where Brand had first seduced her. Apparently it was the place he favored for seduction.

Erica laughed and suddenly ran across the room. Opening the door, she disappeared into the snow. "There are several inches," she called out. "It's lovely, the new-fallen snow."

Deirdre ignored her. She stood up and hurried back inside to dress for dinner.

* * *

The evening's meal consisted of roast pig, bread, berries, apples, and cheese. Erica dressed in a heavily embroidered royal blue overdress, and Deirdre wore a green overdress with an intricate embroidered design in dark thread.

Ivar and Brand sat at either end of the table and Deirdre sat on one side while Erica sat on the other. She glanced at Brand every now and again. It was true he was not treating her as a slave. But still his intentions had been made clear by Erica in the bath. She had spoken of their coming marriage. Still, she vowed she would shed no more tears. She drew on all her inner strength and sat proudly, listening, and now and again joining in the conversation.

"It's still snowing," Ivar said. "And the wind is now blowing from the north. In a few days the water will begin to freeze."

"I cannot imagine," Deirdre said softly.

"The rivers and lakes do not freeze in your land?" Ivar asked.

Deirdre shook her head. "It snows sometimes, but it melts quickly. It does not stay cold for so long."

"Our lakes and river freeze completely, and on the lakes there can be as much as a fathom of ice."

Erica smiled engagingly and leaned toward Brand, touching his arm gently. "When Brand and I were children, we used to skate on the ice. He was quite the fastest skater."

Deirdre felt a chill run through her. Erica and Brand had known one another forever. Still, she forced herself away from thoughts of the two of them. "What is skating?" she asked.

"It is hard to explain, my lady. We have lengths of bone which are specially carved. They attach to shoes. These are used on the ice. We put them on and propel ourselves across lakes and over frozen rivers with long spiked sticks," Brand said.

"It sounds strange indeed," Deirdre murmured, although she was mildly intrigued.

"It's really quite simple," Erica intoned with superiority.

"If you have a good sense of balance. Of course we have skis, too. Mind you, skiing takes even more skill than skating."

"How are skis made?" Deirdre asked.

"They are long narrow strips of wood which are curved on the end. We wax them to make them move smoothly over the snow. You also need spiked poles, like those used for skating."

Deirdre nodded. "What is the purpose, or is it just for sport?"

Brand laughed. "They enable you to move across the snow without falling into it."

"It gets so deep?" Deirdre asked.

"Very deep." Ivar laughed.

"Enough of the weather and our means of winter travel. I expect Cnut will send a messenger soon."

"He will come by sledge now," Erica said. "I must sail tomorrow, or risk not getting home before another storm."

Brand nodded, thinking that in no small way would it be a relief to have her gone. Perhaps, then, he could convince Deirdre that Erica meant nothing to him, save the fact that she was an old friend and now an ally. It would certainly be easier when she was gone. He could feel Deirdre's coldness, and although Erica said she wished him well, he was not at all certain he believed her words. She kept touching him, reminding him of the past and then looking at Deirdre. Was it his imagination, or was Erica intentionally trying to make Deirdre jealous and angry? *Women!* Who could understand them? But whatever else, he thought, Erica and her father were good allies. She will be loyal and later, when he and Deirdre were married, she would probably be a good friend.

Deirdre glanced at Erica when she was not looking. *How sure of herself she must be to leave me here with Brand!* She stood up. "I am not feeling well, I shall excuse myself." Deirdre turned and left the room. She fled toward their room, wondering what she could do and what she must say to Brand. Again she focused on the all-important promise to find Alan.

Erica watched as Deirdre left. It was lovely. An idea was beginning to form, the very beginning of a plan that would mean the end for Princess Deirdre. How nice her skull would look on Halvdan's wall!

Each day that went by made Alan feel more comfortable. He asked for a proper bed for Charlotte, and it was brought. She cleaned and cooked and worked at her loom. They ate their meals together, and in the evenings they talked. She told him all about her life in France, and he, in turn, told her about his life in Meath. And now, he noted with pleasure, when she worked at her loom, she hummed and sometimes sang in French. And she smiled, too. It warmed his heart to see her happy.

He looked up from his work and, realizing the time, began to put his things away. He walked toward the fireplace, where Charlotte stirred a thick soup. For a long moment he stood behind her, then he leaned over and kissed her neck gently as he put his arms around her.

She straightened up and turned suddenly, her mouth slightly open in surprise.

"I did not mean to frighten you. I didn't mean to bring back terrible memories, dear little Charlotte." Suddenly his long-suppressed feeling for her spilled out of his mouth. "I adore you. You are gentle, I worship you. I'm sure you might never want another man after—" He stopped because he could not bear to think of anyone hurting her. She was such a lovely flower.

Charlotte turned in his arms and looked into his eyes. "It is you, Alan, who are gentle." She stood on tiptoe and kissed his lips softly.

Alan felt his heart beating rapidly as he held her.

"I am only a mere mortal," he whispered. "I have loved you from afar and in silence since first you were brought here."

"And I am still a woman," she replied. "Will you be gentle; my sweet love?"

Alan kissed her neck, then her ears. "I shall be as gentle as a spring breeze and as slow as desire. You have only to tell me your needs."

It was as if she nearly fainted in his arms. He lifted her and carried her to the bed. Dinner could wait; at this moment they both felt another kind of hunger.

He slowly undid the cord that tied her robe and pulled it aside, revealing her perfect body. He sighed in ecstasy at the sight of her brown-tipped nipples and her mound of dark hair. It was a forest that surely hid wonderful treasures.

"You are more lovely than I imagined."

She said nothing, but hummed ever so slightly in his ear. He ran his hands gently across her creamy flesh and finally kissed one of her breasts, watching curiously as her brown nipple rose and became hard and firm. It was wondrous! He kissed the other and felt his own skin become hot as perspiration ran down his brow. Her humming turned to a low moan. He reminded himself to slow down, to exercise restraint, not to harm or hurt her. "Am I hurting you?" he asked needlessly as she pressed herself to him.

"No, no. I want you."

He felt himself growing hard; his whole body became tense. Gently, ever so gently, he lifted her on top of him. She moved her knees slightly without a word, crouched over him, the tip of his organ just touching her gateway.

He toyed with her magnificent breasts and took one into his mouth, nursing it slowly, deliberately. She moaned again and lowered herself onto him as he pushed up and into her.

They moved in unison, and he could feel her skin warm and glowing and hear the sound of her breathing in little gasps. Her mouth was slightly open, her eyes closed, and he felt himself bursting forth. He trembled violently just as she let out a low groan and began to quiver. His arms encircled her and they tumbled sideways still together, shaking in one another's arms.

After a time, he kissed her softly and withdrew. "You are beautiful, Charlotte. I hope you are all right."

She nestled in his arms. "You are so good Alan. You have made me want to love again. You have restored me. You are so unlike the others—"

He kissed her again. "Charlotte, you are the first woman I have ever had."

She looked at him and touched his forehead with her hand. "Oh, Alan. I am so honored to be your first."

He kissed her again. "God willing you will be the only one, Charlotte."

"But Lord Thorgills's men will return."

He held her close. "We'll find a way. No one will never hurt you again."

"How can you promise such a thing?"

"I will find a way to keep that promise."

"I love you," she purred, nestling as close to him as she could.

Alan touched her tangled dark hair and held her close, murmuring, "We'll find a way."

Erica hurried down the long corridor toward her father's room. She could not believe he had returned after so long at just this moment. Yet in truth she had expected him.

She stopped before his door, unsure even as she stood there just what she would say. She took a deep breath and knocked on the door.

"Enter!" Lord Radnor called out.

Erica steeled herself. Then she turned the iron bolt and entered her father's bedchamber.

"Erica! You return late at night."

"I was just told of your return, Father."

"I arrived only a short time ago."

Erica pulled her night robe tight.

"There are important matters of which we must speak," Erica said evenly.

"Sit down, my daughter, talk to me."

Erica sat down. Her father was wearing a long red robe. It was of some strange material, doubtless something he had just brought back from his most recent voyage. Where to begin? How to start? "Trouble is brewing," she finally said.

"It's winter," Radnor replied. "Whatever trouble brews will have to wait till spring."

"Wars can wait, decisions cannot."

"Ah, yes, decisions. Go on, tell me everything."

"Brand has returned," Erica said slowly.

Radnor smiled. "Ah, my favorite. And how is he?"

"Much changed," Erica said coldly. "He has brought a woman, an Irish princess. He wants to marry her, and so he has broken our betrothal."

Radnor frowned. "Erica, Brand has obviously not been true to you, but I know full well that you have been untrue to him."

Erica's expression hardened, but she did not wish to reveal herself so much. She waved her hand. "Yes, it is true. But hear me out."

"Go on," Radnor said.

"Brand killed Olaf in a challenge over this woman."

"Ah, we come to the heart of the matter," Radnor said, rubbing his chin.

"Lord Thorgills wants Brand dead, and so does Halvdan. Brand has made Ivar his ally and Cnut as well."

"You know my men will fight with Brand."

Erica stared at her father. His words were no surprise, but she hated hearing them. "Brand betrayed me," she said evenly.

Lord Radnor stood up. "I'm sorry you feel so, Erica. But we will still fight with Brand. He has been fair with you. He has told you the truth. Have you been truthful with him?"

Erica did not answer. Her father was a pig! He would ally himself to Brand in spite of everything! Of course she had known he would. She ran her tongue around her lips. She was beginning to shake with rage, and she fought to disguise it. "No," she whispered.

Lord Radnor shook his head and turned toward his bed. "I must go to sleep," he said. "I've been traveling all day."

He had turned his back on her. Erica stared for a second at her father's back as he prepared to climb into his bed. She saw his bejeweled sword. It was long and sharp. She seized it and moved suddenly. Lunging forward, she stabbed her father in the back.

"Eri—" He did not finish her name as he tumbled forward and fell on the bed.

Erica stared at him. He was gushing blood. She waited, then she went to the door and bolted it from the inside.

She walked slowly over to a pile of cloths and then back to the bed. She withdrew the bloodied sword from her father's back and wiped it clean with the cloth. Carefully, she placed it back in its sheath. Erica turned her father over. His vacant eyes stared up at her.

"Now we can truly discuss the problem," she said, pulling the covers up over his body so she could not see the gaping wound. She bent and closed his eyes, "I do not like your look, my father."

Erica began to set candles around the bed and gradually she lit them till her father lay surrounded by them as if he were spread out on some kind of altar.

Erica pulled a chair up to the side of the bed and sat down. "I will tell the men we are now allied to Halvdan and advise them to set sail for Lord Henrik's. Then I will see to Brand. I'm afraid I shall have to play a double role for a time, my father. I know you don't approve, but you have gone on a long voyage and left me in charge." Erica smiled. "Radnor the Wolf is gone and in his place a cat—yes, the tigress of the snows will rule."

After a long while, Erica stood up and carefully blew out the candles. She discarded her bloody robe and left the room, bolting and locking it behind her.

She went to her own room and brushed out her hair and dressed herself in her finest clothing. She summoned the commander of her father's troops.

"My father rests," she said, walking about the young warrior. "On the first tide tomorrow you are ordered to sail for Lord Henrik's. There you will remain until summoned in the spring to join in a glorious battle for King Halvdan."

The young warrior bowed. He asked no questions though in fact he had many. But he left because he knew that Erica had spoken for her father before, and it did not occur to him that she did not speak for him now.

Thirteen

The winter wind blew out of the north, down the Oslo Fjord, through the pines and across the lakes as it headed for the sea.

The royal hunting lodge near Vest was well protected from the ravages of such inclement weather by the surrounding hills, the tall trees, and the fact that it was covered with turf and built into a mountainside. It offered great comfort and warmth during the ravages of the season.

It was a many-roomed dwelling with each private sleeping room located off the center room. The center room was well furnished and designed as a winter meeting place for the powerful chieftains who paid homage to King Halvdan. In addition to his throne, it had long tables, comfortable chairs, a huge fireplace, and facilities for cooking. Its stone walls were covered with skins and the heads of elk, moose, and reindeer.

The location had been chosen because it was so accessible by land once the ground was covered with snow and ice. Overland travel in winter was in many ways far easier than in summer. Sledges pulled by surefooted horses could move easily through the snow or could be pushed down the frozen rivers by teams of skaters. A series of huts had been built to give travelers shelter at night, and even though the days were short, skiing, skating and sledging were far faster than walking.

Erica had traveled five days to reach Vest. But her journey was mostly over snow and frozen rivers and lakes. She and her entourage had been able to cover over twenty miles a day. King Halvdan's journey from Oslo had been much faster, taking only three days. Lord Henrik and Ingrid, Lord Thorgills's daughter who oversaw his domain while he was in Dublin, had taken more than twelve days to make the journey.

King Halvdan had seated his long, emaciated body at the table and magnanimously signaled the others to join him. Henrik, without the slightest hesitation, took the seat at the far end of the table, leaving Ingrid and Erica to sit on either side.

"You've been to Ivar's den, Erica—tell us what the daughter of the wolf saw."

Erica cringed at the mention of her father. King Halvdan had a way of constantly referring to Radnor. It was his none too subtle way of reminding her that she was a woman and that even though she was a warrior, she owed her position not to her own feats, but to those of her long-absent father. Absent now forever, never to tell her what to do again—Erica thought as she forced a smile. "I saw that our enemies are in good health," she said slowly.

Henrik laughed. "I'm sure you had ample opportunity to assess Brand's health."

Oh, how she hated admitting that Brand had turned to another! It was a humiliation for which she intended to see Brand pay dearly. Indeed he would pay with his life. As for his simpering Irish mistress, she would see her buried alive in rocks with only her head above Halvdan's famous wall. There she could stay till she died as the birds picked her eyes out! How could Brand prefer this woman from across the sea? And almost equally important, how could her father have wanted to continue his alliance with a man who had so humiliated his daughter! Erica's body began to tense as her anger rose. She thought of her father, and had he been present, she knew she would have plunged the sword into him again.

"I had no more opportunity than you would have had,"

Erica retorted. Her voice was cold and filled with the seeth-ing rage that bubbled just below the surface.

Henrik roared with laughter. "Brand was gone so long from you my beauty, don't try to tell us you didn't spend any time in his bed!"

"Brand is a traitor, and he is bewitched with another," Erica hissed. "The rumors you related are all true. He mur-dered Olaf and took his slave girl."

"I did not say he murdered Olaf," Henrik said, contradict-ing her. "I said Brand defeated Olaf in a contest. It is quite a different matter."

Erica scowled at him, hating to be corrected.

Halvdan banged a huge bone on the table, sending meat and spatters of grease flying. "I did not come here to hear of Brand's sexual tastes! What did you learn that is useful, Erica?"

Erica tried not to be unnerved by Halvdan's sudden display of temper, though she knew how dangerous he could be when angered. "I learned he will attack the castle of Lord Thorgills first."

Halvdan glared back at her, then turned toward Ingrid, who was leaning forward in her chair looking for all the world as though she expected him to chop her head off. Ingrid was a strange woman, Erica thought. She was completely unlike Lord Thorgills and his son. She was thin, and her hair was as mousy as was her demeanor. She looked as if she were fright-ened of her own shadow. Lord Thorgills had left her in charge only because he had no choice and because he knew that Hen-rik would keep an eye on things.

"I'm sure we could repulse any attack," Ingrid said tim-idly. "But I have received a message. My father returns in the early spring. He says he wants to kill Brand himself."

"It is a pleasure he will have to fight for," Erica breathed.

"I should not like to be Brand," Henrik said somewhat too cheerfully. He was perhaps the one person there who did not shudder at the thought and sight of Halvdan. But, she reasoned, he was a man. She glanced at Ingrid. Not even Halvdan would want her.

Halvdan made a grunting noise before he added, "Your father's planned return is good news."

"I fear Brand could raise a formidable force," Henrik said thoughtfully. "I do not think we should be overconfident."

"Perhaps Brand is vulnerable," Erica said slowly. She turned to appease Halvdan, who had seemed angry with her. "Perhaps he is more easily defeated in another way."

"Do not be a tease, Erica. It does not become you." Halvdan's eyes were narrow.

Erica shivered. How loathsome he was . . . and yet powerful. Power could be exciting. How ideal it would be if only Henrik would kill Halvdan and take over his forces. Henrik could be both exciting and powerful. But Halvdan was revolting, and he smelled of death. "I did not intend to tease," she said evenly. "I think the woman holds the key to certain success."

"The woman?" Halvdan questioned. His white-blond brow arched, and his pale blue eyes flickered. They were, Erica noted, eyes almost without pupils.

"The woman for whom he killed Olaf. The Irish princess."

"Have you seen this woman, Erica?"

"I have."

"Tell me about her," Halvdan said, leaning toward her. His eyes did not change, but his tone showed interest.

"She is small, about this tall." Erica made a sign with her hand. "And she has long red hair, very long. And green eyes."

Halvdan smiled, revealing once again his rotten yellow teeth. "And her body?"

"Good, well shaped."

"Surely there is more to her than this—to kill Olaf meant much."

"I saw no more to her than beauty," Erica said coldly.

Halvdan stared at her. It was as if he could see through her, and it made her recoil. "So what are you suggesting?"

"That we kidnap her. Brand will come after her. He will ignore Thorgills's domain. Henrik's and mine as well. Such a plan will allow us to concentrate our forces at Oslo, where the girl will be. He cannot defeat our combined forces on home ground."

Halvdan rubbed his chin with his long bony fingers. "It is a plan that has some merit, but let us explore it."

"Are you certain this woman means so much to him?" Henrik asked.

"I am certain," Erica said.

"So tell me, dear Erica," Halvdan said slowly. "If we can kidnap the girl, why can't we kidnap Brand and rid ourselves of our problem entirely?"

A silence fell over them, and Halvdan extended his white-coated tongue and licked his pale, formless lips. "A woman's plan must always be questioned," he said, leaning back.

"It would be suicide," Erica replied slowly. Oddly, she had been ready for this question. "We could not kidnap Brand without taking a force of men with us, and Ivar's castle is well guarded. We would not succeed."

"How do you purpose to get the girl?" Henrik asked.

"I can get into the castle," Erica said, smiling. "I am, after all, their ally. I will find a way to lure her outside the castle walls. I will have two men waiting—they will take her."

"I like all but one aspect," Halvdan said. "I want the girl kept at Lord Thorgills's fortress. I will bring my forces there and so will you and Henrik. Its location is more defensible, and it will be easier to get the girl there. In any case, Lord Thorgills would wish it so. This way his revenge is far greater."

Ingrid frowned. "When shall you bring her?"

"Soon," Erica replied. "But we will not let her where-abouts be known until we are ready."

Ingrid nodded. "I suppose she cannot escape. It is winter, and she is in a strange land."

Erica smiled. "Just keep her locked up."

"Yes, of course," Ingrid said abstractedly.

"We are agreed," Halvdan said, quaffing down some wine. Then he stood up suddenly, tipping over the bench behind him. He turned to Erica and held out his hand. "Come, I am ready for entertainments."

Erica could not look at Henrik. The wretched bastard was probably smiling. At that moment she envied Ingrid. Plainness could have its advantages.

Deirdre, bundled in furs, stepped gingerly through the snow. Here, beyond the castle walls, it was deep and clean-looking. The wind was still, and the sun was shining on a wonderland of sparkling icicles and tall, snow-covered pines, their branches bending toward the ground. The small lake, which the pines surrounded, glistened as if its surface were covered with diamonds. The ice was thick, and she had watched men walk on it, clearing off the snow.

In a moment Brand appeared. He, too, was dressed for winter. He wore a fur hat that came down over his ears, a warm tunic beneath which he wore leggings with fur wrapped around them. He had a fur cloak, and fur on his hands. These were strange things she had not seen until recently. Brand called them mittens.

"Ah, you've come outside to sample the fine winter air!"

In the last month Deirdre had adopted her own set of rules toward Brand. At first she had tried being silent, but it was impossible. She yearned for someone to talk with, and Ivar, who was pleasant enough, was gone a great deal. He loved to hunt and often left his castle for days at a time. So Deirdre had begun talking to Brand, but only in a friendly way.

She sighed. Being only friendly with him was difficult. No matter how betrayed she felt, she had to admit she still loved him. But he had clearly taken her seriously; he had not come to her bed since that night he had taken her. On the one hand she was relieved, on the other she missed him terribly.

Even so, one night she had approached him and asked him

to reiterate his promise to find and free her brother. She had even made it known that if he so promised, she would sleep with him.

"I do not need to be bribed, my lady. I will keep my promise, and I will free you, too."

She had only murmured a thank-you, certain that now he had returned to Erica, he really did not want her in any case.

Brand strode over to her, thinking how ravishing she looked. Her long red hair hung beneath her white fur hat, and her lips and cheeks had grown pink in the cold air. He wanted her so much! But if she did not trust him, if she could not forgive him for not telling her of Erica, then experience told him not to force her. He had tried that once, but he had resigned himself to waiting. He was quite certain she wanted him, too. He was certain she would, in time, return to his arms.

"Did you hear me?"

"Yes, I heard you. My mind was just wandering. Yes, I had to come outside. It is difficult to stay inside so much."

"The sun will not last for long, one must take advantage of it."

"Why has the snow been cleared from the lake?"

"So I can skate," he answered. "Do you want me to teach you?"

"Skate—do you think I could learn?"

"Of course, and to ski as well."

It seemed an age since she had learned anything new, and so Deirdre smiled and nodded. "Yes, oh yes, I should like to learn."

Brand led her to a small bench, half of which was buried in snow. He signaled one of his men and called out for him to bring an extra pair of skates.

In a few moments the servant returned, carrying four long, carved pieces of bone and long, pointed poles. Brand knelt before her in the snow and attached the bone with leather straps to her leather shoes. Then he attached his own and pulled her to her feet.

"Follow me," he instructed.

They plodded through the snow till they reached the edge of the lake. He stepped onto the lake, and she followed, sliding suddenly.

"Oh!" she called out. But Brand had caught and steadied her.

He laughed. "It is ice!"

"I have never seen ice like this. In my homeland the most one ever sees is a thin crust of ice."

Brand handed her the poles. "These are to propel yourself and to be used for balance as well. If you fall, you can use them to help you get to your feet, too."

With that, he left her standing awkwardly on the lake. He glided off, using his poles. He circled three times and called out laughing, "Come on! Try it! You have nothing to lose but your dignity."

Deirdre called back, "I do not care about my dignity!"

With that she launched out and found her balance within seconds. It was easy! She followed him, picking up speed and feeling quite wonderful as she felt the wind in her face. Then, just as suddenly, she lost her balance and went careening into the big snowdrift by the side of the lake.

Brand laughed heartily and came immediately to help her up. "You ought not go so fast at first."

Deirdre could not help but smile. "You go fast."

"I have been doing this since I was a child, you are just learning."

"I will master this," Deirdre vowed with determination.

"You will," he agreed.

Brand could not help thinking that was why he loved her so. She was not just accomplished, but she wanted to be more so, to face new challenges.

Deirdre broke free of him and launched out again across the lake. "Tomorrow you will teach me to ski," she called out.

"It will take more than one day! It's harder!"

"I will learn," she shouted back.

He smiled, knowing she would, and still praying she would come back to him freely. He knew it was his own prerequisite, but she had to come back on her own—she had to trust him, she had to believe he felt nothing for Erica. His father had always taught him that there could be no life without honor and no love without trust. It was a hard way to live, he thought, as he watched Deirdre disappear into the castle.

Erica moved uneasily, then opened her eyes cautiously. Her body ached, and she stretched and listened. She was on a thick fur which was laid on the stone floor at the foot of the king's bed. He had not allowed her to sleep with him, but had rather relegated her, like a slave, to the floor at the foot of his bed.

The details of the evening came back to her, and she felt vaguely nauseous at the memory. He had made her bathe with him and when they got out, he insisted they swat one another with twigs, as was the custom. But he had beaten her harder than was usual. He had laughed and told her the sight of her red buttocks was too tempting. With that he made her kneel on the floor and he had taken her roughly from behind as if she were a dog. When he was satisfied, he had made her lie down on a fur on the floor at the foot of his bed and instructed her to remain there until given permission to leave.

Erica listened. She was certain he was still asleep. How she wanted to run away! But she dared not. Halvdan demanded obedience, absolute obedience, from all his subjects. To disobey him was to invite an untimely and usually quite horrible death. She had no wish to be his victim when she intended being only his ally. It was, quite naturally, an alliance she hoped would be short-lived. Her long-term plan was to convince Henrik that Halvdan must be killed.

Suddenly she heard Halvdan stir and sit up. "Erica!" he growled.

"I am here, Your Highness."

He smiled meanly. "Of course you are. Stand up!"

She did so, and the fur that covered her dropped to the floor leaving her naked.

"Fetch me breakfast and bring it here. Then lie down on my table."

Erica was sure she had gone pale. Was there no end to his perversions? But she did not hesitate. If angered, there was no telling what he might desire.

Deirdre drank from the silver goblet and studied the model that Brand had built of Lord Thorgills's castle and the surrounding area. He sat in the chair and seemed to be thinking about it.

"It is a good plan," Deirdre finally said. "They will expect an attack by sea, not by land."

"It is a harder route, especially in the spring. In the winter we could have gone by ski and sledge. But still, the element of total surprise will be worth the added time."

For days now she and Brand had been skiing. He had praised her on her ability and quick learning. And it was true. She felt competent enough unless they came to a steep hill. Then sometimes she stumbled and fell. But he had spent much time teaching her to fall and to stand again without removing her skis and starting over.

"How does one travel by skis?" she suddenly asked. "How do you know where you are going, the woods are so thick."

"The trails are marked. They are well-traveled trails, Deirdre, hunting trails. Red cloth is tied to the lower branches of the trees to make certain the traveler stays on the trail. And there are shelters along the way."

"But one cannot cross to Lord Thorgills's now because it is across the sea."

"It can be crossed. The sea is frozen. The islands are close together."

"But you wait till spring to fight."

He nodded. "We must. A few can travel easily in winter,

but not the number needed for battle." Brand drank from his goblet. "Shall we work on hills tomorrow?" he asked, grinning.

Deirdre smiled back. "You just want to see me fall."

His eyes were serious. "No, I want to pick you up."

His words were filled with meaning, but she ignored him. "Tomorrow," she said, "I shall show you."

"I look forward to it," he said with good humor.

They were out of the castle as soon as the weak winter sun brought daylight. Brand made her ski far, and then announced, "This is a fairly steep hill. Shall we try it here?"

"What's in that shack down there?" Deirdre pointed off into the distance.

"It's where we keep the sledges."

She nodded and stood still while looking down the hill, taking its measure. Bravely she dug her pointed poles into the ground and took off down the hill.

Brand followed, his body bent slightly, his head down.

But Deirdre floundered and lost her balance; she fell and slid down the hill, her skis in the air. She came to a resounding stop in a drift by the side of the sledge shack.

Brand eased to a stop and looked down at her. Her cheeks were all red from the snow, and even her lovely long red hair was encrusted with wet, white snow.

He bent down. "Oh, you are a sight. A living snowball."

Deirdre straightened up. "You're too perfect," she said in mock anger. With that she took a handful of snow and pushed it into his face.

"Vixen," he exclaimed with good humor. He, too, took some snow and did the same to her.

Deirdre shrieked as the snow dripped down the inside of her cloak. "Oh, it's gone down my dress!"

Brand laughed and took more snow. "I'll teach you to attack me!" He thrust a handful of snow down her dress and she screamed and struggled to her feet, shaking her fist at him angrily.

Brand grabbed her wrist. "Beauty, I cannot resist!" and he pulled her to him, kissing her savagely as she wriggled in his arms, not fighting, but as hungry as he for their long-denied lovemaking.

Brand bent down and quickly untied her skis, then his own. Free of them, he kissed her again and silently swept her into his arms and kicked open the door of the shed where the sledges were. He closed the door behind them, leaving them in the semidarkness, the only light coming from the many cracks and crevices.

"Brand, I—" Her words were lost as he devoured her mouth with kisses. He laid her down on one of the flat sledges, which was covered with a thick fur. He quickly undid her cloak and tunic, leaving her only in her underdress. Her legs were still bound in fur, but above her knees she wore nothing, and his hand moved quickly over her knees, her thighs, and toward her hidden treasure.

"Brand, Brand. . . ." He lifted her dress and found her nipples hard in the cold air. He took one into his mouth and suckled it, brushing it again and again with his tongue. She moved beneath him and groaned with desire even as he toyed with her other nipple, savoring the hardness of it, and remembering the softness of her hidden valley.

"I love no one else," he breathed. "I told Erica—"

"She said, she said—" Deirdre struggled to answer him, to tell him what Erica had told her.

He kissed her again and returned to her breasts. He could not get enough of her. Her skin was so soft, and even here it seemed to smell of roses. He lifted his mouth long enough to speak. "You must trust me. I don't care what she said. I broke it off, forever, Deirdre, forever. Deirdre, I love only you. I have loved only you since we met. I want to marry you."

Could she trust him? Heaven knew she wanted to trust him. She wanted him more than anything save to be reunited with her brother. But no matter. She could not resist him, and she could not live without him. The past weeks had been horrible, she had dreamt of him every night and yearned for him every day. Neither study nor work distracted her.

His mouth on the tips of her breast bit gently and she wiggled just as his hand moved slowly down her, touching her there in that place, and teasing her till she screamed and clung to him desperately, begging for release. His entry was wonderful, and, where his hand had been, the base of him now moved against her, the coarse hair of his lower body rubbing against her, driving her wild with pleasure, with pent-up desire.

Brand wrapped her in his arms as he began to spill his seed into her, and she, in turn, followed him down from the heights of desire, a desire that brought her body a wondrous tension, followed by a glorious release. She shook in his arms, tears of joy forming in her eyes. It was not their first reunion, but each one seemed better than the last.

"I trust you," she said softly. "Perhaps I have been foolish not to listen to my heart."

"I've missed you, Deirdre. I do love you."

Deirdre snuggled close to him. She did believe him. She had to trust him—she loved him too much not to.

The servant brought more wine and filled each of their goblets to the brim. Ivar leaned back and smiled at Deirdre and Brand. It seemed clear to him that the rift caused by Erica's visit had been mended. Brand was once more cheerful and relaxed, and Deirdre's eyes glowed as did her cheeks.

"You haven't yet seen my completed model," Brand said, looking at Deirdre. "Come, I must show you."

He led her from the table, and Ivar followed, bringing with him the carafe of wine.

In their strategy room Brand had appropriated the entire table, which he had arranged to have brought from the workrooms in the castle cellar. It was a large table, perhaps five feet long and four feet wide.

"Heavens," Deirdre breathed as she looked at it. It was something close to an artistic masterpiece. "I have never seen anything like this."

"Knowing one's ground is half the battle," Brand said. He himself was incredibly proud of it. It had taken hours of his time each day, but when Cnut returned, he and the other chieftains would study it, understanding in detail not only Lord Thorgills's castle and its defenses, but every possible approach to it.

Brand had begun by building a model of the coastline, using stones and rocks. He had indicated the inlets and, farther from the castle, he had indicated the place where the vessels would land.

The castle itself he had reconstructed out of wood, showing its walls, which he had built from stones. Behind, he had made the mountains from mounds of dirt and indicated the location of the streams with strips of cloth.

"Here," he said, indicating an area well to the west of Thorgills's castle, "is where our forces will land. We will move overland, across these hills, and then come down this river. We will attack at night, when we are least expected, from the rear of the castle."

"It's ingenious," Ivar said.

"I believe many of Thorgills's men will leave him and fight with us," Brand said confidently. "We will waste no time. I have yet to work out the plan of attack on Halvdan, but it will happen within days of taking Thorgills's castle.

"I have one request," Ivar said slowly.

"Make it, my friend."

"It concerns Ingrid, Thorgills's daughter."

"She has been left in charge, and carried out his will," Brand reminded him.

"Yes, but she is watched. Lord Thorgills does not trust his own daughter, and I know from experience she is very different from the others of his family. She is a plain, but gentle woman."

"What do you ask?" Brand questioned.

"I ask that she be spared and placed under my protection."

"I have no quarrel with Ingrid," Brand said as he smiled ever so slightly. "Do I detect an interest on your part?"

Ivar smiled. "I have always liked Ingrid. I am no handsome devil such as yourself, Brand. Ingrid would make a good wife."

"If she is in charge, she must have control over my brother," Deirdre said.

Ivar nodded. "If so, I imagine he is well. Ingrid is neither cruel nor cold. She treats slaves well. In fact, she usually ignores them."

Deirdre smiled. "I hope you are right."

Ivar rubbed his chin. "Cnut should return soon."

"Within the month, I hope," Brand said. He did not mention Erica. But of course she had to be briefed, too.

Deirdre studied the model. It was like being a bird and looking down on the land. She could imagine everything, how the mountains made of dirt were real, and how densely covered with pine they were. She could almost hear the roar of the sea on the rocky beach. Brand's model was truly a wonder.

"Wouldn't it be wonderful to have a model of everything—to see the land as the birds see it," Deirdre said.

Brand laughed. "Perhaps I shall build a model of this place next winter, when we have peace and Lord Thorgills, Henrik, and Halvdan are no longer a threat."

"Peace," Deirdre sighed. She dreamt of peace and being reunited with her brother.

The snow was now several feet deep, and the lakes, and even the ocean shore, were frozen solid so that one could easily skate or sledge across large distances fairly quickly.

"You're amazing!" Brand called out as he watched his fur-clad Irish beauty ski down the hill, navigating her way around the trees. "It's as if you grew up on them as I did."

Deirdre laughed. "I practice every day, Brand."

"And your hard work shows."

She glided to a stop a few feet from him. "It's good to be outdoors; I think I'm getting used to the cold."

"You are as acclimated as a winter rabbit," he joked.

"I know you have told me about travel in winter, but I would like to experience it for myself. I'm curious."

"You are always curious. I'll tell you what—Cnut will not be back for at least another week. I'll take you on a journey inland to Ivar's hunting lodge. You'll see how we travel and survive."

Deirdre put her arms around him, and he bent to kiss her cold pink cheeks. "It sounds like a wonderful adventure," she said, laughing.

"It will be a cold adventure," he replied, "but good for our health."

"First," Brand instructed, "we must make a pack that can be carried on our backs while we ski. If we were going a greater distance, we might take a sledge, but in this case we will take only our packs."

"But a horse could not pull a sledge in such deep snow."

"No. It would be a flat sledge with handles at the side. A man would ski and push it. It glides easily over snow, so not much strength is required."

Deirdre listened and watched as Brand selected the items to go into their packs. "First, flint."

"Of course, to start fires," Deirdre said. "One would take that if they were going anywhere."

"And a bundle of sticks," he said.

She frowned. "But there are many sticks in the woods."

"Not dry sticks. You need these to start your fire. Once

the fire is going you can use wood gathered from the forest. Each night, you dry out more sticks by leaving them close to the fire. That way you always have some dry wood."

"You're clever, Brand."

He shook his head. "These are skills we all learn at our father's knee. This is a hard land, Deirdre." He laid a pouch on the square fur. "And a wineskin of honey."

"No other food?"

He shook his head. "Only a trapline and a bow and arrows. It is easy to trap in winter, small animals leave tracks in the snow. Most importantly, an ice knife," he said, laying the formidable knife down. Its blade curved, and its handle was made of carved bone. "With this you can carve a hole in the ice, and with this line, baited with a bit of meat, it is easy to catch fish. They're hungry in the winter, and the lakes are teeming with them."

Deirdre watched with interest as he included a small tool with a wooden handle and a metal base. "For digging," he said. "You will see, we'll use it to build our shelter at night."

He wrapped both packs in double squares of fur and tied them securely with leather straps. "These," he told her, "we will carry on our backs, our arms are thus free for our ski poles."

"I'm looking forward to this," she smiled.

"Most women would not. But it is wise you learn how to survive."

"Your people have so many tools—like the tool with which you dig. My people have such an instrument, but its end is made of wood and breaks easily. Of course, they had many things made of metal in King Alfred's kingdom."

"It's called a *schaufel,"* he told her.

"Shovel," she repeated, struggling with his pronunciation. He laughed at her gently. "Almost."

He reached out for her and pulled her to him. "Before we launch out on our trip through the snows of winter, sit by the fire with me and let me tell you about our eternity—let me spin you a tale of the tree of life which reaches to the heavens."

He sat on the fur rug before the fire and pulled her down next to him. She nestled in his arms. "Will we go to Heorot when this battle is over?"

"No, it is deserted and closed. I have no desire to remain in Scandinavia at all. It is Lord Thorgills and Halvdan today who war and sap the blood of honest men in taxes. Tomorrow it will be another. I have told you about a land across the ocean where every man has his say in *The Thing* and where women and children are protected. There is farmland."

"The land where hot water comes out of the ground?"

"Yes. I want to take you there. I want to raise our family there. I've had enough of feuding."

Deirdre snuggled next to him. "I love you," she said simply.

Deirdre and Brand left early in the morning, and before the sun set in early afternoon Brand demonstrated how to catch a fish. After lunch, they skied on, and since the moon was full and the stars bright, they continued even after night fell.

Around eight o'clock, Brand suggested they stop. He chose a spot well sheltered by trees and dug a circle in the snow, piling the displaced snow high around the circle to make a wall. While he dug, he sent her to collect twigs and some large pieces of wood nearby. When she returned, Deirdre found their nest almost complete. With the dry twigs, Brand started a fire, and soon the large pieces could be added. As they were a little damp, they sent billows of steamy smoke into the atmosphere and warmed the area around their little circle. From the double furs around their packs, Brand made them a bed, into which they snuggled together after they cooked the fish and ate it.

"I thought the ground would be colder," Deirdre said as they lay side by side.

"The bottom layer is sealskin. It keeps out moisture and is warm indeed."

He kissed her, and in a moment she felt his hand exploring beneath her furs. It was warm on her skin, warm and taunting.

"We'll freeze if we take off our clothes," she whispered.

He bit her ear gently. "No need to take off our clothes," he told her.

Deirdre tossed in his arms as he toyed with her. It was oddly exciting with their clothes on, and his skill in love-making was proved when they came together through various openings in their garments. Afterward they lay in each other's arms, warm and glowing, while their fire burned on, keeping away animals of the night and warming them as well.

Henrik lay in his bed and watched as Erica dressed. She had long, silky legs, and when they slept together, she wrapped them around his waist. "It is good you came here before returning to Ivar's."

"Timing is all important," Erica said. "One does not want to give Brand time to act before Lord Thorgills and his army return."

"You have a good military mind, Erica. And when you combine it with the hatred of a woman scorned, you are nothing short of dangerous. Frankly, I am glad I am not Brand."

Erica's eyes narrowed. "If Thorgills does not do it first, I shall cut off his—"

"Now, now . . . did you care so much?"

Erica did not answer. It was not really a matter of caring, it was more that he had chosen someone over her. No one seemed to understand that. Her father hadn't understood it. But now her father did not matter.

"Never mind explaining," Henrik said with a wave of his

hand. "But what I do not understand is how you allow Halvdan to humiliate you, and do nothing, but Brand must pay and pay dearly."

"Halvdan is my king, I must obey him."

"If you had your way, you would obey no one. You are afraid of Halvdan."

"And you are not?"

"I respect his power."

"You are not a woman. I have seen what happens to women who scorn him."

"What happens to women who do not?"

She looked away. The acts Halvdan made her perform were indescribable. She hated him. And she hated having to sleep at the foot of his bed. He treated her like a slave. "He's demanding," she answered. The truth was far too disgusting to recount. But she had no intention of discussing this with Henrik, at least not yet.

"When will your father return?"

How she wanted to say never. How she wanted to tell him about her father. "I don't know. He is in the east collecting riches. He is insatiable."

"Perhaps something has happened to him. He did not take many men with him; he left most of them under your command."

Henrik was treading dangerously close to a truth she had kept hidden. She shrugged. "My father is not called the Wolf for nothing. He can take care of himself."

"I'm sure," Henrik said thoughtfully. Then, as a matter of curiosity, "What will you do to the girl?"

"After her usefulness as bait is ended, I shall ask Halvdan to stone her into the wall alive and let the birds pick at her till she dies. I'm certain he will want to amuse himself with her first."

Henrik watched her as she spoke. Her mouth curled slightly, and her eyes narrowed. *I was just beginning to feel sorry for her,* he thought. "I'm glad I'm not your enemy," he laughed.

Erica spun around. "Do not mock me, or you will be my enemy, Henrik."

"Dear, dear. Halvdan did put you in a bad mood."

Erica turned away. One at a time, she thought. Eventually she would be rid of them all.

Fourteen

Ingrid, her hair gathered up in a thin braid, was dressed plainly in a gray overdress. Her skin was a little sallow from being indoors, and she felt less than elated when she looked at the debris around her.

The great hall of the castle was littered with the mess made following her father's return. Where once there had been peace and a modicum of quiet, there was now eating, drinking, raucous laughter, swearing, and much snoring.

She sailed through the corridors, shaking her head and wishing that her father and his men would soon leave. Not that he had ever been a real father, she thought miserably.

Olaf's mother died in childbirth and Lord Thorgills had married again almost immediately. Olaf was four when she was born, and her mother, much mistreated by her father, died when she was eight. Lord Thorgills had not married again. Instead he had a procession of mistresses, none of whom remained long and all of whom loathed him. "But none as much as I," Ingrid whispered to herself. Olaf had begun mistreating her when she was only ten, and she remembered with horror his nightly visits to her bed. She had tried to tell her father, but he did not care. Olaf was never punished, and Olaf continued to abuse her for years.

When Olaf had left for Dublin with her father she had been overjoyed. Indeed, she had prayed to the gods of the sea to take their vessel and maroon them on some distant

isle from which there was no escape. But the gods had not
seen fit to answer her prayers. Not that Olaf would return to
molest her again—for that she apparently had Lord Brand
to thank. Still, her father alone was enough. She could only
stay out of his way as much as possible.

She thought of Charlotte and was glad she had sent the poor
girl to stay with Alan so her father's soldiers would not bother
her as the guards had begun to. It seemed clear to Ingrid that
Alan and Charlotte were perfect for one another, and so she
vowed to allow them a modicum of happiness under her pro-
tective wing. Not that her protection would be worth much if
her father discovered Charlotte. Nonetheless, if her father
asked Halvdan about her leadership, he would hear that she
had been loyal and had, in his place, taken part in the plans
to defeat Brand, Ivar, Cnut, and the other usurpers. Not that
she liked the plans. And what was she to do to help this Irish
princess who would soon be brought? She cursed herself for
not sending a message to Ivar about Erica's plan to kidnap
the Irish princess. But as soon as her father arrived, she had
sent him a message. There was really nothing to do but wait.
I shall be useful when the time is right, Ingrid promised herself.

Ingrid opened the door and looked in on her father. He
was still asleep; last evening's drunkenness had not yet worn
off. She closed the door and continued her rounds. Once
again she felt thankful that Olaf was dead. He was vile, and
she felt nothing but relief that he would return no more.

Twice now she had explained the plan hatched at Henrik's
hunting lodge to her father. He did not seem happy, wishing
instead to storm Ivar's castle and skin Brand alive. "But
Halvdan insists," she repeated over and over. In the end, he
had growled at her to return to her loom, and he would care
for matters of state.

Ingrid passed through the castle kitchen and stopped to
look outside. Across the expanse of snow a thin line of smoke
curled out of the chimney of the sod house where the artist

and scribe, Alan, was working on the stories of Odin. Deciding that she missed talking with Charlotte, she donned her winter cloak and boots. There was no need to remain here. Her father was back and in charge. Besides, he would not wake till late afternoon.

Alan opened the door and bowed as Ingrid came in.

"Do you wish me back in the castle, mistress?" Charlotte asked, a slight tremor in her voice.

"No, not at all. I just came to see you." She glanced at Alan, who looked ill at ease and awkward. "Please don't think of yourself as my slave," Ingrid murmured. "Just—oh, please, sit down or do what you were doing."

"Tea, mistress?" Charlotte asked.

Ingrid nodded and sat down. She could smell the peculiar odor of Alan's paints.

"Is it good to have your father back?" Charlotte asked.

Ingrid shook her head. "It's horrible. And he is in a fearful fighting mood. There will be war."

"War?" Alan questioned.

"War," Ingrid repeated. She shook her head and sipped from the tea Charlotte had brought. "Brand, son of our former king, Jarls, killed my brother, Olaf."

Alan's senses heightened, and he quickly sat down. "Olaf is dead?"

"My half brother. I did not like him. He was cruel."

Alan felt a wave of elation. Deirdre was not with Olaf! But of course she might be with someone equally as bad.

"When did this Brand kill him?"

"In a contest, a sort of duel on the Isle of Man. Brand ran away with Olaf's prize, an Irish princess named Deirdre."

Alan dropped his tin cup, and it fell to the table with a clang. His face went white. "Deirdre? Deirdre is my beloved sister."

"Oh, dear," Charlotte said sadly.

"Brand has taken her—it is said he intends to marry her.

But Erica, who was once Brand's betrothed, has betrayed him. She is kidnapping Deirdre and bringing her here in order to bring Brand to his knees. Brand has gathered a formidable force and will attack us. Eventually your sister will be killed. Erica will not let her live."

Conflicting emotions filled Alan. He could be reunited with his beloved sister only to have her yanked away from him and killed.

Tears had begun to form in Ingrid's eyes. "And Lord Ivar has joined forces with Brand and Cnut. Ivar is—well, we have known each other since we were children and though I am plain and do not think he loves me, I love him with all my heart. But they will all be entrapped—Brand, Cnut, Ivar—"

Charlotte put her arm around Ingrid. "Not if you help us, Ingrid," she said softly. "If we can somehow free Deirdre and send her back to Brand, things will not work out as planned."

Alan smiled at Charlotte, his heart soaring. She was right, there was a chance.

Ingrid looked from one to the other. "It's winter. I don't know how we can manage."

"Is there no way to warn Brand that Deirdre will be kidnapped?" Alan asked.

"It is too late, but I could send a messenger to Ivar revealing their other plans."

Alan nodded. "It is a beginning," he said.

Deirdre left Erica, Brand, and Ivar with three other chieftains inside the castle where Brand was instructing them on the plan of attack. She was familiar with it and did not feel the need to stay. The morning sun was bright, and she had the urge to go outside and feel the wind on her face.

Not even Erica's presence made her ill at ease. In fact, Deirdre noticed that Erica had ignored Brand and not even tried to speak with him alone. Perhaps Erica sensed that she and Brand had made peace and that she believed him.

Deirdre took a well-known trail and began to follow it. It ended by the lake not far from the sledge house, where once they had made love. Brand had warned her not to wander too far alone, but the weather was bright and the day inviting. So many days were gray that she now reveled in the sunshine as she plodded on, using her poles to move across the white snow.

She wore a hat with a special overhang sewn onto it to shield her eyes from the glare of the sun on the snow. "It can blind you," Brand had warned her.

It was quite wonderful, Deirdre thought as she moved along. She loved skiing with Brand, but she also appreciated being alone in the silence of the deep woods. Here and there she saw rabbit tracks or the spoor of some other small animal. It was peaceful here and there was, she believed, a special kind of communication with nature when one was in the forest to enjoy one's self rather than to hunt for food.

Every day since the arrival of the chieftains and Erica she had gone out skiing alone. It was far better than sitting hour after hour at her loom. That activity was better suited to afternoon, when the sun had set and darkness enveloped the white world outside.

"Yes," she said aloud to no one. "This is invigorating." It was most assuredly a winter wonderland. Tiny pawprints paralleled her trail, and crow's feet left patterns in the unmarked snow.

Deirdre stopped short and stared into the woods. There, some twenty yards away stood a doe, its large brown eyes staring at her. It stood stark-still, and so did Deirdre. This was an unexpected bonus! Brand had told her there were many deer in the forest, but she had not yet seen one. "That," he told her, "was because we are always together and talking. They can hear us and run away."

Suddenly, Deirdre was aware of a dark shadow behind her;

the deer started and ran quickly into the dense bush. Deirdre whirled around to see two men and a sledge. She opened her mouth to scream, but her scream was muffled when one man grabbed her and quickly gagged her with a long scarf. The other put a hood over her head as she struggled wildly.

Deirdre felt faint with the sudden darkness and absence of air. She fought with all her might, but they were too strong and lifted her easily and carried her off across the snow on a sledge. *Brand! Brand!* she screamed in her mind. Then, in a moment, she passed out.

It was late afternoon when Brand returned to the planning room. Cnut was already present, as was Erica. Brand peered out into the courtyard, wondering, where Deirdre was. Of course the days were getting longer now, so she was probably still skiing. He smiled to himself. She had taken to the northern climate as if born here.

"How is your lovely Deirdre?" Cnut asked. He turned to glance at Erica's expression and was rewarded with a withering twist of her lower lip. Cnut did not smile, but he wanted to. He had never liked Erica and, indeed, did not trust her. Brand was a fortunate man on two accounts the way Cnut saw it. First, he had found Deirdre and, second, he had rid himself of Erica.

"Skiing I expect. Or perhaps skating. Deirdre can't decide which she likes best," Brand said proudly. It pleased him that she adored winter activities so much.

"Is there so much snow in Ireland?" Erica asked, arching her brow.

"There is hardly any. More rain than anything else."

"Did she learn to ski in Wessex?"

Brand laughed. Except for the far north, there was mostly rain all over the island of Britannia. "No, I taught her only recently. She learns very quickly."

Erica averted her eyes. How she hated it when he spoke

of Deirdre's talents. His eyes fairly shone. If he only knew of her plans for his beloved Deirdre! In the meantime, she reminded herself to be careful. It had been boring as boring could be, but she had stayed with Cnut for the noon meal. Indeed, she had been extremely careful to remain in sight of Cnut, Ivar, or Brand at all times. If she went missing, too, they might suspect her. *No,* she thought happily, *I have planned this well.* Even if they searched her vessel, which was tied below the castle's lower gates, they would find nothing. A second boat lay at anchor three miles north of the castle. That was the vessel that would take Brand's precious Deirdre to Lord Thorgills and dear King Halvdan.

"Where is Ivar?" Brand asked, looking about.

"A servant summoned him. He should be back soon," Cnut explained.

Brand nodded. "We have important matters to discuss this afternoon."

"More strategy? Brand, you plan too well," Erica said. "It is not our way—we fight and we win or we lose."

"Let the gods decide. Is that your theory, Erica?"

"Yes."

"I think it prudent to plan for all contingencies. The gods smile on the man who thinks for himself. I'm sure your father plans all his encounters."

Erica smiled sweetly. In fact, her father had not planned well at all. He had been unable to discern her ambition—but he was gone now and of no concern to her. Still, she could not reveal herself so she feigned boredom and shrugged. "I have not concerned myself with my father's plans. I have indeed pledged myself to you without his knowing."

"One can only admire your independence," Cnut muttered as he turned away. Erica annoyed him—no, it was more than that. He found her irritating and did not trust her. Indeed, he wondered why Brand did, especially since he had confessed his love for Deirdre. Cnut decided he did not believe Erica was unaffected by the sudden turn of events in her life. She was, after all, to have married Brand. And there was, in his mind, the lingering question of Radnor's long voyage. He had been gone far longer than any of his compatriots expected. Something could have happened to him, but somehow Cnut doubted that. Radnor was both cunning and cautious and would not overstep his reach. What struck Cnut as truly unusual was the fact that no one had seen Radnor or returned bearing messages from him. Where once Radnor the Wolf had reigned supreme, now there was only Erica. Cnut turned away from her, but he decided to speak privately with the others about his doubts.

"A messenger has come," Ivar said, as he rushed into the room somewhat breathlessly.

Erica said nothing, but her curiosity was immediately aroused. "And what message might he bear?" she asked.

"Lord Thorgills has returned," Ivar said.

"So soon!" Erica said, hoping her expression did not reveal her relief. Yes, it was perfect. Lord Thorgills would be home when her men arrived with Deirdre. He would understand what to do far better than Ingrid, who was, in her opinion, a somewhat stupid girl.

"The weather must have improved for him to have traveled now," Brand observed.

"You don't seem surprised," Cnut commented.

"I'm not. In fact I'm glad he's back to defend his castle himself. I did not like the thought of attacking when only his daughter was there."

"I can assure you she is well protected," Erica hissed. "More so than she is worth."

Ivar shot Erica a wicked look, but she had turned away and was talking only to Brand. "In any case, when Lord Thorgills is away, Henrik runs all. Ingrid has no mind for these matters."

"No matter," Brand said. "Our plan stands."

"Do we know how many men returned with Lord Thorgills?" Erica asked.

Ivar shook his head. "The message does not say."

Erica burst into laughter. "You have an ill-educated messenger, dear Ivar. That is the most important bit of information of all."

Ivar just stared back at her, trying to control himself. Well, there were things she did not know. *And now,* he thought, *she will never know them.*

"It is a pity we don't know how many ships he brought," Brand said. "But we know the character of our enemy, and that is what is important."

Cnut leaned back. "And now for our decision," he said.

Ivar sat down, and so did Brand. Erica left the window and sat down as well, draping herself over a chair so that most of her left leg was exposed to the thigh, offering whatever little distractions she could provide.

"I've given this matter some thought," Brand said. "I think it wise to consider who will be in charge when we're victorious. This is a matter I discussed first with Ivar, when I arrived."

Erica laughed. "Are we not just going to divide the spoils as usual?"

"I think not," Brand said firmly. "Halvdan is an unjust king and an unjust man. He governs badly. But he has united Norwegian and Swedish factions—and this period of peace has been beneficial to us all."

"He and Lord Thorgills defeated your father," Cnut reminded Brand. "Surely you do not intend mercy?"

"I do not need a reminder of the past," Brand said. "But a secure future is more important than the past. Hear me out."

They all fell silent. Erica continued to stare at him. What was he thinking? More important, how would it affect her?

"Continuity of Halvdan's line, the Yngling Dynasty, would guarantee the loyalty of his subjects and thus prevent an uprising."

"Are you suggesting his son?" Cnut asked, lifting both brows.

"He's nothing but a small simpering brat!" Erica said in an angry tone.

"Harald is said to be a smart lad, well aware of his father's cruelty. I am suggesting that young Harald rule with Cnut and Ivar as his chief advisors and that there be regular meetings of *The Thing* in order that laws may be made and order kept among the chieftains."

"And you and I Brand? What do we get out of this?" Erica asked.

"I am leaving Denmark and Heorot forever. I will go to the new world with Deirdre. You, Erica, have a voice in *The Thing,* at least until your father returns. Most of all, you get peace."

"I object to this!" Erica said loudly.

"I think it's a good idea," Cnut put in. He enjoyed the look on Erica's face. Doubtless she had envisaged herself with all of Halvdan's wealth and vast store of gold and jewels.

"I, too, think it best," Ivar added. "Of course it gives us greater support. There are many who will fight to end a tyranny, but not if they believe it will be replaced by another tyranny. This is why the first question I asked Brand involved what he wanted to gain personally from this revolt."

Brand looked at Erica without emotion. "Well, Erica, that makes it three to one. Harald shall be given his father's throne."

Erica did not answer, but rather gave them all dirty looks.

Her position did not shock Brand. Since his return he had been surprised and deeply distressed by the change in her. She seemed selfish and mean. He remembered her far differently. How glad he was that fate had intervened in his life. Erica was not a woman he would want for a wife.

Brand stood up. "I'm going to look for Deirdre," he said.

Ivar too stood. "I'll go with you," he said smiling. "I have need of some fresh air."

Together they left the meeting room and headed down the stone steps at the back of the castle. As soon as they were out of earshot of the others, Ivar said, "There are things I must tell you, Brand."

"I sensed as much when you followed me."

"I do know with how many men Lord Thorgills returned. He came in four ships and brought four hundred men."

Brand frowned. "You do not trust the others?"

"I trust Cnut. I do not trust Erica."

A month ago—even a week ago, Brand knew he would have argued that she was completely trustworthy. In fact, he had. But now he himself wondered. She behaved strangely— even angrily. "We'll tell Cnut privately and make our arrangements as necessary. We won't tell Erica."

"There is something else," Ivar said slowly.

Brand smiled. "Tell me."

"I asked for Ingrid to be protected. I must tell you that this valuable information came from her. The messenger was from Ingrid."

Brand breathed out slowly. "It is a great crime to betray one's father."

Ivar nodded. "Lord Thorgills is a vile man. He allowed Olaf to abuse Ingrid in a way which is against our laws and our code. She has turned against him justly."

"I see," Brand said softly. "Poor Ingrid."

"I love her," Ivar confessed. "Her heart is beautiful."

Brand smiled. "She'll be protected, I promise you."

"Do not confide in Erica until we find out what is happening."

"I will accept your advice."

They reached the outer courtyard, and Brand began to call for Deirdre. But there was no answer. "It's getting dark," he said anxiously. He sat down and so did Ivar. Both quickly put on skis and Brand led the way as they followed Deirdre's tracks.

* * *

Deirdre sucked in air, filling her lungs and blinking as her eyes adjusted to the light.

"No need to keep you in the dark now," one of her captors said. He was a burly man, with a reddish beard and a steel helmet. "It won't do you any good to scream. We're far from where you were taken, and in a few moments we'll be at sea."

They were on a small vessel, the sort that was used for moving from island to island. Deirdre felt the motion as it was pushed into the water, and in a few seconds, she knew they were in the fjord, and the rowers had begun to row. She shook her head; wherever she was going, she was glad the first part of her journey was ended. She had been gagged and hooded and put onto a sledge. They had moved swiftly over the snow, and her ride had been uncomfortable in the extreme as it was not only a sickening bumpy ride, but her air was restricted. Now her hood had been removed and the gag taken from her mouth. Still, her wrists were tied behind her back and her legs were tied at the ankles. She was lying on her side on a wide, crude bench.

"Where are you taking me?" she demanded.

"To Lord Thorgills," one of them answered.

Lord Thorgills—Alan was there, somewhere. If only she could see him. But she decided not to mention Alan or even think about him for the moment.

"He had me kidnapped?"

"We're under orders from Erica, the daughter of Radnor."

"Erica—" Deirdre breathed her name and felt sick. Erica was privy to everything! Brand trusted her! Yet it was apparent she was loyal to Lord Thorgills. It seemed clear that Brand was walking into a trap! "And I am the bait," she whispered. Deirdre looked up toward the sky. As if he were sitting next to her, she heard her father's last words to her. "Keep your wits about you." Her father was right. Fear muddled the mind just when you needed all your intelligence and guile. *I will not fear,* Deirdre promised herself. She turned her head to the guard. "Please let me sit up, I shall be ill if I lie down." Her voice was soft and she looked into his eyes.

The red-beard laughed. "Sure, untie her. Where can she go?"

The smaller of the two men untied her wrists and ankles and Deirdre pulled herself into an upright position. "Thank you," she said.

"She's pretty," the smaller one observed as he ran his tongue around his mouth.

The red-beard pinched her cheek. "Pity we have orders to leave her alone."

Deirdre breathed a sigh internally. Of course they were probably only to leave her alone so that Lord Thorgills could decide her fate. He would certainly see her as partially to blame for Olaf's death.

"How long will it take us to get there?" she asked, aware that it was vital for her to understand distances. If the chance to escape arose, she vowed she would take it and try to get back to warn Brand—in fact, it was all she could think of.

"Only a day. The wind is good."

Deirdre closed her eyes and thought of Brand's model. She could imagine everything and see it in her mind's eye. "You mean we'll be there tomorrow?"

They both laughed. "Yes, and so will the King Halvdan. He comes to welcome Lord Thorgills."

Halvdan—Deirdre thought about what she had heard of the man. He was said to be cruel in the extreme and Brand had told her he had strange sexual tastes. "Too strange to discuss," he had said.

God help me, Deirdre thought. *I must truly keep my wits about me.*

Brand stopped short. "Look, her ski tracks stop! Sledge marks come from over there."

Ivar swore under his breath. "The sledge must have come from the same direction in which they leave—see, there is overlap here. They must have tried to remain in the same tracks so there would only be one set."

Brand nodded his agreement. He felt ill inside. A terrible picture was taking shape in his mind.

Ivar looked at his friend and knew what he was thinking. "Let's follow the tracks," he suggested. "Perhaps they will give us a clue."

Together they followed the sledge tracks.

"Thank God the night's bright," Ivar said. It had been dark for over half an hour.

"Here!" Brand said. "The tracks turn toward the shore."

They turned as well, and in a few moments were at the edge of the thick woods and facing a rock-strewn shore.

Brand took off his skis and ran gingerly across the rocks. "Here! I can see the marks. There was a vessel here!"

Ivar joined him and put his arm around his shoulders. "Someone has taken her, my friend. Someone who knew her value to you."

Brand could do nothing but stare out to sea. He felt completely numb. "Who would do this?" he wondered.

"I would suspect Erica had she not been with us. I know no one left her vessel—I confess I left guards to watch it."

"How very shrewd of you, Ivar. I would not have thought of doing that."

"I told you, I don't trust her."

"But she was with us and no one left her ship—so who?"

Ivar shook his head. "We must think how this will change our plans."

"We will carry on. I would die for Deirdre, but I can only get her back if I go after her."

"And if Erica is involved, she does not know of the change in our plans," Ivar said.

"We must watch her carefully," Brand said slowly. "Very carefully."

* * *

Erica stood on the balcony watching as Ivar and Brand trekked back on their skis in the moonlight. How wonderfully revealing men were! Brand was somewhat hunched over, hardly his usual posture. He looked defeated even from this distance. As well he should, she thought triumphantly. Erica smiled and turned to go downstairs. *I shall be at the door waiting anxiously,* she decided.

Erica reached the bottom of the stairs just as they came in. "Where is Deirdre?" she asked, with just the proper tone of concern in her voice.

"Disappeared," Brand muttered.

"Taken," Ivar said more pointedly.

"Disappeared? Taken? I do not understand," Erica exclaimed, looking into Brand's face.

"She has disappeared. She was skiing, and she has disappeared."

"Well, darling, she was your slave, maybe she ran away."

Brand scowled at Erica. "She was my lover and soon to be my wife. She would not run away."

Erica shrugged and arched her well-shaped brow. "Why not?"

Brand could not say it. He did not even want to talk with Erica. She had become someone he did not know. She was a strange, devious woman. "I have things to do," he told her as he brushed past her with Ivar in his wake. Perhaps Cnut had some idea—perhaps the three of them could work something out, make a new plan. He only knew he had to do something soon. Knowing Deirdre had been taken by the forces allied against them was unbearable.

Erica watched Brand and narrowed her eyes. Well, little Deirdre would not warm his bed tonight. *Perhaps I will go to him later—he will be lonely and I can comfort him.*

Cnut was waiting patiently when Ivar and Brand returned. "Did you find her?" he asked.

"She's gone," Brand said. "I think she's been kidnapped." He closed the door and turned the lock. "I don't want Erica here—I don't trust her."

"Nor do I," Cnut said. "But then you know that."

"Still, no men left her vessel, and she was with us when Deirdre disappeared," Ivar reminded them.

"Erica has been here and there. She moves like the wind. Could her father have something to do with this?"

Brand leaned against the fireplace. "Perhaps," he allowed. But after a moment of thoughtfulness, he shook his head. "I really don't think so."

"We have time, Brand. Lord Thorgills will wait for us to attack, or he will make an offer using Deirdre as bait. Let me go to Radnor's without Erica's knowledge. Let me see what I can find out," Cnut suggested.

Brand nodded. "Yes. Go."

Cnut smiled. "I will gather my things and be gone within the hour."

Brand lay awake in his bed. He was used to Deirdre next to him. He was so familiar with her softness, so warmed by her responses to him, that he felt deserted and alone. He tossed restlessly; if they hurt her, he would kill them! But he forced himself not to think of such things. He could not allow his imagination to run wild.

Suddenly in the darkness he heard a noise. Brand looked up and, to his surprise, saw Erica moving quietly across the room. She was nude, and her body glistened white in the half-light.

He sat up and she stopped, standing stock-still like a cat. "What are you doing here?" he asked.

"I came to comfort you, Brand. There was a time when—"

"The time is long gone," he replied coldly.

She lit the lamp and stood at the foot of the bed, displaying the long white legs leading to her blond mound and, above that, her flat stomach and slender waist. Her breasts were heavy—far heavier than Deirdre's.

"Is it a time long gone?" Erica asked, cupping her breast in her own hands and leaning forward toward him. "You used to nurse them and kiss them, Brand. I cannot believe you would turn them away—would turn me away."

Her voice was syrupy, and she had moved closer, close enough that he could smell the musky aroma of her body. "Come to me," she breathed.

"No," he answered.

Her expression did not change. "Brand, if she returns, we will not speak of this night. Just one night, a farewell if you like."

"I would rather be alone than with you," he said, deliberately choosing the words that he knew would be clear. "Leave me, Erica, or I shall escort you out."

Her face flushed a bright red and her blue eyes narrowed. "I hate you, you bastard."

"Go away," he said wearily.

"You need me, Brand. You need my father's men."

Brand inhaled. "There are many things I need, Erica. You have none of them. If you choose not to fight at our side, it is your decision."

"I shall go directly to Halvdan and tell him everything!"

"Your vessel is under guard; you will go nowhere."

Her expression twisted, and suddenly she set upon him, beating him with her fists and kicking with her bare legs. "I hate you!" she screamed. "I hate all of you!"

Brand shielded his face and scrambled from the bed. Once on his feet, her blows were easier to deflect.

"I will kill you!" she shrieked.

Brand moved aside. She was surprisingly strong, but fortunately she was unclothed, which made her more vulnerable. At least he knew she had no concealed weapons. Of course, he himself was covered only by a loincloth.

He ducked and then moved aside again. Her fists were

doubled and she was pounding and kicking. He slapped her
hard across the face and grabbed her arm, twisting it so that
she screamed in pain. She stopped flailing and panted heavily.

He forced her forward till he came to the large bowl in
which he had washed before going to bed. The water was now
cold and he pushed her face down into it. She came up cursing
and sputtering. "Perhaps that will cool you off, Erica."

"Bastard! Son of a whore!" she screamed. He bent her
arm a little harder and forced her to the door. He opened the
door and threw her out into the hall, slamming and bolting
the door behind her. He waited. It was silent. She would lick
her wounds—mental and otherwise—and return to her room.

He inhaled and wiped the blood off his face where she
had scratched him. "I hate all of you," she had said. Did she
mean all men? Was she insane to have behaved so? Again
he thought of her father. Cnut was gone, so he could not tell
him of her behavior. Still, he knew she had been drinking.
No doubt by morning her senses would return. If she still
wanted to leave, he would not stop her.

Fifteen

It was a gray day, but the rapidly moving clouds did not bring rain as it appeared they might. The vessel slowed, and oarsmen pulled their oars from the water allowing the ship to drift closer to the rocks. But were they to anchor here? There was no beach, and no wharf.

Deirdre looked up and saw the fortress. So, this was the castle of Lord Thorgills, Deirdre thought as she studied the gray stone edifice. The vessel sailed close to the side of the cliff, then rounded a jutting rock and sailed between two enormous slabs of stone, seemingly entering the mountainside. Her mouth opened in surprise and wonder. It was a huge, hidden grotto, and in the dank murky interior, two vessels lay at anchor. This grotto had not been on Brand's model, and she wondered if he knew of it.

Deirdre blinked in the semidarkness and shivered because of the sudden dampness. She made a face at the smell as well. It was dank, and the odor was most unpleasant. Perhaps, because it was sheltered, the servants emptied the chamber pots into this water. That would certainly account for the unsavory aroma.

On the sides of the cave's stone walls, great torches burned slowly. But they only gave partial light, and everywhere shadows danced like a chorus of ghosts on the rough stone. Here and there water ran down the rock and into the black water of this hidden grotto.

The vessel on which Deirdre entered the grotto was tied with a chain to a huge rock. A wide wooden plank was set between the gently rocking ship and a stone platform that led to a narrow stone staircase.

Deirdre was made to walk across the plank. Then, with one guard in front of her carrying a torch, and the other behind, she climbed the staircase. At the top, a wooden door gave access to the inner recesses of the fortress. Her fur hat and cloak were taken from her by a silent servant, and Deirdre was marched down long, empty corridors, and finally into a large, warm room not unlike the meeting room in Ivar's castle.

Deirdre looked around uneasily. There were two men. One was a large man with high, leather boots and enormously wide trousers which billowed above the leather binding on his legs. He wore a long tunic and gold chains around his neck.

The other man was an ostensibly frightening sight, his physical condition pitiful. He was tall and skeletal with strange eyes. He smiled wickedly at her even as his narrow yellow-ringed eyes seemed to be assessing her worth.

"I am Lord Henrik," the stocky man in the ballooning trousers said. "And this, my dear Princess Deirdre, is the king of all Scandinavia, His Highness, King Halvdan."

"The Black," Halvdan added with a sneer. "For my black and unforgiving heart. My, you are indeed a pretty little present. I shall enjoy you, and enjoy watching you die."

Deirdre absolutely forced herself to stand tall and not react to his brutal threat. With apparent fearlessness, she stepped up to Halvdan, who was not black, but rather yellow with jaundice. "I'm sure you would rather wait and kill me when you can make Brand watch," she said calmly. "In that way you will enjoy it twice as much."

Deirdre's boldness was rewarded as Halvdan's expression changed suddenly. Clearly she had confused him with her suggestion. He had probably expected her to beg for mercy. She stepped still closer till their bodies were almost touching, "Please, stick out your tongue, Your Highness."

Both of Halvdan's brows shot up. "You are a strange girl," he muttered.

"Stick out your tongue!" Deirdre ordered.

Henrik actually laughed aloud. "She is mad, and has a fixation with tongues."

"They have their uses," Halvdan snapped, trying not to betray his curiosity and begrudging admiration of this Irish princess who was either completely insane, as Henrik obviously thought, or extremely brave. His admiration sprang from his belief that she was brave, perhaps even quite clever. Whatever the case, she did not behave as almost anyone else would have behaved.

"Stick out your tongue," Deirdre repeated. "I strongly suspect you are not a well man."

Much to Henrik's amazement, Halvdan actually stuck out his tongue.

Deirdre reached up and grabbed the tip of it with her fingers, pulling it taut. "Lean forward and down, Your Highness. You are much too tall for me to see."

As if she were the queen and he was her serf, Halvdan bent over and Deirdre examined his tongue. "You have yellowish fur," she said slowly. "I have seen this condition before." She let go of his tongue. "You cannot gain weight no matter what you eat, and often your stool is loose and yellowish like your flesh."

Halvdan stood up straight and curled his yellowed furry tongue back into his mouth. "How do you know these things?" he demanded.

"I have knowledge of medicine," Deirdre asserted. She knew full well the Vikings had little or no knowledge of medicine. When someone was wounded in the chest during a battle, they fed the victim onions and then, after a time, they sniffed the wound to see if they could smell the onions. If they could, they assumed the stomach had been pierced and the person would die. In such a case, the person was abandoned. If they could not smell onions, they tended the wound.

"She's a witch trying to avoid her fate," Henrik warned.

Halvdan turned on him viciously. "Fetch Ingrid and leave me with this woman."

Henrik left instantly and without a word.

"I am not a witch," Deirdre protested.

Halvdan nodded. "I do not believe in witches. Tell me about this medicine."

"I learned it from a woman who had lived in the East with the Infidels. They know much, and she taught me."

Halvdan rubbed the end of his long nose thoughtfully. "I have heard of these people and their knowledge."

Deirdre could see his interest growing. What man was not intrigued with his own health? And in this case, she was, in fact, speaking the truth. Emboldened by his response, she said, "I have successfully treated King Alfred, the king of Wessex."

"So, please tell me why my skin is yellow."

"Your skin yellows because the fluids of your body do not cleanse the inside of your body."

"And what causes this?"

"Many things, Your Highness. Sometimes disease, sometimes too much drink." She lowered her voice, "And sometimes something else."

He looked at her steadily, as if trying to penetrate her calm. It occurred to him that she did not seem at all revolted by him or even intimidated by his threats. In fact, she seemed genuinely interested in his condition and had not shrunk away when he touched her.

Deirdre stood on her tiptoes. "Bend down, let me whisper into your ear."

Halvdan did so, a quizzical expression covering his face.

"I believe someone is trying to poison you. I must talk to you alone, later. Do not reveal what I have said; you do not know who your enemies might be."

"We are alone now," he said.

"Perhaps not, people listen . . ."

Halvdan straightened up and for a long time looked into her clear green eyes. It was as if he were talking to her.

Deirdre could feel his change of attitude toward her. She was no longer a 'pretty prize'; now she had some personal value to him.

He walked around her slowly. "You are not afraid of me, are you?"

Deirdre shook her head. "Fear clouds the mind. But truly, I am not afraid because you need me. I can help you."

"And what if I do not harm you just so you can help me? I could let you help me, and then I could kill you."

Deirdre shrugged. "I cannot fight your power. I have no weapons save knowledge."

He walked around her again and finally sat down. "Tell me what to do."

"You will stop drinking wine and mead. And I will prepare some medicine for you. But I must be allowed to walk about freely and unmolested. After all, where am I to go in the dead of winter?"

"Very well," Halvdan agreed. As an afterthought he asked, "Do you tell tales?"

"I have tales to tell, yes."

"Perhaps you will tell me some."

He had actually spoken to her as if she were a person. "I will," she said, not daring yet to smile.

"You sent for me, Your Highness?" Ingrid followed in Henrik's wake. She bowed before Halvdan but only glanced uneasily at Deirdre. Her heart pounded. This was Alan's sister!

"Take this woman and make her comfortable. Get her whatever she needs."

Ingrid's eyes grew wide with disbelief. "Yes, Your Highness. Yes." Before he changed his mind, she turned to Deirdre. "Follow me."

Henrik watched in amazement as Deirdre walked off with Ingrid. Lord Thorgills, who was still asleep, would not believe this, he thought, shaking his own head. Halvdan, a wretched, vile man who was famous for his cruelty and strange sexual appetites, had apparently softly mellowed before this tiny Irish princess who seemed to have a will of iron. He twisted his nose as he watched the two women leave. Erica was a Valkyrie—a fierce female spirit. But this Irish princess was a magical fairy, able to beguile with her soft voice and fearless green eyes. No wonder Brand wanted her!

"Come quickly," Ingrid whispered. "Before he changes his mind. Have you bewitched him? I have never seen Halvdan behave like that. Whatever have you done to him?"

Deirdre herself felt some surprise. "I have not bewitched him," she answered. "I think he is merely fascinated with his own ailments. But make no mistake, he is truly a sick man."

"I can't pretend to understand," Ingrid said.

"Where are we going?" Deirdre asked.

Ingrid smiled. "I have a great surprise for you, Princess Deirdre, one I did not expect to be able to give you."

Erica, bedecked in furs, boarded her vessel for the journey back to Lord Thorgills's fortress. Not that her destination was known to the others. They all assumed she would be going home. The morning sun was high in the sky, and both Ivar and Brand still slept. "Cast off!" she called to her headman. She stood at the rail, feeling the choppy winter sea beneath the boat, watching as Ivar's castle grew smaller in the distance.

"The next time I look Brand in the eye he will have a sword through his stomach!" she said with determination.

"Yes, mistress," her slave replied.

Erica did not even turn to acknowledge his presence. She wasn't really talking to him, she was talking at him, venting her anger in hateful words and even more hateful threats.

Still, she could not say everything, even to her slave. She could not vocalize how it felt to have Brand reject her in the way he had rejected her last night. She could not confess how unhappy she was that she had revealed herself to him—not the nakedness of her body, but the nakedness of her demons. Now he had seen them, and she wondered how much he suspected. And Cnut! Where had he disappeared to? Neither Brand nor Ivar had told her. They were keeping something back, she felt it, and she swore long and low under her breath. A horrible thought swept through her mind. What if they had given her false information? What if they had another plan of attack? What if all she would, and had, passed onto Henrik and Halvdan was incorrect? Halvdan and Henrik would think she had betrayed them! It would be her head on Halvdan's castle wall!

But no. She forced calmness on herself in spite of the searing memory of last night that kept replaying in her mind over and over. "Deirdre," she murmured. "I have Deirdre, and I will make Brand pay!"

Deirdre plodded across the courtyard toward the strange edifice in the distance. From all appearances it was a dwelling inside a hill. This fortress was a strange place. She had been intrigued with the grotto, and this dwelling which rose in the distance also grasped her imagination. It was very like the houses she had seen at land's end when she and Brand had first landed in Britannia. But this sod house was larger.

"What is that?" she asked.

"A sod house," Ingrid replied. "They're very warm in the winter."

Though they had spoken little, Deirdre sensed in Ingrid a sweet gentleness. She was certainly no Erica. In fact, it seemed impossible that Olaf was her brother and Lord Thorgills her father.

"I'm sorry about your brother," Deirdre said, feeling she should say something.

Ingrid stopped short and turned around. Her face seemed

paler than before, her mouth was slightly open, and her eyes had a look of fright that had not been there before. "Olaf—" she repeated his name and shook her head. "He was my half brother. It is wrong to say so, but he was evil, and I shall not miss him. May he freeze in the eternal ice of hell!" Tears suddenly filled Ingrid's eyes, and she turned around and began again to walk toward the sod house.

"I didn't mean to upset you," Deirdre said softly.

"You couldn't know how I suffered—he was evil and unnatural!"

"Your father didn't protect you?"

"No. He is a monster, too."

Ingrid wiped the tears from her face. "I have no time for tears, especially as you are about to be joyous."

Her words suddenly made sense to Deirdre. Was Alan here? How did Ingrid know about them? But before she could ask, the door of the sod house flew open and Alan stood in the doorway, looking much as he had the day they had parted less than a year ago.

"Alan!" She flew into his arms, and he embraced her. "My sister, my darling Deirdre! I never thought I would see you alive again—until Ingrid told me you were with the Viking, Brand."

"Quickly, inside," Ingrid urged. "We cannot let others see us."

Deirdre stepped into the warmth of the sod house and discarded her cape. She inhaled and smelled the long-familiar odor of his paints. It was like coming home! She looked around, her eyes blurry with tears of joy. And then she saw a pretty woman standing near the fire. She was making tea, and she smiled shyly.

"Deirdre, this is my beloved, Charlotte."

Deirdre looked at her younger brother and then at Charlotte and then back again. She hugged him again. "I am so happy for you, my brother." Without the slightest hesitation, she hugged Charlotte. "My sister," she whispered.

"We owe much to Ingrid," Alan explained. "She has been more friend than captor."

Ingrid blushed and looked away.

Deirdre walked to the table and looked at Alan's illuminated pages. They were beautiful. He had drawn dragons and snakes and other Nordic symbols round the pages that contained the legends.

"He is a great artist," Ingrid said admiringly. "We must not forget our danger," she added. "We must make a plan. Our lives hang in the balance."

Deirdre nodded. "I have bought us some time with King Halvdan. But I do not know how long it will last."

"You are a wonder," Ingrid said. "But I warn you, he is completely unpredictable."

Deirdre nodded. "He is also very ill. I believe someone is slowly poisoning him."

"Poison?" Ingrid said in surprise.

"It is most certainly a member of the alliance. It can only be Henrik, Lord Thorgills, or Erica."

Charlotte poured the tea into metal mugs, and they all sat down around the table.

"He has many enemies," Ingrid acknowledged. "And I think even many of his so-called friends are enemies."

Her words, simple, but doubtless true, brought a smile to Deirdre's lips.

"We should all have learned a lesson," Alan said. "We were conquered because we were divided. If King Halvdan's allies are divided, perhaps he can more easily be conquered."

Deirdre smiled. "My thoughts exactly."

"They will use you to get Brand to call off his attack and surrender," Ingrid said to Deirdre.

"Brand will not attack for at least four weeks," Deirdre stated. She turned to Ingrid. "Are all the vessels moored in the grotto?"

Ingrid shook her head. "The coastal vessels are anchored on shore, up the Oslo Fjord about ten miles. That is also near the place where some of King Halvdan's vessels are. There they are protected from winter storms."

"Are they well guarded?" Deirdre questioned.

"I don't think ours are guarded at all," Ingrid said. "But Halvdan's crews are still aboard. What are you thinking?"

"And the vessels in the grotto? Is one of them Halvdan's as well?"

Ingrid nodded. "The bigger of the two. It is his personal vessel."

"Tell us what you have in mind!" Alan pressed.

"I want the three of you to run away and escape."

"It's winter," Charlotte wailed. "We'll freeze."

"You will not freeze," Deirdre replied. "Time is on our side. Now listen, I have a plan. Can you ski, Ingrid?"

"Yes, of course."

"Well, if you put these two on a sledge, you can push it easily through the snow and make good time. You will go to Halvdan's vessels in the fjord."

"I do not understand," Ingrid said. "Halvdan is leaving for Oslo in the morning, and his headman who guards his vessels in the fjord will take us nowhere."

"He will if Halvdan orders it. I will talk with Halvdan tonight. I will agree to go with him to Oslo; you will carry a message from Halvdan to Brand. I'm certain I can get Halvdan to arrange for one of his ships to take you."

"It is dangerous for you to go with Halvdan to Oslo. He is an unbalanced man, very cruel and changeable," Ingrid warned.

"I shall have to take the chance, Ingrid. It is our only possibility of success."

Deirdre took one of her brother's quills. "You will each need a pack with the following items in order to reach Halvdan's vessels." Quickly she wrote down all that they would need.

"Wait," Ingrid said. "What if Erica returns before we leave?"

"I'm sure King Halvdan can control Erica," Deirdre said. "And if he wants treatment for his malady, he will have to control her."

Lord Thorgills tumbled from his bed and stretched. He went to his private bath and submerged himself in its steaming waters.

It had taken so long! So much longer than he had anticipated! Halvdan must have the constitution of a horse, he thought. Not that he wanted Halvdan's death to appear at all obvious. No, it had to seem natural or it would rouse the suspicions of the other chieftains, and he would be forced to fight to keep his position. It was bad enough that Brand, Ivar, and Cnut were raising an army against him.

But they would be defeated, and soon, if Erica was right. The Irish princess would ensure Brand's defeat. He wondered if she had yet arrived. He did remember her, and she was a beauty.

"Yes," he said aloud to the billows of vapor in his bath. "It is all falling into place."

For a year, one of his men, posing as a slave—a gift from Thorgills to Halvdan—had been slowly poisoning the king on his orders. Gradually, Halvdan's skin had yellowed, his eyes had grown paler, and his tongue had grown a furry yellow. He had always been thin, but now it seemed as if his thin yellow skin was stretched over his brittle skeletal bones. And soon, but not before Brand was eliminated, Halvdan would die, apparently of natural causes. And then, Lord Thorgills thought happily, his ten-year-old son, Harald, would meet with a perfectly dreadful accident.

Thorgills smiled. It would be a glorious funeral. Halvdan and some of his less valuable possessions would be buried in one of his longboats together with his son and a few slaves, who would be killed for the occasion so that they might accompany him to the grave. One needed servants, even in

Valhalla. Of course, one of them would be the man he had entrusted to poison the king. Dead men told no tales, and this was a tale he most assuredly intended keeping to himself.

Thorgills emerged from his steaming bath and ran into the snow, rolling vigorously before he hurried back inside to dress. He would have a good noonday meal and after that he would inquire about the Irish princess.

Cnut's crew anchored his knorr at the wharf to one side of Lord Radnor's fortress. It was not unlike Ivar's castle save the fact that the turrets were a little higher and there were two instead of one.

He stepped ashore and signaled one of his men to sound the gong to mark his arrival. It seemed extremely odd that no one was here, he thought as he looked about, his eyes searching the castle walls.

He waited, but even after the sounding of the gong no one appeared. No guards, no warriors, no servants, and no slaves came forth. It seemed that Radnor's castle fortress was entirely deserted.

"Come with me," Cnut shouted, and, with his fingers, he motioned two of his men to follow. If Erica were preparing a fighting force to bring to Brand, where was it? With some trepidation, it occurred to him that the fighting force, Radnor's men, had been sent instead to Lord Thorgills.

Cnut found the main door to the interior of the castle unbarred and he walked in, shouting as he did so. But his shouts only echoed down long empty corridors. The castle was unseemly cold, as if the fires had gone out some time ago.

He stopped and looked in the great hall. Above the fireplace was the head of an angry wolf, mounted and staring with open mouth down on the room.

Cnut's men were as puzzled as he.

"Something is very wrong here," Ulf declared.

"Keep your weapons at the ready," Cnut suggested.

He walked out of the great hall and down the winding hallway toward the bedchambers. His two warriors walked behind him, their eyes searching the shadows.

"It would appear that since everyone is gone, the slaves have run away, too," Cnut said when he reached the great door that barred the way to Radnor's bedchamber.

"It's bolted from the outside and locked as well," he said, looking at the door.

"By all the gods," Ulf uttered. "What is that vile odor?"

Cnut inhaled and smelled the sickly smell of decay. "It's coming from behind this door."

For a long moment the three of them looked at the door. "We'll need a battering ram," Cnut finally said.

The three of them left the door and went in search of a battering ram. Such things were usually kept with the weapons, and, after a short time, they found the weapons room and the ram they needed.

They carried it back to Radnor's door and together they lifted it and ran at the door. It took three runs before the heavy door gave way and broke on its hinges, allowing entry.

Cnut stepped over the debris and into the room. Immediately he covered his nose with his scarf. The smell was hideous—it was clearly rotting flesh. Ulf ran from the room and retched in the hall.

Cnut reached the bed and he looked down at the sickening sight. It was Radnor the Wolf, or what was left of him. His body was rotting beneath the covers.

Cnut looked around. What strange ritual had taken place in this room? There were candles all around the bed. He took his sword and lifted the covers, revealing Radnor's body. The bed was soaked in dried blood from the gaping wound. Radnor had certainly not died from natural causes.

Near the bed, Cnut saw the bejeweled sword and he also saw Erica's robe—it, too, had blood on it.

"She killed her father," Cnut whispered. And then, as if

to make himself believe the terrible crime, he said aloud, "Erica has killed her father."

King Halvdan stood in his private quarters in Lord Thorgills's castle. He squinted and stared into the highly polished metal mirror. He touched his yellowed skin with his hand and grimaced. "Poison," he whispered. Could it be true?

Deirdre entered his quarters and looked about. Lord Thorgills had certainly done everything possible to provide the most luxurious of accommodation for his guest. The bed was far larger than most and was covered with not just any fur, but by sewn-together mink skins. Tapestries from all parts of Britannia hung on the walls, and the many tables were covered with the rich plunder of a hundred Viking raids. "You summoned me," she said softly.

Halvdan motioned her to come in and close the door. Deirdre did as he requested. Somehow knowing what caused his hideous appearance made him seem less ominous. Vaguely she was beginning to wonder if he was as evil as his reputation or if he had, in fact, cultivated his reputation in order to make people afraid of him.

"Have you given thought to my condition?" he asked.

Deirdre nodded. "I have, Your Highness, and I have no doubt you are being poisoned. You must tell me about your food, what you eat, and who prepares it for you. I suspect this is a long-term poison, one meant to kill you slowly and make it appear that you died of natural causes."

Yes, that was how he felt, as if he were dying slowly, as if his life were creeping away. He felt sapped of all energy, and he had seen himself in the mirror. He was decaying like a corpse, though he was still living.

"My food is prepared by my cooks and tasted by a taster. The taster is not ill."

"It must be as I suspect. Your drink is being poisoned. I

believe it to be your wine and mead. Yes, that is most likely it."

Halvdan immediately thought of the slave Lord Thorgills had given him. The slave prepared all his wine and mead. That was it—Lord Thorgills was poisoning him in order to gain full control of the empire. And how very clever! Lord Thorgills had only just returned, so he would not be suspected even if it were discovered that Halvdan had been poisoned. But the slave had been sent a year ago to begin his grisly business, and finally Lord Thorgills had returned. No doubt he thought the time short and his moment of triumph at hand. But Halvdan said nothing, deeming it ill-advised to speak in front of Deirdre.

"I will think and try to remember who serves me."

But Deirdre knew. She had seen the slave pour his wine, and she also knew the slave was a gift from Lord Thorgills because Ingrid had told her. "For now, stop drinking," she advised. "And take this medicine. It is oil of a fish, and will help restore you."

Halvdan took the medicine she offered. "I am returning to Oslo," he said after a moment. He leaned toward her. "I must take you with me."

Deirdre nodded. "I want to go." This was a dangerous game, and she must play it well. "Make peace with Brand," she urged. "I will make a bargain with you."

"I do not bargain, Princess, I command."

"Hear me out," Deirdre said softly. "I will come willingly and treat your illness. I promise you will recover. In return, send Ingrid secretly with two slaves of her choosing, to Brand. Tell him you are withdrawing from your alliance with Lord Thorgills, Lord Henrik, and Erica, daughter of Lord Radnor. Tell him you will abdicate in favor of your son, Harald."

Halvdan tilted his head to one side and studied her. "Is that what Lord Brand wants?"

"Yes. He wants Harald to become king with Lord Ivar and Lord Cnut as his advisors."

Halvdan rubbed his beard. "I will think on this," he said. "If I agree, just how will I keep Ingrid's departure secret?"

"Leave that to me. Just send a message to the captain of your vessels that one vessel must take Ingrid and her two slaves immediately to Brand. Then write the message you will have Ingrid deliver to Brand."

Slowly Halvdan nodded. Then he smiled. "I admire you, Princess, but you are a fool to trust me."

Deirdre looked him straight in the eye. "Your Highness, it is you who must trust me. But, as well you know, I am more trustworthy than Lord Thorgills."

Halvdan smiled ever so slightly and took her hand. She neither cowered nor shivered but continued to look him in the eye. "Knowledge is powerful indeed," he said slowly.

Deirdre's apprehensions did not entirely fade, but still she felt a wave of satisfaction. The wolf, as they said, was among the chickens. Deirdre touched Halvdan's hand in return. "I shall see to Ingrid's departure immediately, but you must keep the others from discovering my absence till nightfall."

Lord Thorgills sat down at the long table beside Henrik. "Where is the Irish princess?" he asked as he took a large egg and sucked it noisily.

"With Halvdan—poor girl. He has such unspeakable appetites."

Thorgills laughed and took another egg. "So early in the evening? Halvdan is probably—"

"Probably what?" Halvdan said as he silently came up behind Lord Thorgills.

"Enjoying the Irish princess," Thorgills finished, although that had not been what he would have said, had Halvdan not appeared.

Halvdan sneered, "Yes, she is bound in my room. Naked and quite helpless. I have been availing myself of her considerable charms." With that he sat down and took a large hunk of bread. "I shall be returning to Oslo tomorrow. I will return with more men to help you defend against Brand's attack."

"Good," Thorgills smiled.

Lord Henrik, too, took some bread, and he spread it with thick, white, whipped butter. "What if Brand attacks before you return?"

"He will not," Halvdan said. "It is still too cold."

"Erica, daughter of Lord Radnor, has returned!" The servant made the announcement from the entrance to the dining hall.

"Now we shall hear Brand's battle plans in detail," Henrik said, grinning.

Erica was not far behind her heralding. She swept into the room, her white-blond hair long and loose beneath her rich black furs.

"Where is the Irish princess?" she asked immediately.

Henrik motioned her toward them. "I can hear the ice in your voice, Erica."

"It is true, I look forward to her unpleasant demise."

"She is bound in my room, recovering from my pleasures," Halvdan muttered. "I shall take her with me when I leave tomorrow."

Erica smiled. How nice that someone else was now the beneficiary of Halvdan's attention. Erica's heart leapt for joy at the thought of the lovely little Irish princess, Brand's beautiful infatuation, being the object of Halvdan's strange affections. "Why do you leave?"

"To bring back more men. Now, tell us the plan, Erica."

"With pleasure." With that she leaned back and began to explain Brand's battle plan in some detail.

Deirdre looked around the warm sod house and felt sad that they had to leave its shelter. Still, it was necessary for them to return to Brand immediately. "I'm pleased. You're all ready to go."

"You should come with us," Ingrid said.

"I cannot. I've made a bargain. Ingrid, I must entrust you with this message to Brand from Halvdan."

"A trap," Ingrid breathed. "You must not trust him."

"I shall leave the trust to Brand. But I must tell you the king has just discovered that your father, Lord Thorgills, has been poisoning him. I believe that Henrik, Erica, and your father are in for a surprise."

Uncharacteristically, Ingrid giggled, and covered her mouth with her hand and blushed. "It is delicious," she whispered. "But never fear, I do not think of him as my father."

"We had better go," Alan said. "I dread it, but still I look forward to it."

Deirdre went with them for a short distance. As they disappeared behind the castle and climbed onto the sledge, large snowflakes began to fall. "Good," Deirdre whispered. "Just in case anyone follows, your tracks will be covered. Ingrid, give the one message to the captain of Halvdan's fleet and the other to Brand. They are clearly marked."

"Be careful," Ingrid warned.

Alan kissed his sister gently on the cheek. "Till we meet soon again, my beloved sister."

Sixteen

Erica headed for the bath feeling somewhat disgruntled. *I've been here for hours,* she thought, *and I haven't seen the Irish princess yet. I wanted to beat her myself.* But then she smiled. She supposed the next best thing was having Deirdre subjected to Halvdan's attentions.

She looked up as she crossed the courtyard. There were huge, soft, fluffy snowflakes falling. It was the kind of snow to be expected in the early spring. Yes, spring was well on the way, and soon it would be time to fight. "I've waited so long," she murmured. And for a long moment she thought of her father and smiled. "Aren't you proud of me," she said to no one.

Erica reached the bathhouse and went inside. Certainly someone had just poured water over the hot coals. The place was thick with a vaporous mist.

Erica disrobed quickly and slithered into the hot water of the bath.

"You're in a hurry tonight," King Halvdan said from the far side of the square bathing pool. "I hardly have time to enjoy you if you move so quickly."

Erica jumped. Halvdan was so devious, he had probably chosen a spot where he knew she would not see him because of the rising steam.

"I would have thought you weary from taking pleasure with

the Irish princess," Erica said with a curious smile. "After all, you have been with her most of the day."

"Are you jealous, Erica?"

The smile faded from Erica's face. He had once again succeeded in verbally trapping her. If she said "no," he would be insulted or feign being insulted. If she said, "yes," he might want to involve her in some unsavory activity. She moved her hand across the rough black rock on the side of the pool, trying to formulate her words.

Uncharacteristically, King Halvdan laughed. "Your very pondering says far too much, my dear."

Erica felt herself going pale in spite of the steam and the heat of the bath. "I simply supposed you were worn out from taking pleasure with the princess."

Halvdan sighed. "Yes, these Celtic woman are very wearing."

Erica could hardly contain herself, "What have you done to her?" Perhaps at the very least he would share verbally with her the torments to which he had subjected the princess.

Halvdan stared at her and licked his lips. "Many things," he replied. "Tell me, dear Erica, are you loyal to Lord Thorgills?"

What did he mean by that, she wondered. Why indeed was he asking? Halvdan seemed different somehow. "But of course I am loyal to Lord Thorgills and to you."

"But are you truly pledged to Lord Thorgills?"

"Yes, I am. I am his ally in all things."

Halvdan smiled again and pulled on his scraggly beard. "All things?"

"Yes, of course. All things."

"I see. Tell me, Erica, do you want to see what I have done to the Irish princess?"

"Oh, yes," Erica said, feeling a wonderful surge of enthusiasm. Doubtless he had her tied up and by now he had probably had her many times in various ways.

"Well, I'm not finished, of course. Tell me, what do you think should be done with her?"

"I think she should be tortured and then buried alive in your wall so that the birds may peck out her eyes."

"A suitable death for someone who goes against me—or goes against you, I suppose."

"It would please me to see her suffer so."

"Well, I shall reward you, Erica. Come to my room, and I shall show you what happens to a woman who wrongs me."

Erica smiled. "I will," she promised.

King Halvdan pulled himself from the bath. "I shall have to go and prepare for you," he told her as he wrapped himself in his cloak.

"When shall I come?" Erica asked.

"Give me an hour alone with her."

"I shall come in one hour," Erica promised.

In spite of the softly falling snow, the sledge moved through the tall pines with ease. But Ingrid, who skied behind it and pushed, felt her arms aching by the time the sun had set. Still, she plodded on through the velvety darkness.

When Ingrid heard the unmistakable sound of water lapping up on stones, she knew she was close to the shore where Halvdan's vessels were at anchor next to those of her father's. She glided the sledge to a stop. "We're here," she said. "And not a moment too soon, my arms are so tired."

Ingrid removed her skis and Alan and Charlotte climbed from the sledge.

"I'm so sorry," Charlotte said. "When we're on the ship I'll rub your arms. It will make them feel much better."

"If only I could ski," Alan said. "I would gladly have pushed you both.

"I really didn't mind," Ingrid told them. "It's just that it's been a while since I pushed a sledge or skied. I hope we shall have no cause to escape again."

"I must learn to ski in any case," Alan said. "It seems an important skill, one which I will need."

"This way," Ingrid whispered as she led them through the

pines on foot. In only a few steps they emerged from the woods out onto the rock-strewn shore of the fjord.

Ingrid called out, and suddenly some twenty armed warriors emerged from below the covered portion of one of Halvdan's vessels.

"Quickly! Ingrid called. "I must see King Halvdan's headman at once! I have an urgent message for him!"

The headman stepped forward, signaling the others to put down their bows. He walked to Ingrid's side.

Ingrid handed him the container with the message from King Halvdan. He motioned for a torch to be brought and when it was, he read the message, not once but twice.

"I am to take you three with all haste to Lord Brand," he said after a few moments. "We are to leave at once."

Alan looked at the knorr. It was smaller by far than the ship which had brought him from Hibernia. He remembered that journey only too well and did not relish another like it. Still, he said nothing as the three of them were taken aboard the knorr.

The headman took them to a sheltered part of the vessel and motioned them inside. "I'll have some mead and food brought," he said after a moment.

"Oh, we are hungry," Ingrid admitted. And she realized as she said it that because of all her physical exercise she was no doubt hungrier than either Charlotte or Alan.

"Here are some covers," he added as he gave them a pile of furs.

Hardly had the three of them settled down when he shouted out orders and the boat began to move down the fjord and toward the sea.

"I hope I won't be seasick," Alan said miserably.

Charlotte hugged him. "You won't be," she said firmly. "I won't allow it."

Ingrid wrapped herself in furs and leaned back against the rough wooden boxes that were packed under the shelter. "Ivar will be surprised that I have done this," she said slowly. "He will say it is out of character."

"You've risked your life and betrayed your father to help us," Charlotte said, touching her arm lightly. "We understand what you have done, Ingrid. And we're grateful for it."

Ingrid turned toward her slowly. "I have wanted to leave for years. My father is a monster, and my brother Olaf was even worse. My only regret is that I stayed too long."

Neither Charlotte nor Alan had need to ask why Charlotte felt so. Olaf's mistreatment of his sister was common knowledge among both the servants and slaves in Lord Thorgills's fortress.

"You have done the right thing," Charlotte told her.

Ingrid squeezed Charlotte's hand. "We must try to sleep. When we awaken we will be at Ivar's."

Charlotte took one of Ingrid's arms. "I promised I would rub your arms," she reminded her.

"I'll rub the other," Alan said, moving to the other side of Ingrid.

Ingrid leaned back and closed her eyes. "This is very nice," she said. "Very nice after skiing so far."

Erica paused before Halvdan's door. She had taken the time to look her best, dressing in a long dark tunic trimmed in black fur. Her long blond hair was loose, and she had brushed it back, and put a dark fur band on it to hold it in place. When she walked, her long legs were bare and showed to the thigh because of the slits in her tunic. It seemed only right that she dress to see the misfortune of the Irish princess. Her lips pressed together tightly as she thought of Brand ejecting her from his bedchamber. Her hatred for Deirdre surged through her. No fate could be too harsh. She took in a long deep breath and knocked.

"Come in," Halvdan called out.

Erica opened the door. She stepped over the threshold into semidarkness and sniffed. She smelled blood. A smile curved around her mouth. Perhaps Halvdan was opening the princess's veins—no, that was too merciful. In any case it was a punishment more common to the French than her own people.

"Come in," Halvdan called out again.

Erica walked farther into the room and blinked as her eyes grew used to the dim light. Halvdan had few torches or candles lit. The room was furnished with massive tables and chests and in the strange light they cast odd shadows.

"Halvdan," Erica said with trepidation. And then in the gloom she saw it. Her mouth opened in surprise, and a scream nearly escaped her lips. On the far wall, with a long sword through the center of his body, was Halvdan's slave, Anders. He was pinned to the wall like a butterfly to a board.

"He displeased me," Halvdan said with a wave of his hand as he stepped out of the shadows and touched Erica's arm.

She let a half scream escape her lips before she forced herself to be quiet. "You startled me."

"I meant to startle you, dear Erica."

"Where is the Irish princess?"

"Deirdre? She is about."

Deirdre? He called her Deirdre? Erica began to shake ever so slightly. Had this Irish princess bewitched Halvdan, too? No, it wasn't possible!

"Seize her!" Halvdan ordered.

Erica whirled about, but there was no escape. Two of the king's own guard grabbed her and held her tightly.

"Why are you doing this?" Erica gurgled.

"Because you are Lord Thorgills's ally in all things, dear Erica."

"I have never done anything to you!"

"You have done nothing for me either. Lord Thorgills is a traitor!"

"A traitor? But I am no traitor!"

"That remains to be seen. I shall be taking you with me in the morning, you and the lovely Irish princess. If you are innocent, you will be punished only for the things you have done. If you are truly Thorgills's ally, you will have the punishment you wished on Deirdre!"

"No!" Erica shrieked, but her cry was cut short by the gag that was put in her mouth.

"Tie her hands and feet," Halvdan ordered. "You shall travel to Oslo in a box, dear Erica. The Irish princess will be tied too, but only for show and only till we leave this place. Think about that while you lie in your box. Think about my wall!"

Erica struggled desperately, but it was no use. She was tied tightly and lifted into a long, wooden box. The lid was closed, leaving her in the hell of absolute darkness.

Lord Thorgills stood stiffly on the wharf and stared into the west. The sun had not yet risen, and it was cold and windy. He hated getting up this early, and he silently cursed King Halvdan, the cause of his misery.

"You're leaving so abruptly," Lord Thorgills said.

Halvdan shrugged. "I came abruptly."

Lord Thorgills forced a smile. Come or go, he really didn't care what the king did. He only swore because high tide was so early in the morning, and the king insisted on leaving at high tide.

Henrik watched as the king's possessions were loaded onto his vessel. He took many crates of wine Lord Thorgills had brought him from France as well as the Irish princess, who was tied hand and foot and carried to a bench amidships.

"She doesn't look as if she's been tortured," Henrik commented.

Halvdan shrugged and marveled at his own reputation. He really enjoyed being feared, though sometimes it was tiring, too. "She's quite pretty; I want her to last a long while."

"Understandable," Lord Thorgills commented dryly. "She seems to be a treasure you don't want to share."

Halvdan looked down his nose at Lord Thorgills. "I don't share," he said flatly.

Henrik watched as they loaded a long box that looked for all the world like a Christian coffin. Vaguely he wondered what cargo it carried, but he decided not to ask. Halvdan did not seem in a good mood.

Halvdan turned without a word and boarded his vessel. "Till we meet again," he said.

"Till Brand is dead," Lord Thorgills added.

Halvdan turned and grimaced. "You will bring me his head for my wall, won't you?"

Lord Thorgills smiled at the thought. "Of course, Your Highness. It will be my pleasure."

With that Halvdan delivered the signal and the vessel cast off. Turning, it headed down the fjord.

The snow had stopped and indeed melted. Outside, the sky was blue and the sea mimicked it, sparkling under the sun like a blue blanket studded with jewels.

The morning meal was spread out on the table. It consisted largely of bread, cheese, and gruel. Ivar sat on one side of the table and Brand on the other.

"You grow more morose with each day that passes, my friend."

"The waiting is hard," Brand admitted. "If I could attack now, if I could do something—"

"In spite of today's weather, it's impossible to attack yet."

"A vessel approaches!" a winded messenger announced as he hurried into the room.

"Cnut must be back," Brand said, tearing off a piece of bread.

"No, it is not Lord Cnut. It is one of King Halvdan's vessels. It flies a white flag."

Hardly had the words escaped the messenger's mouth when both Ivar and Brand were on their feet. They raced together to the parapet, there to view the incoming ship.

"Certainly not a ship filled with warriors," Ivar commented as he pointed to the little knorr bobbing up and down in the choppy sea.

"It's alone," Brand observed as he scanned the ocean in both directions.

"I would have suspected a message from Lord Thorgills under the circumstances," Ivar commented. "What could Halvdan want?"

Brand frowned as he stared at the knorr. Ivar was right. It was Thorgills who had taken Deirdre—surely it would be he who sent the demands.

"Enough of conjecture," Brand said. "Let's go meet our visitors."

They descended the stairs from the parapet all the way to the rock wharf where the waves splashed wildly ashore on the incoming tide. By the time they arrived, the small vessel was being secured.

"Ingrid!" Ivar exclaimed as he recognized Ingrid.

Brand watched, his mouth slightly open. There were two others. A pretty dark-haired woman and, of all people, Alan, Deirdre's brother.

Ivar embraced Ingrid, who hugged him back, and then the two stepped back as if embarrassed with their sudden show of affection.

"Alan," Brand said. "What are you doing here?"

"Deirdre sent us," he replied.

"Deirdre—" Her name hung on his lips as hope sprang in his heart.

"I bear a message from King Halvdan," Ingrid said, handing him the scroll. "We are here with Halvdan's help."

Brand turned to Halvdan's headman who stood nearby. "Have your men rest," he suggested.

"Please, enjoy my hospitality," Ivar added.

"We are to return as quickly as possible with an answer for King Halvdan."

"Refresh yourselves until an answer is prepared."

Brand had unrolled the scroll and was reading it even though the wind blew and the paper shivered in his hands. "Come, we have much to speak about," he told them.

The five of them turned and climbed the stairs to the castle, returning to the room where breakfast waited and the fire was warm.

"Deirdre, is Deirdre all right, Ingrid?"

Ingrid, seeing the anxiety in Brand's eyes, touched his arm gently. "Deirdre is more than all right, Brand. She is very clever and intelligent. I have never seen King Halvdan treat anyone as he treats her. He said he took her for safekeeping. And he has Erica as well. She is a traitor, Brand. She told my father everything."

Brand shrugged. "Everything is not much, Ingrid. We suspected her and fed her false information. But I don't understand. Halvdan is kind to no one. What magic has Deirdre wrought?"

"No magic," Ingrid said. "She discovered Halvdan was being poisoned by a slave given to him by my father. She is treating him. Still, I am worried about her—Halvdan can be unpredictable."

"Your father was poisoning Halvdan?" Ivar said in disbelief.

"My father wanted to be the absolute ruler of all Scandinavia."

"And the scroll?" Ivar asked, turning to Brand. "What does Halvdan have to say?"

"Halvdan offers to meet the terms we discussed earlier as Deirdre has relayed them. Halvdan will step down in favor of his son and Ivar and Cnut will act as advisors for the boy. *The Thing* will be reinstated and laws made and disputes settled when they meet."

"What of Lord Thorgills and Lord Henrik?" Ivar asked, although, in fact, he was certain he knew the answer.

"We will attack as planned. Halvdan will not interfere and indeed may send forces to assist us."

"When will Deirdre be released?" Alan asked.

"When Thorgills is defeated we are to sail to Oslo for the coronation of his son, Harald. Deirdre will return with us."

"Halvdan is intrigued by her medicine," Ingrid said.

Brand bit his lip. "I'll have to trust him," he said after a moment. "There is no choice."

"I think Deirdre will be all right," Alan said. "I feel it in my heart."

Ingrid withdrew a small leather pouch from under her tunic. "Deirdre sent you this," she said, handing it to Brand.

Brand opened the pouch and withdrew the Tara brooch. He smiled and pressed it to his lips. "My good-luck piece."

"We'll need luck," Ivar said. "Lord Thorgills is well armed."

"I'll prepare the message to be sent back to Halvdan," Brand said. "I shall tell him we agree."

Ivar took Ingrid's arm. "Come, dear Ingrid. We have things to discuss, things too long left unsaid."

The servant ran down the corridor and into the room where Lord Thorgills and Lord Henrik sat before the fire. He fell on his face in front of Lord Thorgills, clearly afraid that he would be punished for the bad news he bore.

"What is it?" Lord Thorgills snapped. He had felt irritable all day.

"It is the king's room! You must come at once!"

Lord Thorgills pulled his bulk from the chair and quaffed down the rest of his wine. "I'll have to go; this blubbering fool will never explain why I must come."

"I'll come too," Henrik ventured. "Perhaps Halvdan has left behind something interesting."

"The only interesting thing was the Irish princess, and he took her with him," Thorgills grumbled.

They walked down the corridor and saw that the door to the room where the king had been was ajar. Outside, one of the female servants stood by wringing her cleaning rag and trembling. Tears were streaming down her face as she pointed inside and whimpered.

Thorgills strode into the room and stopped short. He stared at the wall, and his mouth fell open in surprise.

"By all the gods," Henrik breathed. "What's happened here?"

"It's Anders," Lord Thorgills said, staring at the wall where the man still hung.

"Where's Erica?" Thorgills stormed. "And Ingrid! I haven't seen them all day."

"What's going on?" Henrik demanded. "Why has Halvdan killed this man?"

"Because he was poisoning him—on my orders," Thorgills confessed.

Henrik's jaw dropped. "The Irish princess was right. She told him he was ill. She had made him some medicine."

"Halvdan knows," Thorgills said, sinking into a nearby chair. "He knows I have been poisoning him. Somehow, some way, he found out."

"This is a most imprudent thing you've done," Henrik said slowly. It was a monumental understatement, but why anger Thorgills? Halvdan was dangerous enough.

"Be still! I must think," Thorgills muttered.

Another servant appeared and stood silently, her hands folded, her head down. "What is it?" Henrik demanded. "Are there more bodies elsewhere?"

The woman shook her head and began to cry silently. "Neither Lady Erica nor Lady Ingrid is in the castle," the woman reported.

"He has taken them," Lord Thorgills muttered.

"But why? Erica's men remain here, and of what possible use is Ingrid?"

"I don't know," Lord Thorgills replied. "I don't know what's going on here. The Irish princess—I remember. She has a brother, and he is here! I sent him home to copy our legends—he's an artist. Yes, he was put in the sod house to work."

Without further explanation, Lord Thorgills jumped to his feet and took off down the hall, out of the castle, and across the courtyard. Henrik followed, his cloak billowing in the wind.

Lord Thorgills kicked open the door of the sod house. "He's gone!" he shouted. "No one is here! They're all gone!"

"Halvdan will kill us," Henrik said blackly. "You are too ambitious, Thorgills."

"I'd have never been discovered had it not been for that princess!"

"We had better make plans to defend ourselves," Henrik said.

"Defend ourselves! No, we shall attack!"

"Brand?"

"No, Halvdan! We must attack before he readies himself."

"We cannot possibly attack for at least another two weeks."

"But attack we will! We'll kill Halvdan and his son! And I personally will deal with the Irish princess!"

Henrik stared at his ally. Lord Thorgills was a powerful warrior, but he was not a great intellect. Still, attacking Halvdan did seem the best course. In fact, to Henrik it seemed the only course, especially if they did not want to become part of Halvdan's wall.

Ivar had ordered the dinner table set with his finest food and wines. "A celebration of sorts," he decreed. "Not the celebration we will have when we are all together, but a celebration nonetheless because we know Deirdre is safe."

The table bore carafes of wine and mead, roast duck with bread stuffing, pickled herring, fine smoked northern salmon, and turnips and greens from the winter stores.

Brand looked at the others and was painfully aware of his own particular feeling of loneliness. Ivar and Ingrid sat side by side, clearly on the threshold of a long-put-off love affair, and Alan and Charlotte had eyes for no one but each other. He took in a breath—at least he felt Deirdre was safe for the time being. He thought for a moment of Ingrid's account of how Deirdre had handled Halvdan. She was truly one of a kind. But in spite of his initial relief, he still worried about her. Halvdan was cunning and the stories about him unnerving.

"Lord Cnut has returned!" the servant announced. They all turned away from the feast and stood up to greet Cnut, who strode into the dining room.

"Sit down! Sit down! I am no surprise guest. You must have known I would be back by tonight." Cnut looked around. "Ingrid, I have not seen you in years."

"Not since we were children, Cnut. I've left my father. I can live no more beneath his roof."

Cnut embraced her and turned to Charlotte and Alan.

"Deirdre's brother, Alan, and Charlotte, his beloved," Brand said by way of introduction. He turned back to Cnut. "There have been many developments in your absence, my friend. I'll brief you shortly. Were you attacked by Lord Radnor's men?"

Cnut laughed. "There were no men to attack me."

Brand frowned. "Erica is the traitor we suspected, but have all of Radnor's men gone to fight with Lord Thorgills?"

Cnut shrugged. "They are gone, but where they have gone, I cannot answer. Erica is more than a traitor, my friends, but therein lies my tale."

Ivar motioned Cnut to sit down. He poured some wine and sat back. "What did you find?"

"Not what I expected to find," Cnut replied, taking a gulp of wine.

"Tell us," Alan pressed.

"Patience, my Celtic brother. Cnut has a tale, and it is our custom to string out stories," Brand explained.

Cnut took some more wine. "I found the castle deserted. Radnor's warriors were gone as was his fleet. Slaves and servants alike had fled. The halls were empty, yet food had been left on the table, and there were rodents everywhere."

Ingrid put her hands to her cheeks. "Was there a plague?"

Cnut shook his head. "Only a plague of hatred. No, I think everyone fled because Erica never returned. She may or may not have ordered the warriors away."

"We'll find out in time," Brand said. "But continue."

"I found Lord Radnor's bedchamber locked from the outside, but from inside there came a terrible odor."

Charlotte, Ingrid, and Alan all put down their food.

"I had to find a battering ram. We flattened the door, and inside I found Lord Radnor."

"Dead?" Ivar asked in disbelief.

"Murdered. Radnor had been stabbed in the back with his own bejeweled sword. From the trail of blood I would say he was dragged to his bed and laid on it. The bed was surrounded by candles. It was like a terrible ritual of some sort. Erica's bloody robe was nearby—I know it is hers because I have seen her wear it."

"Erica killed her father—" Brand said in a near whisper.

"He had been there for some time. His body was decayed and the rodents had eaten most of his flesh."

"This is the most serious of crimes," Brand said, shaking his head.

"She must have gone mad," Ivar added.

Brand looked at Cnut. "We have learned from Ingrid that Lord Thorgills was poisoning Halvdan. He planned to usurp the throne. Deirdre discovered this and Halvdan has taken her to Oslo to treat him. King Halvdan has turned on Lord Thorgills and offers to meet our demands. We will attack Thorgills in two weeks' time."

"I don't think that Radnor's men will fight with Thorgills when they discover what has happened to their leader," Cnut said.

Brand nodded. "When the battle begins, we must see that the word is spread."

Cnut took some food and began to eat. "Thorgills could be in for a surprise."

Brand looked from one to the other. "It's not wise to underestimate Lord Thorgills. His mind is a tangled web of deceit. He's not a brilliant man, but he is wily, and I for one do not pretend I can outwit him."

Ivar and Cnut fell silent, knowing that Brand was right.

* * *

As soon as they left Lord Thorgills's fortress, King Halvdan ordered Deirdre untied. She stood near the bow of his vessel, looking into the distance as they rounded the bend in the Oslo Fjord bringing King Halvdan's fortress into view.

The fortress castles of Lord Ivar, Lord Thorgills, and King Halvdan were all similar. All three were on cliffs above the water and offered a panoramic view from their parapets. All three had nearby wharves where they moored their vessels, and all three were walled.

In spite of these resemblances, there was a difference. King Halvdan's castle was larger and somehow much darker in appearance. Deirdre soon realized that while the others were built from brownish stone, Halvdan's was built from a black rock. Adding to the ominous quality of the edifice was the fact that its twin towers rose high above the winding water of the fjord, causing them to appear and disappear in the ever-present swirling mist. Deirdre stared at Halvdan's famed wall. She was not yet close enough to see the skulls, nor was she sure she wanted to see them, but the wall itself was daunting. It was high and peaked and made of the blackest stone. As they grew closer, Deirdre realized that the peaks were, in fact, the skulls. Under her breath she said a prayer for the victims, then she turned away. She could not think on such things.

Deirdre was shown into a kind of reception room. It was not unlike the room in Ivar's castle where they often met. This one was sparsely furnished. An angry-looking wolf and two bear heads hung from the walls. On a great perch there was a huge, stuffed bird of prey, a small rodent victim in its hideous talons.

Halvdan followed her and had the long box in which Erica was tied brought in as well.

"You will tell my servants what you require to make your medicines," Halvdan said. "You will be given your own room."

Deirdre watched as a servant put down the box she had brought with her. "I have most of what I need with me," she told him.

"And you will spend some time each day with my son, Harald. Perhaps you can tell him some tales. He is a lonely boy."

"I should be pleased to do so," Deirdre answered.

"And now to Erica. Open the box!" Halvdan motioned to the silent servant, who quickly obeyed. The top was taken off and Erica, still tied hand and foot, was lifted to her feet. The gag was removed from her mouth.

Deirdre looked at her and felt nothing but pity. Erica was deathly pale and shaking.

"Now, how should I punish her?" Halvdan began as he circled her.

"I did not know! I did not know that Lord Thorgills was poisoning you! I am innocent." Her voice was raspy, doubtless from being gagged for so long.

"Innocent is one thing you are not," Halvdan muttered.

He turned to Deirdre. "She wished you tortured and buried alive in my wall. Shall we do the same to her?"

"No, no! Please! I will do anything!" Erica shrieked. "Mercy!"

"I could begin by burning the hair off her head."

"No!" Erica wailed. In spite of being tied, she dropped to her knees and tried to kiss Halvdan's feet.

"What do you think, Princess Deirdre? What shall I do with her."

"I think she should be locked up till Brand comes and you know more of her role in the poisoning and her alliance with Lord Thorgills."

"You see, Erica. The Irish princess is far kinder than you."

Erica looked down. She was still trembling but afraid to speak.

"She does not wish you the harm you wished her." He turned to Deirdre, and with a crooked smiled, asked, "Can't I even pull out her nails?"

"I think she should just be locked up for now."

Halvdan flicked his hand. "All right, for the time being we will just lock her up. Take her to the dungeon and chain her by the ankle to the wall. And, dear Erica, thank the nice princess, won't you?"

Erica shuddered and mumbled her thanks.

"Louder!" Halvdan screamed. "Much louder!"

"Thank you, Princess," Erica said, though she could not look Deirdre in the eye.

"Take her away!" Halvdan ordered.

The guards dragged the sobbing Erica from the room.

"And now you will meet Harald," Halvdan said, turning to Deirdre. "Now that the unpleasantness is out of the way."

Heorot rose out of the mist like a sentinel over the fjord. Brand tied his small knorr to the wharf and, leaving his crew of six behind, began to climb toward his own fortress, his beloved home, the place where his memories played in the corridors and he could hear his mother sing sweet songs on the afternoon breeze.

It was safe now. The pieces on the chessboard were all frozen, everyone knew what the next moves would be, none of them would be here at Heorot. Lord Thorgills's men were long gone, if indeed they had come in the first place. In any case, they would not come now.

Brand walked around the parapet, taking in the view and watching as huge gray clouds moved across the sky, propelled by winds that echoed down the fjord and sounded like a wounded wolf baying at the moon.

Heorot was deserted, but it stood proud—this kingdom that was once his father's domain. He touched the stag's horns as he walked around the wall, and after a time he entered the castle. Long deserted, it was cold and empty.

Yet if he listened, he could hear his mother's voice and see his father's face. He could hear the boy he once was asking a million questions and begging to be taken to sea. The sea was his mistress in those days—she called a siren call—and he answered it as soon as he was old enough to shoulder an oar.

Brand walked slowly through the castle, stopping here and there to remember past incidents. He continued on outside and into the courtyard, where he paused for a few minutes. *There,* he thought, against the far wall, *is where my archery practice took place.* How well he remembered! He used to stand and shoot at a target opposite. He walked to the opposite wall and ran his hand along the stone. It was pitted where his steel-tipped arrows had missed the target and instead hit the rock.

He walked through the gate in the far wall. There was a great mound where there had been no mound before, and he knew that beneath the soil lay a vessel, a longboat bearing his father's royal colors. And inside, his father and mother lay side by side with their household belongings around them.

"I have come one last time to Heorot," Brand said out loud. "I've come to say good-bye my parents. I've come to ask you to guide me."

As if to answer a great clap of thunder roared down the fjord—a spring storm, Thor's voice!

"I'm going from this place, my father. I'm going to another land. But never fear, I have a woman, and she will bear children and your line will not die."

The rain began to fall, lightly at first, then harder. Thor roared again, and Brand let the cold rain fall over him like a baptism.

"We are for each other the way you and my mother were for each other," he said, brushing the rain from his forehead.

Lightning crackled, and once again Thor shook the fjord. But in the sound Brand heard his father's voice—"Go now, my son. Go before it is too late."

Brand turned and walked away. Yes. He felt it. The time was at hand.

* * *

Brand paced the parapet while Ivar surveyed the sea below. The wind was brisk, and Brand turned his face to it as if asking a question. He had come back from Heorot two days ago, and he waited for the right sign.

Brand was only too aware of his growing anxiety. Since his trip to Heorot he had felt a sudden urgency, a kind of sick apprehension. It was a feeling he could not explain since it was based on no known fact. It was just a simple sense of danger—not for his own person, but for Deirdre.

"You want to sail, don't you?" Ivar asked.

"Am I so transparent?" Brand asked.

"You're among friends—you have no need to hide your emotions."

"Were it only a matter of emotions, I would sail in an instant," Brand admitted. Early spring was dangerous. Miscalculation could result in decimation or worse, total annihilation. He and his warriors could take to the sea and be caught in a wild spring storm. It could snow and obstruct their way; it could rain heavily, and they would be mired in mud as they approached Lord Thorgills's fortress. Yet there was the strong feeling that he should go, that he should not wait.

"You know the climate as well as any," Ivar said.

"We are four thousand strong," Brand said. "We are strong enough, my friend. But I cannot allow myself to make the decision to go on the basis of anxiety over Deirdre. I am responsible for the lives of too many men."

"As one of those men, I appreciate your caution, my friend. But there is something to be said for listening to one's instincts."

"I am muddled by love," Brand said, shrugging. "I can't tell instinct from desire."

Ivar laughed. "Then I will make the decision. I say we go now. I say the weather will hold."

Brand smiled. "Are you sure?"

Ivar put his hands in his pockets and looked heavenward. "I am sure."

* * *

The weeks passed slowly for Deirdre. Each day the weather seemed to get a little warmer and each day, she knew, brought Brand's attack on Lord Thorgills's fortress closer. After that, he would come here for her—then they could be together forever. She refused to think of Brand losing, she refused to think of the weather causing yet more delays, and she tried to keep busy enough to make the time pass more quickly.

King Halvdan on her advice, had taken to his bed to rest and recuperate. Gradually, the yellow color of his skin and eyes had disappeared. His tongue had returned to normal, and he seemed content with his progress as he began to put on a little weight.

The most pleasant of her duties was helping to care for young Harald. He was indeed a strange, lonely little boy, deprived now for many years of motherly love and affection. Each afternoon, Deirdre told him stories, and in turn, he told her stories.

The sun had just risen, and Deirdre had finished dressing and was on her way to fetch King Halvdan's breakfast. Each morning she brought it to him, examined him, and gave him her medicine.

She left her room and stopped suddenly, pressing herself to the wall as she heard the all-too-familiar sound of the castle gong.

"Dear heaven," she whispered. The first time she had heard the warning gong was when Malvin had attacked her father and subsequently killed him. The second time was when Lord Thorgills had attacked Malvin. The third time was when Alfred had summoned his army to go forth and do battle with Lord Thorgills. And now she heard it again. For a moment she stood in shocked silence, unable to move. Brand would certainly not attack Halvdan if for no other reason than that she was there—unless of course Ingrid, Alan, and Charlotte had not arrived safely—but of course they had. Brand had returned a message to Halvdan. No, she thought miserably, it

was not Brand. It was Lord Thorgills who was attacking—
Lord Thorgills, or perhaps Erica's father, Lord Radnor.

"We're being attacked, we're being attacked," young Harald
screamed as he ran up to her. "I've never been in a battle
before!"

Deirdre looked into his pale blue eyes. He was half-afraid
and half-excited. "Come," she said, taking his hand. "We
must find your father."

Deirdre took Harald's hand and ran down the corridor toward King Halvdan's chamber.

She opened the door to find the king putting on his battle
dress.

"You're too weak to fight," she said urgently. "Let your
headman do battle."

Halvdan shook his head. "I must lead my own men. If I am
not there, many will not fight. I am much stronger, Princess.
Now, take my son and seek shelter."

"I will tend the wounded," Deirdre offered. "Harald will
help me."

"Yes, I want to help. I want to learn how Deirdre makes
people well."

Halvdan frowned. "Go then to the dungeon. It is the most
heavily fortified part of the castle, and it is where all the supplies are stored. I'll have the wounded brought to you."

Deirdre took Harald's hand. "Come," she said. "We'll be
safe in the dungeon.

Seventeen

Clouds filled the sky from horizon to horizon causing the choppy sea to turn a steel gray as winds whipped up the waves and a late snow threatened to fall.

Brand stood at the bow of his longship, assessing the weather and watching as the near forty vessels cut through the water. It was an armada filled with the warriors he would lead into battle. But if it snowed, the climb up the cliffs could be icy—it all grew more dangerous if the weather turned against them.

Brand was dressed for battle in his steel helmet with the long nose protector, his royal tunic, which was a deep blue, and a heavy leather vest, beneath which his skirt fell over fur-bound legs. Over it all, his warm cloak was held in place by his own heavy gold neck ring. And beneath the neck ring, on his tunic, safely under his cloak, he wore Deirdre's brooch.

He looked from the turbulent sky to the biting sea. This was how it so often looked; this was the weather he knew and could usually predict. In a way, it was a perfect day for a battle—if the weather got no worse. The mood was set by the somber colors of nature, the sun was nowhere to be seen. A battle in the sun was never good; when it grew hot, exertion became a second enemy.

Brand experienced the same feeling he always had before a battle—a kind of excitement, a nervous energy, an apprehension. But apprehension made a man careful.

The ships began to round the bend that took them just inside the Oslo Fjord. He had routed them in such a way as to avoid being seen by lookouts from Thorgills's fortress. They would land on the beach a mile from the fortress and approach it from the back. But this was not the side they had planned to land on when Erica heard the plan. This was the other side, and Brand could only hope that lookouts had all been posted where Erica had believed they would be needed and not where they intended to go ashore.

Brand's vessel was the first to be beached. It was secured, and the men scrambled out. As they did so, he and the other chieftains began to assemble the men on the shore.

"We'll send someone ahead," Brand said. "As we planned, they will scour the outside of the back of the castle and report back within the hour."

A detachment of ten warriors led by Cnut left immediately while the other vessels were still landing and the remainder of the warriors were unloaded.

"If all goes well," Ivar said, slapping his friend on the back, "we will eat our dinner in Lord Thorgills's castle."

Brand nodded and watched as Cnut disappeared into the distance.

"Cnut is a happy man to have Bjorn, his sister's husband, fighting with us," Ivar commented.

"We must find Radnor's headman and tell him about Radnor. I think we can affect a changing of sides in midbattle," Brand said, thinking out loud.

Ivar smiled. "Lord Thorgills will crumble this day," he said with conviction.

Brand paced for a time and checked the hourglass. The hour was nearly up, and Cnut had not yet returned with his report. The same nagging feeling of apprehension that had plagued him before was again beginning to invade his thoughts. Perhaps something was wrong—but what could it be? They had planned so carefully. But hadn't his own father taught him to expect the unexpected?

Deirdre came into his thoughts immediately. He could see

her face and hear her soft voice. Was she in trouble? Was she in some kind of immediate danger? Brand leaned against the side of a pine and for the first time realized that never before had he gone into battle with so much at stake. Before he had been forced to fight for Lord Thorgills, but this time he was fighting to get back his beloved. He was fighting for his whole future, for the future of his family. Never before had he so much to lose and yet, so much to gain. The stakes were greater than the most valuable treasure he had ever sought.

"Brand! Brand!" Cnut's voice cut through his thoughts.

Brand snapped to attention and ran toward his breathless friend even as other chieftains gathered round.

"Lord Thorgills is gone!" Cnut exclaimed.

"Where?" Brand questioned.

"We captured this man—one of Radnor's men. He will fight with us now. He says that Thorgills left on morning tide with a large contingent of warriors. He was on his way to attack Halvdan!"

"Deirdre . . ." Brand let her name escape his lips. She was with Halvdan—he whirled about and shouted, "Back to our boats! We must continue up the Oslo Fjord! We must attack Thorgills from the rear while he lays siege to Halvdan's fortress!" This was a dangerous game where every second counted. A surprise attack from the rear on troops already battle-weary was what military commanders dreamed about. Strategically, it was an ideal situation. Brand sucked in his breath. He hoped they were battle-weary; he hoped that Halvdan's warriors had held them at bay, and he hoped that when he arrived, they would all be easily trapped.

In moments the beach was covered with men who hurriedly returned to their vessels as, one by one, the ships rowed back into the fjord, regrouped, and headed upstream.

Erica opened her eyes and looked around her dungeon cell. She shivered uncontrollably in the dampness. It was a small room, no more than six feet long and five feet wide. But its walls were at least twelve or fourteen feet high. At the very top, on one side was a barred window in and out of which, rats and mice scurried at night, running up and down the wall. Along one wall was a bench, and, near the window, a trickle of water ran down the side of the stone.

In the morning and at night, an unconcerned guard opened the door slightly and pushed some gruel into the cell for her. She had to hurry to retrieve it; otherwise, the rodents reached it first.

For the most part, Erica sat on the bench in the only square of light in the room. She hated the darkness when she could not see the rodents. Her head ached, and again she shivered in the cold dampness. Perhaps Halvdan would leave her here till she died. Perhaps she would be forgotten. It wasn't as bad as being buried alive in his wall, but it was horrible enough. Why didn't he understand how terrified she was of the darkness, how she hated the rodents. Why couldn't he just have killed her?

At that moment, the door opened and her morning gruel was shoved inside. The guard snarled at her, "We're under attack, this may be your last meal!"

Erica strained the length of her chain to reach her meal which was on a metal tray. She picked it up and called after the guard, "Who attacks?" But he was gone and did not answer.

Erica hurried back to her square of morning light on the bench. It was then that she saw a bit of flint and several candles had been put on her tray. "Blessed light," she whispered to herself. She strained her ears—yes, she could hear shouting and battle cries! Perhaps it was Henrik and Thorgills come to rescue her! Perhaps once again she would see the light of day!

Her heart leapt inside her and she wondered if it were possible to get loose and perhaps escape when the guard brought the next tray—if there was a next tray. She examined her chain and shook it. Perhaps if she could find a rock it could be broken. It was only one chain and it was attached to her ankle. Who knew what was hidden in the dark corners of her cell? Erica quickly lit one of her candles and then hobbled to the corner and held it up. She screamed and jumped back, almost dropping the candle.

There, in the far corner, propped up against the wall, was the skeleton of some unfortunate. Its bones had been eaten clean by the wretched rodents, and it lay in repose, the vacant sockets of its eyes staring at her.

Erica shuddered. As if in a trance, she bent down and picked up the skull with two fingers. The bones were so dry it was no longer attached to the rest of the skeleton. She held it at arm's length and examined it. She carefully carried it to the bench, set it down, and put the burning candle inside of it. She smiled and tilted her head, "Father," she whispered. "You've found me."

Erica leaned over and looked at the skull for a long while. At length, she left it and continued looking for a rock. In the corner closest to the door of the cell she found some loose stones that had fallen from the crumbling wall. "Ah," she exclaimed, running her tongue around her dry mouth. She examined the stones carefully and after a few moments selected one she thought big enough.

She returned to the bench and immediately began to pound on what she perceived to be the weakest link in the chain. "It will take a while, Father," she said to the skull, "but I will free myself. Even though you would like nothing better than for me to rot in this cell. No, I will free myself and then I will kill that woman!"

Deirdre had gone to the dungeon with trepidation, but it was not as she had imagined. To be sure, down one dark corridor there were a line of cells and, as she well knew, Erica was in one of them. But the cells were far from the center of the dungeon, which was well lit and quite warm. A good part of it was stacked with supplies consisting of both food and weapons. There were still more weapons at the end of the darkened corridor off which cells were located.

Deirdre had laid out pallets on which to place the wounded, and on the ever-burning fire in the large fireplace she boiled water to have at the ready.

"We've never been attacked before," Harald said, sitting down on a pile of wooden boxes. "I should like to see the battle."

Deirdre put her arm around his slim shoulders. "You're safer here. You must remember, you're the future king."

"They'll kill me right away if they win," Harald said in an all-too-adult tone.

It was a depressing thought, and it saddened her that a child could feel so doomed. Not that she did not know the feeling. Each time her father had marched off to battle she had wondered what would happen if he lost. Her whole life had been spent wondering about her fate. Long ago she had silently resolved that she wanted her own children to know no such fear.

"You must not think of losing. You must only think of winning," she said, trying to make the boy feel better.

"My father is still ill; he is not as strong as he once was."

"Your father has fine warriors. The headman is loyal and skilled."

Harald forced a smile. "I'll try not to be afraid."

"The king is wounded!" a warrior shouted.

Deirdre looked up to see Halvdan being carried down the staircase on a litter by two men. His face was pale, blood poured from his thigh, and he was unconscious.

"Speared," one of the men said breathlessly.

He looked at Harald and bowed. "We are surrounded, young master. But the sun is going down and they will be forced to lay siege to this castle till the sun rises tomorrow."

Deirdre immediately set to washing and cleaning Halvdan's wound. She dressed it and gave him some poppy syrup to help ease the pain. After a time, he opened his eyes.

"We're losing," he muttered. He turned and looked at Deirdre. "You have once saved my life, but this time if you save me, it will be to no avail. Lord Thorgills will come tomorrow. We are already weakened. He will be victorious, and it will all be over. They will kill me and my son."

"We might still win," Deirdre said, trying to sound hopeful as much far Harald as for the king.

He shook his head. "No, we will not."

Deirdre put her finger to her lips. "Save your strength," she whispered. "Your wound is not large. It will heal, and you will live."

"I will live until Lord Thorgills storms the castle and finds me," he repeated.

Deirdre bit her lip. It wasn't going well; she did not need Halvdan to tell her. More and more wounded were being brought. "I must tend the others," she murmured.

Halvdan seized her tunic. "Find a way to save my son," he whispered. Halvdan looked into her distressed face. The truth was, he had liked her from the moment he had first seen her. She had not shrunk from him as others did. But it was more than her bravery, her intellect, and her knowledge of medicine. This Irish princess reminded him in a hundred ways of Harald's long-dead mother. If she had lived, he could never have cultivated his fearsome reputation. But surely life would have been far more pleasant.

Deirdre touched his forehead with her hand. "Have faith. I believe with all my heart that we shall all be saved."

Then Deirdre turned to Harald. "Stay close to me, Harald." He clutched at her tunic and silently nodded.

Deirdre bent over and hugged him. The poor child was pale with fright.

"There!" Erica exclaimed as the chain broke. She shook her leg. Part of the chain was still attached to her ankle, but the chain was broken, and she could walk easily enough. She stood up and began walking toward the door, then turned.

"Good-bye, Father," she said, smiling at the glowing skull. "Wish me luck and revenge."

Erica pulled on the door. The dunderhead who brought her food had not locked it! "What a fool," she whispered. Because she had been chained he had been careless.

Erica carefully opened the door a crack and looked into the dimly lit corridor. There was no one there, so she opened the door wider and crept out, closing the door behind her.

From the direction of the light, she heard the moans of men. But she did not walk toward the sounds or toward the light. Instead, she walked toward the darkness until she came to a pile of stored weapons. She quickly took one of the swords. It was long and sharp. Perfect.

She crept back through the darkness toward the light. Staying close to the wall, she peered around the corner and frowned. What manner of nonsense was this? There were wounded warriors all about, and the Irish princess was tending them like a slave!

Erica waited, taking stock of the entire scene. The princess was alone except for Harald and the wounded warriors. The men were all lying flat, and most groaned with their injuries. Certainly it did not seem to Erica as if any of them would pose a problem. She readied herself, and, with the deathly piercing shriek of a Valkyrie, she sprang forward, her sword at the ready.

"You shall not escape me now!"

Deirdre looked up, startled. She swiftly moved out of Erica's way. "I have done nothing to you," she said. "It is I who put candles on your tray."

"I command you to leave her alone!" Harald said, standing up in front of her.

Erica hit him with the flat of her sword and sent him sprawling onto the stone floor.

"Harald!" Deirdre ran to his side. He was unconscious.

"Get up!" Erica screamed as she poked Deirdre with her sword. "Leave that brat alone, get up and climb those stairs! We're going to the parapet! We're going to Halvdan's wall!"

Erica's blond hair was long and loose. It was tangled and dirty from her ordeal, and her clothes were tattered and torn. Her blue eyes shone unnaturally, as if she were indeed quite mad.

"Let me help the boy," Deirdre begged.

"Leave him, or I shall run him through right here!" Then Erica laughed hysterically. "Let Lord Thorgills kill him!"

Deirdre backed away from Harald but as she did so, she saw him wink at her. He was not unconscious! He was all right!

"I don't know why you tend the wounded," Erica said sharply. "When Thorgills enters the castle, he will kill them all in any case!"

Deirdre said nothing. King Halvdan was only a few feet away. If Erica saw him she would most certainly assassinate him now.

"Move!" Erica screamed, and she waved her sword toward the winding back staircase that led up many circular flights of stairs from the dungeon to the parapet and its surrounding wall.

Deirdre began the long climb slowly. Every instinct in her told her to drag this out as much as possible. Time, she had to play for time. She knew there were other stairs, and perhaps Harald would find help and climb them so that when she and Erica reached the top, help would be waiting.

"Move faster!" Erica shouted as she prodded Deirdre along.

"I can't," Deirdre said. "My ankle is hurt. I can't go any faster."

At long last, they reached the top of the stairs. Both were panting with the exertion of the climb.

"Open the door!" Erica ordered.

With all her strength, Deirdre pushed open the heavy wooden door and staggered out into the early-morning air. Cold though it was, the fresh air awakened her.

In the sky above, the clouds had blown away, and the stars

and moon were bright. To the east, the thin line that marked the dawn was just visible.

In the eerie light of dawn, the skulls which lined the wall stared with empty sockets on the scene below.

Erica prodded Deirdre to the wall. "Climb up there!" she ordered. "Sit between those two skulls."

"Why don't you just kill me now?" Deirdre asked.

"Because I want full daylight. I want you to see yourself falling, and I want to see you land on the rocks below."

Time, Deirdre thought. She had to buy more time.

She did as Erica bade and perched herself between the two skulls. She looked down into the darkness and saw an amazing sight, a sight that raised her spirits and suddenly gave her new hope. Below, an armada of longships disgorged hundreds of warriors. It was Brand! She could not see his banners, but she knew it was Brand. Her heart called out to him as her voice could not, and strangely she felt his answer.

But Deirdre forced her expression to remain neutral. If Erica knew that Brand was coming, she would surely kill her right away. So as much as she wanted to watch the scene below, she turned back to face Erica.

"Hark!" Erica said, tilting her head. "I believe the fighting has resumed."

"So it has," Deirdre murmured.

"I shall let you live to see Thorgills victorious," she said. "Then I shall see you fall on the rocks, though it is much too merciful." Erica laughed. "Let us say I give you mercy in return for the candles."

"Were you able to light them?" Deirdre asked, trying to distract Erica.

"Oh, yes. I found my father's skull. He's dead, you know. I can tell you because you won't live to tell another."

Deirdre inhaled. Lord Radnor was dead?

"Was he killed in battle? Deirdre asked. She vowed silently to try to keep Erica talking. She knew she was spinning out time, but Brand was below, and Harald knew where she was.

"Not in battle," Erica said. "We had a difference of opin-

ion. He wanted to continue to support Brand even after—"
Erica suddenly stopped speaking.

Deirdre felt a cold chill sweep through her whole body.
Erica was truly insane. She had killed her own father!

But still, Deirdre said nothing. She was afraid to move,
afraid her expression might give away the hope she felt in her
heart.

Below, Brand led the charge on the surprised and battle-
weary troops commanded by Lord Thorgills. His men
swarmed like ants around those who besieged the castle.

It was Ivar who seized Lord Radnor's headman and told
him of his master's murder. In an instant, Lord Radnor's men
changed sides as word traveled by mouth through the ranks.
And they were not the only ones, in a short time those defect-
ing from Lord Thorgills were double the number of those
remaining to fight.

As if planned, Lord Thorgills appeared, his dark cloak
swirling in the wind, his ax at the ready. "One to one," he
shouted. "I am for you, Brand, son of Jarls!"

The warriors disengaged, stepped aside, and in a moment
Lord Thorgills and Brand were in the middle of an impromptu
human arena, both armed, both ready, and both with the death
of a loved one to avenge.

Yes, Brand thought. They both did have a death to avenge.
Lord Thorgills was going to avenge Olaf's death and he was
going to avenge his father. But Olaf had died in a fair fight;
his father had died of a broken spirit, having had his life destroyed by Lord Thorgills's never-ending greed.

Lord Thorgills sprang forward, and, holding his shield pro-
tectively, he swung his heavy-headed ax at Brand's head.
Brand deftly stepped back, letting the blow whoosh by him.
He immediately counterattacked with his sword. Thorgills de-
flected the attack with his shield. The sound of their weapons
clashing against the metal of their shields was deafening.
Thorgills's next blow was so forceful Brand had to step back

to keep his balance. Thorgills kept pressing hard, trying to put Brand on the defensive. Brand lifted his shield just in time to deflect the coming blow. In the exchange that followed, their movement created clouds of dust. Brand came so close to Thorgills's face he could see that his enemy's eyes were fired with hatred.

They both pushed against one another, but Brand gave way, letting his sword drop. Thorgills went down to the ground and, with surprising agility for one so large, rolled away from Brand's next blow. But he dropped his shield as he scrambled to his feet.

The crowd gave way, making room for the combatants. Yet all were silent. It was as if collectively they held their breath.

Brand attacked Thorgills's open side, only to have Thorgills's ax deflect the sword. Thorgills quickly delivered a withering slice that almost shattered Brand's shield. Instead the ax partially stuck in Brand's shield. As Thorgills struggled to free his ax, Brand thrust his sword with all his might up into Thorgills's midsection. There was a loud groan as Thorgills doubled over and fell to his knees, his eyes looking blankly at Brand as he fell forward. The crowd's momentary silence gave way to cheers. Brand raised his sword high and smiled broadly as he shouted, "Lay down your weapons, enough Viking blood has been shed this day." Brand sheathed his sword. Thorgills was defeated, Henrik was already dead.

"Lord Brand! Come quickly!" Young Harald ran to Brand's side. "Lady Erica has taken Princess Deirdre to the parapet. She's going to kill her! She's mad!"

Harald led and Brand followed. Breathless, he and Harald, followed by Cnut and Ivar, broke through the door that led onto the parapet.

Erica whirled around at the unexpected noise, and Deirdre, waiting not a second, jumped from the wall down to the relative safety of the parapet.

"Brand!" Erica screamed like a banshee. It was half wail, half angry realization that all the fighting and cheering she had heard from below were not for Lord Thorgills's victory, but for his defeat.

She whirled around, her sword raised, but Deirdre had scrambled out of range. That realization caused her to wail even louder.

Ivar shouted, "You murdered your father, Erica, daughter of Radnor! We all know! It is a heinous crime for which the penalty is death!"

Erica looked from one to the other like a trapped animal, then, screaming, she streaked for the wall and hurled herself over the side.

Deirdre ran to Brand, who embraced her and held her tightly. "I would not have gotten here in time had it not been for Harald," he whispered. "I came too close to losing you."

"He's a good boy," Deirdre said softly.

"For the last few days—it's as if I heard you calling me, Deirdre. A moment came, and I knew we could wait no longer. I did not dream that Thorgills would attack Halvdan. If I had, I would have come even sooner."

Deirdre leaned against him. It seemed like an eternity since they had been in one another's arms. She did not want to move. She didn't care that the others were looking at them.

"It is over," Brand whispered. "Soon we'll be free to begin our new life together."

Several miles from King Halvdan's castle stood the village of Oslo. Normally it was simply a thriving market town, but for the past few days it had taken on a new role, that of host to the first meeting of *The Thing* in many years.

Within a day of Lord Thorgills's defeat, King Halvdan, though still ailing from the symptoms of poison and now recovering from his leg wound, had sent forth invitations to all the chieftains of Norway, Sweden, and Denmark to assemble for a meeting of *The Thing*.

"This is a place transformed," Deirdre observed as she and Brand walked the streets of what had become a new, if temporary, town. Everywhere, there were gaily colored tents, each flying the battle banners of the chieftain to whom they belonged. Everywhere the smell of food permeated the air as the smoke from a hundred cooking fires curled toward the blue sky.

"Have you ever seen anything like this?" Brand asked. "I remember the last *Thing,* but it was small by comparison to this one.

Deirdre shook her long, luxurious red hair. "No, I remember once a fair when it seemed that everyone from Meath came and camped near the river. I was quite young, but I think the event was the coronation of King Malvin."

"We, too, will have a coronation," Brand said.

Deirdre smiled. "Harald is very nervous."

"Even with the best of advisors, his task will not be easy."

"I can see that," she said, looking around at the variety and diversity of people, food, and costumes that seemed to have appeared on the Oslo plain overnight.

"Enterprising women," Brand said. "They're cooking their specialties and selling them."

Deirdre inhaled. "It makes me hungry," she admitted. She took Brand's hand and led him down the makeshift lane between tents, where a great variety of food was being made for the celebrations which would last for several days.

"I must learn to make such things," Deirdre said. "In the new land I won't have servants."

"I don't think cooking is more complicated than the brews and medicine you concoct."

"Maybe not." She laughed. "Mm, what's this?"

"Gronkaalssupppe," Brand said, taking a ladle of it and sipping it. Then he offered some to Deirdre.

"Mm," she said appreciatively. "What's in it?"

"Pork, carrots, leeks, and kale."

Deirdre laughed. "I have much to learn, or my family will starve."

"Please learn to make fish soup first," he said with a smile. "Fish is plentiful where we are going."

Deirdre and Brand moved on, sampling cabbage rolls and roast duck as well as herring in onion sauce and scrambled eggs and eels.

"We must return to the castle now. *The Thing* meets in a few hours."

"But we'll come back?"

Brand smiled. "Of course. A gathering of the chieftains must be seen at night to be appreciated. This afternoon we meet, and it will be dry and boring. But tonight there will be a hundred campfires, storytelling, music, acrobats, and even more food."

Deirdre let him lead her away and back toward where they had left their horses. As the rows and rows of gaily colored tents disappeared in the distance, she knew she would not soon forget this day.

At the hour of three in the afternoon, the gong was sounded to summon the chieftains to the first meeting of *The Thing* in more than fifteen years.

Deirdre, dressed in a royal blue tunic the same color as Brand's, but with more intricate embroidery, stood with young Harald, who wore his royal color of red. To Harald's other side, Brand, Ivar, and Cnut all stood dressed in their refinery.

All around the great hall, 150 chieftains sat on the floor. Each wore the color of his fiefdom, each left his sword and weapons outside as was the custom.

At the sound of the ram's horn, King Halvdan, sitting on his hand-carved wooden throne, was carried in by four servants. He slumped slightly in his chair, as his wounded leg was extended forward. The throne was set down, and all the assembled stood and, hands raised, in unison greeted the king.

Halvdan, still not well enough to speak publicly, motioned to Brand.

"The king has asked me to speak for him," Brand said loudly. "He has been wounded and is still ill. I am to tell you that on this day, our king will abdicate in favor of his young son, Harald Fairhair."

"We would have you be our king!" a chieftain shouted.

"I say the same!" another said, standing. "All stand who say the same!"

As one, the assembled chieftains rose.

Brand raised his hand. "I am honored, but I will not accept this honor. Today, for the first time in fifteen years, we meet. From this day hence we shall meet yearly, or even more often if necessary to decide on just laws, to settle disputes, to debate and to discuss rather than to make war. In Russia, in France, and in Britannia they call us the Viking hordes—barbarians! But we are alone in all of the known world to meet as we meet today. We are the first to come forth and represent the interests of those who serve us and till our soil. We are the first to offer a man accused a trial and a judgment by twelve of his peers. I served a wise king in Britannia who believed ignorance condemns us and that we must learn from our past. I have learned, and it is why I will not accept the honor you wish to bestow on me. Crown young Harald and appoint two of your number, Ivar the Boneless, and Cnut the Fox, as advisors."

Deirdre looked at Brand, and tears of pride came to her eyes. He had told her last night that he would not accept the kingship even if it were offered. Now he kept his word, discarding power for the promise of peace in a new land.

"It is easy to seize power, but to give it up speaks of greatness," Ivar said loudly.

A great cheer went up from the assembled chieftains.

"All who agree with crowning young Harald and appointing Ivar the Boneless and Cnut the Fox his advisors, rise," Brand asked.

Again, the assembled rose.

When they had again been seated, Harald was escorted to his father's throne. He bowed before it, and Halvdan took the crown from his own head and set it on the head of his son. As was his wish, Halvdan was carried away, and young Harald sat on the throne in his place.

"It is too big for me," he whispered to Deirdre. "My crown is tilting."

She smiled back at him. "You will grow into it, Your Highness." She straightened his heavy crown.

Cnut moved to stand on one side of young King Harald and Ivar moved to the other. The ram's horn was again sounded, then the more mundane business of *The Thing* was taken up.

"There must be more than two hundred campfires," Deirdre said as she sat with Brand in front of Cnut's gaily colored yellow tent. As soon as *The Thing* had been adjourned, young King Harald had borne witness to the marriage vows of Brand and Deirdre. "Tomorrow, my wife, we begin anew—we leave all this and travel west across the sea."

Deirdre looked into his blue eyes and took his hand and kissed it, holding it to her stomach. "I am the bearer of new life," she whispered. "I carry your child, Brand."

He turned to her in surprise and quickly kissed her neck. "It is a wonder it did not happen sooner."

She laughed and nuzzled against him. "A wonder indeed," she breathed.

The sun shone brightly as Deirdre and Brand stood on the wharf in front of Ivar's fortress. Box after box was loaded onto their longship.

Ivar, Cnut, and young Harald stood with them, watching as the last of their belongings were put aboard.

"You could have had the kingship of all Scandinavia," Cnut said, looking at Brand. "I don't know if you are a wise man to give it up or a fool."

"I am wise. I want no more of this life," Brand said, as his arm encircled Deirdre's ever so slightly thickened waist. "It is better we go now; it's summer, and we'll have time to get settled before the child comes."

"That's the last box," the head servant said.

Brand embraced Ivar and Cnut, and both he and Deirdre hugged young Harald.

"Be a wise king," Deirdre told the lad.

Harald grinned. "I'm having my father's wall torn down."

Deirdre laughed. "You are already a wise king," she told him.

Brand smiled, lifted her into his arms, and carried her aboard. Charlotte and Alan were already there and waiting to cast off.

Brand set Deirdre down, and they both waved as the vessel was untied and rowers began to move it toward the open sea.

Deirdre leaned against Brand, and she put her hand on her stomach. "Oh, my, our child is moving."

Brand laughed and touched her. "By all the gods, I can feel it! He wants to be off to sea!"

Deirdre laughed and he put his arms around her. "You'll see," he said. "It's a wondrous land, a strange, weird land, a peaceful land."

Epilogue

"I did not really believe all you told me," Deirdre said as she slowly disrobed. It was like a magic wonderland, truly a land of fire and ice, this Iceland.

This turquoise pool was warm and clear, and steam rose from its surface in spite of the cold temperature outside. It was always hot, always steaming, as it bubbled forth from the earth that way, as if somewhere below the surface of the green pastures, a fire was tended.

Deirdre moved into Brand's outstretched arms. His hands slid down to her buttocks, and his lips sought her lovely breasts. "You are just as beautiful now as you were before the child," he said, drawing on her nipple until it was taut.

She moaned in his arms as his hands moved over her, slowly arousing her, teasing her, tormenting her with explorations that, while oft repeated, were always new.

He teased her gateway and softly moved his fingers across her magic spot, increasing his pressure as she rubbed against him wantonly.

He buried his face in her fiery hair. How beautiful she was! How much he loved her mind, her spirit, and her body.

"Take me," she whispered. "And then take me again."

He grasped her buttocks and lifted her gently. She wrapped her legs around his waist and he slid into her, holding her light, lovely body by her buttocks.

"This is quite divine," she whispered, as the steam from

the hot spring swirled around them and a soft snow gently began to fall.

Deirdre threw her head back, and his mouth fastened on her breast. This position was so fulfilling, so intimate that in a few seconds she began to feel the tumultuous pulsating that so filled her with happiness. Brand, too, began to shake his seed into her. "This time for a daughter," he joked.

He held her long after they had both felt the intense pleasure of the their lovemaking. He lowered her slowly till they were both fully in the water except for their heads. He kissed her softly, romantically, and ran his finger round her ear. "I can remember no life but this," he said.

Below this magnificent mountain hot spring was their farm, and Deirdre thought how wonderfully peaceful it was here in Iceland. Alan and Charlotte lived nearby, and here everyone decided what was to be done. There were no lord chieftains and no kings.

"We have truly found peace," Deirdre said.

Brand ran his hand through her hair. "We have found love, my wife."

ABOUT THE AUTHOR

Joyce Carlow lives in Nova Scotia, Canada. Her previous Zebra Romances include *Timeswept*, *A Timeless Treasure*, *Timeswept Passion* and *So Speaks the Heart*. Her newest Zebra historical romance, *Highland Desire*, will be published in December 1998. Joyce loves hearing from readers and you may write to her c/o Zebra Books. Please include a self-addressed stamped envelope if you wish a response.

<u>BOOK YOUR PLACE ON OUR WEBSITE</u> <u>AND MAKE THE</u> <u>READING CONNECTION!</u>

We've created a customized website just for our very special readers, where you can get the inside scoop on everything that's going on with Zebra, Pinnacle and Kensington books.

When you come online, you'll have the exciting opportunity to:

- View covers of upcoming books
- Read sample chapters
- Learn about our future publishing schedule (listed by publication month *and author*)
- Find out when your favorite authors will be visiting a city near you
- Search for and order backlist books from our online catalog
- Check out author bios and background information
- Send e-mail to your favorite authors
- Meet the Kensington staff online
- Join us in weekly chats with authors, readers and other guests
- Get writing guidelines
- AND MUCH MORE!

Visit our website at
http://www.zebrabooks.com